What Others Are Saying about
THE COLDER MOON
By L. B. Graham…

"The heart of Lewis and the world-building of Tolkien dwell richly in the works of L.B. Graham. Prepare yourself for high fantasy charged with suspense and intrigue…"

>—Wayne Thomas Batson,
>best-selling author of *The Door Within* trilogy

"This is a highly entertaining as well as thoughtful contribution to Christian fantasy."

>—Publisher's Weekly

"There is a completeness to L.B. Graham's literary imagination that I don't see very often. He's a world-maker. Barra-Dohn, with its strange technologies and ruthless tyrants and wandering priests, feels like a whole world, a world you can immerse yourself in and not come out for a long time."

>—Jonathan Rogers,
>author of *The Wilderking* trilogy

OTHER BOOKS/SERIES
BY L.B. GRAHAM

The Binding of the Blade (a 5 book fantasy series)
Beyond the Summerland
Bringer of Storms
Shadow in the Deep
Father of Dragons
All My Holy Mountain

The Wandering (a 4 book fantasy series)
The Darker Road
The Lesser Sun
The Colder Moon
*The Elder Star
*planned, but not yet published

Avalon Falls – a crime novel
The Raft, The River, and the Robot – a futuristic/
sci-fi novel with a Huck Finn twist

THE
COLDER MOON
The WANDERING: BOOK 3

L.B. GRAHAM

The Colder Moon
THE WANDERING: BOOK 3
Copyright © 2017 by L. B. Graham. All rights reserved.

For they sow the wind,
and they shall reap the whirlwind.
HOSEA

CONTENTS

Prologue

THE WEIGHT OF IT ALL

Draagan hesitated right before the bridge so that Amintuu could catch up. Amintuu was bigger and stronger, but Draagan, being almost a full year older, was faster. He knew that in his excitement to get to the cave, he might leave his friend far behind, and Amintuu didn't like to be left behind.

When Amintuu had almost reached the bridge, Draagan stepped down from the Arua and tore across the bridge, the sound of his feet on the wooden planks echoing throughout the gorge below as the water of the river rushed quickly on. When he had been little, Draagan hadn't liked to look down since the bridge was so high above the river, but now he was almost eleven, and things like that didn't scare him anymore.

On the other side, he leapt back up onto the Arua field without turning around to see where Amintuu was. The echoes of his friend's feet had already confirmed that he was close behind. The trail hugged the top of the gorge for a while before disappearing back into the trees. Eventually, it found the edge of the gorge again and began to descend, and down, down, down he went, Amintuu somewhere behind.

Near the bottom of the gorge the path ran beside the rumbling river, the churning water splashing up and spraying his feet and legs. On the other side, the path was close up against the almost sheer wall of rock rising far overhead. Draagan looked up as he ran, taking in the wispy clouds cutting across the blue sky like thin white scars. For a Northland Amhuru, this place was almost sacred.

Up ahead, at last, Draagan could see the cascading waters of the Falls. What he could not yet see were the guards, who would be behind the water on either side of the river, but he knew they were there. They were always there. He also could not see Telsiin, not yet, but he knew the Keeper would be there too. Telsiin had promised to meet Amintuu and Draagan there this morning, and this was why he was in such a hurry. Telsiin had to leave again today, and Draagan did not know when he would be back.

When he drew close enough to the Falls to see where the path bent around to disappear behind the water, Draagan saw Telsiin sitting on a rock near the entrance to the cave. His eyes were closed and his arms folded against his chest as he leaned back against the high rock wall. "Telsiin!" Draagan shouted as he ran around the corner, and as he did, the Keeper sat up and his eyes popped open as he broke into a broad smile.

"Little one," Telsiin said, having to speak loudly to be heard above the roar of the water, "where is your friend? Have you come alone?"

Telsiin always called Draagan 'little one,' even though Draagan often objected to the nickname. He did not object today. He was too surprised by the question. He turned and looked behind him, and sure enough, Amintuu was nowhere to be seen.

"Na, Keeper," Draagan said, turning back to face Telsiin. "You know Amintuu. He probably stopped to rest somewhere along the way. He's got the stamina of an ancient bull."

"Sa, Draagan," Telsiin said, still smiling but with a hint of rebuke in his voice. "I know Amintuu. I also know you should not leave your friend behind or deride him for being slower than you are. The ancient bull may not outrace the little fox, but the little fox would be wise not to tug on the bull's horns."

"Sa, Telsiin," Draagan nodded. "I am sorry. I'll go back and look for Amintuu."

"Na," Telsiin said, "Not unless he fails to show up in the next few minutes. If that happens, we will both go. Sit, and we will talk, little one."

"Sa, Keeper," Draagan said as he sat down beside Telsiin. "I am sorry you are leaving today. It seems like you are hardly ever home anymore."

"I will miss you too," Telsiin said, knowing what was on Draagan's heart. "You seem to grow so much while I am gone. The road of a Keeper is hard, Draagan. Honorable, but hard."

"I know, but I still want to be one when I get older."

"I know you do," Telsiin said, "and maybe you will be."

"I hope so."

"Maybe you both will be," Telsiin added, nodding back down the path.

Draagan turned to see Amintuu jogging along between the river and the gorge wall. He looked back at Telsiin. "Do you think we both could be?"

"Who can say what the future holds?" Telsiin said, shrugging. "There are only three Keepers, but there must be three, so who's to say you two won't both be one?"

"Won't both be what?" Amintuu said, drawing close enough to hear them.

"Keepers," Draagan said, rising and grinning as Amintuu approached, eyes wide as well.

"Wouldn't that be something?" Amintuu said.

"Sa," Draagan agreed. "It would."

"Come," Telsiin said, rising too. "We should go in if we are going to see them before I have to go."

Telsiin headed back behind the falling water, and the roar grew even louder. After they passed the waiting guards who only nodded to acknowledge the presence of the Keeper, they entered the cave.

Once inside, they took up the corness lamps and walked through the entrance hall of the dark cave until they found the side corridor that led them to the room where the others were. Draagan followed a little behind Amintuu and Telsiin, but once they were all in the room, he stood still in wonder as he gazed at the dancing rhythm of the replicas of the three Southland fragments, the only three north of the Madri. Their beauty never ceased to fill him with wonder.

One day, he thought to himself, I will be a Keeper and bear one of the three Northland fragments. *One day.*

.　　　.　　　.

Draagan gripped the Zerura on his right forearm with his left hand, gripped it tight and twisted, a mannerism of his that tended to show up when frustration had him in its grip. The moon was bright tonight, but he couldn't see the look on Amintuu's face since his friend was standing with his back to him. Unfortunately, he didn't need to see it to have a fair idea of the expression on it.

"Amintuu," he said. "You're sulking, again. It's no big deal."

"Sa, no big deal," Amintuu said, turning slowly to face Draagan. "Of course, that's easy for you to say since it was your praises the Elders were singing—again."

"You act as though they never sing your praises," Draagan said. "But weren't you the one who earned their praise last week when you brought the biggest deer back from the hunt?"

"Sa, they do praise me for things like hunting," Amintuu said. "But we both know they won't be asking themselves who is the best hunter when they choose who will be Keeper."

"We're both too young to be Keeper," Draagan said. "And besides, there probably won't be a new one for years."

"I don't mean right now," Amintuu said. "And when we are old enough, when they have need of a new Keeper—it will be you."

"I know we used to talk about becoming Keepers when we were little, but you worry too much about it," Draagan said, hoping to calm his friend. "It is out of our control. Like Telsiin always said—"

"I don't want to hear about what Telsiin always said," Amintuu shot back. "He always favored you."

"He what?" Draagan said, growing angry now.

"You heard me," Amintuu said, stepping closer. "Don't think I didn't notice."

"Notice what?"

"And now, you tell me not to worry," Amintuu continued, as though Draagan hadn't even spoken, "which, again, is easy for you to say, since you already know who Telsiin will tell them to choose, don't you?"

Draagan gripped his fragment of the Golden Cord even tighter, trying very hard not to let his anger get the better of him, but sometimes Amintuu made things so hard. He took a deep breath.

"Amintuu," he said at last. "We have been best friends all our lives. I don't know how you can say these things."

"Have we, Draagan?"

"Have we what?"

"Been best friends?" Amintuu asked. "In truth, were we ever friends at all?"

"How can you ask that?"

"I ask, because I do not know the answer."

"You're impossible," Draagan said, lifting his hands and motioning emphatically, his anger working out through his arms and hands and fingers. "I'm heading back. I'll talk to you when you're not in this mood."

"Do what you like," Amintuu said, shrugging, as he turned his back on Draagan once more.

Draagan considered saying something else, thought better of it, then turned and walked away.

．　　　．　　　．

The clouds were thick tonight, Draagan thought, looking upward. The new moon had no chance to shine through them or to penetrate all the way down here to the bottom of the gorge. And so Draagan sat, enjoying the darkness as he listened to the constant roar of the Falls.

"I thought I might find you here," Telsiin said, drawing near.

Draagan rose, as was appropriate in greeting the Chief Elder of the Northland Amhuru. "Chief Elder," he said, "I am honored."

"The honor is mine, to join the newest Keeper in his late night reverie," Telsiin said. "You have no doubt come here to be alone with your thoughts, so if I am disturbing you too much, I can always speak with you another time."

"Na, Chief Elder," Draagan said. "You are welcome. I am glad of your company."

"Then let us sit and talk awhile, as we did when you were a boy." As he said that, Telsiin sat down and Draagan sat beside him.

"We had many good days here, did we not?" Telsiin asked after they had settled in.

"Sa," Draagan nodded, with many fond memories rushing to his mind. "We did."

"And in most of those memories, Amintuu was here with us."

"Sa, he was," Draagan said, and when Telsiin did not say anything to that, he added. "I suppose I shouldn't be surprised that you knew what I had been thinking about."

"Well," Telsiin said. "I know you pretty well, Draagan. I know you both."

"Then you know that sometimes, boyhood friendships don't last into manhood."

"Sa, I know that only too well," Telsiin said, and Draagan could hear sadness in his voice.

"I didn't want it to be like this," Draagan said. "I …"

"I know," Telsiin said, reaching over and squeezing Draagan's knee gently. "And neither did Amintuu. The divide between you both is very deep. The seeds have been growing a long time. I could see them even when you were little."

Draagan sat quietly, thinking about what Telsiin had said. "I did all I could. Are you saying I am partly to blame?"

"I don't know how often any of us do all we could," Telsiin said. As Draagan stirred, Telsiin quickly added, "Peace, Draagan. I think you played a part in this, but I do not think you played an equal part, nor did I say that it was willful. I know you tried, and you tried hard."

"I did try," Draagan echoed, quietly.

"I know," Telsiin said, "and that was a big part of why the Elders chose you to be a Keeper."

"It is?"

"Sa," Telsiin said. "We are Amhuru, Draagan, united by a high and noble calling, but we are also human and therefore vulnerable to all the failings that go with that. To be a Keeper requires more than to bear an original fragment. You must also bear the weight of that calling. Your hard work to keep your friendship with Amintuu alive, even as it fell apart, did not go unnoticed."

"He will see it differently," Draagan said. "He will say you were playing favorites."

"Sa," Telsiin said. "He will, but he will be wrong. I still believe in Amintuu, in his potential, and perhaps one day he will see that."

They sat together, silently, and Draagan looked up as the dark clouds high above parted sufficiently for him to see the slender moon and stars far above them. "It is a time of relative peace for the Northlands, Draagan," Telsiin said. "And hopefully, that will continue. But sometimes, the storm blows up unexpectedly, and the Elders believe you are the kind of man who would be steady, even in a storm."

"In times of peace or turmoil," Draagan replied. "I will do my best."

"I know you will."

"And maybe," Draagan said. "Since the Elders have put their faith in me, that means they may be open to my ideas about perhaps pursuing reconciliation with the Jaens."

"Or perhaps," Telsiin said wryly, "your family's bizarre sympathies for the Jaens have nothing to do with the Elders' confidence in you."

Draagan laughed, and Telsiin laughed too. "All right, I will not push my ideas about the Jaens just now. Maybe after I've been a Keeper for a while."

"Perhaps after you've been a Keeper for a great while."

"Maybe then," Draagan said, growing suddenly sober, "maybe Amintuu will have made his peace with my selection as Keeper."

"Maybe he will," Telsiin agreed. "He has his own gifts, and if he can get beyond this, then maybe one day he will be able to use them without being crippled by envy."

Telsiin rose, and Draagan rose with him. "I think that I'll head back now."

"I will walk with you," Draagan offered.

"There is no need. Stay, and enjoy your solitude. I couldn't sleep the night I became a Keeper either."

"Sa, thank you, Chief Elder," Draagan said. "You know, I wanted this so much when I was a boy, and yet, now that I am older and I have what I wished for, it isn't quite what I expected."

"Things rarely are."

"I hungered for the achievement but did not appreciate the responsibility," Draagan continued. "I did not truly appreciate the weight of it all."

"I do not wish to alarm you," Telsiin said, placing his hand on Draagan's shoulder, "but more than likely you still don't. You will in time."

Part 1

THE BOLDER MOVE

1

A SLEEPLESS NIGHT

Kaden crouched in the snow. He stepped slowly, deliberately, moving with the delicate grace of the hunter. Reaching out, he took the branches of the scraggly bush in his hand and pulled them back so he could reach in. Just ahead his quarry waited. He had avoided detection and there was no escaping him now.

His hand shot out, grabbing Kiki around the waist and pulling her up out of the bush into the air as she shrieked with delight. Her golden curls bounced as her face contorted with laughter. She was very good at hide-and-seek, but Kaden suspected deep down that what she liked most about the game was not avoiding detection but being found again at the end.

"I got you," Kaden said, tickling Kiki's stomach.

"Na! Na!" Kiki screamed at the tickling, which Kaden knew was her way of saying, "Sa! Sa!" for if he stopped, she'd beg him to tickle her some more.

"All right, you two," Nara said, approaching them in the snow with her arms full of the wood they were supposed to be gathering. "Are you going to help or not? Deslo has made three trips already, and you guys are still playing around."

"Sorry," Kaden said with feigned sheepishness as he put Kiki down. He knew Nara wasn't really upset, but he also knew that he needed to help. What's more, he needed to make sure Kiki helped. It was never too early to learn the value of work, to learn that every member of the family had a part to play.

"Yadi! Yadi!" Kiki shouted, holding her hands up to Kaden so he would pick her up and tickle her some more.

"Yadi has to help Noni and Deslo gather wood," Kaden said, "and so does Kiki."

"Na!" Kiki said emphatically, her smile disappearing, replaced by an adamant and angry refusal.

"Sa, Kiki," Kaden said firmly. "Don't ruin the fun we've had. We can play more another time."

Kiki did not protest again, not verbally, but she crossed her little arms and glared at Kaden. He stood still, gazing back, not saying a word, trying to maintain a firm but not cross countenance, and for a long moment they just looked at each other. Eventually, Kiki relented. He could see it first in her eyes and face as they softened, and then she took a sudden step forward and hugged him around the legs.

"Come on, Kiki," he said as he tousled her hair, "let's get some wood."

They built their evening shelter on the lee side of a large rock, where the snow was only a few inches deep. It was a lovely spot, actually, as the edge of the bluff overlooking the choppy waves of the dark sea was not but thirty yards away, and the sound of the water crashing on the rocks below came up through the twilight as they huddled close to their fire for warmth. The rest of the Amhuru camp was a little north of them, and the twinkling campfires dotted the snowy landscape.

"This is so strange," Kaden said, glancing sideways at Nara. "Isn't it?"

"Isn't what, darling?"

"This, the snow, needing a fire for warmth, being in the Northlands, all of it," Kaden said. "Growing up in Barra-Dohn, I never really expected I'd see snow, let alone cross the Madri or do almost any of the things we've done."

"The world is a vast and wondrous place," Deslo said from across the campfire. "At least, that was what Gamalian always used to say."

"Sa, he did," Kaden nodded, remembering the man who had been both his tutor and his son's.

"There was no snow, Delo?" Kiki said, using her old name for Deslo even though she could pronounce his real name accurately now. She looked up at her brother from where she sat in his lap. "Where you grew up?"

"Na, Kiki," Deslo said. "There was no snow. Lots and lots of sand, but no snow."

Kiki looked down at the snow lying on the ground beside them, as though puzzled by this notion of a world without snow. She reached down with one small hand and grabbed as big a handful of snow as she could. She brought it up to her face and peered at it, a small palm-shaped snowball, pressed into almost solid form by the pressure of her hand. Then, without warning, she tossed it into the air in a fit of youthful exuberance, giggling. The small clump fell in the darkness behind them.

"Snow!" Kiki cried as she clapped her hands together.

"Sa, Kiki," Nara said. "We know you love snow, but please don't throw it around while we're cooking supper."

Kiki giggled again, but she nodded her understanding as she leaned forward and reached out with her cold, wet hand to dry it by the fire. They sat quietly, waiting for their dinner to cook, each of them tired from the long day's march. Snow might be fun to play with and in, but it sure made for tough walking when it grew deep. Kaden hoped that, when they turned inland on the morrow, they would find easier hiking.

"Tchinchura says we leave the shore behind tomorrow," Deslo said, as though reading the thought on Kaden's mind.

"That's what he told me too."

"And then it's just a couple days to Berran's Point."

"Maybe not even two full days," Kaden said. "It depends on the conditions, I think, and how much the weather slows us down."

"But either way, two nights from now we should be there, right?"

"I think so." Kaden could hear an eagerness in Deslo's voice, a longing, almost, but he wasn't sure why. They were all tired of traveling, but there wasn't anything new about that. Since the fall of Barra-Dohn five and a half years ago, they'd been on the move pretty constantly, even if most of it had been on board *The Sorry Rogue*. He thought probably there was more to it than that, but what it might be, he had no idea.

Not long after dinner, Nara and Kaden stood. "We're going for a short walk, but it is time for bed, Kiki," Nara said. "Say good night to Yadi and Noni."

"Good night!" Kiki called, blowing kisses across the fire.

"Good night," both Kaden and Nara called back.

"Delo," Kiki said as Nara and Kaden started away. "Tell me a story about where you grew up tonight, please? And tell me why there's no snow."

"All right, Kiki," Deslo said, "I'll tell you a story about Barra-Dohn."

Kaden and Nara walked out into the chilly darkness beyond the reach of the fire's warmth, heading south, away from the main camp, with the bluff and the sea beyond it on their left. Nara's hand fumbled in the dark for a moment, but soon she found Kaden's hand and took it in her own, and for a little while they walked in silence.

"You said we'd be all right," Kaden said a moment later, "and we are."

"What do you mean?" Nara asked, looking up at him. "All right about what?"

"When you told me you were pregnant with Kiki," Kaden said. "I started freaking out because we were living on a ship and had no permanent home, and you told me it would be all right—that we didn't need a palace because we had found each other. You were right."

"I know," Nara said, smiling. "Although, I wouldn't mind a few nights in some kind of shelter. These nights keep getting colder."

"Well, Deslo's right," Kaden said. "We should be there by the night after tomorrow. At least, that's what Tchinchura said this morning."

"I can't wait," Nara said.

"Nara," Kaden said somewhat abruptly, "Do you think Deslo is all right?"

Nara didn't say anything right away, and when she did, what she said caught Kaden offguard. "I think he's a bit heartsick."

He looked over at her and almost stopped walking, but she never broke stride and he kept going too. "You mean, over a girl?"

"Sa, darling," Nara said. "Over a girl."

"Zangira's daughter?" Kaden said, confused. "But he hasn't seen her since we were in Azandalir."

"Shaline was her name," Nara said, "and Deslo did like her, but I didn't mean her."

This time Kaden did stop, and Nara stopped with him. He frowned as he turned toward her. "Olli?"

"Congratulations," Nara said, wryly.

"But she's too old for Deslo."

"I'm not sure Deslo would agree."

"And he couldn't stand her when she first came on board," Kaden added quickly, feeling a little defensive, though not exactly sure why. "I know he didn't, because you pointed it out to me."

"My dear, darling husband," Nara said as she stepped forward and put her arms around him. "I love you, but honestly, sometimes you're just hopeless. I know you grew up in a palace, and that life was … different for you, but do you really know so little of the human heart? Have you never seen the appearance of dislike mask something more … affectionate?"

"Perhaps," Kaden said, pulling Nara in for warmth. He thought about what she was telling him. Olli and Deslo had certainly seemed to bury the hatchet after they crossed the Madri, or perhaps even before, while they were staying at Azandalir. In fact, they had spent quite a lot of time together, which had seemed natural, given their ages. They didn't spend nearly so much time together now, that is, not since the arrival of Maarta, the young Amhuru …

"Oh," Kaden said out loud. "How did I miss that?"

"I have no idea," Nara said, and then she reached up and kissed him.

"So what do we do?" Kaden said when she was finished.

"We don't do anything," Nara said, "except love him as best we can. I've dropped hints to see if he wants to talk about it, but I don't think he wants to. So, we give him his space."

Kaden nodded. "All right, I can do that."

"Let's head back," Nara said. "It's just too cold out here."

.   .   .

Deslo sat up in the dark. What a strange dream that had been. He'd been in a vast, snowy field at twilight, with Rika and Gamalian, both of his old tutors, and they'd all been throwing snowballs at one another. And not only had they been doing that, they'd been laughing and playing, obviously enjoying themselves. Very odd, given not only that Gamalian was dead and Rika had suddenly left their company weeks and weeks ago, but that he would dream of them together—they hadn't liked each other at all.

Almost, Deslo thought as he gazed up through the darkness at the night sky, he could have thought that this was a dream like those that had plagued him while crossing the Madri. It was surreal enough, but it wasn't very sinister, and those dreams had a darker feel to them. This one had been pretty cheerful, really, save only the strange howl at the end, just before he woke up.

The night stars were bright and plentiful, stretching across the canopy of the night sky. The moon was bright too, and it looked almost full, though Deslo could see it wasn't. It had started to wane. Around it, though, he could just make out the grey ring they had seen there more prominently before, tonight just a faint, misty halo. Tchinchura had said that the Northland Amhuru called this moon—when surrounded by that grey ring—a cold moon, but Deslo didn't really know what that meant, unless it just indicated that the grey ring showed up only in winter.

By the position of the moon and the condition of their fire, though, Deslo could tell he'd been asleep only a few hours. It was still a long time until daylight. He groaned, because he felt wide awake and knew it would be hard for him to go back to sleep. He'd pay the price for his wakefulness tomorrow on the march.

He stoked the fire and added a bit more wood. As long as he was up, he thought he might as well. Before long, he had the fire going pretty well again, the embers having ignited the new fuel. The fire grew hot, and he wondered if the change in heat might wake either of his parents where they slept on the other side. Kiki wouldn't wake, he thought, looking down at the little bundle next to him. She could sleep through just about anything.

"Deslo?"

He turned to see the source of the whispered greeting, and there was Olli, arms wrapped tightly around her, standing not far from the fire behind him.

"Can't sleep either?" she added when he didn't say anything.

"Na," he shook his head.

"May I join you?"

"Sa," he nodded, and she approached and sat.

"I saw someone stoking your fire," she said, once she had sat down, "and as I was tired of sitting alone in the dark, I thought I would come see who was up."

"Just me, I'm afraid," Deslo said, turning from Olli to gaze down at the flickering orange flames.

"Well, I'm in luck that it is just you," Olli said, a little playfully. "We haven't talked in ages."

Deslo wasn't sure what to say to this, so he just nodded as he stared at the fire. Olli once again took up the burden of conversation in the face of his silence and said, "Did you hear that howl a little while ago?"

Deslo looked up. "Howl? How long ago?"

"I'm not sure," Olli said, looking a little surprised at Deslo's sudden interest and intensity. "Not too long."

"I thought I was dreaming," Deslo said, almost to himself, then added to clarify. "I mean, I was dreaming when I heard it. I thought the howl was in the dream. That must be what woke me. What did it sound like?"

"Creepy and unpleasant," Olli said, reaching her hands out to warm them. "I'm sorry, but that's all I can tell you. One of the unfortunate things about spending most of your life on an island, in a cave, is that there are a whole lot of sights and sounds in the larger world that I still can't identify."

"That's all right," Deslo said, hearing the apologetic tone in Olli's voice. "I didn't grow up either on an island or in a cave, but I'd probably be just as hopeless since I grew up by a desert in the Southlands. Whatever lives around here is probably something I've never seen or heard either."

"Well, the watch didn't seem overly concerned about it," Olli said. "They must have thought it sounded too far away to need investigating, or perhaps they knew what it was and it didn't worry them. I would have asked Maarta, but he was asleep and I didn't want to wake him since he's got to stand the last watch."

Deslo glanced back at the fire. An afterthought. Once, he had been the one Olli addressed her questions to in the face of the many unknowns she encountered almost daily, but he'd been reduced to an afterthought, a plan of last resort when Maarta wasn't available. Deslo thought about the young Amhuru, feeling something perhaps quite close to hate.

"I wish," Olli started, perhaps seeing the look on Deslo's face as he had turned away. "I wish we could all be friends again."

"We are friends, Olli," Deslo said without looking up. "You and me."

"And Maarta," Olli said hesitantly, but also hopefully. "Can he not be your friend too?"

"Why does it matter if Maarta is my friend?"

"Because I love him, Deslo."

Her words hung in the air between them. They hung silent and un-wavering in the cold stillness of the night. It wasn't exactly news, as he had seen it in her eyes, known and feared the truth of it. But to hear the words spoken aloud, spoken by her own mouth, it was like someone had hit him in the stomach. Hard. For a moment, he found it difficult to breathe. At first he didn't realize that Olli had started talking again.

"... I know this isn't what you want to hear, Deslo, but it is true, and I would like it if you could at least try to be friends again, with both of us."

He turned to look at her. Her blond hair was pulled back so that the fire illuminated the entirety of her lovely face. He opened his mouth to speak, then realized he had no idea what to say. He closed it again and looked back at the comforting flicker of the fire.

"You'll always be important to me, you and your family," Olli added. "I'll always be grateful for what you did for me and my people on the island, killing the gorgaal and setting us free."

Deslo started shaking his head, and he almost raised his arm to wave off the words that Olli was saying. He didn't. He knew she thought she was being comforting and it would hurt her if he did, but he could find no comfort in anything she said. What comfort could there be? She loved someone else, and it didn't matter if she was grateful to him or if he was important to her. Olli didn't love him.

"Look, Olli," he said finally. "I don't know that there's much use talking about this. You feel the way you feel, and I feel the way I feel, and I don't know what either of us can do about it."

They sat in silence, warming themselves by the fire. After a little while, Olli suggested that perhaps she ought to go back and try to get some sleep after all. Deslo agreed, saying that he should probably try to sleep again too. She rose, but she didn't walk away.

"You know," she said, and he could almost hear the internal debate in her about whether or not to continue. That made him curious to hear what she was thinking of saying, but it also brought the slightest sense of dread. "You may yet see Shaline again."

He tensed. He hadn't been expecting that, and Shaline's name did not bring the comfort he imagined Olli thought it might, only a different kind of discomfort. "I don't know, Olli. I'm not sure how likely that is."

"I know," Olli said. "I'm just saying you shouldn't automatically assume that you won't. Once we take care of the Jin Dara, you will be free to go south again, and ..."

Her voice trailed off, and with good reason. Who could know what lay beyond that 'and'? Ever since the collapse of Barra-Dohn, the Jin Dara—finding, stopping, and hopefully killing him—had defined his life and his family's lives. Forgetting for a moment the difficulty of ever achieving that goal, and even how long it might take, what would he or any of them do then?

"I don't know, Olli," Deslo said at last, looking up. "You're right of course, I might see Shaline again, but it is hard to imagine taking care of the Jin Dara, as you put it, let alone what comes after."

"I know," Olli said. "And I'm not saying you will see her again. I just wouldn't give up hope."

"Thanks," Deslo said. He turned away from her. "Sleep well."

"Sleep well, Deslo."

He listened to the soft crunching of her footsteps in the snow. It grew faint, and then disappeared.

For a long time, Deslo sat by the fire, the thoughts and memories in his head dancing in sync to the rhythm of the flames.

2

BERRAN'S POINT

Two days later, in the late afternoon, they caught their first glimpse of Berran's Point. It sat on a slight rise, giving it excellent sight lines with which to survey the surrounding land. The wall was a tall, log stockade affair, which rose perhaps twelve to fifteen feet into the air and ran around the small, fortified settlement in something approaching a perfect square. Kaden could not see a gate, but that did not surprise him. Tchinchura said the fortress had been built facing the wilder, more desolate wastelands to the west, which seemed to go by the odd name, Graymere.

As they drew closer, Tchinchura slowed and turned to Kaden. He pointed toward the fortification and said, "Smoke, do you see?"

Kaden peered at the sky ahead and did see smoke rising, in more than one column, in fact. The sky was overcast, and the swirling smoke was less easily visible than it would have been against a blue sky, which was perhaps why Kaden hadn't noticed it yet. Now that he did see it though, he had a sudden, sinking feeling that something was wrong. It was cold out, to be sure, but those columns of smoke gave the impression of coming from some pretty large fires.

Kaden was going to ask Tchinchura what he thought was going on, but up ahead most of the other Amhuru, who had also been observing the rising smoke, started running toward Berran's Point with weapons drawn.

Those who didn't run toward Berran's Point ran back toward them. Telsiin was with this contingent, and it was he that addressed Tchinchura.

"Keeper," the Northland Elder said, "you should stay with us until we know what is going on. We must not endanger the fragment you bear."

"Sa, Elder," Tchinchura said with a slight nod, acknowledging his willingness to wait until more was known.

Nara, who held Kiki in her arms, moved in closer and Kaden put his arm around her. Deslo stood a little apart, gazing at the smoke rising from Berran's Point, perhaps wishing he were among the Amhuru who had gone on ahead to see what was happening. All alike stood quietly, watching the small fortress, waiting.

They didn't have to wait long. Shortly after the Amhuru disappeared around the corner of Berran's Point, one of them reappeared there and waved urgently for them to come. As they set off at a jog, Kaden reached over and took Kiki in his arms.

Once past that corner, the uncertainty Kaden felt turned quickly to horror. No sooner did Kaden see that the gates were thrown open wide, than he saw what lay inside them. Charred and blackened buildings sat smoking here and there, explaining the smoke. Almost miraculously, though, the stockade walls appeared to be untouched by the fire that had burnt the buildings.

The real horror, though, came when Kaden saw what was hanging from the wooden walk that ran around the inside of the stockade wall. Bodies—naked, bloody, and flayed, each of them suspended by a solitary ankle. All of them, maybe seven or eight total, had golden hair. All were missing a limb. Just one for each—either an arm or a leg—but all of them. None bore jewelry, not any more.

Kaden, when he had begun to process what he was seeing, turned away from the open gate and reached up instinctively to cover Kiki's eyes, though the look he saw there and the quivering of her lips suggested he was too late, that she had glimpsed what lay within. He saw the look on Nara's face too, and he walked a few steps away, outside the wall, motioning for her to follow.

They huddled together beside the strong wooden wall, and Kaden handed Kiki back to Nara. Kiki clasped Nara tightly as the child buried her head against her Noni and cried, and Nara tried to soothe and comfort her. All the while, Nara's eyes searched Kaden's face, as though hoping to find answers there, but he had none to give. A hollow, sinking emptiness yawned within, and Kaden suddenly felt overwhelmed by despair. There really was no safe place in this world for them anymore. They had come all this way, crossed the Madri, all for nothing. They would die in this cold and barren place, die and be forgotten.

Kaden closed his eyes, for the world had begun to whirl around him, and he suddenly felt unsteady, like he might fall down. Reaching out, he balanced himself against the stockade wall. How long he stood like this, he didn't know, until he heard Deslo's voice and opened his eyes.

"Yadi," Deslo repeated.

"Sa," Kaden said, standing up straight but reaching out for Deslo, as though the feel of Deslo's shoulder beneath Kaden's hand would provide comfort and strength.

"They've found the Keeper, Asantii."

"Sa?" Kaden said.

"He's dead," Deslo said, matter-of-factly, then added. "His left leg is gone."

"Gone?" Kaden asked, the world around him beginning to whirl again.

Deslo nodded. "Another original is missing."

.   .   .

Taking down and gathering the bodies of the dead did not take long. As sunset was just a few hours away, no thought was given to a permanent resting place for them, and they were stacked in a pile behind one of the smoldering buildings of the fort, under a blanket, in a corner at the back. In the morning, the Amhuru would decide what was to be done. For now, more pressing matters confronted them.

Nara and Kiki were huddled inside a large storage shed, one of the two remaining structures that had not been completely destroyed by fire. One of the walls of the shed had been scorched, but for whatever reason, the fire had died out instead of spreading, leaving the shed and the foodstuffs stored within intact. The refuge it provided from the sights and smells of Berran's Point was real even if incomplete, and Kaden had himself struggled to leave that refuge and join the gathering of Amhuru outside, but left it he had.

The smell of charred wood and, worse, charred bodies, was strong in the open courtyard inside the gate, but as the Amhuru gathered and squatted there, Kaden was aware he could detect the less palpable but equally real scent of fear. The fact that he had never detected anything quite like it in all his years around Amhuru since leaving Barra-Dohn only heightened the growing sense of panic that he fought hard to suppress. If they were afraid, these who stood unflinching before almost anything, what hope remained for him and his family? For the world?

Curiously, Deslo, who squatted beside him in the gathering, showed no signs of either fear or panic. In fact, the look on his face was, if anything, only harder and more determined. Kaden didn't know if he should be proud of his son's strength or anxious that perhaps he didn't grasp just how potentially devasting the loss of a third fragment really was.

Telsiin squatted in the middle of the courtyard. His arms clasped his knees, hugging them tight, as he seemed to stare distantly at the patch of dirt and snow in the open space before him. On his left, Amintuu squatted, next in seniority among the Northland Amhuru, and on his right was Tchinchura. Both glanced occasionally at Telsiin, but neither would speak until he did first.

Kaden and Deslo squatted in the outermost ring of Amhuru, but they had placed themselves in this ring as close to the spot where Tchinchura was squatting as possible, instinctively. Likewise, close by, though a little farther to the side, Marlo and Owenn also squatted, their physical location reflecting well both their inclusion in the counsels of the Amhuru but also the fact that, welcome or not, they were Devoted, not Amhuru.

Olli and Maarta, on the other hand, were directly opposite, and as they waited in the somber stillness, Kaden noted that Deslo's attention seemed pretty evenly divided between Telsiin and Tchinchura in the center of the circle, and Olli on the opposite side. Remarkable, Kaden thought, the contours of the human heart and the power of its desire, even in the face of other things, no matter how dire.

"A Keeper is dead," Telsiin said at last, "and we thank Kalos for Asantii's life and service, as is good and right, even if his death grieves us and the loss of the fragment frightens us."

"Sa, Elder," a few of the Amhuru murmured quietly nearby, most of their heads bowed, as though sagging beneath a heavy weight. "Sa."

Even the silence seemed to hang heavier now than it had before, if possible, and though Kaden had never met Asantii, he felt grief over his brutal death welling up within. Grief, and guilt. He gritted his teeth and punched the cold, hard ground. He thought he had dealt with these feelings, settled this inner conflict, but he couldn't help feeling that Eirmon bore a large portion of the blame for what had happened here. Had his father not betrayed Zangira and Tchinchura on the walls of Barra-Dohn, not only would his city still be standing, but the Jin Dara would most likely be dead. And if the Jin Dara were dead, Kaden thought, how many other things that had gone wrong with the world would not now need fixing?

Hardly had this thought passed through his mind, when Telsiin spoke again and Kaden's attention was pulled back to the Elder.

"Do we think the Jin Dara has been here?" Telsiin asked, surveying the other Amhuru.

Kaden glanced around at the watching faces. The possibility that the death and destruction they had found here had been anyone but the Jin Dara had not occurred to him. He saw in the eyes of the other Amhuru that he was not the only one surprised by the question.

"Do you not?" one of them asked.

"It would be a remarkable coincidence," another said, "if Asantii came here to hide his fragment from the Jin Dara and someone else came and took it from him, would it not?"

There were murmurs of agreement. Many heads nodded. To which, in the end, it was Tchinchura who replied, not Telsiin.

"We could quibble over the word coincidence, since I am not sure such a thing exists in the world that Kalos rules." Some nodded again, agreeing with Tchinchura, and all waited for him to go on. "But I understand what you mean and if I may use the word the same way, I might say coincidence of this magnitude is indeed possible. It brought all three Southland fragments to the same city at the same time, and only a hair's breadth separated the possible outcomes of recovering the two that were lost and losing the one that was retained. I know, for I was there.

"As it turns out, of course," Tchinchura continued. "Neither of those things happened, but the experience left its mark on me. When it comes to the Cord and its power, anything is possible. The Jin Dara is not the only one who desires it."

"True," Amintuu agreed, "but should we not assume that the one known to be looking for fragments has taken it, unless we have a good reason to think otherwise?"

"There is good reason, I think," Telsiin said, "to be skeptical that what has happened here was the work of the Jin Dara."

The Amhuru listened quietly, their attention once more on their Elder. "It was Naalsen," Telsiin said, nodding at an Amhuru who was squatting not far away, "who brought word to us of the ambush at Casmir. He was certain the Jin Dara had been there and had captured at least some of the other messengers alive. We figured the Jin Dara would target Draagan, whose hiding place was closest to Casmir, which is why we chose to come to Berran's Point and Asantii, since he was farthest from Casmir and we presumed Berran's Point the safest rallying place."

"We may have been wrong," one of the Amhuru said.

"We may have been," Telsiin agreed, "about Draagan being the Jin Dara's target. But even so, he should not have been able to get here from Casmir before us."

"This is true," Amintuu agreed, "unless Naalsen was wrong and the Jin Dara wasn't in Casmir. Maybe this was a trap."

"I wasn't—"

Telsiin interrupted Naalsen's protest. "Naalsen may have been wrong, of course, but we do not yet have reason to doubt his testimony, other than what we have found here, which is my point."

"And my point," Amintuu said, "is that what we have found here is reason to doubt his testimony. A Keeper and seven other Amhuru were here. It would have taken a very powerful enemy to kill them all."

"And that is what we know," Telsiin said, nodding at Amintuu. "Whoever attacked Berran's Point was very strong. But before we assume it was the Jin Dara, we should remember where we are, and that there is another, perhaps much more obvious possibility—"

A howl ran out in the dim twilight. All the Amhuru together turned to look through the open gates, and what Kaden saw there was like nothing he had ever seen. In the middle of the large open field beyond the gate of Berran's Point crouched a creature that made him shudder. The body was distinctly man-like, though it was covered with hair, but the head was unmistakably wolfish. The long snout and large ears had an especially lupine character, but the eyes! They were piercingly golden, and they stared with open and ferocious malice at the gathered Amhuru.

Kaden barely had time to see the creature, to begin to take it in, before a voice cried out, "The gates! The gates!"

The Amhuru nearest to them were immediately on their feet and running, scrambling to shut and bar them. As they ran, the rest drew weapons and started to clamber up ladders onto the walkway that ran around the fort so they could peer over the stockade walls. Kaden rose uncertainly, also drawing his axe, glancing from Deslo back to the storage shed in which Nara and Kiki were resting.

The gates behind him slammed shut with a crash.

3

THE GRAYMIR

The sun had set over Berran's Point. The day, which had been struggling under the shroud of gloominess that the clouds cast over the land anyway, darkened still further. As the light faded, the howls grew.

Perhaps, Kaden thought as he listened to the cries echoing from outside the stockade, that word 'howl' was too uniform. There was a diversity of animal sounds rising now from the world outside their walls; that was for sure. Some were like howls, others were more roars or growls, he supposed, but all of them brought goosebumps to his skin and made Kaden long to have even the partial daylight from earlier in the overcast day back. They were alone in the dark, trapped in the same fort that had failed to save Asantii and the Amhuru with him.

Kaden's first instinct was to shelter in the shed with Nara and Kiki, but he quickly realized this was a mistake. The shed was small and full of storage shelves. What little space there was for people, Nara and Kiki already occupied, for Nara had stretched out on the floor with her back against one of the walls, and Kiki was curled in a ball upon her. There was barely enough room inside the shed for Kaden to stand, and that was right inside the doorway. The longer he stood there, the more like a fool he felt. He could keep neither Nara nor Kiki safe by standing over them. His place was outside with the rest of the Amhuru.

As though reading his mind, Nara looked up and nodded, giving her consent. "Go, stand with Deslo. Defend the walls."

Kaden stooped, leaning over them. He couldn't quite reach Nara's face, but he kissed the curly blond hair on Kiki's head and then looked up from his daughter to his wife. He wanted to promise that they'd be safe, but he couldn't do that. In the end, he said the only thing he could think to say, "Kalos is with us."

Kaden ducked out, and quickly he surveyed the scene inside the fort. Most of the Amhuru were on the walkway, though a few were gathered just inside the gate, bracing for the possibility of attack. He didn't see Deslo anywhere around on the ground level, but when he looked carefully at those who had stationed themselves above, he saw his son standing at one of the corners that commanded both the front and one side of the fort.

He had not yet decided where he would go, when he felt several Amhuru seize hold of the Arua. Remarkably, despite their strength and the firm hold they took, he felt their control and mastery challenged by someone or something outside the fort. Could those things, those monsters, could they have the ability to manipulate Arua too? Was that why their eyes were golden? Did they somehow bear Zerura, and if so, how?

If Kaden had thought that his world had faltered when they arrived to find the fort smoldering, the Amhuru dead, and the original fragment of the Golden Cord missing, then it really staggered now. It reeled as the men inside the fort struggled with the power arrayed against them outside of it. It reeled, and Kaden sought desperately for understanding of this incredible turn of events.

The Golden Cord was the only fragment of Zerura the world had ever seen, right? The six fragments and their replicas were controlled by the Amhuru and always had been, except for those periods of time when ambitious men had briefly taken one away—like his father, Eirmon, before, and like the Jin Dara now. Those men might experiment with the fragments, and those experiments might bend the natural order of things, but those changes made with the power of the Cord were not permanent, were they? How could an animal—if indeed these things were animals, Kaden thought—have eyes like an Amhuru who had worn Zerura from birth?

Kaden ran to the nearest ladder, climbing swiftly up to the wooden walkway. He moved along it, intending to head all the way to the corner where Deslo stood. But as he walked along, he realized afresh what he had noticed upon approaching the fort, that the sightlines were good and his vantage was unobscured. He suddenly halted, staring out over the large open field before the fort.

The wolf-like creature still crouched in the middle of the field, and scattered about beside and behind it was a striking array of creatures, at once both very similar to each other and very diverse. There were more than a few that were likewise covered with greyish hair and which had the same wolf-like traits of the one who appeared to be their leader, while several others had brown or black hair, with heads that resembled bears. Some looked doggish, and still others had dark, fierce, feline features, like panthers perhaps.

And yet, despite these differences, there was a sameness about them too. All of them had the same striking golden eyes, and all of them, below the neck, seemed roughly proportioned like men, just covered with hair. Or, Kaden supposed, perhaps more accurately, fur.

Kaden peered at the hands of the wolf-creature at the front. They were definitely hands, not paws, as he could make out what appeared to be long, separate digits, though again, they seemed to be covered with hair. He couldn't see clearly enough in the growing dark to know what kind of nails capped those digits, but he easily imagined that they were sharp and long and capable of ripping a man open.

Though the struggle over the Arua had continued during his musings, Kaden felt that the hold the Amhuru had upon it had grown. This fact seemed to him confirmed by the renewed howling that arose from the odd, golden-eyed creatures. The wolf-captain, as Kaden now dubbed him, leapt forward, howling, and the others began to follow. Immediately the Amhuru began to twist and pull and ripple the Arua out in the field, so that the wolf-captain and the others behind him could feel the violence being done to it. They howled still more, screaming their animal screams, but they stopped advancing.

Kaden turned and hurried along the walkway toward Deslo, noticing as he drew near that Maarta and Olli were also coming along the walkway toward that corner from the far side. They converged at the place where Deslo stood, and each of the four greeted the others with quiet nods and then took places side by side, leaning up against the top of the stockade to watch the bizarre creatures as they howled.

At last, Kaden turned to Maarta and asked, "Do you know what these things are?"

"They're Graymir," Maarta said, all the while keeping his eyes glued on the creatures in question. "I think."

"I thought the Graymere was a where, not a what," Kaden said.

Maarta turned then, a slight smile on his face, lightening the somber mood a bit. "Yes, the Graymere is a place, but the Graymir are the people who live there."

"People?" Deslo asked, joining in, and Kaden swallowed the complaint he was going to make about the terms sounding exactly the same, since he was far more interested in his son's simple question than the confusion about the label given these creatures.

Maarta shrugged, glancing back out over the stockade wall at the Graymir. "Yes, despite some of their features, I think they are, in essence, people. At least, that's how I was taught to think of them."

Olli leaned in close, against Maarta, but she looked at Deslo when she said. "I know they look nothing alike, but they make me think of the gorgaal."

Deslo nodded, and Kaden found himself nodding too. The gorgaal had been made by the Jin Dara through his experiments with the power of the Golden Cord, and those experiments had involved people, so Kaden understood why Olli would say that. He suspected that these Graymir, though, with their brilliant, golden eyes, were something quite different. They seemed like wielders of Zerura, not victims of its power run amok, like masters, not servants.

Darkness settled over Berran's Point and those gathered outside it. The howls had diminished, and in the eerie silence Kaden wondered if the creatures had withdrawn. The Amhuru maintained their firm grip on the Arua and continued twisting and rippling it beyond the walls of fort, so he thought it unlikely the Graymir would approach any nearer in the dark. However, any hope that the creatures might quietly be leaving disappeared as torches began to appear at a distance around the entire perimeter of the fort, not just in the front.

It was odd, thinking of those things holding torches, and he could see, even this far away, that they were holding them. Their beastly faces appeared strange and surreal in the flickering light, but even so, the mere act of having and holding fire confirmed for Kaden what Maarta had said. No matter what they looked like, these things were a kind of people.

The creatures kept their distance, no doubt deterred by the hold the Amhuru had on the Arua field, but as the night stretched on, they set more and more things on fire. They had evidently collected a number of branches that they burned in small clusters between one another, contributing to the feeling that Berran's Point was surrounded by a ring of fire.

The Graymir even seemed intent on burning the wisps of grass that rose here and there above the snow, but they didn't have much luck getting it to light or to stay lit when they did. They threw burning sticks and flaming cones from the nearby pine trees into the field that lay between them and the fort, but if these were serious efforts to burn the wet grass or start some kind of larger blaze, they failed.

Kaden wondered what they might have accomplished had there been no snow and the time of year been different. If everything had been a bit hotter and drier, the Amhuru might have been burned out of the fort, though he supposed there were those among the Amhuru who could probably summon rain to extinguish the flames or wind to blow them back the other way.

When it became apparent to Kaden that the standoff between the Amhuru inside the fort and the Graymir outside didn't look like it was going to end anytime soon, he headed back down to the storage shed to check on Nara. He found her dozing, snoring softly, while Kiki likewise slept upon her. He contemplated waking Nara to tell her of the things he had seen, but decided against it. There would be time later.

But as he turned to go, Nara woke with a start and, sitting up with a slight jump, she cradled Kiki tightly as she said, "Kaden?"

"Yes," he answered her, "it's just me. Sorry."

"It's all right," she said, yawning as she settled back against the wall. "What's going on? Tchinchura looked in on us a little while ago, but he didn't say much."

So Kaden sat in the doorway and told her what he had seen and what Maarta had said. He had no answers for the inevitable questions that followed, and in fact he found himself giving voice to some questions of his own. "I wonder how they overpowered Asantii and the Amhuru who were here before us, assuming that they are the ones who did?"

"Maybe they got in the fort somehow and caught them unawares," Nara said.

"Or maybe there are just too many of us here now for them to over-power," Kaden replied, thinking of the brief battle he had witnessed for control of the Arua.

"If that's the case," Nara said, "maybe they'll give up and go away."

"Maybe," Kaden said, hearing and understanding the hope in her voice, even as something else occurred to him. "Though, if they did kill Asantii, we won't be able to just let them go. We'll have to try to get back what they've taken."

They didn't either one say anything else to that. Hunter or hunted, since the day they'd fled Barra-Dohn, their lives had been in constant motion. Kaden was tired, bone-weary in fact, and he knew Nara was too. Whatever hope he'd harbored for Berran's Point—that perhaps with two original fragments in one place and a large collection of Amhuru, that maybe here might be a place of refuge, at least for a while—well, so much for that. That dream had died with Asantii.

"I'm going to stretch out here, just outside the door," Kaden said. "Why don't you try to get some more sleep? Who knows what comes next and when you'll have shelter again?"

"All right," Nara said, as he backed out of the door far enough to lie down in front of it. As he settled down, she added, "I love you, Kaden."

"I love you too."

"We're still all right, you know."

He smiled in the darkness. Here they were, in a mostly burned-out fort, surrounded by a bizarre race of beast-men, or something like that, their already-uncertain future looking increasingly bleak whatever the morning brought, and she was trying to reassure him. So much for being her protector and provider. He glanced through the doorway into the darkness at the back of the shed where he knew she would be watching him, even if she couldn't make his face out in the dark either. "I know. Let's get some sleep."

·   ·   ·

Kaden woke to the grey half-light of a winter's morning in the Northlands. Remembering where he was, he sat up, looking first to see Nara and Kiki still asleep in the shed, and then glancing around the fort to see what he could see. Several Amhuru were up, walking on the raised walkway, while some others stood not far away, talking near the gate. Still, from even a quick survey of his surroundings, Kaden could tell the Graymir were likely gone.

Even as that thought passed through his mind, he realized that he couldn't feel anyone manipulating the Arua field, and that confirmed it. He was relieved, to be sure, but his exchange with Nara in the night kept him from overreacting. If they were gone, he imagined it was only a matter of time before some or all of the Amhuru went after them.

Kaden rose, stretched, and walked around the inside of the fort. He hadn't had much of a look around the ground level the previous night, and he surveyed what remained of the burned-out buildings now. In one of the corners near the back of the fort, he found Marlo and Owenn sitting and talking quietly beside a small fire. They greeted him pleasantly, and he joined them.

"We have just made some jonda," Marlo said, holding up the small metal pot that he had been warming over the fire. "I'm afraid it won't be quite so good as what we used to make in Sar Komen, but you are welcome to a cup if you would like."

"Yes, please," Kaden said with genuine enthusiasm. Jonda was one of the few new tastes he had found in the Northlands to which he had taken almost immediately. "If you have enough to share, that is."

"We have plenty," Marlo said, pouring Kaden a cup of the hot, dark liquid, and passing it to him.

Kaden held the cup lovingly, letting the heat from it warm his hands, savoring the rich fragrance of the jonda. "This is a treat," he said, as he raised the cup to his lips and took a slow, deliberate sip.

They started to share with one another their impressions of the preceding night, but they did not get far. Tchinchura approached, and he told them that Telsiin was gathering the Amhuru to discuss their situation and their options. Kaden felt his heart sink. Tchinchura might speak of options, but he saw few choices ahead.

As they had gathered and squatted in the open space near the gate the previous afternoon, the Amhuru once more circled around Telsiin, Tchinchura, and Amintuu. Kaden had sensed alarm and fear the first time, and while there might still have been some of that in the assembly, he sensed more of a renewed resolve this morning. The hardened, impassive faces had returned, and the Amhuru seemed once again themselves. Kaden took a deep breath, straightening up and pushing away his despair. They would, as always, do what had to be done.

"It would seem," Telsiin said, "that the death of Asantii and the others was not the work of the Jin Dara after all, unless he somehow recruited the Graymir to do his bidding, and that seems … unlikely."

"I agree, Elder," Amintuu said, nodding. "I see no evidence that the Jin Dara was behind what happened here. He is a Southlander, and I find it hard to believe he has even heard of the Graymir yet, let alone had time to contact and recruit them."

"And why would the Graymir help him if he did?" another added.

"Why have they come forth from their hiding places in the Graymere at all, for that matter," yet another said.

"Patience," Telsiin said, motioning for quiet as murmurs spread quickly through the gathering. "That is another question altogether, though one we must soon attend to."

Telsiin turned to Tchinchura, fixing him with his gaze. "You know this Jin Dara better than we, you and the other Southlanders you brought with you. Do you see his hand at work here?"

Tchinchura did not answer right away. He stared at the ground thoughtfully, as though carefully ordering each word he would speak. After a moment, he looked up at Telsiin. "I find it hard to know what I have seen, for the creatures who gathered outside this place last night are unlike anything I have ever encountered. I know the Jin Dara can both alter and command the animals of a place, for I have seen him do that, but I don't even know if what I saw last night were animals. They wore the faces of animals, cried out to the wind and sky, to the moon and stars like animals, but they had in other ways the form of men.

"Elder," Tchinchura continued, "for myself, and for my Southland friends, will you not now tell me more about these Graymir?"

Telsiin considered this for a moment, then nodded toward Tchinchura. "I feel some urgency to decide a course of action, and there will no doubt be time to tell this tale in more detail at a later time, but you are right. Without more knowledge of the Graymir, you will find it difficult to speak to the likelihood that the Jin Dara has found and manipulated them. So let me tell you their tale in brief.

"The Graymir were a ferocious and war-like tribe who inhabited the Graymere, obviously drawing their name from the wild and desolate lands they inhabited. Long before our forefathers stretched forth their hands and created the Madri, they had established for themselves a reputation that kept all but the hardiest souls far from their lands. In fact, this fort and others like it were built as part of a network of outposts, set to watch their borders, so that the neighboring lands might be warned should the Graymir come forth.

"At any rate, there is no need to recount all that they did to earn their reputation. After all, the Graymir then were not like they are now, not as you have seen them. That did not happen until a mysterious group of wanderers, who many believe were trapped on this side of the Madri when it was created, happened upon the Graymir and merged with them. These wanderers brought with them dark rituals and ancient secrets that the Graymir exploited as their first step toward what they have become."

Telsiin paused, looking up, and Kaden saw that the Elder was staring at something just above and behind himself. He looked over his shoulder, and Kaden was surprised to see Marlo standing, the only one of all those in the circle on his feet.

"Devoted one?" Telsiin said, tentatively. "Do you have something to say?"

"Their name," Marlo said quietly. "Do you know what name these wanderers went by?"

Telsiin nodded. "I do, for my father and my father's father passed it down to me."

"What was it?"

"They were called the Far'n Gael."

In the silence that followed, Kaden glanced back at Marlo. The Devoted's eyes were closed now, a pained look that spoke to Kaden for all the world of something very much like devastation on his face.

"That name is known to you, I see," Telsiin said.

"It is," Marlo answered, opening his eyes at last. "All too well."

"Then perhaps my story really begins with you, for very little is known of the Far'n Gael among the Northland Amhuru anymore. All knowledge about them, save only the name, has passed out of living memory. Will you tell us what you know?"

For a long moment, Marlo said nothing, and then Telsiin spoke again. "Devoted One, you are, I understand, a Guardian of Truth. Much of the

Old Ways has passed from the world, and few remain who remember them. But, if you are indeed a Guardian, I invoke as an Elder of the Amhuru our ancient rights. Will you not speak of these Far'n Gael? Will you not share with us this portion of the truth you guard?"

"Yes," Marlo said. "I will."

4

THE FAR'N GAEL

About the beginning of all things," Marlo began, "the world has long since forgotten, save only for a few of the Old Stories, which are handed down as myths and legends."

"A few?" Deslo said, leaning over and whispering to his father, his eyebrows raised.

Kaden smiled, understanding what Deslo meant. He also recalled the many afternoons he had spent under the bright Aralyn sun in the courtyards of the royal palace in Barra-Dohn, listening to Gamalian tell him another of the Old Stories. Still, he wanted to hear what Marlo had to say, so he silently lifted his finger to his lips and Deslo smiled back as he also returned his attention to the Kalosene, who continued …

·   ·   ·

… and some of the Old Stories that are still told are themselves incomplete. For instance, though many still speak of Kalos' decision to place Zerura in the ground to generate the Arua field and regulate the growth patterns of all things, they do not remember the whole reason why. They typically speak of the Dark Things, the Jin Dara, that would grow out of control on occasion and become monstrosities that terrified our forefathers. They forget, though, that oftentimes these Dark Things were not accidents, but the deliberate creations of men who practiced the forbidden rituals that Telsiin has mentioned.

They also forget how these men came to learn these rituals, and so I must tell you both something of the Far'n Gael, as well as something of the one they serve.

When the universe was young, and Kalos had not yet made man to govern this world, he first made the Haladriim, or 'the Bright Ones' as they are often called. He gathered a handful of starlight in his mighty, out-stretched hand, and he breathed life into it. Each individual ray became a Haladriim. How long the Haladriim served Kalos in peace and content-ment at the dawn of time, we do not know. All we know is that it did not last.

The Old Stories tell of Nekron, one of the Bright Ones, who grew weary of serving Kalos. He wanted to rule, not serve, and he sowed discon-tent and corruption among some of the Haladriim. A great war followed, and though Nekron was defeated, the war continued, only in other ways and on other fronts.

It was Nekron who first showed one of our ancestors how to manip-ulate the growth cycles of living things in a world without Arua. Nekron taught the dark rituals that gave his followers the power to blur the line between man and beast—a line that Kalos had forbidden any man to cross—and to create the Dark Things that terrorized the world. Those who were drawn to this power, who rejected Kalos and chose instead to worship Nekron, became the Far'n Gael, whose name means 'children of the shad-ows.' They are the legion of the lost, the ancient enemy of the Kalosenes, for we were first formed as a group, distinct from other men, to oppose the Far'n Gael.

I know this may be hard for you to believe, you who live in a world where the Kalosenes are reclusive outsiders, who avoid the petty conflicts of men and renounce the wars of kings and nations that care for nothing but power. Indeed, as a child of this age, it is hard for me at times to believe this, but we were once an elite military force, commissioned to fight a long and difficult war against the Far'n Gael.

This ongoing war between the Kalosenes and Far'n Gael was one of the fronts in the ancient war between Kalos and Nekron, and it lasted for many generations. The Far'n Gael were a powerful foe, and the power they wielded was psychological as much as physical, for they bent the world around them in awful ways, distorting much that Kalos had made, includ-ing themselves.

A major campaign against the Far'n Gael was raging a long, long way from Aralyn when Kalos and His Temple were profaned and the Golden Cord was first separated into its current fragments. In fact, this campaign concluded not long after your Amhuru ancestors first started traveling throughout the world. The campaign was very successful and the power of the Far'n Gael seemed crippled, so much so that when the Kalosenes of the Southlands found that the Far'n Gael did not rise again to trouble them or the world at large, it was both natural and plausible that they would believe the enemy had been finally defeated, once and for all.

And yet, if what Telsiin says is true, then this is not so. It sounds now as though a remnant of the Far'n Gael did indeed survive that last campaign, only they were north of the Madri when it was created. I think that there were those among the Kalosenes who suspected that something like this might have happened, but most wanted to believe that the Far'n Gael had perished and the menace they represented was gone for good. It is with great sadness that I say, from what we saw here last night, that I know now this cannot be the case. These Graymir certainly appear to have learned much that the Far'n Gael, and perhaps only the Far'n Gael, could have taught them.

·　　　·　　　·

Marlo stopped talking, and the Amhuru remained silent, watching the Devoted as he stood gazing deeply at nothing in particular, as though lost in the collective memory of the Kalosenes. Telsiin nodded slightly, head bowed, murmuring something silently to himself, and then he looked up at Marlo.

"You have answered a riddle as old as I am, Guardian," Telsiin said, and he looked up at the hazy, grey sky above them, though Kaden could see that it was really into the past and not the sky that he peered. "When I was a boy, my great-grandfather once told me that the Bright Ones were the messengers of Kalos. I asked him, 'Who are the Bright Ones?' and he told me, 'They are the children of the stars.' I did not know what to think of that, and he died not long after. Of the Bright Ones, and of Nekron, I never learned anything from my other ancestors."

Telsiin turned to Tchinchura, "Are tales of them told in the Southlands among our people?"

Tchinchura slowly shook his head. "I have never heard of them nor this story before today."

And then, before all the watching eyes of the Amhuru, Telsiin rose, walked to Marlo, and bent down on one knee with his head bowed, like a supplicant. "Guardian, forgive us for forgetting these things, like the world around us has forgotten them."

"Elder," Marlo said, quietly and gently, "You need not ask my pardon. I don't know if Kalos is offended by this or not, but it seems to me that we have each persevered in the tasks we were given. You and your people have labored to guard the Cord, and we have labored to guard the truth."

"Ah, the Cord," Telsiin said, rising and turning with something like a wry smile to the rest of the circle. "If we are to be judged for our work protecting the Cord, I am afraid we are still in trouble."

A smattering of laughter followed, and Kaden saw that even those who did not laugh smiled at the Elder's joke. It was one of the things he appreciated about the Amhuru. Even in somber times, they didn't seem to feel it necessary to be only serious, all the time. In Barra-Dohn, or at least in Eirmon's household, laughter was an offense if the King was in the wrong mood.

"The Cord," Telsiin said again, but it looked to Kaden like the Elder was talking to himself even though he said the words out loud. "We shall have to figure out what to do about the missing fragment, but not yet."

He looked up, and his glance swept over the assembly, but it finally fixed on Marlo. "You have spoken of the Far'n Gael, that we might better understand the Graymir and the task before us, but there is more to this story that you do not know. I will complete the tale, but it is a story of shame for me and my people."

Kaden could see a shift in the Amhuru, given the laughter that had only just died down among them, and as he glanced around the group, he saw looks of embarrassment and discomfort. They knew what Telsiin was going to say, and they were ashamed. Kaden looked back at the Elder, curious about what he could say that would make the Northland Amhuru look like that. Telsiin began ...

.   .   .

... The Far'n Gael came north, this the stories of my people confirm. Their strange ways drove them to keep their distance from most of the more populated regions, and I suppose, though I do not know this for sure, the Devoted who were in the Northlands when the Madri was created would have warned us about them also.

At any rate, however it happened, they eventually found the Gray-mir, and the two peoples essentially merged into one. The Graymir had always been wild, and their lands always forbidding, but the stories that came from there then were like nothing anyone had ever told before. Horrible stories. Frightening stories. But even so, they were stories of strange powers, and more to the point, stories that held a strange power for some of those who heard them.

One of those caught in the spell of those stories, who started to dream of the power these Far'n Gael had brought to the Graymir, was a man named Charfiin. Charfiin was an Amhuru. In fact, Charfiin was a … Keeper.

You understand, I'm sure, that it takes time under any conditions to realize that a Keeper is missing. In Charfiin's case, it took a great deal of time, for he long planned how to give himself the maximum time to make good his disappearance into the Graymere and cover his tracks. It took, not years, but decades to find him, and by the time our forefathers knew where he had gone, Charfiin had been among the Graymir for so very, very long. They had spent years and years experimenting with how Zerura could enhance their dark rituals and add power to their secret ways.

Recovering the fragment that Charfiin had taken with him into the Graymere was the most difficult task the Northland Amhuru ever faced—save perhaps, what faces us now with the coming of the Jin Dara. And though the mission to recover his fragment was successful, it came at the cost of many Amhuru lives. In the end, though we believed then and still believe now that the Graymir had a vast store of Zerura fragments made from Charfiin's original, we had to withdraw from the Graymere without that store. Where they hid it and how exactly they used it, none of us were ever sure.

The rumor, though, about how they used it, spread by those who had penetrated into the Graymere and escaped alive, was that they would grind small portions of Zerura into a very fine powder and ingest it by first mixing it in water and then drinking it. The Zerura, taken in that way perhaps, aided them in their attempt to manipulate the growth patterns of the world around them, as well as in their quest to mix human and animal elements within themselves. And if the store of Zerura they built up over the years Charfiin lived among them was big enough, then they might still have access to it.

.   .   .

Telsiin had finished talking, but Kaden was mesmerized by his tale and its implications. He thought of the wolf-captain from the night before and his golden eyes, and he could imagine that creature sprinkling gold Zerura dust in his cup and drinking the water down before howling at the pale white glow of a winter's moon. If anyone but Telsiin, Elder of the Northland Amhuru, had told him this tale, he would have assumed it was a story invented to scare children before bedtime and thought he was being teased. But Telsiin had told it, and Kaden had little choice but to believe it.

"I understand that the Graymir are dangerous—both the people and the place," Trajax said, and Kaden smiled just a little as he watched the Southland Amhuru stumble a bit over the names that had given him pause the night before. "But if the Northland Amhuru knew a large store of Zerura was hidden away in there, how could they just leave it?"

"This was long, long ago," Telsiin said, and Kaden could hear understanding, not defensiveness, in his voice, "and I was, of course, not there for those deliberations. I was always taught that it was a very difficult decision, but that since so many had died simply trying to find Charfiin and get the original back, it was believed by the Elders to be the right decision. There were just too few of us, too many of them, and the Graymere itself fought for them. It is a fearful place."

Telsiin hesitated here, and Kaden found himself looking past the assembled Amhuru toward the gate, as though he could see outside and beyond it. He wondered what this Graymere was really like, that Telsiin would use those hushed tones when he spoke of it. There was a good chance he would soon find out, he supposed.

"And," Telsiin continued suddenly, "remember what I said before, places like this were built and maintained, with Amhuru help, to keep an eye on both the land and the people who inhabit it."

"Do raids like this happen very often?" Marlo asked.

"No," Telsiin said, shaking his head. "Rarely, in fact. I can't remember the last time an outpost was attacked by the Graymir."

"Then why here?" Marlo asked. "Why now?"

"Perhaps," Tchinchura said, "Elder Telsiin has given us the answer with his story. No matter how big a store of Zerura the Graymir had originally, if they have been using it steadily and routinely in their rituals ever since, then surely their supply has run low. Or perhaps, it may even have run out."

"Asantii's piece," Amintuu said, rising. "That's it! They came for Asantii's piece. They can replenish their entire supply now that they have another original."

"But how did they know an original was here?" Maarta asked, and Kaden nodded, for that question also was on his mind. "After all, Asantii was only just moved here to protect him from the Jin Dara."

"I don't know," Amintuu said, "but it makes perfect sense that they would come out of their land and attack the fort for it. A prize like that would be worth the risk."

"Perhaps they didn't know," Tchinchura said, and all eyes swung once more toward him. "After all, they did take off the limbs of every Amhuru that was here in order to remove every fragment of Zerura."

"Of course they did," Amintuu said. "Why leave any behind?"

"Perhaps they were just being thorough, even though they knew Asantii bore an original," Tchinchura said. "Or, perhaps they were being thorough because they thought every ounce of Zerura they took here would be precious, that these were all replicas like the Zerura fragments in their own stores."

"Then it is possible that they don't yet know they have an original," Telsiin said.

"They may not," Tchinchura agreed. "But if they know what they're doing—and it appears they do—once they cut it, they will realize what they have."

"And then they will retreat as fast as possible to the very heart of the Graymere," Telsiin said, "and we will have to make war on the entire Graymir population to get it back—like before."

"They will head back as fast as they can anyway, won't they?" Amintuu said, almost scoffing.

"Not necessarily," Tchinchura said. "They know there are more Amhuru here after last night, so they know there is more Zerura within their grasp. Who can say what they will do?"

"But they've gone," another Northland Amhuru said. "Doesn't that mean that even if they don't know exactly what they have, they're heading home?"

"It might," Tchinchura agreed. "Though they may just be heading back to their nearest outpost for reinforcements. Perhaps they are seeking help to return and claim more pieces."

"We don't know where they've gone or why," Telsiin said. "And we're not going to know before we have to make our decision about what to do now. I think that we have to assume the worst, that they know what they have and are heading even now back into the heart of the Graymere. That means the time for talking has past. We must decide who will go in pursuit, and who will stay. For you, Tchinchura, must not go, and enough must stay with you to provide a reasonable defense should they, or others intent on harm, come for what you bear."

And just like that, all matters of history, all speculations about what the Graymir did or didn't know, did or didn't intend, simply disappeared. All that mattered now was who was going and who was staying.

.   .   .

Kaden stood on the walkway, overlooking the tall stockade wall. The Amhuru party going after the Graymir was moving across the open field, but he wasn't really watching the whole party. He was focused on just one of them.

Deslo jogged near the back, a little behind Maarta and Olli, and beside Marlo and Owenn, who had been equipped with meridium soles for this trip, since they would need to move fast to keep up with the Amhuru. He was glad the Devoted were going. They had been together for so long, he felt like Deslo would be safer with them, though he knew that in a battle, Deslo was as likely to have to defend them as the other way around. His son was a boy no longer.

Kaden watched Deslo jog away, and he felt a pang of worry. If the Graymir, and the land of the same name, if they were as dangerous as Telsiin indicated, then there was a good chance some of those Amhuru weren't coming back. Maybe none of them were.

He thought about the day they went ashore at the island of dreadful daylight, about bringing Deslo with him as they faced the gorgaal on the beach, and then later when they fought those ferocious creatures by the Manor House. He had known that would be a dangerous day too, but this felt different. This time, he wasn't going to be there. This time, Deslo was on his own.

He knew that wasn't literally true, that Deslo was surrounded by other Amhuru, not to mention Marlo and Owenn, but he wasn't there. It bothered him, sending Deslo off and not going himself. He felt he should be there. It was a father's job to keep his children safe.

But that was why he couldn't go. He turned from the outside and looked down at the burned-out storage shed. Nara and Kiki were not in it now, for they had gone back to the cookfire near the rear of the fort to help make food for those who remained. They were his responsibility too, and he couldn't stay and watch over them and at the same time go with Deslo.

And of course, Tchinchura was here, and that too was his responsibility. He had become an Amhuru to help recover what the Jin Dara had taken, and to avenge himself on the man who had destroyed Barra-Dohn. Along the way, that motive of revenge had been not exactly replaced, but subordinated to a better, higher motive: To protect the last of the Southland fragments and the one who bore it.

Kaden sighed, glancing back over his shoulder one more time at the Amhuru party disappearing in the distance. He was so glad he had finally found and built a relationship with his son. At long last this, even in the midst of the collapse of most of the things he had held dear. But, at the same time, he had not quite understood the pain of love, and of letting go. He felt it now, and he prayed a silent prayer that Deslo would not be lost to him again. "Let him come back, alive and whole. Let him come back."

5

A SPARK OF AN IDEA

Draagan leapt up off the Arua, planted his right foot firmly on the smooth trunk of the Trillaga Tree, and pushed up as hard as he could. He reached for and grabbed the lowest branch, and in a moment he had pulled himself up onto it. From there, he scurried up and farther up, using the trunk to help him reach from branch to branch until he was at least forty feet above the jungle floor.

There Draagan crouched on a limb, gazing out and down at the jungle ahead, scanning forward as far as he could, though the thick canopy of leaves made it difficult to see much of the ground. That was all right, for there were other ways to see what was going on below. There, off to his left and about a half mile away, a localized fluttering of birds, mostly the bright red and green Cappas so common in this part of the jungle, lifting up off the branches they were perched on into the morning sky, told him what he wanted to know. The Najin had gone that way. He swiftly climbed back down.

Draagan signaled silently for the other Amhuru who were spread out around him, almost invisible in the jungle. They had left only the wounded of their own number behind at their stronghold, for Draagan knew this might well be their best chance to recover the fragments of the Golden Cord that had been stolen. He led them forward, motioning for them to follow, as he set out in the direcion of the flutter of birds he had seen from above. He ran, thinking about both these Najin and what he had learned about them and their leader.

From one of the wounded men they left behind shortly after their fight two days earlier, he had learned the name they used for themselves. The man lay dying from his wounds, and Draagan and another Amhuru had knelt beside him to see if they could learn anything about who were the attackers and the man they served, before he died. He was defiant, even attempting to spit in Draagan's face—and failing—while proudly proclaiming that he would tell them nothing, that he was 'Najin.' He said that, over and over, clearly proud of the word. Before long, though, he died and said nothing, proudly or otherwise, ever again.

Literally, Najin meant 'sons of the dark,' which fit, Draagan supposed, as it was a dark business trying to take and reunite all the fragments of the Golden Cord. And yet, the golden clothes they wore seemed incongruous, given the name, though he assumed the color choice was a fairly obvious tribute to the Zerura they wore.

Beyond their intent, what was really dark about them, Draagan reflected, was the one they followed. Draagan thought of him, the man he had wounded with his steel blade, and once more found himself wondering if the man was dead, wondering and hoping. Breeson's scouting party had determined nothing more than that the Najin were carrying him, and also that there might be a chance, if the Amhuru moved fast and Kalos favored them, of taking back the missing originals.

Draagan ran along the surface of the Arua, scanning the jungle ahead for any movement and listening for any sign that would indicate the presence of the Najin. He did hope that their leader was dead, but he had to admit that it seemed unlikely. They had left behind their dead and fatally wounded, and he suspected that they would have left him behind too, taking only what he bore, had he also been dead. Perhaps they carried his dead body with them out of reverence, but these Najin did not strike him as terribly sentimental.

More birds fluttered upward, somewhere not far ahead. He heard their cries and the flapping of their wings, and he veered left in pursuit. As he did so, he saw, almost too late, a half dozen colorful Cappas diving toward him, their wings outstretched and their sharp beaks open.

He dove to the side as the Cappas swooped. They angled sharply back after him, their claws and beaks searching for a place to grab and tear his skin. More birds joined them, and he saw among them other kinds beside the Cappas, and he knew instinctively that this was not a random attack. The Najin had sent them, which meant they were aware of the pursuit. The Amhuru would not have surprise on their side if they closed on the Najin.

Draagan had more immediate problems, though, and he drew knives with both hands, struggling furiously to hold off the birds that had gone mad in their bloodlust. There were too many for him to fend them all off at once, and he felt the piercing strength of talons rip and dig into his shoulder. He let himself drop from the Arua and, twisting in the air, he hit the ground with a thud, crushing the Cappa between the weight of his body and the hard ground.

Then Draagan felt something else, not the talon or beak of a Cappa, but the twisting of Arua by a man bearing Zerura as he bent the field to his will. He realized he had been feeling it for some time, only gently at first, but now it was no longer gentle, and if he was right, the one messing with the Arua was drawing closer. The Najin hadn't just sent the birds to slow him down; they had used the birds as a diversion. They were coming. They were attacking.

Draagan leapt back up onto the Arua, and as he did so, he saw one of the Najin, the mysterious men in gold, moving in the distance, running at an angle toward the place where he now stood. He moved back, swinging with the blade in his right hand and slicing through a diving Cappa's outstretched wing, and lifting his left hand to his mouth to whistle twice in a shrill, high blast. Then he ran.

They had to fall back. Coming had been risky, very risky. The Najin each bore two fragments, and they knew how to use them. Only the close quarters in the stronghold and the surprise wounding of their leader by Draagan and his steel blades had turned their first encounter in favor of the Amhuru. Their hope on this mission had been for surprise, but now all hope of surprise was gone. As much as they wanted to retrieve the two originals the Najin had, they could not afford to lose a third, and the fragment around his right forearm was an original.

The slightest of movements out of the corner of his eye was all the warning Draagan had. The knife was on its way toward him even as he turned to see the Najin throw it. Draagan turned hard away, and as he did, he saw the knife turn to follow him. They could redirect the trajectory of their weapons, he thought as he dropped suddenly down off the Arua field.

He hit the ground at an awkward angle and his hip exploded with pain—pain that Draagan had to ignore if he was going to survive. He spun, knife in hand, preparing to throw. The Najin had also dropped from the Arua and was closing fast. Draagan threw the steel knife, but the Najin was not fooled. He made no attempt to redirect it. He only dodged quickly left, allowing the blade to sail by him.

Draagan now had dodging of his own to do, as the Najin hurled another knife his way. At this short distance, Draagan knew his choices were limited. If the Najin could redirect the blade mid-flight, he couldn't simply dodge left or right, for the blade could follow and strike home. He ran toward the nearest Trillaga Tree and dove behind it, listening as the blade struck its smooth surface with a thwack. He rose, threw one of his meridium blades at the Najin, who again dodged.

This time, though, the blade didn't simply sail past the Najin, as Draagan immediately summoned it back into his hand. As he did so, he reached over and pried the Najin's knife from the trunk of the Trillaga, so that when he caught his own knife, he was once more wielding two blades. This time, though, he threw neither. Instead, he ran directly toward the Najin, closing the distance between them rapidly. If the other had the advantage in his control of the knives in the air, Draagan would finish this at close quarters.

The man, another knife of his own now out and in his hand, saw Draagan coming and grinned. It was a wide, eager grin, and a moment later, the men crashed together at full speed. They tumbled to the ground, and Draagan found the Najin to be strong and wiry, slick with sweat from the humid jungle air. The struggle was intense but brief, as Draagan moved to finish the encounter swiftly, slipping his hand through the man's defenses with remarkable speed and agility and driving the Najin's own knife deep into his chest, burying it up to the hilt.

The Najin's lifeless body slumped to the ground as Draagan pushed out from under him. He wasted no time, though, with deliberation. He turned and headed back toward the stronghold. His first duty was to the fragment of the Golden Cord, and in his judgement, the Amhuru could not continue with their current mission and keep it safe.

He whistled two more short, shrill blasts, and he ran as fast as he could go. He hoped the others were close behind, but he couldn't wait to see. They would need to see to their own safety and escape.

·   ·   ·

Not long after dark the following day, Draagan and the other Amhuru who had survived the encounter with the Najin—which were most of them, thankfully—returned to their stronghold. They passed wearily through their new, makeshift gate, which they closed and barred. The first thing they did was set the watch, just in case the Najin had followed them back.

Draagan thought it unlikely that they had, but he would not take any chances. While listening along the way home to the other Amhuru speak of their encounters with the Najin, those who had indeed encountered them, it sounded less like a comprehensive attack meant to destroy, and more like a quick counterstrike meant to scare the Amhuru off their trail.

Well, Draagan thought, if that was their goal, it worked. He slumped to the ground with his back against the sturdy wall of the fort, and he second-guessed his decision to retreat. The enemy had probably been weary and nervous, no doubt just as worried that the Amhuru would take from them the two original fragments that they had as Draagan was worried that the remaining Najin would take the one he bore. Perhaps, if he had re-organized the Amhuru after the Najin attack and returned to the pursuit, perhaps they would even now have reclaimed them.

Perhaps. But of course, perhaps was double-edged word. Perhaps not. It was also true that if Draagan had not retreated, he might be dead and the enemy might now have three originals. Perhaps. What would have hap-pened if he had behaved differently was impossible to know, though of course that didn't keep Draagan from wondering about it.

Breeson walked over and slumped down next to him, letting his arms dangle on top of his drawn up knees. He looked over toward the great hall, where the gaping hole created by the *salandra's* entrance and shattering of the gate still stared at them. Breeson looked from the great hall to Draagan. "It really stinks in there now. That thing is foul."

"Three days of rotting under a hot sun," Draagan said.

"How in the world are we going to get it out of there," Breeson said.

"One piece at a time," Draagan answered, his characteristic grin returning.

Breeson smiled and shook his head. "What a revolting prospect."

"At least we're alive to do it," Draagan said. "Given what we were fac-ing, we weren't any of us sure we'd live to see this day."

"Sa, that's true."

"So," Draagan continued, "I'll deal with removing the rotten carcass of the *salandra,* if need be."

"If need be?" Breeson asked. "Is there any if?"

Draagan did not answer immediately. He looked from Breeson to the dark opening into the great hall. He hadn't given a lot of thought to what would come next, as everything had been about the Najin, about whether to give pursuit, and about whether they had the strength and numbers to take back what had been stolen.

They hadn't been able to do that, so he needed to plan his next move carefully. The man who had faced him in the great hall might be dead, or he was more likely just seriously wounded, but in either case, the original that Draagan bore might still be in great danger.

"I can'na stay here, Breeson," Draagan said at last. "The only question is whether any of you should. And if we all go, I suppose the Great Croc can be left where he is."

Draagan suddenly stood, and Breeson, as though caught in the sudden expenditure of energy, rose with him. Draagan looked at Breeson as he nodded his head in the direction of the great hall, "If the world is ending, there is no great need to clean up the mess inside. If it isn't, well, then those who survive what lies ahead can come back later and haul out the bones."

With that, Draagan strode swiftly away.

. . .

The thick layer of clouds made the night feel extra dark. Draagan felt like he should be running, but only a fool would run through this jungle in the absolute dark. He made his way as swiftly as possible, yet carefully, and Breeson stayed close behind.

Another flash of lightning ripped through the sky, illuminating their surroundings for the briefest of moments, then as it faded to darkness, the accompanying thunder crashed overhead and decayed to a deep rumbling. It started to rain. It poured down with a fury, the sound of the drops slamming into the thick leaves above almost as loud as the thunder had been. In a matter of moments, they were drenched, every scrap of clothing on them absolutely soaking wet.

"Great," Breeson murmured.

Draagan ignored the sarcasm and flashed his companion a broad smile that he probably couldn't see through the shroud of utter blackness around them. Draagan turned his face upward and closed his eyes involuntarily as the large drops struck his face with what felt like angry vigor. He opened his mouth and drank in the warm rain.

For what felt like a very long time but was probably less than an hour, they traveled in the downpour. And then, as suddenly as it had begun, it ended, and they were once more left in the stifling dark, only the air felt even warmer and thicker and more humid than before.

With the departure of the rain, the veil of silence that had seemed to hang over them lifted, and Breeson came up beside Draagan. "Do you think it will work?" he asked. "The diversion?"

Draagan disliked speculative questions about the unknown, but he knew that, for Breeson, it was a nervous habit, something to say when he wanted to talk. Draagan also knew that what he answered was less important than that he answer. "I don't see why it shouldn't. The others will leave from Min Luna at the mouth of the river, and if it is being watched, as I'm sure it is, they will be spotted."

"And since the next closest large port is almost three weeks away through difficult terrain, they should assume we are all there," Breeson added.

"They should," Draagan agreed, "and I hope they do. Otherwise this long walk will have been for nothing."

"Not necessarily nothing. If they know the original has gone elsewhere, at least they won't know precisely where, unless they're watching all ports equally."

"I can'na imagine they have the resources for that," Draagan said, "and if they do, we are in some serious trouble."

"We're already in some serious trouble," Breeson said. "Though I have this feeling you are already working on a plan, even if you haven't shared it with me yet."

"I'm not sure I would call it a plan, exactly," Draagan said, and he laughed, for he could imagine Breeson's look as he said those words. "Call it more of a spark of an idea that might one day grow into a plan."

"Whatever you want to call it," Breeson said, "would you care to tell me what it is?"

"It's not so much a *what* as a *who*."

"A spark of an idea is a who, not a what?" Breeson asked, confused.

"I meant my idea refers to a who, more than a what."

"Go on," Breeson said, encouraging Draagan to continue.

"Well," Draagan said. "I don't know if I killed their leader. I suspect not, but even if I have, their retreat seemed orderly and efficient, so there may well be a good second-in-command that we now have to contend with.

"Either way, the man I encountered, the man who crossed the Madri with two fragments of the Golden Cord, he was a ruthless and determined man—as I'm sure his closest companions are. I don't see any use in hiding from men like that. Sooner or later, they'll just find me."

"They already did, didn't they?" Breeson said, not so much asking a question as voicing his agreement.

"Exactly," Draagan said.

"So if hiding won't work, what are you thinking? And how is this about a who, not a what?"

"Hunting, Breeson, that is the alternative to hiding," Draagan said, and for the first time since leaving the stronghold, he stopped. He stood still, and Breeson stood beside him, only a couple feet away, but almost invisible in the dark. "And if you are going to hunt a man like that—men like that—then you want someone with you who is as ruthless and determined as they are."

"Yes," Breeson said, a little warily. "I take it you don't mean other Amhuru."

"No, I do not," Draagan said. "We are, by our natures, protectors, not hunters. I can'na argue with Elder Telsiin's decision to split up the Northland Keepers and hide our fragments, as I don't bear his responsibility and the decision wasn't mine to make. I mention it only to illustrate my point. Hiding—protecting—it is our first instinct."

"Who, then?"

"That, Breeson, is the question."

There was silence again, though not far away on their left, a chorus of frogs sung from the muddy banks and shallows of the river. Draagan listened to their song, hesistating to answer Breeson's question. He knew his answer would sound crazy, and more than that, he knew it might actually be crazy.

"Well," Breeson said, impatient for the answer. "Are you going to tell me? Or do I have to wait and see?"

"The Jaens," Draagan said at last. "I am going to visit the JaenSing."

"The JaenSing?" Breeson said, echoing him, and Draagan noted that though he sounded stunned, his voice was at least steady. "You're serious?"

"I am serious."

"They're the most ruthless, ambitious, dreaded mercenaries in the Northlands!"

"Precisely."

"And they hate the Amhuru."

"Also true," Draagan conceded.

"Will they even see you?"

"They will see me," Draagan said. He thought about saying more, but he decided against it. He wanted to offer the history between his family and the Jaens as a reason his plan might work, but he wasn't really sure that was true, so he said nothing further.

"Are you sure about this, Keeper?"

"I am not," Draagan said, and he started forward again. "But we have a long journey ahead of us, which will allow me lots of time to reconsider, if need be."

"Or perhaps," Breeson said, "to have a different spark which might lead to a slightly less dangerous idea."

Draagan smiled, and for a moment, he walked silently along in the darkness. Then he said, "Breeson, do you remember playing First & Last as a child?"

"Of course."

"If you ask most of our people what it takes to be good at First & Last," Draagan said, "They would offer answers like reflexes, balance, quickness, and of course the ability to manipulate Arua, but I don't think any of those are the key."

"You don't?" Breeson said.

"No, I don't. Those things are important, obviously, but I have seen children win games of First & Last who were outmatched by their opponent in all those things."

"What's the key, then?"

"The secret, I think, is to know that your choices in the game—as in, say, combat, or even more broadly, life itself—are never limited to just two. It's rarely as simple as the right move versus the wrong move, the cautious move versus the bold move, attack versus retreat. Oh, it might be occasionally like that, but usually it isn't. Usually, there are choices within the choices.

"The best players of First & Last seem to instinctively realize, that even when the situation calls for boldness, there are multiple options, and they never make the bold move. They make the bolder move."

"That's how an overmatched player can win?" Breeson said. "Make the bolder move?"

"Sometimes you are overmatched so much that no move will save you," Draagan said. "Let us hope that is not the case here. But, sometimes, when the momentum of the game is against you, and all hope seems lost, it is the bolder move that can save you, and does."

6

INTO THE GRAYMERE

The first day out from Berran's Point left Deslo wondering what all the hushed tones about the Graymere were about. The landscape didn't change that much, and he didn't see what had caused all the fuss. The snowy plain and grey skies were much as they had been for the last several days before arriving at Berran's Point, and they made good time jogging along on the Arua. Nightfall came, the tracking party took watch in shifts, and Deslo slept soundly.

The dawn came. The sun rose. Deslo stretched and stood, inhaling the brisk morning air, oddly excited. After so much sailing and walking that seemed to have no larger purpose than getting somewhere new to hide, he was invigorated at the thought of doing something else. They were tracking those bizarre creatures that had gathered outside the fort—hunting them, even. As hard as it was to believe, those things had taken an original fragment of the Golden Cord, and he was giving chase to get it back.

"Morning, Deslo."

Deslo turned to see Marlo stretching. Owenn was rolling up the thick blanket he slept on. Both Kalosenes had slept nearby. Deslo was pretty sure that either they had offered to watch over him, or Kaden had asked them to. They had stayed close but not too close throughout the previous day, and they had settled on a spot to sleep that was not only near Deslo, but it was strategically placed between him and the edge of the camp.

"Good morning, Marlo," Deslo said, smiling at them. "Good morning, Owenn."

Not that long ago he would have been annoyed or even offended by the notion that the Kalosenes felt a need to watch over him, but not anymore. If they wanted to keep an eye on him, that was fine with Deslo. Their presence on this expedition was comforting. Of all those who had escaped from the collapse of Barra-Dohn on *The Sorry Rogue*, they were the only ones here, and that meant more to him than he cared to admit. Tchinchura and Deslo's family were back at the fort, Rika was gone, and he hadn't seen Zangira in years.

Ordinarily, at least recently, thinking of Zangira would simply have made him wonder about what had happened at Azandalir, about Shaline and her family, and ultimately about his own confused feelings for her and for Olli, but another benefit of being included in this tracking party was that those things seemed both old and distant. Olli and Maarta were here too, but there were more pressing matters before them all.

He knew part of being Amhuru was leaving behind what you could not control or change and doing the job at hand. The pre-eminent commitment as Guardians and Keepers of the Golden Cord clarified these matters at times in a way that both bound them to that one central task but also freed them from the misgivings and confusions of others. That there could be freedom in being bound was not a concept Deslo had understood when he had undertaken the ceremony to become an Amhuru apprentice, but he was beginning to understand it now.

"… I don't think he's listening."

Deslo heard the tail end of Owenn's observation and realized he'd missed something Marlo had said. He smiled sheepishly and apologized, "I'm sorry, Marlo, what did you say?"

"Nothing important," Marlo said with a smile of his own, waving his hand as though to dismiss Deslo's apology. "I only asked if you had slept well."

"Very," Deslo said. "And you?"

"Not well," Marlo replied. "I'm not used to shoes of any kind, and those meridium soles were a little tricky yesterday."

"Oh?" Deslo said. He hadn't thought about what wearing meridium soles would be like for the Kalosenes. "You did well keeping your balance on the Arua field. I didn't see either of you fall off."

"Yes, but I had to really concentrate, and when we stopped last night, my ankles were sore. They kept me up."

"Mine too," Owenn said.

"Maybe today will be better," Deslo offered, trying to be comforting.

"Maybe," Marlo said, "though I suppose we're in for some new problems once we enter the Graymere, which I gather should be pretty soon."

"I suppose so," Deslo agreed. His heart sank. They weren't in the Graymere yet. The relief he'd felt the previous day about the similar terrain had been premature. He took a deep breath. He was not a child. He was an Amhuru apprentice. He would do what must be done and face what must be faced, whatever it was.

Whether the Amhuru leading the tracking party had known it or not, Deslo had no idea, but they had camped the previous night with the edge of the Graymere just beyond the horizon. Consequently, they had only just begun to move out when he noticed the changes begin. They were subtle at first: less grass, more trees, but stumpy and leafless, a general sense of barrenness and desolation, though if pressed Deslo wouldn't have known entirely why the world around him felt more desolate.

They began to encounter a good deal more water. Not streams or lakes or springs or anything that was at all appealing, but dark pools, often crusted with ice around the edges, some of them large and all of them reeking. Deslo had been exposed briefly to some swampland in the Southlands during their travels, and he would not have called what he encountered in the Graymere a swamp. It seemed more boggy than swampy, though again, he wasn't sure if he could have articulated just what the difference between swampy and boggy was.

Perhaps the difference had something to do with the strange mist that lay all around them now. Like the pools of dark water, the mist wasn't uniform, but rather it was sometimes thick and high and nearly impenetrable to their eyes so that visibility was almost non-existent, and at other times it was thin and low like the merest wisp of cloud had fallen from the sky and now lay still upon the ground. And yet, however much the mist might change, it was always there, a constant companion with every mile deeper into the Graymere that they passed.

The combination of the mist and the dark pools of water created an unexpected obstacle to their movement on top of the Arua. Some of the pools were deep enough and affected the Arua field enough that going over them was risky. Deslo had learned during his time in the Northlands that ice on a lake might not be equally thick, and while it might support you in one place, it might be too thin to hold you in another. The Arua over some of the pools was like that. Since the mist sometimes hid the pools that lay below, they could not move swiftly and be sure of their footing. Accidently stepping off solid ground and into a pool of water was one thing, but tumbling off the Arua and falling several feet before plunging into that same pool was quite another.

So, after they had stopped for a break and some food around midday, they made the decision to head out on foot. They would move slower, but it would also be safer. At least, that was what they thought, and Deslo understood the reasoning. Even so, having spent most of the morning traveling above the mist, except in those places where it was very thick and high, he did not especially enjoy walking through the mist now. If only that had been the worst of it.

The further into the Graymere they went, the more extensive the dark pools seemed to be, and while they found in most places a path through the network of pools, they sometimes got turned around and came to what looked like a dead end. The Graymir had left tracks that they could follow pretty well when the mist did not obscure them, but since there wasn't always clear enough visibility, sometimes after the mist lessened sufficiently, they realized that the Graymir must have gone a different way. The tracking that had been easy the first day became considerably more difficult, and Deslo began to sense the growing frustration among the Amhuru leading the expedition.

But neither the mist nor the slowness it created was, from Deslo's perspective, the worst—that was the water. More and more they found themselves accidentally splashing into pools, in front of them, beside them, or at times even behind them when they were forced to reverse their course and backtrack. Deslo didn't mind water, but water that smelled this foul and could barely be seen through the mist disturbed him. Whenever he stepped in, he would scramble back out as fast as possible, and Deslo saw from the way the others reacted to getting wet that he wasn't the only one who felt that way.

He understood then, all too well, why silence fell over the whole group early in the afternoon when they reached a place where the mist was fairly thin, the tracks of the Graymir fairly obvious, and the way ahead appeared unavoidably to lead through one of the large, dark pools. Solid ground could be seen in the distance, on the other side, but none of them had any idea how deep the water might get between here and there, nor if the Arua could be trusted all the way across.

A scout was sent, and Deslo watched as he passed through the water, which thankfully never got more than waist deep, though that seemed quite deep enough. He reached the other side and signaled that there were tracks there, so the rest of the Amhuru moved to follow, and Deslo with them. He took a deep breath and waded in, determined to get through this as quickly as possible, and he was a little more than halfway through before the first Amhuru up ahead cried out in pain.

The Amhuru seemed to flounder, splashing the dark water around him in all directions. Immediately, others started moving toward him, but he was not the only one to cry out. More shouts rose from among the others making their way across. Deslo felt panic seize him, even as he saw it taking hold of some of the others, and all moved either to get across and out as quickly as possible or to help those who were crying out. Deslo started to run as best he could while half-submerged in the dark, stinking water.

He was only half a dozen steps away from the opposite shore when he felt the bite. Sharp, tearing teeth ripped through his pants and sunk into his calf. He cried out as the others had, and he waited for the small, round mouth to close and pull a chunk of his calf away with it. Whatever it was, though, that had bitten him, seemed content to simply clamp on and hang there. He pushed forward, splashing ahead even more desperately.

He felt something smooth and thin and strong slip around his leg just a little further up from the place where he'd been bitten. It was like a large string or a small rope, and it wrapped around and around and around, and immediately it began to constrict like someone was pulling it tighter and tighter.

There was also, coming from the thing that had latched on to him, a strange pulsing. The creature was sucking in rhythmic pulls that were very, very strong. What was it and what was it doing? Deslo's panic deepened. He had to get out of this death-water and get up on the shore.

He saw men scrambling out ahead of him, and one of them had something clamped on his leg too. The sight of it almost made him vomit. A long black body like that of a snake was wrapped around the leg, just below the knee, and a bulbous knot that must have been the head was simply attached to the leg. It must have been all jaw and teeth, from what Deslo could see, a mechanism designed simply to attach to the host while it sucked whatever it needed into its long body.

Deslo felt suddenly light-headed. He faltered a bit, stumbling forward in the water. A big, strong hand caught him under his arm and yanked him back up. He knew he was about to pass out; he only wanted to be on land when he did it. The blackness rose and he felt a loss of control of his feet, his legs, his arms. He started to fall forward, and as he slipped into the blackness he remembered thinking that at least he was falling mostly on solid ground.

.   .   .

As Deslo fell, he was strikingly aware that he was entering a dream. He was literally falling into it, falling into sand, and while his brain told him that this should annoy him, that he had never liked to get sand in his hair and clothes—it was so hard to get out again— nevertheless, he didn't mind. There was something about the warm softness of the sand that was quite welcome, and the gritty feel of it sticking to his hands and face was not as bad as he had remembered.

He pushed himself up, though, and brushed off as much of the sand off his skin as he could. Ahead lay the open gate of Barra-Dohn, and even though he knew this was a dream, he wanted to go inside. He hadn't been here in such a long time. A sudden, deep, and painful homesickness welled up in him. Tears fell from his eyes. He couldn't remember why he had left, and this was very upsetting. There must have been a good reason, he thought, but he couldn't seem to grab hold of it. He seemed sure he was un-likely ever to return, but once again, he didn't quite remember why.

The city was much like he remembered, only the streets were empty. Perhaps it was early in the morning and everyone was still in bed. The sun felt high in the sky for that to be true, though, and in the end, he didn't worry himself over the riddle much. He thought that he would like to walk on the Arua, so he could get where he was going faster. Even though he didn't have meridium-soled shoes on, he thought he'd try. Sure enough, he was able to step up onto the Arua and run quite fast in his bare feet, and without pausing to figure out how he could do this, he did.

He zoomed through the empty streets of the city, only gradually be-coming conscious that he didn't actually know where he was going. He thought it might be good to see the palace again, perhaps go inside and find his old room, but he wasn't sure how to find it. None of the buildings around him, now that he looked carefully, were familiar.

Dark clouds gathered in the sky. The sun was lower, and night approached. The lights should have been coming on, their faint bluish glow beginning to dot the cityscape, but there was nothing. Fear rose inside him. He wanted to get inside before it grew dark, but as he ran down street after street, he couldn't find the palace, or anything at all that might serve as a reference point. Suddenly, his feet slipped from the Arua, and again he felt the sensation of falling.

.   .   .

When Deslo opened his eyes, his head was being cradled in Olli's lap, and she was smoothing his hair gently. He stirred, almost trying to pull away, but she shushed him and held on tight. "Easy, Deslo," she said. "You've been crying out in your sleep. Just rest now."

Deslo closed his eyes and did as he was told. He was shaken, a little disoriented, and not altogether unwilling to let Olli hold his head and stroke his hair. "What happened?"

"Owenn got you when you started to go down," she said. "And he pulled you up and through until he could get you out. One of those things had gotten ahold of you."

"What are they?" Deslo asked, looking up at Olli with curiosity and thinking of the awful thing he had seen attached to the leg of the other Amhuru and not much wanting to think of it on his own leg. He couldn't feel the strong sucking sensation or the teeth that had dug into him, so he assumed that, while he had been unconscious, Owenn or Olli or someone had gotten it off.

"I don't know," Olli said. "Some kind of really big, really deformed, really disgusting leech, maybe? They seemed mostly to just want to get on, take hold and suck as much blood out as fast as possible."

"Leeches?" Deslo echoed her, confused. He'd encountered leeches before, but they'd been nothing like these things. "Blood?"

"Yes," Olli said. "They got quite a bit in a small time, a surprising amount really, which is why everyone who had one passed out, or nearly everyone. The blood just about exploded out of them when we were killing the awful things. It was revolting."

It did sound revolting, and Deslo felt pretty sure that it was better he'd been unconscious when the thing had been removed from his leg and killed. And since it sounded like he wasn't the only one that had passed out, the fact that he had didn't bother him, especially since he had dreamed of home. Yes, it had turned unpleasant at the end, but not like the dreams after crossing the Madri, not like the land of broken dreams.

Deslo started to sit up, and immediately the lightheadedness came over him again. "Easy," Olli said. "Best to lie still."

He had come to that juncture, however, where the awkwardness of having Olli touching him now outweighed his enjoyment of it. He looked at her and said, "Thanks for whatever you did, Olli, but I think I'll just lie back now."

She seemed to understand all the things he didn't want to say, and she smiled, gently sliding out from under him. He was glad that she understood, and that she didn't say anything further as she rose and went among the others, presumably to find Maarta.

He looked around, and nearby, he saw Owenn lying asleep. Marlo sat beside him. Marlo saw Deslo look over and smiled.

"Is Owenn all right?" Deslo asked. "Did he get one on his leg too?"

"Actually," Marlo said, "he got one on each leg."

Deslo frowned. "But Olli said he caught me when I started to fall and he pulled me out."

"He did."

"With two of those things attached to him?" Deslo couldn't help but marvel.

"I'm telling you, Deslo," Marlo said, shaking his head, "Owenn is a tough guy to bring down."

"I guess so," Deslo said, and they laughed together as Owenn slept on.

The day was growing late, and after their experience crossing the pool, Amintuu and the Amhuru decided it would be best to camp where they were. They had not made very good time, and Deslo felt sure that any headway they had made the previous day had been lost today. He lay on his side, looking back across the water, back the way they had come, feeling decidedly unhappy about the fact that, in the morning, they would be headed deeper into the Graymere. Any sense of excitement and adventure that he'd felt before was now long gone.

7

RED TREE

Deslo's first night sleeping in the Graymere mist passed uneasily. He moved in and out of restless dreams that, when morning came, he could not remember, and he would have been glad of this except he couldn't decide if the reality he had woken to was actually better. For the first time since crossing the Madri, he thought that maybe bad dreams weren't so bad. On the other hand, he was pretty sure he didn't want to see any more of the Graymere, and he wished now that he hadn't been so quick to volunteer. He thought of his family back at Berran's Point and wished he were there.

He forced himself to sit up, though, because whatever he might want, he was an Amhuru apprentice. He pulled up his pant leg and looked at the makeshift bandage his leg had been wrapped with after the thing from the day before had been removed. His blood had soaked it and turned a rusty red overnight. He wanted to lift it up and see the wound underneath, but he thought maybe the wound would open up again, so he let it be. He'd give it more time.

The group prepared silently to move out, the determination of the previous day now combined with a sobriety that was almost palpable. Moving deeper and deeper into the Graymere, in the possession of those strange beasts that had encircled Berran's Point, was an original fragment of the Golden Cord. Whatever assumptions they'd each one brought on this journey, Deslo suspected that the reality of just how difficult this was going to prove was only now beginning to sink in.

They moved out, picking up the trail from the previous day. The mist was light and the ground visible, so they had little difficulty at first, which temporarily buoyed their spirits. This lasted up until they reached the first place where the trail ran straight into the murky bog, and they all knew, without anyone needing to say a thing, that they had to cross through the water again.

Amintuu, for the first time since leaving Berran's Point, moved among them all, taking up in a visible and personal way the role of leader that Telsiin had entrusted to him when the team had been assembled to follow the Graymir. He encouraged, he directed, and they drew together to hear him.

"Have your knives out," he said. "Stay close, but not so close you don't have room to operate if one of those things bites you. Sever the body if you can, as quickly as you can. We'll remove the heads when we get across. If you need it, get help. Don't wait. Together, we'll be fine."

They assembled on dry land, facing a stretch of water that was not quite as large as the one they had crossed the night before. On Amintuu's signal, they started across, moving at almost a sprint from the very beginning. Hopefully, whatever advantage they might lose because of noise or disturbing whatever lurked in those waters was compensated for by the increase of speed.

Deslo's heart pounded as he splashed into the water. Marlo and Owenn were beside him, and they moved quickly, keeping pace. He waited, expecting to feel the bite of another of those things any moment, the sharp teeth sinking into his flesh again. The water got deeper, and the closer to his waist it got, the more his pulse raced. Ahead on his left an Amhuru reacted, his arm swinging down, his knife swiftly cutting through the water and hopefully whatever swam beneath its surface.

More Amhuru were now thrashing, cutting, fighting off unseen threats. Still Deslo felt nothing, and he moved forward, going around an Amhuru that had almost stopped to attack whatever was attacking him. He could see the other shore not far away, and hope leapt up in him that he might make it through unscathed. Then, beside him, Marlo cried out.

It was one of the hardest things Deslo had ever done, but he turned from the dry land and stepped toward his friend, who was reaching down in the water by his right leg. "What is it? Are there two?" Deslo called.

"Yes," Marlo snarled as he hacked away. "My other leg."

Deslo didn't stop to think about what he was doing, but his hand shot down into the dark water, feeling desperately around for the body of the creature that had bitten Marlo. His hand found it, curling around the leg, and with a deft, swift motion Deslo cut through the body, severing it from the head that remained attached.

"Thanks," Marlo gasped, moving forward again, and before long, they were out.

Deslo could see on both Marlo's legs, bulbous black heads now ending in short stumpy bodies, still leaking blood out of their open wounds. The rest of each creature had been left behind in the dark water. Marlo went to work with his knife to pry open the jaws and remove the heads, and Deslo turned back to see if anyone else needed his help.

All seemed well in hand, though, as each of the Amhuru who had been attacked like Marlo was out and dealing with the attached heads of the creatures, and those who had not been were hovering nearby to help as needed. Before long, they had ascertained that all were able to proceed without delay, and they headed out at a good pace.

Two more times that day they came to places where they had no choice but to cross the water, but both of these were far shorter crossings than the first two, and few had trouble getting across. On the second of these, though, Deslo was bitten again, but this time he was ready for it and cut the creature's body off himself. Removing the head was painful and unpleasant, but he was determined to do it on his own, having seen it done now a couple of times. Olli appeared as he was about to pry open the jaws, offering to do it for him, and while he was tempted by her offer, he passed.

That night as they camped, the mood among them all had changed yet again. A quiet confidence had returned, and Deslo shared it. He realized that the strange creatures in the water were surely not the only thing the Graymere would throw at them, and likely not the worst, but having faced them again, and knowing how to handle their attack, he was reassured. He thought about the difference a day could make, as well as the difference between the known and the unknown. For the first time since leaving Berran's Point, he found himself wanting to talk, even as he lay in the deepening dark.

"Marlo?"

"Yes, Deslo."

"I heard what you said when you were talking about the Far'n Gael, about Nekron and the Haladriim, but I didn't understand it. How could Kalos hold a handful of starlight, or breathe life into it?"

"Ah," Marlo said, and then it was quiet, as though he was thinking. All he said when he spoke again was, "I don't know."

"That's not an answer, Marlo," Deslo said.

"Sure it is," Marlo said, laughing, "It just isn't the answer you were hoping for."

"Well," Deslo said, "Breathing life into starlight sounds made-up. My old tutor, Gamalian, would have said this was exactly the kind of thing that proved most of the Old Stories weren't true."

"I see," Marlo said. "And why is that, exactly? Is that just because I can't explain it? Because I also can't explain exactly how Zerura generates the Arua field or regulates the growth cycles of all living things, but it does."

"That's different," Deslo said.

"Why?"

"Because it is," Deslo said after a moment, searching for just how he could explain the difference.

"To quote you from a moment ago, Deslo," Marlo said before Deslo could find what he was looking for, "that's not an answer. I think it feels different to you because you have experienced the Arua, and you have seen Zerura's power. Even now you wear some, but you can't explain how it works. You have knowledge, but there is mystery in your knowledge. Maybe there is always mystery in knowledge."

"The sun rises, the sun sets," Deslo said. "There's no mystery there."

"No?" Marlo said. "Where'd the sun come from? Who made it, and when, and out of what? And if no one made it, where did it come from? What was here before it? Should I go on?"

"No, but it still feels different," Deslo said.

"I know it does," Marlo said. "To me too. I think that is because I have seen the sun, and felt Arua, but I have never seen one of the Bright Ones, not personally. But I am not sure I want to limit what I accept as truth to my own experiences. That seems illogical, and perhaps dangerous."

"Well, let me change my question, then," Deslo said. "Maybe you don't know what the Haladriim are, but what do you think they are? Do they have bodies? Did Nekron? And if so, what would a body made from starlight be like?"

Marlo laughed again, and Deslo could hear Owenn laughing too. "I have no idea, Deslo. I know that the Old Stories suggest the Bright Ones have been seen by men. Not just Nekron, but others of the Haladriim as well. Beyond that, I can't say. I have never seen one, and the stories I know of them don't speak in detail about their bodies."

"Do they say where Nekron lives, or even if he is still alive?"

"They do suggest he is still alive," Marlo said. "That much I know. He was defeated, but not killed. Where he lives, I couldn't say. The Old Stories are vague on just how the Haladriim exist in time and space."

"I have heard," interjected Owenn, and Deslo was momentarily taken aback by Owenn's decision to wade into the conversation as more than a bystander, "that Nekron, during the long war between the Kalosenes and the Far'n Gael, sometimes appeared to leaders on both sides in the likeness of friends or loved ones or even enemies long dead—to manipulate them."

"He can change form?"

"That's what I learned as a boy," Owenn reiterated, but added no more.

"I had forgotten that," Marlo said, agreeing with Owenn. "But I have heard that too. There were some among our ancestors who gave credible reports of encounters with those they knew to be dead, and some of the Guardians of Truth came to believe that Nekron was behind it, that while the dead cannot rise and return, it might be possible for a Haladriim, like Nekron, to mimic them if he desired."

"Maybe the Jin Dara is Nekron!" Deslo said, the thought bursting out of him in a rush. He sat up, suddenly possessed of the idea and convinced that their adversary was in fact this ancient nemesis of the Kalosenes.

"That's an interesting possibility, Deslo," Marlo said, and he seemed to chew it over, deep in thought, as Deslo stared at him. Eventually, he said, "But I don't think so. While Nekron may be able to assume the appearance of the dead, this Dagin Orlas wasn't known to any of us, and it is hard to imagine just what advantage he would gain by assuming the form of a man who grew up in relative isolation, unknown to the world.

"What's more, I don't think Nekron would need the Golden Cord to be powerful, the way the Jin Dara seems to need it. I believe the Jin Dara is who we think he is."

"Oh, I just couldn't help but wonder, you know," Deslo said, feeling a little disappointed, though he supposed it was probably good news that their enemy wasn't an ancient and powerful being made from starlight.

"It is good to wonder," Marlo said. "I don't know if knowledge always involves mystery, but I do think knowledge always begins with wonder."

Deslo couldn't think of anything else he wanted to ask Marlo about Nekron or the Haladriim, so he said good night. He lay in the dark, wondering what he would do if he saw someone he knew to be dead, or what a handful of starlight might feel like, and if it would have any weight. Before he knew it, he was asleep. Graymere or not, he slept soundly.

.　　　.　　　.

The next day, the terrain began to change. The dark water didn't disappear, but they did not encounter any other large bodies that needed crossing. Instead the water lay all around in smaller pools, often connected by small rivulets like tiny canals that could be stepped over to get past. The relief Deslo felt at the change was significant, although there was always a little bit of uneasiness when he had to step over the black water.

The other big change in the terrain was the proliferation of gnarled, nearly leafless trees. The few leaves the trees had were black, as was the bark on the trunk and thick branches. The only splash of color to be found came from the vines that hung over many of the branches and dangled from the trees. They were red, not a bright red, but a deep crimson that seemed only a few shades removed from the black of the tree bark.

The trees grew more plentiful, and between them and the boggy water, the path wound a great deal. However, the soft springy turf, frosted with a light coating of snow, showed the tracks of the Graymir pretty readily, so at least it wasn't difficult figuring out where to go, even if the way ahead sometimes felt as confused and desolate as this whole place. Deslo kept almost as wide a berth from the trees and those hanging vines as he did from the bogs and the dark water.

Early in the afternoon, the Amhuru up ahead, strung out along the winding path, stopped their slow jog and grew both still and quiet. They hadn't been loud as they went along, but now they were absolutely silent. Deslo saw several heads looking, not around them, but up. He looked up too, trying to see what had brought them all to a halt. All he saw, though, were thick black tree limbs, criss-crossing beneath a deep grey sky.

He glanced to the side at Marlo and Owenn. Owenn, noticing perhaps the questioning look on his face, put his large hand on Deslo's shoulder and gripped. He nodded up and to the right, pointing with his other hand.

Deslo gazed further up into the higher branches of the trees, but still he saw nothing except for a small cluster of short red vines that hung together.

One of the vines curled, appeared to bounce a bit, and then moved along the branch.

Deslo looked at Owenn in surprise, and Owenn nodded. He had seen it too. Deslo gazed back up into the branches. The cluster of short red vines weren't vines after all. They were tails, attached to furry black creatures that blended in with the trees perfectly. Deslo had seen a few monkeys in his travels, but none that looked quite like these. For one thing, these were larger and, from what he could see, they had large snouts poking out of their faces. And what was a little disconcerting once Deslo realized it was that the small cluster was clearly watching him and the others, even as they too were being watched.

Deslo scanned the branches above in every direction, and he began to realize the cluster of monkeys Owenn had shown him was not unique. There were several similar groups at varying heights above them, as far as he could see in all directions. The Graymere was alive, not just below them in the dark recesses of the boggy water, but above them in the branches of the trees.

Just then, one of the monkeys in the cluster Deslo had been examining opened its rather large mouth and called, *hro-hro-hro, ah-ah-ah!* That same call then echoed from other branches all around them, and a flurry of motion in the treetops interrupted the silent watchfulness below. The Amhuru at the front of the line began to jog forward, but as the party moved out, Deslo found himself looking up as often as he looked ahead to see where next to go.

Deslo soon realized the monkeys in the trees above were following them, or at least shadowing them. They stayed as high above them as the trees allowed, but as the Amhuru moved, so did they, swinging from tree to tree and scampering along the long, thick branches. He wasn't sure at first if he was imagining things, but he realized none of the movement he saw above was heading away from them, as one might expect from most wild animals who would scatter when men approached.

As the late afternoon turned to evening, there was a shift above them, and the monkeys, seemingly in concert, all at once began to move down in the trees, until they were only a few feet above their heads in the lowest of branches. They came like a swarm, most of them directly ahead of the Amhuru in the direction they were heading, so that the men up front turned aside and moved to the left. The loud calls of *hro-hro-hro, ah-ah-ah!* began again, and this time it was so close as to be almost deafening.

Deslo glanced up at one of them not far above his head, and inside that large mouth that ran the whole length of its long snout he could see rows of sharp, jagged teeth. These monkeys were nothing like the cute, trained monkeys he had seen on occasion during his travels, performing in the streets of places like Brexton. The eyes that stared at him from out of the trees were dark and unblinking and seemed to convey a deep and irrational malice, while those powerful claw-like hands that gripped the branches, Deslo imagined, could do a lot of damage to his soft, vulnerable flesh. He drew his knife.

Deslo glanced ahead, and he saw that he wasn't the only one. Most of the others had weapons in hand, and as they rounded a bend in the new path they had chosen, they emerged into a clearing, a larger open area than any they had been in all day, possibly even since entering the Graymere at all. At the far end was the biggest tree Deslo had yet seen. It dwarfed the ones they had been walking beneath all day. The trunk was massive, knotty, and gnarled, and lots of those red vines drooped from its enormous branches, concentrated most heavily near the trunk.

As the Amhuru moved into the clearing, the monkeys attacked. They swung out of the trees and descended upon them, a host of furry, screaming monsters with red tails and a single tuft of red fur on top of their heads. Deslo quickly lost any sense of what was going on around him as he fought ferociously to keep the creatures coming for him from sinking those awful teeth into his arms or legs and to keep those strong claw-like hands from grabbing hold.

He buried his knife in the chest of a monkey coming straight for him, and as he summoned the blade back into his hand, he drew his axe with the other hand. A dark blur, glimpsed in the outermost extremity of his peripheral vision, led him to whirl quickly around, and just in time, as the swinging monkey's hand missed his head by the narrowest of margins. Years of training with Tchinchura and the others paid off now, as Deslo's reflexes were razor sharp and his reaction immediate. A deft counterstroke severed the hand. The creature howled.

There was no time to celebrate. More were coming. Deslo felt himself giving ground, moving deeper and deeper into the clearing, as were the other Amhuru. Wave after wave of the shrieking creatures descended from the trees, until finally the onslaught seemed to slacken. There were still plenty of monkeys around them, but Deslo could see them moving up higher into the tree branches. He exhaled with relief, just as the ear-splitting scream echoed through the clearing.

He turned, surprised to find himself much nearer to the massive tree than he had thought he was. He was even more surprised to see one of the Northland Amhuru held fast a couple of feet above the ground by almost half a dozen red vines. Then he saw with horror what had made the poor man scream.

In the middle of the tree's trunk, an especially large and gnarled knot had opened wide to reveal a gaping maw of a mouth, with teeth the size of Deslo's hand. Two of the vines held one of the Amhuru's arms firmly in an inescapable grip and were feeding it into the mouth, inch by inch. The tree-mouth was flaying shirt and skin, sinew and muscle, all but the bone, right off the man's arm. Blood, much the color of the vines themselves, was already seeping out of the open mouth and running down the outside of the tree.

Deslo was not the only one to have noticed what was going on, and several of the other Amhuru were trying to fight their way closer to the tree, but the host of vines that had been harmlessly dangling a moment ago had become a maze of living cords seeking to tangle and tie and restrain. The Amhuru, and now Deslo among them, hacked away at the vines, but they were surprisingly tough to cut.

The tree-mouth had consumed the Amhuru's arm right up to the shoulder, and Deslo watched as it, remarkably, seem to stretch and expand further while the vines fought to feed the man headfirst into the opening. The Amhuru, despite the pain and the devastation to his arm, fought with mounting urgency, kicking with all his might and trying to free his other arm to brace against the tree-trunk—anything to keep his head out of the gruesome, snapping mouth.

Deslo, already tired from the skirmish with the monkeys, wielded his blades faster and harder, trying to push through the red vines, thinking that if he could just get a hold of the man's ankle, get a good grip, then perhaps he could help to keep him out of the snarling mouth until more help arrived. And then, one of the vines swept below his defenses and wrapped around his ankle. Deslo felt himself being picked up off the ground.

It didn't last long, as Amintuu himself leapt to his rescue, severing the vine that held him and pulling him back. Deslo was about to throw himself at the vines again to continue the work of hacking through, when Owenn took hold of him and held on tight. "It's too late, Deslo."

Only then did Deslo look up, and he immediately wished his hadn't. The Amhuru's head was gone, inside the terrible tree, and the vines were busy pulling the other arm and shoulder as tight as possible so they could feed the rest of the body in through the mouth. Something in the Amhuru's shoulder gave way, and Deslo heard the pop of it dislocating before it started to disappear into the tree.

The clearing suddenly grew quiet. The screams from the man being eaten by the tree had stopped. The screams from the monkeys in the branches above them had stopped too. The Amhuru backed slowly away from the carnivorous tree and from the vines that did not seek to ensnare another so much as to make sure that the tree could finish its meal.

As the stunned feeling that had swept over him with the descent and attack of the monkeys began to subside, Deslo surveyed the rest of the party, and he saw that very few had been injured. He couldn't imagine how the relationship between the tree and the monkeys worked, but he understood without needing to be told that the monkeys had come, not to kill them, but to divert them into the clearing and to drive them back to the tree so that it might feed.

Deslo also noticed, as he scanned the Amhuru, that Amintuu was visibly furious. Deslo had observed before that Amintuu was more expressive than most of the Amhuru he knew well, but this obvious, unbridled emotion was extreme, even for Amintuu.

As Deslo watched him, Amintuu turned from the tree and scanned the rest of them. "Stay in groups of three or four, and don't wander far, but gather anything and everything that will burn."

There was silence for a moment, and then another Northland Amhuru started to say, "But if we make a fire, the Graymir—"

"We will deal with the Graymir," Amintuu said in a voice that would brook no opposition, "but first we will deal with that tree."

It was almost dark before they had gathered enough materials to make a large fire, and that was only the beginning of their difficulties. Getting the materials up close to the tree meant cutting and hacking through those red vines, which whipped around in a frenzy whenever they tried to approach. Twice they almost got control of another Amhuru to feed the tree-mouth, which sat closed and dark with a large swath of blood-red bark below it, and both times the Amhuru had to turn their efforts to rescue instead of revenge.

They did, though, eventually get their revenge. They managed to get most of the fuel they had gathered up against parts of the massive trunk, but since so much of it was damp, starting the fire proved challenging. Amintuu would not give up, though, and eventually, they had it going. They retreated to a safe distance to watch the fire burn.

Slowly, at first, it grew. Flames began to lick up the sides of the tree. They rose higher and higher, starting to catch the lowest hanging branches and the vines that hung from them. Through the growing flame, Deslo could see the bloody mouth, and as the fire grew stronger, it opened again.

The tree began to scream, and its screams echoed through the whole of that surreal, interminable night.

8

A MEMORY OF SAND

Deslo moved forward doggedly. Ten days into the Graymere, he knew that, if nothing else, he had to pay attention. Innocuous things here were not innocuous. They could and would hurt him, even kill him, given a chance.

The most vivid example of that so far had been the frogs. Small, with a skin of bright if pale yellow, the frogs liked to climb on the trunks of the trees and hop down out of the branches. They would have been cute if not for the fact that wherever they touched human skin, pus-filled sores would swell and grow, almost immediately. And if they found their way onto your shirt or pants, you were still in trouble, since eventually whatever they secreted would soak through the garment and have the same effect.

Once infected, the sores had to be lanced and drained over and over for almost two days before they would even begin to heal. The skin on the sores was so sensitive that this was an excruciating process. Deslo winced just thinking about it, glancing at the almost-healed spot on the back of his hand where one of the frogs had landed just a few days ago. To make things worse, if you weren't careful when draining the sore, and if you got too much of the puss on another part of your skin, a new sore would form there too and the whole process would start over.

No, the frogs hadn't been the scariest part of the Graymere so far—that had been the red tree, for sure—but they certainly illustrated the need for vigilance the most. Any moving thing, anywhere around him, received Deslo's full attention.

And yet, he was so tired. Paying attention to every moving thing was becoming difficult. Restless nights full of bad dreams combined with long days that required constant vigilance had taken their toll. After crossing the Madri and getting stuck in 'the land of broken dreams,' he had thought that he would hate nightmares for as long as he lived, but here, escape from the reality of the Graymere, even if it meant stepping into a nightmare, was welcome. The dreams wouldn't kill him; this place just might.

Deslo rubbed his eyes and yawned as he marched behind Marlo. Just ahead of Marlo, Olli walked with Maarta. He didn't know if she had stopped paying him her motherly attentions because of his quiet but firm resistance to them, or because this place had started to take a toll on her too. Either way, he missed them. Maybe being here day after day would have been bearable if he could have laid his head in her lap at night and gone to sleep with her hands stroking his hair.

Deslo realized he was staring at Olli and looked away before she could notice. He thought maybe he'd rather swallow one of the little yellow frogs and have those awful sores spurting pus all over the inside of his throat and stomach than be caught staring at her. He didn't want to have any more late night conversations about what could or couldn't be between them.

Deslo pushed thoughts of Olli from his mind, allowing the need for hypervigilance to take over. He thought about nothing, save only the path ahead, the trees and their branches, the dark black pools of foul water. He glanced around him wearily, but also warily, determined to prove capable of enduring this awful place. Whatever might lie ahead, he would survive it and return to his family with the others.

Late in the day, the party approached a clearing, much smaller than the clearing where they'd found the red tree, and also much different in other ways. There were earthen embankments anywhere from a couple feet high to several, and they formed a sort of perimeter around an internal space where the Amhuru found the remnants of small fires. Deslo could feel the excitement rising in himself and the others. It was a camp or outpost of the Graymir.

Deslo noticed the others drawing their weapons, and he drew his axe. Amintuu made silent motions directing them to spread out and search. Deslo went where directed, following Marlo and Owenn. He realized as they moved quietly through the clearing that just because the fires hadn't been lit in the last few hours didn't mean that the Graymir weren't nearby. The fires could have been used the previous night, and whoever had kept warm by them could still be close at hand.

Just ahead, one of the small firepits lay with a few charred remnants of firewood, now little more than flaky charcoal. He passed his hand over the remains and thought he detected, perhaps, some residual heat. Over the firepit hung a large cookpot. Deslo examined it. Two metal posts rose out of the ground on either side of the firepit, and at the top, both opened into a 'Y' shape, across which another metal pole was laid and from which hung the large cookpot.

Deslo peeked down inside it, and a sudden whiff of the smell rising from it almost made him gag. The cookpot wasn't empty. Inside lay water every bit as murky as the water in the boggy pools, only it looked thicker, and sticking out of it was a long white bone, like perhaps a bone of a hand, though Deslo couldn't tell if it was a fingerbone. His imagination immediately tried to show him what the bone might be attached to below the surface of the awful stew, and he pulled his head away to avoid wanting to gag again.

"You all right?" Marlo asked, whispering.

Deslo nodded, then quickly whispered back to change the subject. "This set-up doesn't look like something the Graymir would carry around with them."

"I agree," Marlo said. "This is probably a waystation of sorts. I wonder if it is just an empty spot Graymir traveling parties use when on the move, or if it is a manned outpost and the residents simply aren't here at the moment."

"That's the question." Owenn added.

"Sa," Marlo agreed, and they moved on through the camp.

Other than the three small firepits and the cooking apparatus, though, they found no real sign of enduring habitation. If the Graymir stayed here year round, they had built no shelter, though Deslo wondered if they needed it. He thought about the wolf-captain, and the idea of him sitting in a chair beside a crackling fire late at night was almost comic. No, he reckoned the absence of something he would consider adequate shelter didn't tell him very much about whether this was a manned outpost of Graymir or not.

Before long, most of the Amhuru had gathered near the center of the camp, though Deslo knew some of the scouts had moved out into the

Graymere around the camp as well, to see what they could see. Amintuu and the other Amhuru stood, weapons in hand, watchful and ready to move at the first sign of a threat. But no threat came, and eventually all of the scouts returned.

"They were here," one of the scouts said, reporting to Amintuu, "as recently as last night for sure, maybe even early this morning."

"Are we any closer?"

Deslo listened to Amintuu's question, holding his breath. Ten days in this dreadful place, and no hope of getting out unless the answer to this question was—

"Sa, I think so," the scout said.

Deslo exhaled.

"However," the scout continued, "It looks like they've split up."

"Split up?" Amintuu asked. "They've gone separate directions?"

"Sa," the scout said. "One group, which definitely appears to be the smaller of the two, seems to be heading deeper into the Graymere, more or less like we have been all along. The other, the larger, seems to have moved out in an arc from here, perhaps to avoid us, but ultimately heading back the way we've come."

"There's something else," another of the scouts chimed in. "I think that party is larger than the one we've been tracking."

"Perhaps," said the first scout.

"Sa, perhaps," the other agreed. "Not a lot larger, maybe, but I think it is larger."

Amintuu nodded, stroking his smooth chin with his powerful hand. "So, there were Graymir already here, and some of them have joined with those we've been following and have doubled back, while some have gone on."

"That's what it looks like," the second scout nodded. "And one last thing. In the place where the tracks from the larger party of Graymir turned back the way we've come, there was a large furrow in the ground, a mound of loose turf as though it had been pushed up from underneath. I set my foot on it and it sank back down and might have fallen still further if I hadn't taken my foot off of it. The furrow ran from there along with the tracks as far as I could see."

Amintuu looked puzzled, and for a moment, he just stood there, considering what the scout had said. "Do you have any idea what this furrow-thing was?"

"I can'na tell," the scout said. "The result of digging or burrowing along the path, maybe? But made by what or whom? There was no time to look more closely. We wanted to report back about the two sets of tracks."

Amintuu nodded, and now he walked as he thought. The other Amhuru silently parted to make room as he paced back and forth. "The smaller party is taking the Zerura deeper in, they think to safety. The others are either a diversion to get us off the track of the smaller party, or they're going back to attack Berran's Point again, since they know there are Amhuru with more Zerura there."

"Maybe both," Marlo said. "Maybe attacking Berran's Point is the diversion. They think we won't risk the lives of those we've left behind to recover something that wasn't even stolen directly from us."

"They're wrong, though," Amintuu said quietly, but in the silence of the Graymir camp, they could each hear him perfectly. "If the fragment Asantii bore is out there, with the smaller group—and if we can catch up to them before they meet up with any more Graymir—this is our best chance to get it back. We have to go on."

Deslo's head drooped. He didn't say anything, didn't object or protest, because he knew Amintuu was right. He'd sworn always to value the protection of the Golden Cord above all other things, even his own life, and he would die in service to Kalos and to protect the Cord. But still, the thought of moving deeper into this nightmare landscape while a large party of Graymir headed back, possibly to attack the fort that sheltered his parents and sister, was hard to bear.

He felt a strong hand on his shoulder and looked up in surprise to see that it wasn't Owenn, but Amintuu. The Northland Amhuru was standing before him, looking down on him with compassion. "Tchinchura is a Keeper, Deslo," Amintuu said, "and I would not chase Asantii's fragment if I thought in doing so we would lose his. Take heart, I am still in contact with Telsiin, and I will send a message about what we've seen and surmised. The fort will not be easily taken."

Deslo nodded and held his head up, because he knew everyone was watching, but he was not consoled. A Keeper and several Amhuru had failed to hold Berran's Point against the Graymir once already, very recently, which is why he was out here. And, while the two Southland

Amhuru who had crossed the Madri along with Tchinchura, Calamin and Trajax, as well as Telsiin and a few of the Northland Amhuru, were there at Berran's Point with his family, the majority of the Amhuru were here with him. Even though Amintuu could speak through his fragment to Telsiin, as Tchinchura and Zangira had so long ago when he was a boy, the Amhuru at Berran's Point would be greatly outnumbered if an attack came.

Amintuu stepped away from Deslo, turning his attention back to the group as a whole. "We will track the smaller party, and even though it will mean being a little less careful and taking some risks, we can'na catch them unless we move faster."

There were nods and murmurs of agreement. They knew what he was saying, that he understood they could not increase their speed without decreasing their safety, and they accepted this fact. What had to be done, had to be done.

"Don't take any foolish risks, though," Amintuu added. "We've been in the Graymere long enough to notice shifts in the terrain, shifts in the flora and fauna, and if you see something new or different or dangerously familiar, take precautions."

Again there was broad consent and agreement, and there was no need for Amintuu to speak further. The Amhuru scouts led the way out of the Graymir camp, and soon Deslo found himself jogging at a rapid pace through the Graymere, trying to watch all directions at once—up and behind and to both sides in equal measure—trying to notice if the world around him moved too much, if the dark water in pools looked or smelled differently, if the trees were clustered unusually, or even if the deep grey of the sky above was different than it had been.

And in this complete preoccupation with the Graymere, Deslo found a way to set aside if not forget his fear for his family. They would have to take care of themselves. He could not help them.

·   ·   ·

Kaden held on tightly to Kiki's hand as he followed Trajax out of the gate. She squeezed his hand as though to say, I know, Yadi, I know. Kaden nodded and smiled at Calamin as the Amhuru began to close the gate once they were through.

The last few days had been mild, and while there were still patches of mushy white snow scattered outside the walls of Berran's Point, most of the meadow around them was dominated now by the tall, brown grass that had previously just poked through the snow here and there. The turf underfoot was not as hard as it had been, and from time to time Kaden set his foot down in small puddles of run-off as the water inevitably wound its way downhill in search of the sea or at least a local stream or perhaps an underground aquifer.

"Kiki," Kaden said as they walked quietly behind Trajax, heading down the slight slope toward the edge of the wood there. "You have to stay close to me, and I mean close, like, if I say to come to me you can come to me by the count of three close."

"Sa, Yadi," Kiki said, looking down at her feet as she walked.

Kaden almost stopped his spiel there. They'd been over this after the last time she came out with him, when she'd wandered off just far enough that when Kaden looked up from what he was doing he couldn't see her. Even though finding her had taken only a few minutes, in those few minutes he'd felt a surge of panic run through him that he hoped never to feel again. Kiki had been apologetic and abashed, both when Kaden swooped her up and held her close, chastising her for wandering off, and also when Nara had gently forbidden her to leave the fort when she'd heard about the incident later.

It had taken almost a week for Nara to relent, and in the end it had been Kaden who persuaded her to let Kiki come again. He would look at her gazing at the gate, like a caged animal gazes at the world beyond its bars, and he realized that while the walls of Berran's Point looked to him like protection, to Kiki they looked like the walls of a prison.

In the three weeks since Deslo and the others had left in pursuit of the missing fragment of the Golden Cord, those who had remained at Berran's Point had dedicated themselves to the project of repairing what could be repaired and rebuilding what could not. That required occasional excursions outside, like this one, in search of suitable timber, but those excursions were always carried out with specific goals in mind, and no one strayed far or stayed outside the walls for long, just in case the world outside the fort was not as quiet as it appeared.

Still, despite all the work to be done, for a little girl in that burned-out fort there was almost nothing to see or do, except when Nara set her about some unimportant task so she'd have something to do. Kiki would do these things faithfully, but even though she was but a child, she seemed instinctively to understand they were busywork, with no larger purpose than to keep her occupied.

So Kaden had argued for Kiki to be allowed outside the walls again. He would take her, he would watch her, and he would bring her right back when he had found what he and Trajax were looking for—timber of about the right size and girth to be a rafter in the building they were restoring. And now, as they walked down the hill toward the wood, Kaden felt compelled to go over again the conditions of Kiki's inclusion in this expedition.

"When Trajax and I find the tree we're looking for, we'll have to cut it down and get it ready to carry back," he said. "I won't be able to hold your hand then, and I'm trusting you to stay close by."

"Sa, I will."

"And don't forget that Noni asked if you would find a few branches of firewood to bring back to her."

"I won't forget."

"Good," Kaden said, thinking that he'd probably said enough.

They were walking behind Trajax, now almost midway between the fort and the wood, when Kiki said, "When can we go somewhere else, Yadi?"

From the forlorn tone in her voice, Kaden understood that she wasn't talking about going somewhere other than the wood when they left the fort, but leaving the fort and moving on to some place else altogether. He thought of Kiki's short life, lived entirely in the context of their wandering since crossing the Madri—a life of ships and sojourns, camps and forts—and he wished he could promise her that better things lay ahead, but that he could not do.

"I can'na say," Kaden said, almost surprised to hear the Northland slang come out of his mouth. "We certainly can't go anywhere until Deslo and the others come back."

Kiki looked up at him. "Is Delo all right?"

He heard the concern, and he shared it, so he squeezed her hand and said, "I think so, Kiki. There are a lot of Amhuru with him. I'm sure he's fine."

"I miss him," Kiki said.

"Me too," Kaden said, and he was about to say that he was sure Deslo missed Kiki, when he saw something moving in the distance, across the large open field.

Kaden stopped, and he turned to tell Trajax to stop too, when the Amhuru nodded and said, "I saw it."

"What was it?"

Trajax shook his head. "No idea."

They stood, peering across the field, while Kiki stood, peering up at them, no doubt wondering why they had stopped here, out in the middle of the field, well short of their goal. Kaden scanned the horizon, and then he saw what looked like bits of earth spraying up into the air. Looking more closely, he thought he spied a ridge or mound that he didn't remember seeing there before, not much higher than the tall brown grass. Was someone digging something? And where were they?

"You see that, Trajax, right?" Kaden said. "Kind of like a mound or ridge, and it seems to be growing longer."

"I see it, and it is getting longer."

Kaden had locked in on it now, and as he gazed, the ridge extended forward at a steady if unspectacular pace. He could see the spray of dirt and chunks of earth tossed up by the rippling ground, and he had the sudden realization that he'd seen something that looked an awful lot like this before. He stepped back in time, into a memory of sand.

He could see the desert beyond the walls of Barra-Dohn, the rippled furrows of sand created by the hookworms pushing through beneath the surface. He could see the sand sprayed up into the air by the force of the powerful drive of the worms, could see the sand in their wake settle back down once they had passed. Something out there was pushing through the much denser ground outside Berran's Point like the hookworms pushed through the sand, only the displaced dirt and clay couldn't just settle back down once it had passed like the the loose grains of sand could. But what had that kind of power, the strength to drive through hardened soil and earth as though it were sand?

He stared at the ridge, moving steadily across the meadow in the direction of Berran's Point, and then another memory swept over him—of the hookworms sent against his army by the Jin Dara. Not simply their size and number, nor the death and mayhem they had created, but he remembered the reports he had heard of the hookworms that had gone beneath the mighty walls of Barra-Dohn and pushed up even through paving stone to break free inside the city.

He looked at the growing ridge, and then at the fort, and he turned in a single, swift motion to grab Kiki and swing her up into his arms, calling to Trajax as he did so, "We have to go now!"

"But Yadi," Kiki protested, "the wood—"

"Not today, Kiki," Kaden said.

And he ran.

9

NOT ALONE

The gravel crunched underfoot as Shaline walked around the small public garden. This port—Casmir, the sailors had called it—was larger than the others they had visited since waking from the awful dreams she had fallen into when they crossed the Madri, and Shaline had found this garden and decided to stay here while Trabor looked for a smithy.

Their ship's captain had been reluctant to let Shaline and Trabor go ashore when they first arrived, but it was a big port and the first mate had reported that this was the kind of city where 'all kinds' milled the busy streets. Shaline and Trabor had pressed their case that in a port like this, two teenagers, even with golden eyes, were not likely to cause much of a stir, and at last the captain had relented.

Now Shaline stood before a rosebush that looked at once beautiful and forbidding. The buds were large and lovely, a light pink in the clear afternoon light, but the thorns that lined the stems were jagged and large, much larger than any thorns Shaline had ever seen, though she knew her experience was quite limited, having spent most of her not quite 18 years on Azandalir.

The rose drew her toward it, despite the thorns, and she leaned closer to smell it. Its fragrance was both sweet and strong, and as she closed her eyes to savor it, she found herself confronted with memories of her most vivid dream from the crossing.

In the dream, she had opened a large, ornate door into a luxurious room. Stepping inside, she realized that this was her bridal suite. She crossed the floor to the large bed with a light blue silk canopy and pulled the soft fabric aside to gaze in at the lovely white bed. She moved around to the foot of the bed, slipped off her sandals and sat there, gazing at the beautiful sitting area opposite the large bed, illuminated by two large candelabra.

Only after she had taken all of this in did she notice what she was wearing, a simple but elegant white dress. Around her neck hung a necklace with a single blue stone in a gold setting, and on her right wrist was a matching bracelet. Her hair had been pulled up into an ornate braid and wrapped around her head, and she could smell a faint hint of jasmine coming from it.

The door she had come through opened again, and gazing through the opening in the canopy on that side of the bed, she could see her husband enter. He was obscured from the shoulders up, but she blushed as she realized, even without seeing his face, that it was Deslo coming to join her. He was carrying a single rose in his hand. Impulsively, she scooted back onto the bed so that she was no longer sitting on the end as she had been but reclining upon its full length.

She watched as he drew near to the side of the bed where she had first parted the silk to look in on the bed herself. His strong hand reached down to do the same, and a moment later the fabric was brushed aside and she got her first glimpse of his face.

It was terrifying.

The shape and form in many ways was that of Deslo, but his eyes had no color at all. They were black like darkest midnight, when the clouds have shut out every star that ordinarily shines in the nighttime sky. They seemed useless, like the eyes of the blind, and yet her skin crawled as his face seemed to find hers and fix upon it.

Worse than the eyes was his mouth, which was open, gaping really, with large, jagged teeth, unevenly distributed on the top and bottom. As she stared in horror and dismay, she realized that drool was running out of his mouth at both corners, dripping steadily from his chin in two places. And, as she looked more carefully at the two rivulets of drool, she noticed that blood was mixed with the saliva that ran down his face.

Shaline screamed as this nightmare-Deslo leaned toward her, his dead eyes leering, his fanged mouth snarling, as though he wanted to take a bite out of her, to sink his teeth into whatever part of her soft flesh he could reach. She scrambled out the other side of the bed, ripping down a large portion of the blue silk canopy, and she turned to see a door on the far wall—the mirror image of the one she had come through on the other side. She ran to it and swung it open.

Shaline stood up from the rosebush in the public garden, shuddering at the memory of that awful dream. Here, she could push the memory away. When she'd been trapped in the seemingly endless nightmare-filled sleep after crossing the Madri, the dream had gone on and on. In the dream, the door she went through to get away from the nightmare led back into the bridal suite, and she would step through, instantly forget all that had just happened, and then repeat the whole event again and again and again, until it was inevitable that long after she had awoken, every last detail was burned into her mind and memory.

She wasn't sure if she had been stuck in this dream any longer than the others, nor would she necessarily have said that it was the scariest or most dangerous of the bad dreams that had haunted her, but it was definitely the most vivid and the one that disturbed her the most. She wondered if she would ever be able get the awful sight of nightmare-Deslo's terrible face out of her memory, and if she couldn't, what seeing him again would be like, if she ever did see him again.

Shaline wanted very much to see Deslo again. She didn't doubt that. It had surprised her somewhat, once he and his family had left Azandalir, just how much she had missed him, but she had. That her subconscious had placed him in her dreams as a groom, coming to her as his bride, wasn't entirely surprising, but that he had shown up as a monster was. She hated the memory of the dream, hated that it had spoiled, even a little bit, the happy and cherished memories she had of him. She had been prepared, she thought, for whatever the crossing might entail, but she had underestimated just how awful the Madri was and how even now, two months after she had awoken, it still dominated her waking life.

She turned from the rosebush and walked a little further down the gravel path. She came to a very different bush, much fuller of leaf with small white buds scattered all over it. Shaline did not know what kind of bush it was, and she leaned in to smell the scent of its flowers. She did not care for it and moved on.

As she walked, she thought of her father—her Yadi, she corrected her inner voice, knowing she had to become more comfortable using North-lander terminology—as she often did after being reminded of her own dreams. She wondered what dreams plagued him as he lay asleep on their ship, and she hoped that whatever he dreamed about, his memories of her mother were not being used against him as her memories of Deslo had been used against her.

She hoped that her Yadi and the other adult Amhuru would start waking up soon. She and Trabor, along with all the other Amhuru under twenty were already awake. Fortunately, the ships that had borne them north across the Madri were owned and run by old sailing families that had long aided the Southland Amhuru, and they trusted them completely. Otherwise, it would have been a fearful thing for the whole community to place itself in such a vulnerable position as they now were.

As it was, Shaline both liked and trusted the captain on their ship and his first mate, and she never felt unsafe around either of them. The sailors, down to a man, readily obeyed them both, and all were respectful to her and the others, so Shaline did not worry about any of them. Of course, even if any of them had been troublemakers, she doubted that they would bother her, since all of them knew she was Trabor's sister.

She thought of her 'little' brother and smiled. He was not much more than fifteen and a half now, but he had grown half a foot in the last year and filled out, so that he was only a hair shorter than their father and his shoulders were just as broad. What's more, not only did he have a powerful man's body, but he had a very skilled man's hands. He trained with both knife and axe daily, and his command of both the weapons and the Arua had become impressive. Just a few weeks ago, Shaline had watched him at work onboard their ship, and she almost hadn't believed what she had seen.

Trabor had taken a board—as he often did—and attached it to the outside wall of his small cabin. It was by the starboard rail, not especially close to anything anyone needed access to, so he was left alone to practice. Shaline had been sitting, halfway down the length of the main deck when he started, but as he proceeded, she had risen and drawn nearer to get a better look.

Trabor drew his knife and leaned in to the board, and what he then did Shaline couldn't see. Carving something, no doubt, but it couldn't have been very large, as Shaline couldn't tell what it was. Then he measured off a fair distance from the board with his feet and then turned to face it. He drew his axe, took aim, and threw it.

The axe struck the board with a *thwack!* He did not go and pry it out of the board, but stood, concentrating, until he summoned it back into his hand. Shaline watched in awe. Her command of the Arua onboard the ship was minimal at best. She didn't think she could have called a meridium-coated feather from six feet away, let alone replicated her brother's mastery. She moved closer, as though drawn, noticing as she did, that many of the sailors on the deck were ignoring their work and watching Trabor as well.

Seven times in all he threw the axe, and each time it hit a little lower, a little more to the right. After the last time, he did not call it back into his hand. He walked to the board and pried it out as he stood, examining the board. He nodded, indicating his satisfaction, so preoccupied that he did not hear Shaline come up behind him. She too examined the board, and when it dawned on her what she was seeing, she gasped. Only then did Trabor turn around.

He had made seven horizontal notches in the board with his knife, stair-stepping down from the top left of the board to the bottom right. Each notch was small, perhaps only an inch wide. Now, splitting each of the notches in what appeared to be the very middle, was a new notch, made by the axe blade. As Shaline scanned them all, her naked eye could not see any difference in the distance to the left and to the right of all seven vertical marks made by the axe.

"That's impossible," she said softly to him as he looked at her. "You've split them all equally."

"Not all of them, I'm afraid," Trabor said, sounding, not dejected, perhaps, but disappointed. "The second to last one isn't quite right."

Shaline looked at the one he indicated, puzzled, unable to see any inequity in the two sides of the horizontal line. She even stooped and felt the notch with her fingers. "Trabor," she said, "they're exactly the same length."

He frowned. "No they aren't, the top part is clearly shorter than the bottom part."

Shaline stared at him, looking for evidence that he was joking and saw that he wasn't. She stood and swiftly surveyed the other marks a second time. Sure enough, though she hadn't noticed it at first, she now saw that each of the vertical notches he had made with his axe in the other six marks were also evenly divided above and below the horizontal notches that he had made with his knife. Looking again at the sixth one, she saw that Trabor was right; this one wasn't perfect.

"Brother," she said, a trace of awe in her voice, "surely you are master of that axe. You are amazing."

Trabor smiled at that, and then he made new marks and did it all again.

Shaline stopped in the middle of the public garden. She was alone there, as the busy inhabitants of Casmir obviously had more pressing things to do today than linger in the public garden. She thought of her little brother, no longer little, who certainly could take care of himself and did not need protection—and yet she worried about him.

He had a man-sized body, and with it he had developed man-sized talents for using both axe and knife. She was an Amhuru, and with these things, she was most pleased, as any Amhuru would be. What she worried about was the man-sized hatred that had also grown in Trabor. Ever since the Jin Dara had come to Azandalir, destroying it and killing their mother, Trabor had changed. The good-natured boy was gone, or at least he was buried deep within the serious-minded man. He showed up now and again, suddenly and without warning, but he would disappear again, just as quickly. Shaline missed him, and she worried about what the hate would do to Trabor—what perhaps it was already doing.

There was a sense in which they all hated the Jin Dara. They had come here, crossed the Madri, not just to recover the missing fragments, but to make him pay for what he had done. She understood that, but she also understood that the hatred in Trabor had become something deeper, something closer to obsession. The practice with the axe and knife, they were not merely skill development for Trabor. They were rehearsals, practice for a moment much desired and anticipated. Over the last two years, he had talked less and less, even as he practiced more and more.

She did not know what all this was doing to him. Perhaps nothing, and yet she was afraid. Yet another reason why she hoped and prayed that her Yadi would wake up soon. She needed his wisdom for this, as for so many other things.

·　　　·　　　·

Draagan and Breeson walked along the dirty streets of Kaldar. Breeson had never been here before, since he had come to Draagan and their jungle fortification from Telsiin via the larger and much nicer port at Min Luna. Kaldar was less reputable and far more likely to have the kind of captain who would be willing to take them anywhere in the vicinity of the JaenSing's headquarters.

They had found that man on their third night here, a short, surprisingly ordinary looking fellow with neat and nondescript clothes. He didn't look expecially daring, but he hardly flinched when Draagan explained where he wanted to be taken. His negotiation for their fare was tough but not unreasonable, and he had been flexible about their desire to depart the following day. All in all, Breeson had wondered more than once as he lay awake in his bed the previous night if Captain Daugen wasn't hiding some deep dark secret, or if he might not be luring them out into the middle of the sea before trying to murder them in their beds.

Of course, Draagan didn't seem at all concerned, which comforted Breeson somewhat. He had come to realize over the last few months that Draagan, even for an Amhuru, was unusually capable and perceptive. This was not entirely a surprise, as Draagan's whole family was legendary for being both exceptional and eccentric. For just this reason, he had been excited to be selected by Elder Telsiin to be the emissary to Draagan with the news of the second Madri crossing. He would be able to aid and perhaps get to know the legend. Now, here he was traveling as Draagan's lone companion on a quest to find a group of men that almost any other Northlander would go to great lengths to avoid.

They found *The Starfish* with little difficulty, and the vessel like its master and its name was surprisingly ordinary. The crew was capable and efficient, and none of them looked like the kind of riffraff that manned the vessels of smalltime smugglers or less reputable merchants who traded in stolen or illegal goods. What this ship and its captain and crew had been doing in a town like Kaldar, Breeson couldn't guess, and in the end, he didn't care.

Once they stowed their belongings in their cabin, Breeson and Draagan went up on deck as the ship slipped away from its berth at the quay and headed out of the harbor for the open sea. The jungle fortress they were leaving behind had proved less than safe, but now that Breeson had a better grasp of just how powerful their adversary was, not to mention the lengths Draagan was willing to go in order to withstand him, he wondered if they weren't jumping out of the frying pan into the fire.

Draagan leaned on the rail next to Breeson and gazed out at the sea, as the water beneath them surged rhythmically up and down. He turned to Breeson, and for the first time since coming aboard *The Starfish,* he spoke. "We are not alone, you know. It may feel like it, but we're not."

Breeson looked at Draagan, his golden eyes intent but unexpressive. He waited for the Keeper to continue, and eventually, Draagan obliged. "I know that to most of our people, my family is seen as a bit odd."

Here, Draagan smiled and even chuckled a little bit. "And I know, just as well, that our reputation is deserved. My family has some strange traditions. Come, Breeson, I will tell you a story, and it may help you to better understand this strange fellow you have fallen in with …"

                        .   .   .

When I was five years old, my Yadi told me a story. He said, when he was five years old, his Yadi, my Grandsire, came and told him a story. My grandsire said to him, that when he was ten years old, his Yadi packed up some supplies and led him on a journey, ten days into the wilderness.

They crossed the great open plain northwest of the village, and they journeyed for days through the great forest. On the other side of it, they crossed a mighty river, and ascended to a high plateau, and beyond that, at the last, they climbed a tall mountain. Near the top, nestled beneath the crag, a small mountain lake was there. My Grandsire's Yadi uncovered a small boat hidden in the reeds and paddled my Grandsire to the island in the middle of the small lake.

Once on the island, my Grandsire's Yadi put his hands on his son's shoulders, looked him in the eyes and said, "You are my son, and I love you. Whatever happens, I love you. You have your Zerura and your weapons. You have your training, your knowledge, and your wits. You will feed yourself, defend yourself and find your own way home. When you return, I will greet you as one man greets another. And, if you do not, you are still my son, and I still love you."

At that point, my Grandsire's Yadi got back in the boat, crossed over the lake, and walked away. My Gransire, at ten years old, was left alone to fend for himself. He found his way home, and when he arrived, his Yadi was the first to greet him. From that day forward, his Yadi treated him like a man and not a boy.

This story my Grandsire first told my Yadi when he was five, and he told it to him regularly in the years to come. When my Yadi turned ten, he went on his own accord to my Grandsire and said, "I am ready. Take me to the lake."

They went. Ten days they journeyed, until at last they arrived at that same mountain lake. My Grandsire uncovered that same boat, and he paddled it across to the island, where he bid my Yadi farewell with the same words, and then he left. My Yadi found his way home, and when he arrived, my Grandsire was the first to greet him.

This story my Yadi first told me when I was five, and he told it to me regularly in the years to come. When I turned ten, I went to my Yadi on my own accord, and I said, "I am ready. Take me to the lake."

My Yadi took me northwest across the great open plain, journeying for days through the vast, dark forest. On the other side, we crossed the mighty river, the flow so strong I could barely keep my head above the surface as we crossed, but I made it, and on the far side, we ascended to the high plateau. We crossed it in the bitter wind and cold, and beyond it, at the last, climbed the tall mountain. Near the top, nestled beneath the crag, I finally saw that small mountain lake. My Yadi uncovered the small boat hidden in the reeds and paddled me to the island in the middle of the small lake.

When we were on the island, I felt a curious mixture of pride and fear. I could not stop trembling. My hands were shaking, and I could feel the tears well up in my eyes. My Yadi put his hands on my shoulder, looked at me, and he said in a strong but tender voice, "You are my son, and I love you. Whatever happens, I love you. You have your Zerura and your weapons. You have your training, your knowledge, and your wits. You will feed yourself, defend yourself and find your way home. When you return, I will greet you as one man greets another. And, if you do not, you are still my son, and I still love you."

Then my Yadi got back in the boat, paddled across the lake, and walked away. He did not look back. I watched him until I could see him no more, and then I watched still longer. I built a fire, lay beside it, and cried.

In the morning, I started my journey home. I hunted and fished, I navigated by the sun and the stars, and four times I fought off wild animals—three times in the dark. When I finally reached the outskirts of our village, I looked up and saw my Yadi waiting, watching for me. When I saw him, I ran to him. I was weary. I was faint with hunger. I was weak. Still I ran, and my Yadi caught me in his arms and greeted me as one man greets another. From that day forward, I was still his son, but I was also a man.

But that is not the end.

Many years later, when my boy was four, almost five, I went to my Yadi. I said, "Yadi, my son will soon be five. I know it is time to begin to prepare him for the test, but I don't know if I can do it. I know now what it is to be a father, and I don't know how you did it, how you left me."

My Yadi looked at me, and though there were tears in his eyes, he was smiling. He said, "When you were almost five, I went to your Grandsire and said much the same thing. That was when he told me, that after he paddled across the lake and walked away from me on the island, he doubled back once he was sure he was too far away to be seen. He returned to the lake, only down the shoreline a ways, where he could hide in a small copse of trees. There he waited and watched me from the shore.

"When I left the island to begin my journey home," my Yadi continued, "Your grandsire shadowed me all the way home. He always stayed out of sight, but he was never far away. When, at last, I drew near the village, he ran ahead, changed out of his clothes, and prepared to greet me."

When my Yadi finished telling me this story, I stared at him in wonder. "You were there the whole time?"

"I was there the whole time. I would not have interfered, even if you were in serious danger, unless I was convinced that it would kill you. You had to face the danger of the journey alone to know your own strength."

For a moment, I felt cheated. It was only a moment, but it was there. He must have seen some of that in my face, for he said. "Your courage is not diminished by this fact, nor is your accomplishment. You did not know I was there."

He was right, and I suddenly realized that this was good news. I would not have to leave my son. I could take his journey with him. I could watch over him as my Yadi had watched over me.

My Yadi said, "It is good for a son to know both that he is strong and that he is loved. It is good for all of us to know that we are not alone."

10

THE GROUND BENEATH MY FEET

Kaden ran for the gate, holding Kiki tight. Trajax easily outpaced him, as he was unencumbered, and Kaden was glad to find the gate open when he reached it. Barely had he passed through when Trajax slammed it shut.

Whatever Trajax had said to the gatekeeper, the Amhuru inside were already scrambling, leaving their work and drawing their weapons. "Up the ladders, up the ladders," Kaden shouted, lifting Kiki up above his head so she could grab hold of a ladder almost halfway up to the walkway that ran around the inside of the walls. "They're tunneling in."

Kaden could see some of the Amhuru look askance at him as he said that, but he had no time to explain the strange feeling of utter certainty that this was precisely what the long, growing furrow in the field meant, especially since he had no idea just how he could be right. He had to find Nara and get her up onto the walkway too, before the Graymir broke through.

He didn't have to look long. Nara came running, her eyes fixed above Kaden's head. Only then did Kaden notice the frightened little girl frozen on the ladder, having moved neither up nor down since he let go of her. He looked back at Nara as she drew close, "We need to get up to the walkway. Now."

Nara nodded to him but looked at Kiki. "Kiki, sweetheart, climb up. Noni is coming."

Kaden stepped aside from the base of the ladder, and Nara started swiftly up. Kiki finally started to climb too, and he started up after Nara. Soon all three of them stood on the walkway.

Kaden instinctively guided his wife and daughter away from the ladder, both to make room for others, but also because he assumed that when the Graymir broke through, the ladders would quickly become the center of the fight.

As they made their way along the walkway, Kaden heard Tchinchura calling and turned to see the Amhuru running along behind them to catch up. Kaden reached forward and put his hand on Nara's shoulder so she stopped, and then he turned.

"I think you're right," Tchinchura said as he approached. "A second tunnel appears to be approaching from the northeast."

Tchinchura pointed past Kaden, in the direction of the back corner of the fort toward which Kaden had been moving. Kaden turned again and for the first time looked over the wall in that direction. Sure enough, a second furrow, just like the first, was rippling through the field that lay there between Berran's Point and the woods in the distance.

Kaden turned back to Tchinchura, "From up here we can inflict maximum damage, while staying out of reach."

"Take Nara and Kiki to the corner," Tchinchura said, nodding his agreement. "We will hold the ladders and keep the Graymir below."

Tchinchura turned back, calling out instructions and pointing around the walkway at the various ladders, and the Amhuru moved to positions appropriate to defend them against the coming assault. Kaden followed Nara and Kiki to the corner, and there they waited.

The furrow approaching that corner was moving steadily, and while Kaden knew it would not take long for it to reach the walls and pass beneath, it seemed to take an eternity. He gripped his axe, waiting, looking back and forth between the approaching furrow and the open space just inside the front gate on the opposite side of the fort, wondering where they'd break through first and how great the flood would be when they came.

The furrow behind them reached the wall, and Kaden held his breath, assuming the question of which tunnel would break through first had been answered, but he was wrong. As he turned back toward the inside of the fort, he saw the dirt and mud inside the gate being flung to the side as the ground there bulged upward. A great brown head broke through the bulge, along with two massive, powerful claws, and a furry body followed.

The earth seemed to fall away to both sides as the creature emerged out of the large hole he had created. It was much larger than a horse, though smaller than an Omojen. It was longer than an elephant, but not as tall, and the enormous brown head seemed to be all nose and mouth. Kaden could not see any eyes.

A flurry of axes and knives descended upon the creature from Amhuru close to the spot where it had broken through. It roared with pain as the weapons struck it and were summoned back into the hands of those who had thrown them, and the animal moved sidewise away from the hole he had come out of. His powerful forelegs began immediately to dig, spraying dirt way up into the air all over the space behind it as it began to burrow downward.

The bizarre animal was apparently the answer to the mystery of how the furrow had been made. But Kaden's attention to it ended then as two other things happened and became, at once, far more pressing. Out of the first hole that the creature had opened inside the gate, Graymir began at last to pour forth. The first one to rise from the ground into the fort was a large bear-man, who came out snarling in rage and defiance of the fort's defenders.

He was greeted by an axe and knocked back from the hole, but what became of him Kaden couldn't have said, for the ground just fifteen or twenty feet inside the corner, below where he stood, had begun to tremble. Now he saw up close the power of the tunneling beast. It broke through the earth, showering dirt and small rocks and all manner of debris as it rose like a hookworm from the sand, bursting into the air after a Romaia lizard.

Very quickly, the world immediately below Kaden's feet consumed his attention entirely. His axe was among those that struck the creature as soon as it emerged from the hole. In fact, he had the presence of mind to aim deliberately for one of the two claws that first rose into the air, and it hit the claw right in the middle, even as two or three more axes took the beast in the head. It roared as the other had, and the sound split the air, echoing through the fort. Kaden summoned his axe back with all the force he could muster, hoping desperately that if they could fatally wound the creature or prevent it from being able to dig its exit tunnel, perhaps it might plug the hole it had made.

Kaden's hope proved vain. The onslaught of the Amhuru's axes slowed the creature, for he wavered where he was, rocking back and forth, half in the hole, half out, yet he nevertheless scrambled forward after a moment. And as he lumbered free of the hole, another round of strikes from the Amhuru on the walls struck him hard, and his legs seemed to collapse below him as he fell to the ground, a tremendous groan escaping his giant frame. It struggled to rise, but failed, and Kaden turned away from it to face the first Graymir now leaping out of the hole.

If it was not the wolf-captain, it was a Graymir who looked very much like it. Its lupine head shot up through the opening, but the creature did not linger there, as it must have pushed off one of the sides of the hole it was emerging from, so that it sommersaulted backwards out of the opening. Kaden saw an axe and a knife fly through the space above the hole where the wolf-captain had been for no more than the briefest of moments, and he hesitated to throw his own weapon, wondering if he should take aim at the beast wherever it might land or focus on the next one to emerge.

Kaden made his choice, aiming for the wolf-like Graymir who had landed, crouched, arced its back and howled such a high, wailing howl that the air seemed to shake with it. He threw his axe and as he did, he felt the Graymir take hold of the Arua. Kaden's axe seem to slow, though it didn't stop, and the wolf-man swung a powerful arm and knocked it away once it drew close enough, then the thing whirled and knocked away a knife coming from another spot up on the walkway.

Kaden reached out for his axe, calling it back to his hand. The ability of the Graymir to affect the Arua had been known to them after their first standoff three weeks ago, but control that precise was a surprise, at least to him. If the Graymir could nullify their ability to strike from a distance and forced this confrontation into a hand-to-hand situation, the Amhuru would be in trouble, for Kaden had no doubts that they would soon be outnumbered and quite possibly overrun.

Movement flashed below him as a Graymir leapt out of the hole in the direction of the corner where he stood. The Graymir landed and whirled to the side, so Kaden couldn't see its face, but the large orange-furred head looked feline, and Kaden planted his axe firmly in the back of its skull. The blow was quite forceful, given how close the Graymir was, and the beast sank instantly to its knees, pitching forward face down in the dirt and mud.

Some of the Graymir, like the big cat-man Kaden took down, were dealt with summarily upon their emergence into the fort, but some like the wolf-man evaded harm long enough to clear the hole and make room for more, and soon they had proliferated enough that all was chaos below. Those that came through relatively unscathed used their ability with the Arua to defend themselves, and soon the predicted assault on the ladders began.

Since there was a ladder on every side and all were attached to the walkway, the Amhuru were spread thin, barely two per ladder, but the narrow rungs created a vertical bottleneck that made them just as deadly for the Graymir as the holes had been. The Graymir were completely exposed to the weapons of the Amhuru as they climbed, and Kaden saw more than a few fall mid-climb to rise no more.

For his part, Kaden kept doing as much damage to the Graymir coming out of the hole as he could, but the flow of the creatures had slowed. It appeared that most of the Graymir who were coming were already inside Berran's Point. The Graymir who had survived the Amhuru gauntlet to get out of the tunnel into the fort scattered away from the holes toward the ladders. Kaden stood, sweating profusely, holding his bloody axe and wondering what he should do, now that the battle had shifted away from him. He didn't want to leave Nara and Kiki, but there were too few defenders on the walkway for him to do nothing.

Just at that moment, Nara grabbed his arm with one hand and pointed past his ear away from any of the ladders, toward one of the burned-out buildings the Amhuru had been restoring. "Look!"

As Kaden scanned the lumber and other materials scattered on the ground, it took a moment for him to see what Nara was pointing at. Just the other side of the building, he could see the wolf-man directing two of the bear-like Graymir forward toward the walkway. Both were carrying massive poles that had been cut as central supports for the building, poles that would take two or perhaps three Amhuru to lift and move.

As soon as Kaden saw this, he understood and knew what he had to do. He ran along the walkway toward the spot they had chosen, a spot that was neither close to any of the ladders nor easy to see from above, given the cluster of burned buildings around it. He ran, hoping he could get there before any of the Graymir could scramble up those impromptu ladders.

He saw, just up ahead, both poles come to rest, jutting up just a little bit above the walkway, leaning in on an angle. He also saw on the nearer pole that one of the bear-like Graymir was halfway up. Kaden ran toward it, and placing his foot on the pole, pushed it with all his might—not out, but to the side, in the hope he could just slide it sideways so the pole and Graymir would fall and take out the other pole at the same time.

He didn't know if the pole was just too heavy with the added weight of the Graymir, or if it was being held by someone or something below, but he couldn't get it to topple over. The head of the Graymir was almost up to the walkway, and the bear-man looked up as Kaden swung his axe downward with all his might. The blade hit its mark with full effect, and Kaden had to wrench it free with a jerk, which he did just in time, for the Graymir's grip on the pole immediately relaxed as it plummeted down to the ground.

Kaden was able then to push the pole sideways, and as the Graymir on the other pole was closer to the ground, the force of the first pole hitting the second did succeed in dislodging both, and they fell sideways. The wolf-man, which had grabbed a smaller piece of lumber, suddenly hurled the long, makeshift spear at Kaden. He dropped flat on the walkway as it whistled past.

Kaden could see from his prone position the wolf-man searching for another weapon in the pile of materials, and the bear-man starting to pick up one of the poles again. He was gathering himself for whatever would be necessary to repel the next attempt to gain the walkway, when a howl from across the fort froze the Graymir in their tracks. A second howl unfroze them, but when they started moving again, it was not to move against the walkway, but to scramble for the hole and descend back into the tunnel that led under the corner of the fort and outside the walls of Berran's Point.

The Graymir were defeated.

Weary, Kaden stood over the body of the dead creature that had made the second tunnel. It had never risen from the place where it fell, and now it lay, immense and still on the muddy ground. The other one had managed to escape, tunneling under the wall and away while the battle inside Berran's Point raged on, but this one would never tunnel again.

Standing closer, Kaden was struck anew by its size. His initial assessment had been basically right. It was larger than a horse and smaller than an Omojen. A normal grey elephant was probably the closest size comparison that Kaden could think of. What struck Kaden more than the creature's size was that he still couldn't see any eyes on the long, shaggy brown face, unless they were buried deep beneath the thick fur. Kaden was curious, but he didn't really want to touch the thing. They would probably all have to touch it, eventually, for the tunneling beast posed quite a conundrum. What to do with this enormous carcass?

The exhausted Amhuru had spent the last half hour carrying the dead Graymir—almost twenty, in all—outside the gate. They had to work in shifts, so that half the Amhuru could stand guard while the other half carried bodies. Now the Graymir lay piled outside on what smaller, loose lumber could be found, and the pyre would soon be lit beneath them.

But this fellow, he was quite another thing all together. The bear-like Graymir had required three Amhuru to be carried out, but Kaden doubted if this creature was going to be carried in any fashion. If they had any beasts of burden, he would have suggested dragging it, but they had none. He suspected that, in the end, they would be the beasts of burden, and only with all the Amhuru in Berran's Point in a harnass would there be sufficient strength to get the job done. Perhaps not even then.

As it turned out, though, the problem of the tunneling beast was postponed until the morning. Evening was approaching, and more important than moving the creature was collapsing the tunnels that now stretched in three directions out from the fort, as the escape tunnel for the first of the burrowing beasts also had to be dealt with. Standing on the walkway, working together, the Amhuru were able to manipulate the Arua enough to exert downward pressure on the long furrows, so that they collapsed in on themselves.

The end result was that now three gullies stretched out from Berran's Point toward the woods, like three streets stretching out into a city from the central market place. The Amhuru knew that the creature that had escaped could always make a new one, and if the Graymir had more of those things available, they could too, but collapsing the tunnels was still necessary. None of them were going to sleep tonight, not as long as those tunnels were there. The thought of the long dark corridors lying open for Graymir and other things to scurry through was just too much.

Unfortunately, collapsing the three tunnels also meant that now, in the three places where the tunnels went under the walls, there were gaps beneath the foundation that needed to be addressed, lest they also be used against them as a means of entry. While the main force of Amhuru worked to fill those gaps, Telsiin summoned Tchinchura and Kaden to join him on the walkway above.

"We are in your debt," Telsiin said, surprising Kaden by addressing him first, rather than Tchinchura.

"Not at all," Kaden said, not knowing quite what to say, and not entirely sure what Telsiin was referring to. "I did very little, actually."

"You saw and immediately understood what was happening," Telsiin replied. "That gave us time to get up on the walkway. Had we been caught at ground level, it may have gone ill with us."

"Trajax saw the furrows too," Kaden said, still unsure if he deserved Telsiin's praise. "It wasn't hard to figure out what was happening, once I had a moment to process what I was seeing."

"Kaden comes from a world full of sand," Tchinchura said, smiling with what Kaden would almost have called a smirk. "And he assumes that others who do not come from such a world would have recognized what he saw, just as he did. And yet, I have been to Barra-Dohn, and I have seen some of the great creatures that burrow in the sand there, but even I might not have made the connection to what I saw outside the fort as quickly as he did, as we are a long way from such a world."

Kaden conceded the point. "You are welcome, Elder. I am glad I could be of service."

Telsiin nodded graciously, and the conversation quickly moved on to other things, namely, what to do now. On this front, they quickly agreed, and Telsiin summarized their thoughts succinctly when he said, "We will cease all attempts to repair and restore Berran's Point. We have only one job here, and that is to guard what Tchinchura bears. We erred by distracting ourselves from this task, even a little bit. As long as we wait here for the others, we will focus our time and attention on fortifying, standing guard, and making sure nothing threatens the Golden Cord again."

Later, when the sun had set, Kaden and Nara sat talking quietly in the dark while Nara stroked Kiki's head as the child slept in her lap. "Will they try again?" Nara asked, and then added, as if her meaning had been unclear. "To get in?"

"I do not know," Kaden said, "but it seems unlikely. However they surprised and defeated those who were here before us, they will not surprise us."

"And so many of them died," Nara said. "Surely they won't risk it again."

"True," Kaden said, but he wasn't so sure. He had no idea how many of these Graymir there were, so he had no idea how many they could muster and throw at the fort, or how callous they were about their losses. If the Zerura inside the fort was valuable enough to the Graymir, then they might be willing to pay a high price in their own blood to take it.

"They've been gone for so long," Nara said. Kaden heard the worry and knew it was Deslo and the others she now referred to.

"I know," Kaden said, and he stroked Nara's hair even as she stroked Kiki's. "You know what Telsiin said when they left, that the Graymere is vast and difficult to travel through. Their mission may take quite a while. At least we know Deslo is still alive and well."

"Yes," Nara conceded. "But it sounds so awful."

There was nothing Kaden could say to that, for truly, the reports about the Graymere had sounded awful. He hated the thought that Deslo was out there, but he could do nothing about that now.

"Kaden?" Nara whispered.

"Yes, my love," he replied softly.

"I feel so unsettled. The world was already so uncertain, and after today, I don't even know if I can trust the ground beneath my feet. I don't know how much longer I can go on like this."

"I know," Kaden said. "But as you have so often reassured me, we can trust Kalos, even in a world of uncertainty."

Nara leaned over and gently kissed Kaden on the cheek. "At least we are facing the uncertainty together."

"Yes," Kaden said. "At least we are together."

Together they sat in the dark for a long time.

11

THE ALTAR OF NEKRON

When the topography of the Graymere began to change, Deslo was delighted. The black, boggy pools began to disappear, replaced as a staple of the landscape by frequent protrusions of rough, dark rocks which jutted from the ground like jagged bones poking through decaying flesh. The company of Amhuru treated the rocks with great care, steering clear wherever possible, but as yet, these outcroppings had not tried to kill them.

They were passing a large boulder at that very moment, sticking out of the ground at a slight angle, pointing up at a sky that seemed always to be grey and miserable here, and which today looked especially like rain. Deslo trusted neither the boulder nor the sky, for almost a month in the Graymere had taught Deslo that nothing in this land could be trusted, and as it had rained frequently over the last week and a half, soaking them again and again, he had little doubt that today would be any different.

The trees in this part of the Graymere were small, they reeked of decay, and their limbs were blunt and stubby. They didn't feel like swamp or jungle trees like the red tree had. There were no vines, nor were there any high branches in which poisonous frogs or red-tailed monkeys could hide. Still, the Amhuru gave them a wide berth, but neither the trees nor the rocks showed any signs of hosting life of any kind.

Initially, this had only fueled Deslo's delight, but after some time of it, Deslo began to wonder if his happiness upon leaving behind the by now more familiar parts of the Graymere had been premature. Though he felt less threatened with the imminence of death in this terrain, nevertheless the silence and emptiness of death seemed to dwell here more fully, and that fell upon him and all their company with every step.

The oppressive heaviness of the landscape, though, was not enough to completely obscure the good mood he'd been in since Amintuu heard Telsiin's message that morning. Almost ten days had passed since the Graymir's surprise subterranean assault on Berran's Point, and there had been no further attacks. Deslo hoped, as they all did, that perhaps this meant the Graymir would now leave the fort alone.

As he thought about that attack, Deslo still felt a sense of pride when he considered the role his father had played in repelling it. It certainly seemed like Kaden's quick action had been instrumental in preserving the fort. He was the one who had seen the bulging ground and figured out that something very strong was plowing along underground toward the fort and might well intend to go under the walls. He had rallied the Amhuru, getting them up the ladders to the comparatively safe walkway that ran around the top of the fort. Just a moment's hesitation in either recognizing or rallying might have cost them the battle.

Like his father, Deslo had strong memories of hookworms and other things that could plow through the sand that surrounded Barra-Dohn, so he could imagine how Kaden had seen what he did and interpreted it. He also understood how those who only knew, or primarily knew, the harder soil of this land, might not have been able to make those same connections. Olli, for one, had marveled at Kaden's insight, and her wonder had been gratifying to see. Deslo felt as though his own status in the group had risen, simply by association.

The Amhuru did not treat him like an outsider, like he didn't belong, or even like he wasn't an authentic Amhuru apprentice—but Deslo sometimes felt that way nonetheless. He was a Southlander in the Northlands, which was a factor, though he imagined even Tchinchura and Trajax and Calamin felt that. They, at least, had called Azandalir home and had been raised Amhuru, so whatever displacement they felt here, Deslo knew they didn't doubt their place in the world.

He was different. Like his father and Olli, he was an outsider brought in to the Amhuru world, grafted in, as it were, and he was the youngest of the three. He was of age, but he knew most of the Amhuru saw him as a boy. It probably didn't help that the two Kalosenes obviously considered it one of their duties on this journey into the Graymere to keep an eye on him. Both the fact that they were not Amhuru and the implication that he needed protecting couldn't help.

Olli, on the other hand, spent most of her time with the Northland Amhuru because she spent most of her time with Maarta. Deslo felt he could see the subtle barriers between her and the Northland Amhuru disappearing with each passing day, and more to the point, she seemed to slip further and further away from him. Their days spent together as two young apprentices after the Madri crossing, both on board *The Sorry Rogue* and at the farm near Sar Komen, were now a distant memory. She walked not more than twenty yards ahead of him, but she might as well still have been living in the cave below the mountain on the island of dreadful daylight. She was lost to him.

The ground underfoot began to rise, and it rose steadily for some time. They had seen in the distance, not long after the landscape shifted, that a small cluster of very tall hills, or perhaps small mountains—Deslo didn't really know where the one began and the other ended—lay ahead, and that the path the Graymir was taking appeared to head that way. They now seemed to be entering the foothills of those small mountains, and as Deslo scanned the horizon, it certainly seemed to him that the road forward must invariably lead upward.

Looking ahead and up, Deslo suddenly shivered. The Graymere was so much more open here, and though they were careful, moving both stealthily and quickly, Deslo felt exposed. How could the Graymir, who knew this land and would be moving up on to high ground first, not see them and know both their number and location? Perhaps they had come this way for just that reason, to find a place to turn the tables, to become the hunters rather than the hunted.

Then so be it, Deslo thought as he pushed ahead. Without conflict, the Amhuru were never going to recover the fragment of the Golden Cord that the Graymir had taken. Blood would be shed, and if the Graymir wanted this to be the place, if they had chosen to fight on this ground, then Deslo and the Amhuru would meet them in battle. The Cord must be recovered and protected. This was their mission. This was their calling.

Deslo smiled as the words of his thoughts echoed in his mind. He might not always feel like a real Amhuru, but he was beginning to think like one.

·   ·   ·

They had been ascending in earnest for some time now, and Deslo felt the weariness in his calves, which had not yet grown accustomed to the constant climbing. The day had grown late, though how late was hard to say, for the darkness was due as much to the thick, dark clouds that rolled tumultuously overhead as to the hour. Not far away, Deslo could see flashes of lightning in them, and he suspected that the storm they were going to unleash would come soon. He didn't hold much hope that it would miss them, but there was always a chance.

They were moving in single file along the fairly narrow path, making their way through the rocky ridges and climbing up and up toward the pinnacle of this hill that felt like it was just a bigger version of the rocks and boulders they had been passing these last few days. The ground beneath Deslo's feet was very, very hard, a big change from the softer turf they'd traversed for most of their time in the Graymere.

Deslo felt more sheltered here than he'd thought he would. The rocky side of the hill rose sheer and high above them, and they hugged that wall closely as they walked. Deslo couldn't imagine anything moving up or down that sheer rock face with ease, and as he gazed up at it again, he figured that if the Graymir were up above them, they would not be able to attack them without coming back down the path, and if they did that, the Amhuru in front would spot them long before they could fall upon them.

Deslo heard the distant rumble of thunder, and he turned from the rock face on his left to peer out over the land through which they had just come. The Graymere stretched out in the distance, a forlorn and dark land. The stench of it wasn't so bad up here, but looking at the decay as it spread out for miles and miles in every direction, Deslo thought maybe the wind that gusted along with those dark clouds must reek with it. It was depressing to think that even if they were successful, they'd have to go back down and pass through all that awfulness again, but so it was.

And then, almost without warning, the ground beneath their feet began to level out. The path rose less steeply for a while and then not at all. They had crested the main peak and now followed a winding trail that still moved through high rock, though on both sides of them and not as high as earlier. The trail both rose and fell at times, and when it did fall, the feeling of moving downward felt alien to Deslo after the long steep climb. Alien but welcome to his weary legs.

The first sign for Deslo of the clearing up ahead was a sound, not a sight. He heard the soft but now clearly recognizable sound of knives being drawn, and he took hold of his own axe and knife without hesitation. Always on guard, it would be wrong to say that he started paying attention to what lay ahead or to what might be moving on top of the rock walls on either side of them, but he did pay more attention, and soon he saw the clearing into which they had quite suddenly come.

The rock walls opened up on both sides, but they did not end. Rather, they curved around in both directions, creating a large ring of stone around the clearing. The ground here was basically solid rock, though Deslo could see that some form of dust or ash or both covered the rocky ground to varying depths in the great open ring. There was no grass, no bushes, no trees—no living, growing things of any kind. The only living thing that Deslo could see was a Graymir—a large, wolf-headed fellow—squatting on top of a large stone altar that sat right in the middle of the clearing.

Seeing him there, alone on the altar, staring at the assembled Amhuru with piercing eyes of yellow-gold, brought back the shiver Deslo had felt earlier. Then, Deslo had only imagined that he was being watched by the Graymir, but now he knew he was being watched. He gazed around the open space, and he searched above the stone walls, all for evidence of more than one Graymir, but he found none. Still, he did not believe for a moment that this audacious creature, crouching still on the altar, was alone.

And then Deslo noticed that the Graymir on the altar was not entirely still after all. Its arm, which Deslo thought had been at its side to start with, was slowly moving forward and up, and there in the air, dancing to the unseen rhythm of its own hidden music, was a piece of Zerura. Not any piece, of course, for Deslo knew without question that this was the original fragment of the Golden Cord that the Graymir had taken from the Northland Keeper, Asantii, in their raid on Berran's Point.

Deslo stared, entranced, struck at once by the beauty of the Cord and its dance, but also by the hideous claw extended beneath it. So strange, to see the pure, living matter that generated the Arua and governed the life cycle of all living things contrasted with such an abomination—the mixing of things human with things animal—the trademark of the Far'n Gael and now the Graymir. Deslo burned with anger. That claw, that hand, had no right to touch the Cord.

"Welcome, travelers," the wolf-man said loudly, in a raspy, growly voice. He rose from his crouch so that he stood at his full height, looming like a statue on top of the altar. "Welcome, Weight-Bearers. Have you also come to worship Nekron at one of his High Places?"

Deslo understood the words clearly enough, but the tone of the voice he could not read, whether it was serious or sarcastic. Amintuu's tone, however, was very clear.

"Never."

"Then why have you come, Weight-Bearer? Force-Wielder?" The Graymir's voice rose, and he continued in a rush. "You—children who either do not understand the power of what you possess, or who fear it—why have you come?"

"To take back what you have stolen."

The Graymir threw back his head and laughed, only the laugh turned into a howl in the middle that rose high into the darkening sky and echoed across the mountain. Deslo had a sudden, incongruous thought as he felt the chill from the howl subside, that he would never hear the words 'howling with laughter' the same way again. He pushed the thought away.

"That may be why you followed us, Weight-Bearer," the Graymir said, "but it is not why you have come. Nekron, Lord of the Dead, has brought you here—"

"Nekron isn't Lord of the dead," a voice said from right beside Deslo, and it took him a moment before he realized that it had been Marlo who spoke. He stepped forward and pointed at the Graymir. "Kalos is Lord of both the living and the dead."

The Graymir's head swiveled from Amintuu to Marlo, and as Deslo was right beside the Kalosene, that glance of the yellow-gold eyes seemed to catch him up in their sweep as well. Deslo swallowed in fear. Then, the Graymir laughed and howled again, both louder and longer this time, until the last echoes died away and silence fell upon them once more.

"When your blood is spattered on this altar and we feast on your flesh while we burn your hearts as an offering to Nekron, then you will see who is Lord of the Dead."

"Maybe you will kill me and spread my blood upon your altar," Marlo replied, "but that would prove nothing, for if Kalos wills my end upon this mountain, then surely it will come to pass."

"You worship in vain if you worship a god who cannot save you."

"I did not say cannot."

The Graymir made a sudden swiping motion with the claw that did not lie beneath the undulating length of the Golden Cord, as though he had lost patience with Marlo's quibblings and wished the Kalosene to be quiet.

To emphasize the gesture, he turned not just his head but his whole body in Amintuu's direction and addressed him specifically with what he said next.

"Nekron has brought you," he said. "Long has it been since we have had such worthy sacrifices to lay upon his altar. There is no return from here for you, for none who come to the Altar of Nekron from the outside, ever return."

As the Graymir said these final words, the other Graymir that Deslo had known must be nearby suddenly appeared. They came, leaping and climbing onto the stone wall that ran in a ring around the clearing, so that like the Graymir in the center, standing upon the altar, they loomed above the earth, contrasted against the grey sky, like a museum dedicated to terrible statues of animals mixed with men.

The Amhuru did not retreat to the narrow path behind them, but they did slide closer together. For a moment, the two groups—the one in a tight cluster, the other in a large circle—stared at one another in silence. And then Amintuu stepped forward and hurled his knife at the Graymir on the altar.

The wolf-man leapt into the air, dodging the knife and landing on the ground beside the altar. Amintuu summoned the knife back into his hand, and as the blade flew back across the clearing, the other Graymir leapt down from the rim of rock with roars and howls that made the Graymir's earlier howl seem like a whisper.

Deslo braced for the battle. Whatever Marlo said, he hoped Kalos' will was not for his blood to be spattered on the altar of Nekron. He didn't feel quite ready to visit the land of the dead just yet, even if Marlo was right and Kalos, not Nekron, was Lord of it.

·   ·   ·

The battle that followed on the mountain between the Graymir and the Amhuru unfolded so chaotically that, to Deslo, it was less like an unfolding story and more like a quick succession of violent, visceral images and experiences. The first of those was the cacophony of sound, as the shrieks and howls and roars of the various Graymir mingled together, the precursor to their furious onslaught.

But that cacophony was followed by streaks of light or, at least, of knives and axes flying in all directions, looking like streaks of light as they contrasted vividly against the dark rock and the dark ash and the dark sky. Those knives and axes, gleaming with the threads of Zerura that ran through them, grew wet with the dark blood of the Graymir, and that early impression of streaks of light faded as the sound and sights that surrounded Deslo grew increasingly grim.

He became embroiled in the fight himself, and at times he lost completely any larger, more global feel for the battle being waged all around him as his attention became more telescoped upon his own situation. He found himself fighting desperately to keep from being ripped open by a Graymir whose head was black as midnight and looked for all the world like that of an enormous cat with terribly large teeth. The cat-man was remarkably quick, and Deslo was hard pressed to avoid both being torn open by its claws and being bitten by those teeth.

Deslo, who from the beginning had been almost purely on the defensive in his encounter, suddenly dropped down to a low crouch himself and slashed his axe across the leg of the creature, so that it screeched in pain and fury. Deslo had hoped to provoke the cat-man's counterstroke, and when it came, rather than dodging the blow, Deslo used the force of it against the Graymir and drove his knife straight into the center of the raging creature's claw.

Deslo was knocked back, despite his good knifework, and the claw of the Graymir hit his shoulder and cut it open in three long gashes, but his knife had gone in deep. Deslo could feel the creature's agony when he wrenched it back out. The Graymir stumbled back, and Deslo whirled forward, swinging his axe for the killing blow, which he struck swift and sure across the Graymir's exposed neck.

Beyond the sounds, the sights, and even the tactile experience of the battle, the next sensory impression that struck Deslo about it was the growing struggle for control of the Arua field. There were too many Graymir to fend them all off, using their axes and knives from a safe distance, and as more and more of the combat came down to close quarters like Deslo's fight with the cat-man, control of the Arua became more and more important. The Graymir seized and tried to hold the Arua, Deslo realized, not so much to use it against the Amhuru, but to try to keep the Amhuru from using it against them.

It didn't work, though, as Deslo felt the Amhuru regain control of the Arua, working in concert to grab hold, and then to use the invisible field to slow and sometimes even stop their enemy, tying them up, as though in unseen cords. Deslo, emboldened by what he felt, reached out himself, took hold of the Arua with his brethren, and contributed what strength he had to keeping mastery and control in their hands.

And then, Deslo felt and saw something even more striking and powerful than all that had happened so far. He felt one of the Amhuru—glancing round he thought he saw Amintuu, striking down a Graymir with his axe in one hand and raising his other hand to the sky as though to take hold of it—the Amhuru seemed to take hold of the dark clouds above them, rip them open and summon down the lightning and the rain.

It wasn't like a gradual sprinkling leading to steady rain leading to a heavy deluge. It was the descent of a sheet of water which covered them all, instantly soaking everyone on the mountain and turning the ash and dust to muck and making the rocky surfaces slick and treacherous. The lightning fell three times, striking the altar of Nekron each time, so that smoke from burning stone rose into the sky, the offering of the empty altar to an angry sky.

For all of them the rain was a complication, but for the Graymir who depended on their animal-like quickness and reflexes to counter the Amhuru's superior mastery of the Arua and their Zerura-laced weapons, it was disaster. Their footing became unsure as they slipped and slid on the rocky ground and walls. The battle, though grim, turned increasingly toward the Amhuru.

But even as it did, Deslo saw a Graymir coming up behind Olli where she stood side by side with Maarta near Nekron's altar, embroiled in a fight of their own. The Graymir, slender with a doggish head like a giant mastiff, raised a great paw-like hand to strike her from behind, and surely he would have taken her unaware had Deslo not driven his knife deep into the creature's back. It shuddered and howled, so that Olli swung to see the Graymir just a foot or two behind her, and with beautifully quick reflexes she drove her own knife deep into the Graymir's neck, silencing him for good.

The Graymir slid sideways, slumping down against the altar, and it did not escape Deslo's notice that a healthy amount of the thing's blood spattered the stones. He looked at the dark stain on the dark stones and nodded as he turned to Olli. She nodded her head in return, all the thanks he needed or she had time to offer, and they were both moving once more through the battle to do what needed to be done.

Not long after that episode, the battle wound to a close, as the few Graymir the Amhuru had not yet killed turned almost in unison and ran.

The Amhuru followed across the clearing, axes and knives flying in all directions, and very few Graymir, Deslo thought, managed to get away.

The battle had not been without cost for the Amhuru, either, as three of their number lay dead and all who had fought there bore a cut or wound of some kind. Even so, the last image that struck Deslo, the final impression in that tumultuous assault on his senses, was an image that in any other context would have been gruesome and terrible. In that moment, though, where utter euphoria and terrible battle-fatigue come together, it was to Deslo both splendid and wonderful.

He turned in full-body weariness and exquisite relief to see Amintuu standing upon the altar, the fragment of the Golden Cord held out at shoulder height in his hand, just as the Graymir had held it. Still it danced, beautiful and golden, to the music hidden from all ears but its own. However, Amintuu's other hand was not empty. It was also extended, even higher, and in it the Amhuru held up the head of the wolf-man for all to see.

The battle-frenzy was still full upon Amintuu. Deslo could see it in his golden eyes, so he was not surprised when Amintuu called out to the Amhuru, to the few Graymir who had survived and were scrambling to get away, to the dark sky itself, saying, "Hail, Nekron! Lord of Nothing!"

And with that, Amintuu hurled the severed head across the clearing, where it struck the slick stone and skidded eventually to a halt. And there, as far as Deslo knew, it may still lie.

12

I'M SO THIRSTY

Deslo used both hands to half grip, half trace the slick rock wall in the pouring rain. The path beneath his feet was very slippery—he'd already gone down twice in their descent—and he knew that the other side of the path was a drop over which he did not want to go. So he, like all the Amhuru, was hugging the sheer rock wall as close as possible as they made their way, single file, back down the mountain.

A flash of lightning overhead briefly illuminated the fearful dark, and Deslo took heart that the end of their descent looked to be not that far away. He had grumbled inside about the climb earlier, feeling the burn in his legs from the steep ascent, but this was far, far worse. Then, they had enjoyed light to guide their steps, the path had not been wet and slick, and they had not been burdened with the staggering weariness of battle fatigue that sweeps in upon you like an angry wave at sea once the temporary strength and energy of your battle euphoria has run its course.

They could have stayed the night, he supposed, in the clearing where the battle had been fought and the altar of Nekron stood. It was flat, spacious, surrounded by rock walls that could be easily patrolled by the watch, and there was no chance of losing footing due to darkness or slipperiness and pitching over the edge of the mountain. And even beyond all of those advantages was the fact that they could have gone to bed almost without delay.

But, even now, as his body cried out with every groping step of the treacherously slick, dark descent, crying for sleep that had already been deferred far too long, he did not regret their decision to leave nor relish the alternative to stay. None of them had, which is why there had been no discussion of doing it. In the moments following the battle, it was as though they held silent convocation and unanimously agreed to brave the path down the mountain in the stormy dark rather than remain for one more moment in that awful place. They took up the bodies of their fallen brethren, ignored the slain Graymir, and started almost immediately to make the slow, winding descent despite the pounding storm and almost impenetrable dark.

At long last, they reached the base of the mountain, and here, with their backs against the great, sheer wall of rock, they set up camp in the first open spot large enough to hold them. They appointed the first watch not only to keep an eye on the open Graymere beyond the mountain, but also to guard the path they had just descended against the unlikely event that they had been followed down. And Deslo, though not happy about being in the second of the three watches, nevertheless settled down and immediately fell asleep.

Deslo woke for his watch, tired and grumpy, convinced that no time had passed at all since he'd laid his weary head down. Even so, he took up his position without audible complaint and manned his watch as the seconds creeped by with excruciating slowness. What made matters worse was the fact that his tired brain seemed unable to think of anything except the hug and kiss Olli had given him after the battle. He would think of the soft touch of her lips on his cheek, but always that thought was followed by the memory of Maarta's firm embrace, as he clasped Deslo to himself.

He'd had tears in his eyes, and Deslo found that image oddly compelling. He didn't like thinking about how Maarta felt—it was certainly easier to simply focus on his own feelings—but he had to acknowledge as he recalled that moment that Maarta certainly seemed to genuinely love Olli. This didn't change how Deslo felt, but it made it a little harder to resent Maarta. Not impossible, but harder.

His watch passed uneventfully, and he gratefully returned to his spot and lay back down. Once more, he quickly fell fast asleep. This time, though, his sleep was marred by fitful dreams of blood and battle, only he wasn't in the dark world of the Graymere, for he had exchanged it for the bright world of Aralyn. He found himself fighting in the sand outside the walls of Barra-Dohn, surrounded not only by a wide array of Graymir, but by hookworms and rhino-scorpions too. He felt instinctively that he had to hold the enemy back, to win this fight and keep them from the gate, or the city would fall.

He was not alone. At least one other soldier fought with him, and they worked together to cut down the enemy, matching them stroke for stroke. And then, just as victory seemed assured, he turned to strike the next Graymir before him, only as Deslo raised his arm to strike it down, he saw that it was Olli. At least, it was a cat-like version of Olli, growling and eager to rip him open. Still, he hesitated, unable to strike her, even in his dream, and when he tried to move, to run away, he realized he was stuck. His legs were sinking in the soft sand, which had come up over his ankles and soon would rise above his knees. He couldn't strike, and he couldn't get away.

Then the soldier he'd been fighting with, side-by-side and back-to-back, struck her down with a single, powerful, violent blow. Deslo, suddenly and inexplicably free from the sand, wheeled around in shock and even grief to see the face of the man who had defended him, and in doing so, had killed cat-Olli. He thought as he turned, just for a second, that it would be Maarta, but it wasn't. It was Eirmon, his grandfather, the long deceased king of Barra-Dohn. He stood, grinning at Deslo, bloody axe in hand.

Deslo woke with a gasp to the murky light of morning in the Graymere. He sat up, rubbing the sleep from his eyes vigorously, as though by doing that he could rub that last, haunting image of his dream from his memory. It remained, of course, and Deslo decided that getting something to eat was a higher priority than forgetting his dream. He was as hungry this morning as he had been tired last night.

The long march that day passed like a blur through nondescript rocky terrain, bearing no further signs of life now than it had when they passed through it before. For the first time it occurred to Deslo that someone would have to lead them out of the Graymere, to remember how they had come, for the further they went this direction the less would remain of the tracks they had made on the way in.

He certainly hoped the Amhuru charged with this task didn't lose their way, for Deslo felt weariness like he had rarely felt it before and didn't want to be here a moment longer than was necessary. He realized that this weariness was about more than the previous day's physical exertion. The tension of pursuing the Graymir and the stolen fragment of the Golden

Cord had grown with each passing day, so much and so steadily, that Deslo hadn't even understood it until he now felt the relief that it was gone.

Today at least, they made good time, and that night as they camped, Deslo found the Amhuru to be unusually talkative in the fading twilight, their relief to be on the way home triumphing for the moment over their shared fatigue. He tried to engage Marlo and Owenn in some good-natured speculation about how long the trip back to Berran's Point would take, suggesting that their desire to get out of the Graymere might motivate them to travel just as fast if not faster on the way back, but his attempts gained little traction with either Kalosene, who both nodded or smiled to acknowledge him, but who said little themselves.

"What is it, Marlo?" Deslo asked. Owenn's relative silence was commonplace, but Marlo almost always had something to say. "Why so quiet tonight? We won. We got it back."

"Getting the fragment back is great," Marlo said. "But even though we won, as you put it, I am troubled."

"Why?"

"Did you not see the Graymir, Deslo? Their bodies twisted and transformed from not just years of mixing human and animal traits together, but generations?"

The words stung, and Marlo's tone was impatient, almost angry. Deslo recoiled as though slapped. Marlo was almost as consistently gracious as Tchinchura. He never spoke to Deslo or anyone this way. Deslo was about to apologize for bothering the Kalosene and head somewhere else when Marlo, as though guessing his intent, reached out and put his hand on Deslo's arm.

"I'm sorry, Deslo," he said, and Deslo heard contrition in the Kalosene's voice. "I shouldn't have spoken to you that way."

"It's all right," Deslo said, trying to put Marlo at ease and not to sulk over it.

"It isn't, but thank you for your understanding," Marlo said, giving Deslo a half-hearted smile, then he added. "You should just ignore me tonight."

"I could," Deslo said, "Or you could tell me what's bothering you. Tchinchura tells me that learning to watch and listen are as important to being an Amhuru as learning to wield an axe and handle the Arua, so you'd be helping me with my training to tell me what's troubling you."

"That was well done," Marlo said, and this time his smile seemed less forced. "I sometimes forget, Deslo, how much you have grown since the will of Kalos cast our lots together. Fierce in battle, gracious in manner—I think, were he here tonight, Tchinchura would be proud of his apprentice."

Deslo nodded, accepting Marlo's compliment, but he could see Marlo had more to say. He waited and did not speak.

"You heard my story of the Far'n Gael, right?"

"Yes."

"Our first encounter at Berran's Point," Marlo said, "made it clear to me that even if the name, Far'n Gael, has been lost to the ravages of time, if they have been absorbed into these Graymir, even so, the practices of the Far'n Gael live on. I thought I had come to terms with that, but hearing that creature last night speak of Nekron, with adoration and with awe, chilled my blood."

Marlo paused, and they sat quietly until he continued. "It's not that I thought Nekron was dead—I'm not even sure if Haladriim can die—but last night was a vivid reminder that there are forces in the world opposed to us, and to all the servants of Kalos, that are even greater than the Jin Dara."

Deslo thought about this for a while, and then he said, "But we won last night, Marlo? How great can Nekron be?"

Deslo had almost said, 'Even if he's real, how great can Nekron be?' but he caught himself. He didn't want to get sidetracked on that issue with Marlo.

"It's true we won a battle last night," Marlo said. "But we have no idea how many Graymir there might still be, or how powerful they are when all together. Their ability to bend and manipulate the Arua as evidenced by how they've transformed and developed their own bodies suggests that there is a good bit of power at work somewhere.

"What's more, the problem of the Graymir may be localized here, to the Graymere, but it would be foolish to think Nekron is contained here. As a Haladriim, he may go where he sees fit."

"You're worried he's helping the Jin Dara, or that he will help the Jin Dara." Deslo watched Marlo carefully as he spoke, looking for his reaction, but the Kalosene gave little away. "You said earlier that you didn't think the Jin Dara is Nekron, but that doesn't mean that they aren't or wouldn't work together."

"Even short of working together, by which I assume you mean some kind of partnership, I could envision Nekron aiding the Jin Dara simply because it suited his own warped purposes."

"Which are?" Deslo asked. "I still don't understand what exactly this Nekron wants."

"I'm not sure anyone but Nekron knows what Nekron wants," Marlo said. "But generally, Nekron's history suggests that what he wants, most of all, is to bend or even break what Kalos has made whole. To make his own twisted kingdom, a dark mockery of Kalos' beautiful order, for whereas Kalos delights and finds beauty in order and life, Nekron prefers chaos and death."

"So, what help do you think he could give the Jin Dara?" Deslo asked. "What power does Nekron actually have?"

"Both good questions," Marlo said. "And I wish once more than I had answers. What troubles me about the stories of Nekron I can remember, are the tales of subtlety and deceit. Nekron was perhaps at his best, his most effective, when he worked behind the scenes to divide, to mislead, to entice or to tempt. He was, or is, a master of these things, and he bred much mistrust among the Kalosenes in our war against the Far'n Gael and did much damage before his plots and deceptions were unmasked."

Deslo thought about that, trying to imagine what Marlo was describing, but found it difficult to see how such a thing could be done. At least, he found it difficult to see how it could be done now, in this situation. The Amhuru were such a small, dedicated, and tight community, infiltration or whatever it was Marlo was describing sounded unlikely if not impossible.

"Well," Deslo said at last, "it is good and wise to be on guard."

"Yes," Marlo agreed. "Without and within."

Deslo thought about that conversation the next day as they continued on, but by the next evening, it had faded from his mind. Soon, they had left behind the rocky portion of the Graymere, and the black bogs and their stench were back, along with the larger trees and all the living things that went with them. The Amhuru were careful, but they could not entirely avoid the Graymere's dangers.

Still, there was a sense among them, which Deslo shared, that the Graymere was like a snake that had been defanged. It might coil around their ankles and frighten, but its power to strike and to kill had been removed. Sure, the red tree could kill, and maybe other parts of the Graymere could too, but it just didn't hold the same power and sway over them that it had initially. They knew its tricks, they had passed through once before, and more importantly, they had retrieved what they came for. And so the days passed, and with each step, Deslo thought of little else beyond the end of their journey, of leaving this awful place behind and returning to Kiki and his parents.

.   .   .

Amintuu sat up in the dark and rubbed his eyes with trembling fingers. Her voice, again. It couldn't be her voice. Couldn't be, but he'd heard it, three nights in a row. In a dream, a vision, a trance, a memory—something. Whispering. Softly. So softly.

"Yadi, I'm so thirsty."

Melaane. It had been almost twenty years. And yet, he remembered it as though it were yesterday.

She was sickly from birth. So small, so fragile, but so beautiful. When Melaane smiled, the whole world was brighter. Amintuu's wife teased him that Melaane had only to open her eyes and look at him and his heart was in her hands.

He denied it, but it was true. He seemed somehow to know that her time was short, that every moment was precious, holy. He wanted to make every day she had perfect, and he had done his best. In the end, he had lost her as he feared he would, far too soon.

The fever came upon her quickly. In the morning, she had been fine. No signs of sickness or anything unusual. By the afternoon, she was burning up and bedridden. By nightfall, the Elder who had come to see if anything could be done sighed and told them that it would not be long.

Amintuu waited by Melaane's bed as she tossed and turned, mumbling jibberish in her fever-induced fits. Sweat glistened on her tiny face, and her hair was soaked and matted with it. She was restless and obviously in pain. Amintuu was helpless. He could not save her.

Right before the end, though, she stopped tossing and turning and lay still. Her eyes opened, and she looked at Amintuu. Recognition showed in her look, and she pleaded with him in the softest of whispers, dry and raspy in her weakness. "Yadi, I'm so thirsty."

And then she died. She lay, eyes wide open, staring at nothing, until Amintuu closed them. The heat left her fevered brow as quickly as it had come. By dawn, she was as cold as ice.

Melaane. His Melaane. How could she be here, in the Graymere, whispering to him, calling to him, "Yadi, I'm so thirsty"?

This place. This dark, forlorn and dreadful place. Perhaps it was getting to him, breaking him down. He couldn't let it get the best of him. After all, they were so close to getting out, to being free of it at last.

He sat up. It felt early, perhaps an hour or two before dawn. Surely it was the third watch. He looked around. The camp was still, but he could see Owenn, the big Kalosene, leaning on the great axe he carried, standing watch. Owenn glanced his way, no doubt drawn by Amintuu's movement, and he nodded silently when he saw Amintuu looking at him. Amintuu nodded back.

He started to lie back down but stopped, reaching down instead to feel the fragment of the Golden Cord where it lay, coiled around his left leg, just above the knee. He traced the smooth Zerura with his finger, feeling for the persistent pulse that was now just an echo of his own heartbeat as the fragment was synced to him. He still bore the replica of the original that Draagan bore, wrapped around his right forearm—though Telsiin had recommended against it—and the feeling of both pieces was not obviously or dramatically different, but it was different. Subtly so, but also, intoxicatingly so.

There was so much power. He could sense that if he called upon them both, if he combined them both, remarkable things would be possible. Not just for him, but for anyone who wore two fragments, even two replicas.

There had to be some way to convince Telsiin to reconsider his stance on the Amhuru wearing multiple pieces of Zerura. There had to be. The Jin Dara had two fragments—assuming it wasn't more by now, assuming that Maccado and Draagan had evaded him so far—and the Graymir had almost taken the one he now bore. If the Graymir had succeeded in taking this one, and if the Jin Dara took a third, then the Amhuru would have had only two. Then there would have been little they could do to counter the Jin Dara's power. It would have been too late.

This could never be allowed to happen. While the Amhuru still had the advantage, still had more fragments, could still combine more pieces than the Jin Dara's soldiers could combine, this war had to be fought and won. Telsiin's overly scrupulous fears about breaking rules that clearly weren't made with this possibility in mind would lose them the Cord and possibly bring ruin on the world. Surely after this close call with the Graymir, the Elder could be made to see that. Extreme measures had to be taken.

After all, it wasn't as though Amintuu was suggesting that anyone combine original fragments. Surely as long as they didn't do that, then they could combine replicas, just this once. When the Jin Dara was defeated, they could go back to the old way, give up the extra pieces. It wouldn't be easy, perhaps, having worn multiple fragments and felt their power, to relinquish them, but the Amhuru would not be seduced by the same allure that had seduced the Jin Dara. They were bound to the Cord, bound to Kalos.

Amintuu knew, though, that if he was going to make this argument, that questions about what to do with the *cadeen* would arise—again, assuming that Maccado still had it. Even Amintuu didn't know if making and distributing replicas of the *cadeen* was a good idea. Surely if they made replicas of the piece he now bore, and of Draagan's piece, and the Southlander Tchinchura's piece, then distributing those three and wielding their combined power should be enough to defeat the Jin Dara's forces.

But, Amintuu thought, as long as extreme measures were being taken, perhaps even the *cadeen* should be used. For if three pieces gave them an advantage against the Jin Dara's two, then how much more would four give them?

He lay back down, shaking his head almost involuntarily. He knew without considering the thing any further that to suggest it would only hurt his main argument. The Amhuru had to combine replicas like the Jin Dara's men were doing, and debates about the *cadeen* and its place in their tradition would hurt his case. Maybe, once the bulk of the Amhuru had come around to his side, had seen the wisdom of his proposal, perhaps then he could suggest that replicas of the *cadeen* be made. Not worn, of course—just made and kept nearby to be used only in the utmost emergency. Yes, Amintuu thought, the Amhuru might consider that, once the initial reluctance to combine replicas had been overcome.

Amintuu lay thinking about the issue for some time. Telsiin treated the question as though it was settled, but now that Amintuu was a Keeper, he had the authority and the right to present the idea once more. He knew Telsiin would acknowledge this, but he suspected that the Elder would still oppose him. What's more, he knew there were many among the Amhuru who would follow Telsiin, even if they saw the sense and force of Amintuu's argument.

Of course, there were no insurmountable barriers. Facing a crisis of this magnitude made all things possible. If Telsiin and his influence should become the only thing between the Amhuru and doing what was necessary to win their war with the Jin Dara, then steps could be taken. Telsiin could be dealt with.

The Amhuru had to have power equal to the challenge the Jin Dara presented. The Cord and its protection was everything. Sometimes even an Amhuru could lose sight of that fact, as he believed Telsiin had. Amintuu had not, however, and even if he was the only one, he would do anything that was necessary to defeat the Jin Dara and retrieve what he had taken.

13

JOY AND SORROW

Two months ago Nara stood in this spot and watched Deslo and the rest of the Amhuru party sent after the Graymir dwindle and then disappear into the distance. Since that day, she had walked and paced with a barely contained nervous energy, traversing every traversable square inch of the fort. She walked up and down the length of the ground below, back and forth from side to side, and up here, on the walk, she had gone round and round this fort countless times. Walking couldn't get Deslo home any faster, but for some reason, it helped her deal with her anxiety while he was gone.

Now she stood, stone still, rooted to the spot. She had come up this morning, not long after Elder Telsiin passed along the message that he had heard from Amintuu, that he and the others had left the Graymere behind and that they hoped to press on quickly all day and be back at Berran's Point by nightfall. Kaden had persuaded her to come down for a while at lunchtime, since nightfall was yet a long way off, but she had felt the tug of her deep longing pulling her until at last she drifted back up with Kiki in the early afternoon to resume her watch.

Kiki didn't last long. She couldn't see over the wall without help, and even if Nara did lift her up, there was nothing to see of any interest to her—just the mushy meadow, now devoid of snow as the spring thaw was underway, stretching into the distance as far as she could see. Kiki flopped down on the walkway next to Nara, and after her third complaint about being bored, Nara gave her the choice to remain in complete silence or to go down to her father. Kiki opted to go down, and Nara was left once more alone upon the walkway.

Nara's legs had grown tired, very tired, but still she maintained her quiet vigil. If she had been asked why it was so important to her that she be standing here when Deslo and the others came into view, she wasn't sure she could have found the words to explain the strange urgency inside her. So she was glad that no one did ask. She thought once, when Kaden came by to give her some water and to see if she needed anything else, that he might ask, but he didn't. She was grateful, and she would thank him for that later.

Nara watched the sun drop low in the west, then dip below the horizon, but she didn't move. No word had come yet that they weren't arriving tonight, and unless it did, she would remain here even after the darkness fell and the slender moon showed up to give her light. Her boy was coming home, not because Berran's Point was home, but because she was home. She and Kaden and Kiki, they were home to each other, and when Deslo had gone away, she had lost a piece of herself. She was ready to be whole again.

She yawned and stretched and was about to turn around to glance below and see if she could see Kiki or Kaden, when she thought she saw movement across the meadow. She was suddenly alert and rigid, leaning forward over the wall to peer into the grey twilight. Yes, she had seen movement. Men were running above the Arua, coming toward the fort. She stood, watching, searching, until she could see Deslo toward the back of the group.

Her heart leapt inside her, and after standing here all day, after all her waiting and stillness, she raced to the nearest ladder and almost fell off it, she scrambled down so fast. She rushed to the gate, opened it with barely a word to the Amhuru standing watch before it, and ran out into the meadow.

The meadow was mushy indeed, and her feet squished as she ran. It was so muddy, in fact that she lost her shoe in the muck, but she didn't care and she didn't stop. She ran, heedless of the discomfort and imbalance with her shoe gone, and twice she almost slipped and fell. She didn't care if she didn't look graceful to those behind her or ahead—her son had come home.

At last the party approached, and the Amhuru near the front saw her and moved wordlessly to either side so that she passed through their midst. They parted, she saw him, and then she stopped. Deslo stopped too, and for a moment he stood on the Arua as they stared at one another. Then she rushed to him, and he stepped down to receive her embrace.

She held him close, burying her head on his chest, as tears of joy slipped down her face. He hugged her too, but after the initial embrace, she could feel his hold relaxing, so she let go and stepped back a half step to look at him. He was looking at her strangely, perhaps quizzically, perhaps sheepishly, and Nara thought maybe he was a little uncomfortable with being made a spectacle before the Amhuru.

"I'm sorry," she whispered, leaning in again, "I didn't mean to embarrass you."

"Don't worry about that," he said gently. "The others have gone on, anyway."

Nara glanced behind her and saw that it was true. The Amhuru had kept going toward the fort, and so had the Kalosenes, though they were clearly lingering behind a bit, as though uncomfortable intruding on Nara and Deslo's reunion but also uncomfortable leaving them behind completely. Nara also saw Kaden and Kiki on their way out from the fort, and she was glad. She took Deslo by the hand and started back toward them.

"Noni," Deslo said as they walked. "Where's your shoe?"

She looked down. While both feet and ankles were spattered with mud, the missing shoe was obvious, and she understood the strange look from Deslo earlier. "I lost it on the way out here," she said. "Let's keep an eye out for it on the way back."

"No need," Deslo said, pointing forward.

Nara looked and saw Marlo holding her shoe up to hand it to Kaden as they passed each other. She turned to Deslo with a smile. "Come, let's go see Yadi and Kiki."

"Yes. Let's." They took a few steps and Deslo added. "It's good to be back."

She smiled at him again and squeezed his hand. It was true, and there was nothing further that needed to be said.

·   ·   ·

Lying down that night inside the walls of Berran's Point, Kiki sound asleep beside him, Deslo thought that whatever might be wrong with the world at large, all was well with his world. When they had passed the edge of the Graymere, leaving that nightmare-land behind, he had felt as an imprisoned man must feel upon release—free and unfettered, with endless possibility in front of him. It was true that all who went in hadn't made it back out, but he had survived and the fragment of the Cord had been retaken. He rejoiced, knowing he would soon be back with his family.

Now he was back, and though he didn't have the slightest idea what was next for any of them, he didn't mind the uncertainty. A man could, he had come to realize, deal with a great many unknowns in his life, if but a few things were sure and certain. Those things could provide an anchor in the midst of life's storms, even when sorely tested by the vagaries of time and fate.

Telsiin, though, did not waste time the following day, making no concessions to either time or fate or their vagaries. Now that the fragment had been returned and the surviving Amhuru had been reunified, decisions had to be made. So the Elder gathered the whole group together, and the most fundamental question was laid before them—to move on to their next destination as planned, to stay for a while and gather their strength, or to revisit their plan entirely?

The debate that emerged among the Amhuru was like no other Deslo had witnessed. Ordinarily, spokesmen emerged for the various options being argued, trying to persuade others to join them and see the matter their way, but this wasn't like that. Sometimes, the same person would make points in favor of opposite views, or even suggest later in the conversation reasons to refute what he had said earlier. There appeared to be genuine openness to any possibility, combined in equal measure with genuine skepticism about all possibilities.

Deslo watched and listened, wondering what he would choose if the decision were up to him and feeling very glad that it wasn't. He noticed, as he observed the proceedings, that Amintuu was curiously silent. He had sometimes agreed with Amintuu in past discussions like this, sometimes not, but Amintuu had always had a strong opinion and had never been silent. Deslo wondered why the Amhuru sat, staring at the ground in the center of their circle, saying nothing.

Deslo thought back over the last few weeks, realizing that the change in Amintuu did not begin today. A quiet determination had fallen on all of them as they made their way as quickly and safely as possible back through the Graymere, but the shift in mood had affected Amintuu perhaps even more than any of the others. He did not insist on being in front, but he accepted and embraced his new role as Keeper of the recovered fragment, allowing the rest of the Amhuru essentially to serve as a dedicated body-guard, keeping him in the center of the party and as far from any danger as possible.

Maybe that was it, Deslo thought. Maybe the weight of his new re-sponsibility hung heavily upon him. Deslo couldn't imagine what it must be to wear an original fragment of the Golden Cord, especially now, with the Jin Dara out there, trying to take them all.

If that was indeed the case, Deslo thought, it might be a good thing. Amintuu had struck Deslo as one who liked to be listened to, to be heeded, and perhaps just the smallest suggestion that he didn't much like being dis-agreed with. He wasn't obvious about it—after all, he was an Amhuru—but when the will of Telsiin or the group went against him, Amintuu seemed to chafe under that authority in a way he didn't see in other Amhuru like, say, Tchinchura.

Maybe now, though, Amintuu was getting a lesson in the respon-sibility that Tchinchura bore and, in a way, that Telsiin bore, for though the Chief Elder did not bear an original piece, he bore responsibility for them all. Maybe this silence on Amintuu's part was evidence of newfound humility.

The discussion of their options had come to an impasse, and there was clearly no concensus. Telsiin was on his feet, pacing in the middle of the gathering. At last he stopped, and he said, "When the first message was sent to the three Northland Keepers, right after the first Southland frag-ment crossed the Madri, the instructions I sent included a mandate that whatever happened, if the situation had not been resolved in five winters, I appointed a time and place for all three Northland Keepers to gather.

"That way, we would know if all three original fragments remained under our control. That way, we could take council given whatever we had learned about what to do next. It was a fallback contingency that I never expected to need, as it was unimaginable to me at the time that we would not have dealt with whatever lay before us.

"I wonder, though," Telsiin said, now looking not at them, but over their heads and at nothing in particular, since only the timber wall of the fort lay where he was gazing. "Now that almost three years have past since

I sent those messages, I wonder if our wisest strategy isn't simply to send messengers to the *The Sorry Rogue* and *The Lion's Mane* to meet us at the nearest port, to get on board those ships, and to stay on them at sea as much as possible until the time comes for that rendezvous.

"At that point, if Draagan and Maccado have survived, then we can all take counsel together."

"And if they haven't?" Amintuu said, entering the conversation at last. "If one or both have fallen and if the Jin Dara has taken what they bear?"

"Then we are lost already," Telsiin said. "And to go in search of them would likely only take us to him and hasten our fall."

"But if we could come to them in time? If we could save them?"

"But how can we know that?" Telsiin asked, raising his arms in a gesture of something more like helplessness than anything else. "How can we know we're not just doing the Jin Dara's work for him? Gathering the remaining fragments for him?"

There was nothing further from Amintuu, and all were silent. After a moment, Telsiin said, "I will not make a decision today. I will consider the matter further. After our near miss here, though, with the Graymir, I am inclined to concede that we have tried our best and are, for the time at least, defeated. To retreat, regroup, and fight another day is my inclination."

There were several nods of agreement among the Amhuru, and Deslo knew as he looked around him that, while Telsiin might be saying the decision would come later, the matter was already decided. From what Deslo could see, the Elder had almost unanimous support for what he had suggested.

For himself, Deslo embraced the idea far more warmly than he would have two months ago. He had thought himself fed up with life at sea on *The Sorry Rogue,* and by the time they arrived at Berran's Point, he was once more so used to being on solid ground that he could happily have never boarded another ship in his life. But, after spending the last two months in the Graymere, the prospect of being back at sea wasn't so bad.

Deslo waited for the Elder to give formal permission for the gathering to disband, but he didn't. Instead, Telsiin said, "Before we disperse, there is one other thing, but it is not my place to share it. Maarta?"

At the mention of Maarta's name, Deslo tensed. He couldn't move, and he stared as the young Amhuru stood and walked over to Telsiin. He reached the Elder, and without saying anything, motioned to Olli to come up and join him.

No, Deslo thought. Not this.

Olli joined Maarta at the front. He put his arm around her shoulder as she slipped her arm around him.

"Just a week into the Graymere," Maarta said, "Olli and I were talking one night, and we said to each other, we said, 'if we live long enough to get out of there, we are going to get married, without delay.'"

No. No. No.

"Well," Maarta said. "We talked to Elder Telsiin this morning, and he's going to perform the ceremony tonight. We'd like you all to come to our wedding."

Maarta grinned. The Amhuru laughed and cheered. Deslo felt like screaming.

Soon, the happy couple was surrounded by well-wishers. Laughter filled the fort. Deslo rose and walked away.

.   .   .

It came as no surprise to Kaden, given Nara's almost maternal relationship with Olli, that Olli wanted Nara close by during the ceremony. And so, he found himself near the center of things that night too, as he stood close to Nara with Kiki between them. Kiki did well during the ceremony, holding Kaden's hand and staying quiet, seeming to understand that this was not a time for any of her many questions.

Where Deslo was during the ceremony, Kaden didn't know. He had made himself scarce the whole day, wholly absent from the preparations underway for the wedding, for the feast afterward that would be a feast in name only since their food supplies were low, and for the structure in the fort that was the least damaged from the earlier fire to be transformed into a bridal suite. Kaden thought he saw Deslo at one point during the ceremony, at the back of the gathering, but when he turned to look for him again, he wasn't there.

The ceremony ended, and Telsiin pronounced Maarta and Olli husband and wife. The Amhuru crowded around them again to congratulate them. They moved to the wedding feast, and though the supplies were scant, the warmth of the community around the table wasn't. They each shared the feeling that they had survived a near disaster here, and their

celebration over that survival easily fed their willingness and desire to celebrate Olli and Maarta's union.

The meal over, there was both singing and dance, and Kaden observed
both the similarities and the differences between the music of the Northland Amhuru and the music he had witnessed on Azandalir. Both were
festive in their own way, but also serious in their own way, mixing joy and
sorrow.

Not long after the music began, the older Amhuru began, playfully at
first and then almost forcefully, to push Maarta from the circle of dancers.
Kaden came to understand it as a ritual, whereby the Elders of the community pushed the new husband to take his bride to the bridal chamber.
Responsibility to the community was bred deep in the Amhuru, but there
was a time to lay down your duty to the group and take up your place in
your family.

Maarta did not need much convincing, and after just a few of these
half-playful, half-forceful attempts to remove Maarta from the dance, he
took Olli's hand and led her toward the back of the fort where the building
stood. The Amhuru cheered briefly and then returned to their dancing.

A large fire was burning near the front of the fort, and the bulk of the
Amhuru either sat beside it or danced nearby or took their turn patrolling
the walkway above and guarding the gate below. Eventually, Nara lifted
Kiki, who was already asleep with her little head on Nara's shoulder, and
told Kaden she was going to bed.

"I'll be along soon," Kaden said, and Nara nodded. He did not need
to explain why he wasn't coming right away. She understood that Olli and
Maarta's joy was Deslo's sorrow, and she knew what he must do.

Kaden didn't know if Deslo had been at the ceremony, but he knew he
hadn't been at the feast or the festivities after. It was inconceivable that he
was anywhere near the building serving as the bridal suite at the back, so
Kaden knew he must have taken refuge somewhere on the walk above. He
climbed a ladder and, sure enough, quickly discovered Deslo at the front
of the fort, sitting with his back against the timber wall, his knees drawn
up against his chest with his arms around them, his head down in the dark.

"May I sit with you?" Kaden asked.

The barely audible grunt that came from Deslo could have meant anything, so Kaden decided to take it as a yes. He slid down beside Deslo, so
that he too could lean against the timber wall. For a long time, they sat and

neither said anything. Kaden was thinking about what exactly to say when, unexpectedly, Deslo spoke first.

"She's lost to me."

"I know," Kaden said, and in that moment, as he both heard and felt the heaviness of his son's sadness, Kaden knew what to say.

"When I was young, not much older than you," Kaden began, "I fell in love with a girl named Addi. Her family was among the lower nobility of Barra-Dohn. Your grandfather wasn't thrilled with my interest in her—he thought her beneath me—but I think he left us alone at first because he hoped the situation would resolve itself, that I would tire of her."

Deslo didn't speak, but Kaden could see through the dark that he had lifted his head and was watching.

"I didn't tire of her, though, and when it became clear that I was serious about marrying Addi, Eirmon began his campaign against her. He tried logic and argument, he tried to defame her character and plant doubts in my mind about her faithfulness—he tried everything. But, with every attempt to separate us, I clung to her all the more.

"And then, after weeks of constant conflict about her, he just stopped. For one, brief, golden day, I thought I had won. I met Addi in the market, and I told her I thought Eirmon was giving up. We cried tears of joy at the thought that we might at last be together, but … I never saw her again.

"What I didn't know was that Eirmon had offered Addi's father an enormous sum of money if he would carry out certain political and mercantile ventures in Golina. Part of the deal was that he would take his entire family with him. Addi's father knew, I'm sure, that he was being bribed to keep us apart, and while I hated him for taking Eirmon's money, I know now he had little choice. It wasn't just the money. Eirmon wasn't someone you said no to, especially a man in his position.

"And so, he took the money and left. I never even got a chance to say goodbye. Not long after, Eirmon picked Ellenara as a suitable wife for me, and we were married within the year. When Addi eventually returned, I wouldn't see her. It was too painful. She and her family ended up moving to Amattai—I wouldn't be surprised if Eirmon had something to do with that too."

"Noni mentioned her to me, once," Deslo said. "It was maybe a year or so before the fall of Barra-Dohn, and I was venting about you. Usually,

I vented about why you didn't love me, but that night, I was venting about why you didn't love her."

Kaden listened, feeling the slight pang of regret that always accompanied conversations like these with Deslo. Those days were behind him, but he was never able to think about his behavior then without pain.

"She told me a little of what you just told me, though she never mentioned the girl's name," Deslo said. "She wanted me to understand that grandfather had wronged you, that what was going on in our family was more complicated than the three of us."

"Your Noni has always been a wise woman," Kaden said. He added, "I hope I don't need to say this, but what Eirmon did to me, it doesn't justify what I did to you, or to your Noni. You know that, and you know I know that, right?"

"Yes," Deslo said. "I know it, and I know you know it too."

"Good," Kaden said. "I didn't bring this up to justify my past misbehavior. I just wanted you to know I have some idea of what it feels like to lose someone."

Deslo nodded in the dark, and then he said, "What do I do, Yadi? I don't know what to do."

Kaden put his arm around Deslo, pulling him close. Deslo began to cry, and Kaden rubbed his son's back gently. "I don't know what to tell you, Deslo. This is a pain I can't fix, and I can't take it away. I am afraid it must be borne."

After a few moments, when Deslo's tears had slowed, Kaden continued, "I will say that there is hope. Two things should be added to the story I just told you about Addi. The first is that I love your Noni very much. It has been a long time since I regretted losing Addi, so don't ever believe that you can't love again. You can.

"The second is that if I had married Addi, as I had hoped and planned, I would never have had you in my life. There would have been no Deslo and no Kiki. There may have been other children, different children, but there would never have been you, and I would have missed out."

"You wouldn't have known that you missed out," Deslo said, wiping the tears from his eyes as he sat up.

"No, I wouldn't," Kaden said, smiling. "But, nevertheless, I would have missed out. That's yet another reason I'm glad now that I didn't get my way with Addi. Perhaps there will be a day when you hold your own child in your arms, when you will know quietly within yourself that, had you married Olli, you would never have had this child to hold and to love."

"Perhaps," Deslo said.

It was enough, Kaden thought, for Deslo to at least conceive of a future without Olli. He knew it would be little consolation at the moment, with the wound fresh and raw. What could Kaden say that would make this night all right for his son, he who knew full well the futility of offering words to comfort the wounds of a broken heart? There was little he could say or do, other than to be here and to hold Deslo.

And so they sat in the dark, against the wall, for a long time. After a while, Kaden's thoughts turned back to the discussion from the morning. He hoped they would do as Telsiin had suggested and head back to the ships soon. He hoped they would leave this place far, far behind.

But where they would go then, and what they would do, and how they would defeat the Jin Dara, he had no idea.

14

HALFWAY HOME

Maccado heard the whistle and started immediately down the dusty mainstreet of Barden. The lookout had spotted a wagontrain, the first in several weeks, and he and the others would need to take refuge in the usual place.

He found four of the other five already in the stable. They were waiting at the foot of the ladder that led up into the loft. He stopped at the door and glanced behind him. The last of their number was coming and would be here soon. Maccado looked back toward the ladder and nodded, and the others started to climb.

He joined them a moment later, taking his spot by the front wall of the building, where a small knot in the wood made a perfect hole through which to view the street and the large warehouse opposite the stable where the long wagon-sleds would be stored and locked overnight while the horse-teams that pulled them would be liveried here, right below them.

The street and the warehouse were all he could see. The tiny town of Barden lay along the street to the east of the stable, but none of the buildings could be seen from the hole through which Maccado peered, nor could the large, sprawling prairie that lay west of the stable and the town. Barden existed because the wagon-trail across that prairie existed, and all the horses that pulled the great wagon-sleds and the men who drove them had to stop somewhere. Who had decided that place would be here, or when, or for what reason, Maccado had no idea.

The waiting always made Maccado tense, and today was no different, but eventually the wagontrain came into view, and he watched as the great wagon-sleds loaded with cargo were navigated through the vast front doors into the warehouse for safe keeping. The long wagon-sleds glided smoothly above the ground as they were maneuvered into place, and the tired horses were unhitched and led into the stable. Soon the relative quiet of this building, almost as large as the warehouse across the street, had been thoroughly broken by the sound of horses being cared for.

The sound of horses Maccado didn't mind, but their smell was a different matter. The horses always entered, smelling of that stale, sweaty smell of horses on a long journey, and that was the best part of their odor. It only got worse from there. For Maccado, who had experienced almost no contact with the animals before, his admiration for the beasts was severely blunted by the many warm days he had spent in this loft, trapped in the close air and stench of this place.

Eventually, though, the hubbub down below faded and disappeared, as the horses had been taken care of and the workers left to grab their dinners, save only the one who would take the first watch at the stable door. Darkness fell on Barden and on the Amhuru hiding in the loft, and Maccado sat in the scratchy hay, fingering the *cadeen* where it circled his brow. To keep it safe, he would have endured far worse than the stench of this place.

Maccado slept, and the faint light of morning was streaming in through his eye-hole when he awoke. The stable workers were already at it down below, preparing the horses, and soon the teams were being led out. Maccado watched through the hole as they were hitched back up to the wagon-sleds, and as they reformed their long caravan and started west across the prairie that Maccado could not see.

For a long time, several hours in fact, Maccado and the others stayed put. They would not risk the possibility of coming down too soon, only to find a rider returning from the wagontrain for some lost item to purchase, for some good that had been forgotten or suddenly become necessary. So, it was already late afternoon when the whistle came from the lookout on the western side of town, and Maccado and the others made their way to the ladder and went down.

All that time in the loft, not one of them had spoken. They had long practiced what was as close to absolute stillness and silence as a man could achieve, and whenever a stranger came to Barden, they never let down their guard. Now they relaxed, and smiles and words returned. They walked together back down the mainstreet toward the heart of the town, and Maccado wasn't sure which he wanted more—supper to satisfy the growling in his stomach or a bath to try to wash the horse-stink away. Fortunately, both were waiting, so he joined in the laughter and the talk. They were free again until the next caravan came, and that could be many weeks away.

Maccado joined in with the others, but under all the laughter and the talk there was a growing sense of unease. When he'd first come to Barden, he'd not known what to expect or how long he would be here. Whatever he'd thought, though, he had never expected to be here so long, and since the messenger had come bringing word that all the fragments were in the Northlands, no further word had come. Rightly or wrongly, he always associated the size of almost any problem with the amount of time it took to solve, and any problem that his brothers couldn't resolve in the years he had been in hiding here was a very big problem indeed.

.   .   .

The Jin Dara lay in the tall grass, far south of both Barden and the dusty wagon road that ran through it. The caravan had passed on several hours ago, and he waited with Devaar to see what would happen next. Now it was well toward evening, but a small cluster of men exited the stable and walked east into the town.

He turned to Devaar, who no longer wore any Zerura, and to the Najin beside him who did but held a looking glass as Devaar did. It was interesting to the Jin Dara to compare how much more improved his own vision was with the others. He didn't need a looking glass to see the men walking down the street, but he couldn't make out a great deal of detail. Perhaps with the aid of the glass, the Najin could, but it had become clear that in general, the extent of the others' improvement was not even close to the magnitude of the Jin Dara's.

Of course, his first thought was that this was the difference between wearing two original fragments and wearing two replicas, but he wasn't so sure anymore. Even among the Najin, who all wore replicas, differences in abilities like this were beginning to emerge. How to explain that?

He had two theories. Perhaps it was connected to a difference in the men themselves. Perhaps the Zerura only magnified, in a way, the native abilities that he and his men already had, so that while all might improve their ability to see, those who had possessed better eyesight from the beginning perhaps improved more. Future tests on new recruits might help prove if this theory was true, and he made a note to himself to talk to Devaar about it later.

The other possibility was that some men improved faster because they practiced more frequently or with better focus. This made sense to the Jin Dara, because there was a correlation in most of life between hard work and good results, so why not with the use of Zerura? Maybe the more you used it the more it transformed you. Certainly this would help explain his own superior senses, as no one had practiced with Zerura as frequently or for as long as he had. Not among the Najin, certainly, and quite possibly not among the Amhuru either.

Devaar lowered his looking glass. He turned his head toward the Jin Dara and nodded. The Jin Dara acknowledged the nod and then turned back to look at the town. "Brilliant, isn't it?"

"What is?"

"Hiding in plain sight," the Jin Dara replied. "Really brilliant."

"Or really foolish," Devaar said. "There are only half a dozen of them, in a tiny town with no defenses. That jungle fortress was much more forbidding."

"Yes," the Jin Dara conceded, "but it was also much easier to find. For all the power the Zerura gives us, we still have to find the Amhuru before we can take the fragments from them. The fortresses and strong places of the Northlands would always be first on the list, wouldn't they?"

"Sure, because they're defensible, just like this town isn't."

"Yes, but if we never find it, we can't attack it."

"We did find it."

The Jin Dara turned back to Devaar and glared. It wasn't an angry glare, but Devaar's grin slipped from his face. "You're thinking like a soldier—what can I defend? I'm talking about thinking like, I don't know, a thief—where can I hide? And why not? Perhaps they know now that there is no place strong enough to defend, that their only hope is to never be found."

The Jin Dara turned back to face the town before he continued. "I mean, think how we found this place. Rumor reached us of a small cluster of Amhuru passing through a small town near the eastern terminus of this road, and only after combing several other towns along the trail not far from that one, did we find a second report that confirmed our suspicion—but those sightings were more than a year old at the time. Do you remember what we did next?"

Devaar shrugged. "Sure, we sent a few scouts west."

"Yes, all the way west, like to the far western end of the caravan trail, because we learned there were no strong places of the kind we've been discussing anywhere along the road and assumed they intended to travel all the way to the other side and then move on from there."

The Jin Dara paused in his telling, reached for a tall stalk of prairie grass and pulled it. He started chewing on the end, absent-mindedly. "But no one at the western end of the trail remembered seeing a party of Amhuru pass. So, I thought they'd given us the slip, made it through unseen and moved on, who knows where. I almost let it go, Devaar. You understand?"

Devaar didn't answer.

"I almost let it go," the Jin Dara repeated. "On a whim I sent a couple scouts to work the road itself, to see what they might find. It was a complete afterthought. One I didn't expect to yield any benefit. We got lucky, Devaar, and brilliant strategy isn't less brilliant because blind luck foils it."

"I see your point," Devaar said. "And I don't disagree that it was clever. But it was risky, and now that we've found them, it seems fair to say the gamble has failed."

"Yes," the Jin Dara said simply. "It was a gamble, and it failed."

"Tonight then?"

"Tonight," the Jin Dara answered, still watching the town. "We won't let this one slip away."

·   ·   ·

Just before the blast of wind shattered all the windows in his room, Maccado felt someone grab the Arua, seizing it with such violent force that he woke from a dead sleep. There was no time to speak or move or do anything else. The wind hit the building, blowing glass all over the room. Maccado shielded his eyes with his arms, but he could feel shards cutting his arms and face.

The whole building shook. In fact, it seemed to rock, as though the wind was lifting the building, tilting it. Then the wind stopped and the building settled back down. Maccado stood, fully aware that there might be nothing he could do. Their ruse had been unmasked and the enemy had come. Unless he had come alone or with very little help, he and his men were far too few to hold him off. He had to fight, to save the *cadeen* if he could, but secrecy had been their only real hope.

As he stood, another blast of wind hit the building, but this time from the opposite direction, and Maccado heard the sound of shattering glass as the windows on that side were blown in. The house definitely moved again, and he felt the floor beneath his feet tilting the opposite way from what it had just a moment ago. Maccado could not yet see his enemy, but he could still fight him. He reached out through the *cadeen,* hoping to seize the Arua and take it back, but the strength of the enemies' hold did not afford him much hope.

.   .   .

The Jin Dara watched the systematic destruction of Barden from a comfortable distance. The fight no longer hung in the balance as the brief attempt by the Amhuru in Barden to take back control of the Arua from his Najin had failed a few moments ago. Of course, this fight had never really hung in the balance very much. It had been effectively over before it began.

Still, Devaar had insisted he remain well outside Barden with a small escort of Najin, and the Jin Dara had not argued with him. He felt the scars where the knives of that Amhuru had cut him more than a year ago, and he felt the shiver of fear that had run through him then run through him again. He had been a hair's breadth from death that day, and he would never forget it.

In a way, he owed that Amhuru a debt of gratitude. Wearing two fragments, feeling the constant thrum of their power—he had started to believe that he was invincible. He still believed he would be, once he wore all six. Indeed, invincible might not even be a strong enough word. To wear not two but six, to have his whole body wrapped in Zerura? Would he not then be more than a man? A god?

Perhaps he would be, but he wasn't a god yet. That Amhuru in the jungle had taught him this, and it had been a valuable if painful lesson.

Even so, the Jin Dara had spent a great deal of time considering the things he would do to that man when he caught up with him again. They would not be pleasant things.

The kitchen knife is king, until it meets a sharper blade.

The Jin Dara had heard those words in his nightmares for months. They still ran through his head, but now instead of taunting him, they motivated him. He would become that sharper blade, and he would cut the Amhuru to pieces.

. . .

Maccado lay in the middle of the dusty road. He was being restrained both physically and through the power of the men who encircled him, all of whom were helping to hold him with their manipulation of the Arua field.

Barden lay in ruins, and the bodies of his brothers and most if not all of its townsfolk lay scattered. Maccado tried not to look at the dead. They had all known the risk, but he grieved for them. He had known the risk too, and he knew that in all likelihood, he would soon join them.

He sensed more than saw that another had come. There was a shift in the formation that surrounded him, and a man passed through. So this is he, Maccado thought. The true enemy.

The man walked over until he stood over Maccado. Maccado lay still, neither looking up to see him, nor looking away to avoid him. At last, the man spoke.

"You have something that belongs to me."

The man bent over to take the *cadeen,* and as he did, Maccado struggled as hard as he could, and the response from those holding him was both immediate and painful. When he was again subdued, the man quickly and firmly pried the *cadeen* off of his head. It was at that moment that something inside Maccado broke, and the tears came. He had failed. He had lost the *cadeen.* He prayed that death would find him swiftly.

He waited, but nothing happened. When the tears stopped, and his eyes cleared, he glanced up and realized that the man holding the *cadeen* appeared to be paying no attention to him. He was simply standing, gazing at the *cadeen* as he held it in his hand.

"Bring him," the man said as he turned to walk away. "Time for some new experiments."

. . .

The feel of the Zerura wriggling up across his chest almost tickled. It moved up and up, and then down the slope of skin that led to his neck. He already had Zerura around his neck of course, so the new fragment kept moving, up over his chin and onto the Jin Dara's face.

When it reached his forehead, it stretched around his head until it had formed a complete but tight circle. It pulsed and thrummed, and when it fell into sync with the other two, the elation and wonder that the Jin Dara felt was indescribable.

He reached up, unable not to. His fingertips stroked lightly the Zerura on his forehead. So beautiful. So wonderful. So much power.

It struck him as he felt the new piece, that it was too early to wear a crown. He was only halfway home. He would have to remind himself of that fact daily, lest he once more fall into the trap of overconfidence.

Still, halfway was halfway. When he had put on the second piece, he had feared that doing so would kill him, for the Old Stories said that gathering the fragments of the Golden Cord was forbidden and that terrible things would happen if you did. Of course, nothing terrible had happened.

Consequently, he had been less afraid this time, and once again, nothing had happened. He was not surprised. The Golden Cord was not a holy relic, not the gift of some imaginary deity worshiped long ago. It was just Zerura, the living matter that created and regulated the Arua field. Not magic, just matter. How it had been discovered and mined, he didn't know and didn't care.

All he knew was that he now had half of the Cord. When he had it all, the world would bow before him.

Part 2

THE DEEPER CUT

15

A FAVOR

Draagan walked around the room where he had been left. They had locked the door after showing him in, and as he had no idea how long he would need to wait, he figured he might as well have a look around.

The room was large, even a little luxurious. There were several plush, comfortable chairs placed on a large, ornate rug. A sideboard on the far wall had meat and bread, cheese and fruit, as well as both water and wine. He picked up the bread and ate it as he ambled around the room.

He hoped that Breeson had been shown to a room as nice as this one, and that he was being fed and generally treated well. He had reassured Breeson on numerous occasions that he believed they would both be fine, that even if the Jaen brothers rejected his proposal, he didn't think they would hurt either of them. He hadn't lied exactly, as he did believe they would be all right, but he had, perhaps, exaggerated the degree of his connection with the eldest of the Jaens.

Now that he was here, waiting to be seen, he wasn't entirely without his reservations. This had always felt like a very bold idea, but here, walking around in this room, it felt more like complete lunacy. What had possessed him to come? Why would the Jaens do what he was here to ask? Would he do it if he were in their shoes?

Draagan glanced down at the fragment of the Golden Cord wrapped around his right forearm. Risking his own life was one thing, but risking the Cord was madness. If something happened here, if he died and the fragment of the Cord that he bore, which he was responsible for, if it fell into the hands of the JaenSing, then he would have weakened the Amhuru in their hour of greatest need. More than the personal shame that he would bring upon his own name, he could not bear that thought.

And yet, he knew there was nothing he could do now. He would have to go through with this plan. This whole town was run by the JaenSing. In fact, he would have been greatly surprised if even the mid-sized port where Captain Daugen and *The Starfish* had dropped him and Breeson off wasn't also controlled by the JaenSing, even though it was a good twenty miles away. He doubted if anything happened in either place or anwhere in between that the Jaens didn't know about. Now that he was here, he would not leave without their knowledge and permission, that much he knew.

The door behind him opened, and Draagan turned to see a man enter and close the door after him. His hair was short and grey, and he wore a neatly trimmed beard. His eyes were a pale, bright blue. He was tall and had a powerful build.

The man was alone, but he walked confidently over to the sideboard and poured himself some wine. If he had glanced at Draagan upon first opening the door, Draagan had missed it. He hadn't looked over yet and didn't look at Draagan until after he had his wine in hand, and then he walked to the nearest of the plush chairs and took a seat. He examined Draagan then, looking at him over the rim of his cup with those intense eyes.

Draagan had not seen Meldriic Jaen in a very long time, and yet he was sure this was he. Those eyes were memorable, but it was the left ear that was the true giveaway. The top third or more was completely gone—it had been bitten off by some wild animal when Meldriic was a boy, if Draagan remembered correctly. Draagan had never forgotten the mutilated ear.

"My men say I should hang you from the roof," Meldriic Jaen said.

"That would not be very hospitable."

"They wonder if you're an assassin."

"They took my weapons when I came in," Draagan said. "What am I going to kill you with?"

That brought a hint of a smile to Meldriic's face. "Yes, because we all know how helpless Amhuru are without their weapons."

The smile disappeared, and Meldriic Jaen stared hard at Draagan. "You told my men you know me, but I've never seen you before in my life. You have exactly one chance to give me a really good reason why I shouldn't hang you and your friend from my roof. If you know anything about me and my family, you know we don't love Amhuru, so don't lie again. I won't hesitate to cut out your lying tongue."

"I didn't lie, Meldriic," Draagan said. "We have met, but I was only a boy. It would have been more accurate, I suppose, to say our families know each other. My grandfather always said it was a miscarriage of justice that your grandfather was stripped of his place among us and sent away."

Meldriic leaned forward, staring at Draagan again. "Kaarnin is your father?"

"Was," Draagan said. "He is dead."

"I'm sorry to hear that," Meldriic said, still watching Draagan closely. "I liked your father."

"He liked you," Draagan said.

"Really?" Meldriic said, leaning back in his chair and taking a sip of his wine. "I thought he didn't approve of us."

Draagan shrugged. "You can't really think any Amhuru would exactly approve of the JaenSing—"

"Well, what did they expect?" Meldriic snapped, cutting Draagan off. "Did they think we'd become fishermen? Shopkeepers? Farmers?"

"I don't know what anyone else expected," Draagan said, "But my grandfather always said he had hoped your grandfather would accept the decree of the Elders, graciously, perhaps lay low and take up some honorable calling until enough time had passed for those who believed in him to raise the matter again—hopefully with a better outcome."

"Lay low," Meldriic Jaen scoffed, but he looked away, almost wistfully, perhaps considering the 'what if' inherent in what Draagan was saying.

"Anyway," Draagan said, thinking they'd said enough about a distant past that neither of them wanted to discuss. "My father did like you. He may not have liked the JaenSing, but he respected your father and believed you had greatness in you."

Meldriic Jaen continued to stare, not at Draagan, but at a painting on the wall that showed a group of men, standing shoulder to shoulder with a forest behind them. When he spoke, his voice was soft and distant. "What is your name, son of Kaarnin?"

"Draagan."

"Why are you here, Draagan?"

"I have a favor to ask."

Now Meldriic turned back to look at him. "A favor?"

"Yes."

"You must be Kaarnin's son," Meldriic said, then added dryly. "Only his offspring would be so bold as to come here, little more than a stranger, to ask a favor of the Jaens."

Draagan smiled. "It isn't just any favor. It carries with it great risk and even the likelihood of death."

Meldriic laughed, then took another drink. "You really don't have to make this more challenging than it already is, you know."

"I know," Draagan said. "But you see, I am not the liar you said I was, and the truth will come out sooner or later."

"All right," Meldriic said. "I'll hear you out. But tell me, you wouldn't have come unless you thought you might succeed. What makes you think I would even consider helping you? Our grandfathers were friends, to a lesser degree our fathers, but we are not. I have no interest in dying for you."

"I'm not asking you to die for me," Draagan said.

"Then what?"

"Two reasons. The first is that if you do what I ask, and if you or any of your brothers survive, I think the way may be clear for the Jaens to return."

"Who said we want to return?"

"Maybe you don't," Draagan said, "but I think you could, even given the, shall we say, less than admirable family business for the last few generations?"

Meldriic grunted. "And the other reason?"

It was Draagan's turn to stare at Meldriic. The moment of truth had come. "Someone has taken two of the Southland fragments of the Golden Cord. The other Southland fragment has been brought across the Madri, and the two missing pieces crossed shortly after. All six are in the North-lands. The thief, he wants them all—I know, because he almost killed me to take the one I guard. If he gets them—well, you know we can't let that happen."

"Protecting the Golden Cord is no longer my problem," Meldriic said, but Draagan could hear that he was shaken. Good. There was hope.

"If he gets the rest of the Cord, it will be everyone's problem, yours included. You know that."

"Well, what do you want from me? What's your plan?" Meldriic said, and then added hastily. "And since when do the Amhuru ask help from outsiders?"

"Since now," Draagan said. "And I have no plan, not exactly. We would need to gather a lot of information first to make anything as concrete as a plan, but I do have an idea—a dangerous, possibly foolish, absolutely mad idea. If there's any chance for it to work, it would have to be carried out by men who haven't been raised wearing Zerura."

"So the Amhuru are out."

"Yes, the Amhuru are out," Draagan agreed. "These men would also have to be about as tough as men could be—otherwise they wouldn't stand a chance."

"So of course," Meldriic said, "you thought of us. How flattering."

"And," Draagan added, "I think that to work, these men would have to really believe, deep down, in the mission of the Amhuru. Otherwise, they might just be tempted to kill this man and take his place."

Meldriic didn't say anything to that. He sat, staring at Draagan, and the Amhuru found his mood difficult to read.

"My father and my grandfather believed there was still honor in your family," Draagan said. "So I have come to you as a supplicant. If you agree, and if you succeed, you might just save the world."

"Well," Meldriic said, rising and walking to the sideboard to refill his cup. "I guess I better hear your idea so I can consider this favor."

．　　　．　　　．

Zangira sat in the front of the small landing boat, wrapped in a blanket and clutching it tight, while Trabor did the rowing. He wasn't cold, but he was shivering. The feeling of the water underneath as the boat bobbed up and down made him shiver. It reminded him too much of the dream.

Zangira had gathered from the others that his experience of the Madri had been a little different. Like the others, he had moved from one terrible, repetitive dream to the next, trapped in the same sequence over and over until it almost drove him mad. Unlike the others, there was one dream among all the rest that kept returning, again and again, interspersed with increasing frequency among the rest.

In that dream, he found himself crawling out of the sea onto a large, flat piece of wood that was perhaps six feet by six feet. He was anxious and desperate, but he had to be careful since the piece of wood was so small, lest he tilt it too far in any one direction and slide off, back into the water. He crawled slowly to the middle of the makeshift raft and curled up there, relieved and happy to have escaped, but from what he didn't know.

The sun rose and baked down upon him. The wood grew dry and hot to the touch. His clothes and his skin grew dry too, so much that his skin cracked in places and was raw and sore. His lips became so dry that it hurt just to open his mouth and his throat so dry that he couldn't swallow.

The sun hung directly above him for what felt like hours, maybe even days. He would glance up, looking for some indication that it had moved, and he would find none. He began to despair that it would ever set, that there would ever be any relief. He covered his eyes with his arms until he was too tired and weak even to lay them across his face. He rolled onto his side, feeling the hot wood sizzle as it touched the exposed skin on his face and arm and leg.

The sun continued to bake him, but at least he could open his eyes and not have to see it. He stared straight ahead, beyond the edge of his little raft, at the pitching up and down motion of the sea. The water looked so cool, so inviting, so deliciously wet. He thought if he could just scoot close enough to the edge, and then dip his hand in, the water might provide some cool relief for his dry skin and parched throat.

Something, somewhere deep inside him, resisted that idea. Someone, sometime had told him not to drink this water, but that was crazy. Why shouldn't a man dying of thirst drink water? Zangira marveled at some of the foolish things adults sometimes say to children. He started to scoot toward the side of the sheet of wood.

The progress he made along the very hot board was painful, and splinters kept digging into his skin as he slid inch by inch across the wood. He was not to be deterred, however, and he kept his eyes focused on the water. At long last, he reached the side, at least close enough that he could reach over the edge and dip his hand in the cool water. He raised himself up on one arm and leaned toward the edge.

Suddenly the board lifted up out of the water, pitching Zangira sideways off it and into the sea. He fell into the water with a splash, and while it was an enormous relief on the one hand to be in the cool water, something inside him panicked. He shouldn't be in here. It was dangerous.

As he kicked and splashed, thrashing weakly in an attempt to stay above water and not lose sight of the board, he felt something massive glide along the side of his leg. It went on and on, and he could only imagine the incredible size of the creature that was swimming past him.

The board was just out of reach, and he made as though to swim a stroke or two to get closer, when the same creature, or maybe another, passed below him again, this time moving between his outstretched legs. He could feel it, rubbing against the inside of both legs, now wriggling ever so slightly back and forth.

When it cleared him the second time, Zangira mustered all the energy he could and lurched across the few feet that separated him from the board. He took hold and pulled himself up with a mighty heave until he was completely out of the water. Relief washed over him, and he crawled to the center of the board, where the dream started all over again.

The little boat glided into the shallows, and Trabor leapt out into the surf. He came around front, grabbed the prow and pulled it in until Zangira could step out easily onto almost dry ground. Then Trabor gave the boat another pull or two to make sure it wasn't going anywhere. Zangira meanwhile limped up the beach until he was well clear of the water, and he dropped to his knees in the sand.

The sand was soft, and it wasn't bobbing up and down. It felt so solid, so safe. Zangira closed his eyes and reveled in the softness of the sand, in the total and complete lack of movement of his body. Dry ground. A shadow passed above him, and he looked up at Trabor. "I'm awake, right?"

"Yes, Father. You're awake."

Zangira nodded, then said, "Yadi. You should probably start calling me Yadi."

"Would you like me to help you up, Yadi?"

"No, not yet," Zangira said. He rolled over onto his back where he lay, stretched out on the beach. "I think I might stay here for a few minutes. Sit. Join me."

Trabor did as Zangira asked, sitting down beside him. Zangira knew that in one sense, they shouldn't linger here, as there was work to be done. But it felt so good to lie still in the cool sand. Even business as important as his could wait a few minutes, couldn't it? Besides, lying here, free from the distractions on the ship, helped Zangira to think.

He knew what he had to do, he just didn't know how to do it. He needed to find Tchinchura, or at least news of him. Almaren, already weakened by age and devastated by the destruction the Jin Dara brought to Azandalir, had not survived the Madri. And, though Tchinchura was not the next oldest of the Southland Amhuru, the Elders that remained had convened a special council while still at sea and decided that Tchinchura must take up in this time of emergency the role of Chief Elder.

And that meant, of course, that Tchinchura would need to relinquish possession of the last Southland fragment of the Golden Cord. It would pass to Zangira, who had been groomed most of his life for this task. He had never expected to take possession of an original fragment in times such as these, but so it was.

However difficult his task might be to do, it was simple enough to grasp. They needed to find Tchinchura, and with his help and the help of the Northland Amhuru, they needed then to find the Jin Dara and recover what he had stolen.

Of course, Zangira had no idea where Tchinchura was, or even if he was still alive. He had awakened only a few days ago. Still, it was better to be awake, and to be faced with a seemingly impossible task in the real world, than to be lost in the desolate mind-prison of the Madri. Terrible things might lie ahead, but he never wanted to go back there.

16

IN MOTION

Draagan was ushered out through a door that led to a large side yard. The garden here was surprisingly well cared for, given the nature of the Jaens' business. Draagan caught himself and pushed that thought away. It was irrational to think that interest in gardening was limited to any particular kind of person.

The man who ushered him out pointed in the direction of the lake that was downhill from the house, and he said. "Down the stairs. End of the dock."

The door swung shut, and Draagan was alone. For a moment, he hesitated. No one was there. No one was watching. He could simply go, get away, reconsider his options from a safe distance.

No, he thought, he couldn't. He had brought Breeson here, and he couldn't leave him. Whatever happened, whatever Meldriic and the Jaens decided, he had to see this through.

He started walking in the direction the man had pointed, toward the bottom of the hill, and soon he spied the stairs the man had mentioned. He didn't know for sure that Meldriic would say no, but it had been four days since they had talked, and he had seen no one in all that time other than the man who brought food to his room. In those four days, he'd had time to entertain every conceivable doubt and reason why coming here had been a really, really bad idea.

At the top of the stairs, Draagan halted. Down below, on the dock that jutted perhaps twenty-five or thirty yards out into the lake, Meldriic Jaen was standing by himself, gazing out over the water. Draagan looked back at the large house, wondering if he was being watched, and if so, by whom or by how many. He glanced back down at Meldriic alone on the dock. He appeared unconcerned about meeting with Draagan alone, as he had the night of Draagan's arrival. Draagan had to admire the man's toughness, and it made him think that if Meldriic agreed to undertake what Draagan had asked him to do, maybe he could actually do it.

Draagan started down the stairs toward the lake. They were broad and made of stone, and Draagan couldn't help but wonder at their existence as he started down. The hill was tall and steep, and the work that would have been required to put so many large stone stairs here seemed excessive, given that there was so little at the bottom of the stairs to find. Perhaps once there had been more than a dock here.

Or perhaps, Draagan thought, the dock was all that had ever been here, but it was what they unloaded at this dock that required some serious, sturdy stairs. He didn't know what it would be, but even as the thought occurred to him, he knew that this was the answer to the riddle.

He thought maybe Meldriic might turn around once he started out onto the dock, but that didn't happen. So Draagan walked out until he stood beside him, and he waited, staring at the lake too.

Eventually, Meldriic turned to Draagan and said, "You have greatly overestimated my desire and the desire of my brothers to rejoin the Amhuru."

"Have I?" Draagan said, watching Meldriic out of the corner of his eye, even as he stared straight ahead.

"You have," Meldriic replied. "You need to understand this, Amhuru. Even if you could have arranged it, which I doubt, we neither want nor need to be restored. When you leave in a few moments, you can take that message with you to anyone who cares."

Well, Draagan thought, at least he doesn't mean to kill me. But does he mean to make a play for the fragment I bear? Would he dare?

"You have not entirely misjudged us, however," Meldriic continued. "We do not care about you, but we do care about the Cord. We will do what you suggest."

Draagan almost didn't believe what he was hearing. He turned now to look at Meldriic, who stood, studying him carefully. "My answer surprises you. You thought we would decline."

"I feared that you would," Draagan said, "but I am glad you have not."

"It was a close thing. Your arrogance almost cost you your life."

"My arrogance?"

"You presented your request as though we would want—no, more than that—as though we would need some way to redeem ourselves in your eyes, in the eyes of all the Amhuru. We owe you nothing. It is you who should apologize to us. This is why we reject your offer of restoration. We reject it utterly."

Draagan listened to the quiet intensity in Meldriic's voice. He nodded. "I am sorry. I did not mean to offend."

"I know, and I intervened with my brothers that you might be spared—out of respect for your father, and perhaps out of a growing if grudging respect for you."

A slight smile appeared on Meldriic's face and then disappeared.

"I thank you," Draagan said simply, acknowledging what was surely meant as a compliment.

They stood, and after a few moments, Draagan asked, "When will you head out?"

"In a few days. We have some things to put in order, and then we'll be on our way."

"All five of you?"

"All five of us," Meldriic said. "I thought maybe we shouldn't all go, in case things go wrong, but in the end, we felt that if we are going to our deaths, we should go together."

"If you succeed, how will we—"

"We'll find you."

Draagan nodded again. He would have to trust that the Jaens, if successful, would seek him out and not try to keep what they recovered. He wasn't sure what other option he had.

"And you?" Meldriic asked. "Where will you go now?"

"I don't know," Draagan said. "There are no safe places."

"No," Meldriic agreed. "I guess not."

They stood a little while longer, and then Meldriic turned to leave. "When you climb the stairs, head past the house to the road. Your companion will meet you there."

Meldriic walked away, and when he was almost to the foot of the stairs, Draagan called after him. "Meldriic?"

He turned, and Draagan said, "Thank you, and may Kalos guard you and keep you."

Meldriic looked at him for a moment, nodded, and then turned and started up the stairs.

·   ·   ·

Amintuu stood on the deck of *The Lion's Mane* and wiped the sleep from his eyes. He gazed up at the nighttime sky, at the soft moon and lovely stars, and he wondered how they could look so still and so beautiful when he was clearly going crazy.

Melaane had come to him again, as she now did every night. Amintuu had plugged his ears when she first started pleading with him, "Yadi, I'm so thirsty." Over and over she called to him, until at last he had been fully awake. Driven to distraction, he had thrown back the covers and rushed from the cabin out into the open air where he now stood, trying once more to understand what had come unstuck in his mind.

At first he had hoped that leaving the Graymere behind would take care of this new development, but when the nightmares and visions continued throughout their march to the port and their rendezvous with *The Lion's Mane* and *The Sorry Rogue*, he had realized that whatever had started in the Graymere, it hadn't ended there. Amintuu had dared to hope as they set sail that perhaps the cleansing winds and endless forgetfulness of the open sea would settle him, but that hadn't happened either. Now he doubted if any distance traveled or time elapsed would set him free. He was a prisoner to the memory of the person he had loved the most and lost, and with each and every night he relived that loss.

The sound of the waves pounding up against the side of the ship suddenly came to him, and he leaned over the rail to gaze down at the babbling waters. In the smallest fraction of a second that it took him to tilt his head downward, he knew with immediate certainty both that there was a way out of this nightmare and that he was more than willing to take it. No, that he was going to take it, now.

Amintuu gripped the rail, tensing for the moment when he would use it to help catapult over and into the sea. He took a deep breath. The ship would soon leave him behind in the dark and, given sufficient time, he would tire enough that he wouldn't be able to stay afloat. Then there would be an end.

"Would you really take one of the original fragments with you to the bottom of the sea? Have you forgotten completely who you are?"

Amintuu looked down the rail in the direction of the voice—that lovely, terrible voice. "Melaane? Are you really here?"

A small figure, shrouded in darkness to a surprising degree given the brightness of the moonlight, took a step nearer along the rail. It certainly looked like Melaane, though she was paler than Amintuu remembered. "Why do you flee from me, Yadi? Why don't you answer when I call?"

"You're not … real. You're dead."

"Yes, I am dead," Melaane said, "but I am also real."

"I don't understand," Amintuu said, his mind reeling. "How can this—"

"We don't have much time. The captain stirs and will soon join you on the deck. I have been sent with a messge—"

"What message? From whom?"

"If the Cord is to be saved, you know what you must do," Melaane went on, ignoring Amintuu's interruption. "You have known for some time now."

A chill rippled down Amintuu's spine as he gazed at the image or apparition or vision of Melaane. He hadn't noticed her doing so, but she must have taken a step back, for she was starting to recede. He thought of stepping toward her, but he was rooted to the spot, unable to move or speak.

"You know what you must do, Yadi," she said again. "The Cord must be saved, whatever the cost."

She slid away still farther, and as she did, a cloud moved across the face of the moon and the dark grew deeper. When it passed, and the moonlight returned as bright as before, she was gone, but Captain Kanns was approaching as Melaane had suggested he would. His white hair and beard appeared silvery in the shining moonlight.

"Trouble sleeping?" Kanns said as he drew near.

Amintuu looked at the captain and blinked, but he was still dumbstruck from his encounter and said nothing.

"Amintuu? You all right?" The captain looked concerned.

"I ..." Amintuu stumbled as he spoke. "I think I may have been sleepwalking."

"That's a bad habit for a man at sea," Kanns said with a grin, stroking his goatee. "I'd advise against it in future."

"Yes, of course," Amintuu said, rubbing his face with his big hand. "I think I'll return to my cabin. Try to get back to sleep."

"It might be good to lock your door," Kanns said. "That doesn't stop all sleepwalkers, but it does work for some."

"That's a good idea," Amintuu said. "Good night, Captain."

"Good night."

Amintuu turned and walked away. When he was back in his cabin, he did lock the door, though not because he was afraid of sleepwalking. His daughter was dead, and whoever or whatever had appeared to him on the deck, it was silly to think locking the door could keep it out, but it made him feel better to do it. An ineffectual measure was better than nothing.

And yet, as he lay in his bunk, staring into the darkness above his bed, it wasn't his visitor that preoccupied him, but the message. She had known, or it had known, what thought tormented him. But how? How could it have known what Amintuu was wrestling with? How could a message be sent from the dead to the living, and who would send it?

As Amintuu lay, the thoughts in his head going round and round, he wondered if perhaps there was another way to make the nightly visits from Melaane go away. Perhaps, if he did what he had been contemplating, what this ghostly visitor had urged him to do, perhaps he would be left alone.

Perhaps he would, and perhaps he would help secure the support he needed to take the necessary steps toward saving the Cord. The Southland Keeper, Tchinchura, he might be a problem, as he had seemed to side with Telsiin on the issue of combining replicas, but then again, he might not be. Perhaps he hadn't so much sided with Telsiin as shown deference to the Chief Elder of the Northlands. Perhaps it was respect and manners more than agreement and support. And even if it hadn't been, maybe he could be persuaded.

Either way, the immediate issue was Telsiin, as Amintuu had known for some time. Perhaps his inability to stop the tragedy of Melaane's death had driven him to imagine these visits, in which she was spurring him on to avert another, even greater tragedy. Yes, that must be it. He had to do what he had feared doing.

He had balked at acting on this, at raising his hand against another Amhuru, but the spirit was right. The Cord had to be saved, whatever the cost.

.   .   .

Rika pulled the *swaani* across her face. When she'd first encountered women wearing the *swaani,* she'd looked at them with disdain. Why would she choose to wear a long scarf that not only wrapped around her long and beautiful hair but covered her face from the nose down? Especially in hot weather, she found the idea ridiculous. But when she'd first held one, she'd found the fabric remarkably soft in her fingertips and almost alluring. Wearing it, she realized that it was actually comfortable in any weather. Over time, she'd come to see the advantages of passing through a town almost invisible, as indeed, a woman wearing a *swaani* could become if she chose muted colors and a simple wardrobe.

She drew the *swaani* tight and stepped back into the line. She'd passed through two checkpoints already in the last ten miles, and here was a third. She knew she must be getting close. The men in green with the golden fist insignia were carefully examining every traveler, every merchant, and though they weren't exactly advertising their presence, the soldiers fanned out in the trees on either side of the road weren't exactly hiding either. Krayton couldn't be far now. She'd probably reach it the next day, or at worst, the day after.

A merchant with a substantial cargo moved forward past the checkpoint and the line shuffled forward. There were perhaps three or four parties ahead of her, and none of them looked to have quite as much to inspect as the merchant who had just been let through. Rika waited calmly.

She wasn't especially given to either anxiety or excitement, and yet her calmness surprised her just a little bit. She had come so far, traveled so long, that to be so close at last—she didn't know what to think, and maybe that was it. Maybe at some subconscious level she was blocking the excitement for fear that he wouldn't be here.

That was possible, of course. She had no doubt after all the reports she'd gathered and all the rumors she'd heard that Krayton was a base for the Jin Dara, maybe the very headquarters, but that didn't mean he'd be there. He had not crossed the Madri and come to the Northlands to turn a mid-sized town into a fortress and hang out. He'd come for the Golden Cord, and she didn't doubt for a second that he would do anything and go anywhere to get what he wanted, whatever the risk.

So would Rika, which was why she had to find him.

The line shuffled forward again, and Rika shuffled with it. She was close enough to hear the conversation with the pair of travelers currently being inspected. It consisted of the same basic questions they'd answered at the earlier checkpoints. What are your names? Where are you from? What is your business in Krayton? Do you have any weapons? And so on.

The two men answering these questions were clearly nervous, and Rika listened with bemusement as they stumbled over their words. They had no business in Krayton, they said. Their uncle had a farm thirty miles past Krayton. He had broken his leg and they were coming to help with the harvest, etc.

When at last the two men were waved through, the party in front of her with half a dozen men and women moved up to the inspection point. Rika would be next, and now the butterflies that had come at the other checkpoints returned. Without actually going through the internal debate, she found herself wondering what she should tell the man who would question her. Should she give the same, simple story she had given the others, or had the time come to reveal herself?

She was close enough to the checkpoint now to see there were multiple transports here. Like the sliders she'd grown up with in Barra-Dohn, these required a fuel, though here it would be corness and not the sage oil the sliders had used. But, unlike the sliders, these were larger transports, capable of carrying perhaps half a dozen people instead of just one or two. Maybe if she told the soldier who she was and why she was here, they'd give her a ride to Krayton. She smiled at the thought. She was tired of walking.

Of course, there were risks that went with telling the man her business. This might be as close as she ever got. But, Rika knew that whether it happened here or in Krayton itself, she would never get to the Jin Dara without telling the truth. There would come a point where she'd have gone as far as her cover story could take her, and she would have to put her chips on the table. She knew that, but that didn't necessarily make her eager to do it any sooner than she had to. Still, she found herself wondering if it wouldn't be better to just come out with it. Maybe lying her way through all the checkpoints and revealing her real purpose once already in Krayton would be a mistake. It was hard to know. No, it was impossible to know. She would just have to choose.

The party in front of her moved on. Her turn had come, and she stepped up to the table where the official was seated with soldiers standing quietly on either side. The man had not yet looked up as he was writing something on his paper. Rika took a deep breath.

"Your name?" he said, still not looking up.

"Rika Elandras," she said.

The man scribbled something down. Still no eye contact. "Where are you from?"

"Barra-Dohn," Rika said. "Once one of the mightiest cities in the Southlands—that is, until the Jin Dara leveled it using the power of the Golden Cord."

The man was looking now, his eyes wide with wonder.

"I know, because I was there at the time," Rika continued. "I barely escaped the city's ruin with my life. I have traveled a long way to find him."

The man's eyes narrowed at that, and Rika hastened to add. "Don't misunderstand me, I haven't come for revenge. If I had, would I tell you all this?"

The man visibly relaxed, but Rika could see with her peripheral vision that the two soldiers behind him and to both sides had stepped closer. "Then what is your business in Krayton?" the official asked.

"I told you," Rika said, working hard to be sure her tone didn't betray any impatience. "I have come to see the Jin Dara."

"Why do you think he would see you?" the man said softly. "What is your business with him?"

"He will see me," Rika said, "because for many years I traveled in the company of the Amhuru who bears the third Southland fragment of the Golden Cord. In fact, I crossed the Madri with him. I can help the Jin Dara find him and perhaps some of the Northland fragments as well."

The official said nothing and for a long time stared up at her from his seat. Then, he turned and motioned to a man standing some distance away, a man who looked like an officer, not a soldier. He walked over, bent down, and listened as the official whispered in his ear—all the while keeping his eyes steadily upon Rika.

When the official was done speaking to him, the officer motioned to Rika and said, "Come."

She followed him toward one of the transports. When they reached it, he said, "Get in," and she did.

He got in too, and in a moment they were speeding down the road, past the party of travelers who had just gone through, past the two men headed to their uncle's farm, past the merchant and his wares.

The officer did not look at Rika, and he did not speak. He simply drove the transport, looking straight ahead.

Now, Rika found, both the anxiety and the excitement that were absent at the checkpoint had come. She didn't know if she was on the way to see the Jin Dara, or headed to some secure location to be interrogated—perhaps both. Either way, she had finally set the plan in motion, and soon, if all went well, she would behold the Jin Dara face to face.

17

THE COLOR OF POWER

Rika couldn't believe how fast things were moving. The transport, once in Krayton, had gone straight to the Jin Dara's private residence—a large, somewhat sprawling building set apart a little from the town center. At least, Rika had gathered that this was the Jin Dara's private residence, as the conversation between the officer who had brought her here and the one who received them indicated this was his headquarters while the Jin Dara was in Krayton.

The conversation had been brief and, once concluded, the officer who had brought her turned the transport around and headed back the way he had come. Whether he had other business in Krayton or he simply returned to the checkpoint, Rika never knew. Nor, to be honest, did she care. She was standing not twenty feet from the door to the house that contained the Jin Dara. She felt nervous, to be sure, but mostly, she was beside herself with excitement. Her destiny lay inside. She could feel it.

The officer led her inside and into a small sitting room, where a pair of men watched her enter but said nothing to her. They stepped out into the hall with the officer for a moment and then returned when he left and shut the door. Rika did not hear what they talked about, but she assumed they had been asked to watch over her, which they did. They helped themselves to a drink out of a tall, silver pitcher, but they didn't offer her any. She didn't mind. As long as she got her chance with him—that was everything.

Now that the door was closed, she examined the men. They settled down into their seats, drinks in hand, and paid her little attention. They wore simple golden uniforms, as had the officer outside. The officer who had driven the transport in from the checkpoint had been in gold too, now that she thought about it. Most of the other soldiers she had seen had been dressed in green. She wondered about the difference, assuming that the men in gold must be part of some trusted, special unit.

That thought reminded her of Eirmon and his Davrii. How proud Eirmon had been of them, his private guard. And yet, they had not been able to save him. When the Jin Dara had come, and when Barra-Dohn had fallen, there hadn't been anything that could save him, Rika mused.

Thinking about Eirmon and the fall of Barra-Dohn brought that day back to her in a flood. She had often marveled over how she had been saved from the wreckage of that great battle even though she was in Eirmon's prison when the assault began. She, the king's prisoner, had survived, while Eirmon, the king himself, had not. How ironic. How amusing. She started to laugh, but she stopped when the soldiers turned and stared at her. She clasped her hands together and stared down into her lap, trying to look submissive and uninteresting. She wanted to be noticed, of course, but not by these men.

She managed to keep still, keep her head down, and keep control of her fluctuating emotional states, but not without some difficulty. Just moments after starting to laugh out loud, she almost started to hyperventilate, the memory of being locked in Eirmon's dungeon being a little too real as she sat here, watched by guards, perhaps just moments from her death.

That's right, she thought, she could be on her way to death, with or without a detour to see the Jin Dara first, and that thought reminded her of the dead guards that Eirmon had flaunted before her when he confronted her and Barreck. She'd mastered her fear at that moment, managing to spin the situation as best she could to claim ongoing loyalty to Eirmon, and even though the ploy hadn't worked, she had been pretty proud of her composure later. Of course, as she sat in the dark cell down below the palace later, she had also trembled in fear at the thought of her impending execution. She trembled again now, but she managed once more to master herself.

She tried to take deep breaths without being obvious about it. Stealing glances at the guards, she reassured herself that they were once more ignoring her. Calm thoughts, she told herself quietly, think calm thoughts.

The mental pep talk didn't exactly work, as she suddenly thought of standing before the Jin Dara and imagined having just a moment to explain herself and impress the man who must be the hardest man in all the world to impress. Not really the calmest of thoughts, but she breathed out and then, once more, silently inside her head, started to rehearse what she would say, given this chance. The mere routine of going over those words began to calm her. She closed her eyes to concentrate, and she was still sitting with her eyes closed, going over and over her prepared remarks when she heard the door to the room open again.

"Bring her," a voice said as she opened her eyes, and the next thing she knew, she was on her feet and following the two men in gold and another man she had never seen before down a long corridor.

. . .

The Jin Dara slouched in his high-backed chair, his right leg dangling over its soft, stuffed arm. He reached down and picked up the flagon of wine from the table and took a drink, savoring the full, sweet mouthful. The wine near Krayton was very good, some of the best he'd ever had. Of course, the world as a whole seemed brighter, sweeter, better—ever since he returned with the third fragment of the Golden Cord more than half a year ago.

He sat the flagon down, tore off a chunk of bread, and ate. What to make of the message he had just received? A survivor from the collapse of Barra-Dohn? Here, in this house, waiting to see him? A woman who claimed to have traveled with the Amhuru who bore the third Southland fragment? A woman who claimed to be able to help him find that fragment?

The obvious question was whether she was telling the truth or not. If not, then why tell this lie? To get close to him? To try to harm him? A survivor of Barra-Dohn—if that much was true—might well want revenge for what he had done. But, as the woman had apparently said herself when revealing her intention to meet with him, why would she admit to being from Barra-Dohn if it was vengenance she sought? Why not hide the fact?

Further, the fact that she claimed to have traveled with the third Southland fragment seemed to validate her story. The Jin Dara knew that this fragment had been in Barra-Dohn on the day that he crushed the city. He knew this with certainty, beyond all doubt, even though he never saw the Amhuru who bore it or the fragment itself. However, he had no idea how many other people had known this. The Amhuru were always discreet about the location of the originals, so he felt sure only a few would have known it was there. This woman appeared to be one of those few.

But if she was so deep in the counsels of the Amhuru that she knew an original was in Barra-Dohn when he was there and had escaped its collapse along with that original, why would she betray them? Why would she come to him? This was the part of her story that the Jin Dara did not believe. She might be telling the truth about her escape from Barra-Dohn and about her travels with the third Southland fragment, but he could not believe she was telling the truth about why she was here.

The safest thing, then, would have been simply to have her killed. Even if he couldn't imagine what a single woman, bearing no Zerura, might be able to do to him, that didn't mean he wasn't missing something. (Cursed Amhuru and his steel knives, the Jin Dara thought. Now he doubted everything, even though he wielded power beyond his own wildest dreams.) And yet, his curiosity was strong. He wanted to meet this survivor of Barra-Dohn, hear her pitch, see what her real business was here, learn if she would show her hand. He could always kill her after the meeting. In fact, he imagined he probably would.

Of course, there was always the remote possibility she was telling the truth. Perhaps she had traveled with the Amhuru, and perhaps she had decided to betray them. If that was the case, and if she really could help locate any of the other fragments, then hearing her out would be well worth his time.

The door to his receiving room opened, and Devaar led the woman inside. Two more Najin stepped in behind her, as Devaar crossed the room to stand beside him. The woman looked nervous, and her attention seemed torn between him and the much mangled form of the Amhuru he had 'planted' by the window to experiment on. It was understandable, of course, as both of them were visually striking these days.

The Jin Dara smiled as the woman struggled visibly to stop looking at the Amhuru and to focus her eyes on him. She was a pretty thing, he thought, and though she was clearly disconcerted by what she was seeing in front of her, he could feel the ambition radiating from her as she looked at him. It was something in her eyes that fixed on him at last and did not turn away.

This would be interesting, he thought, and reached again for his wine.

.   .   .

Nothing in any of her hundreds of daydreams about this moment had prepared Rika for what she saw when the door to the room at the end of the hall opened and she was ushered inside. On the far side of the room, slouched in a chair, sat a man whose eyes and hair were golden like an Amhuru, but, unlike an Amhuru, his face had a golden sheen too. It wasn't uniform. His forehead and cheeks seemed shinier than the rest of his face, but there was a definite golden tint to his whole complexion.

She glanced at his neck and his arms and hands, the other easily visible patches of skin, and they showed at least flecks and streaks of gold too, though not as thoroughly as the face. She wondered if the circlet around his head, which might be a fragment of the Cord, was the reason for this. Eirmon's fragment had been worn on his leg, and it hadn't occurred to Rika that one could be worn on the head, but the man clearly had something bright and golden around his. From what she knew of this Jin Dara, wearing Zerura like a crown didn't seem entirely out of character.

All this she took in pretty quickly, before the grotesque monstrosity by the large window on her right took her attention away. At first, she didn't realize it was a grotesque monstrosity at all. It just looked like a tree of middling size, and it drew her attention because she couldn't figure out how or why a tree would be inside the room. But as she looked at it, she saw very quickly that something was very, very wrong with this tree.

There were only two main branches, extending up and out to opposite sides of the trunk, and as she looked at them, she saw five smaller branches extending out from the end as though they were five elongated digits extended out from two wooden hands. This thought led her to recognize that the top of the tree between the branches looked a bit like a distorted head with budding leaves where one might expect to find hair. The trunk also had a ridge down the lower half, so it looked not unlike two legs fastened together and covered with bark. And at the base of the tree, the roots that spread out from the trunk and then broke down through the floorboards into the darkness underneath, appeared to be divided into two sets of five like splayed toes extended way beyond any natural length.

She looked back up at the 'head' of the tree with a mixture of growing fascination and horror, wondering if she could discern any facial features there, and sure enough, a knot protruded from the center at just about the place where the nose would be, and just below it was a roundish opening that might have been a mouth. She stared, momentarily unaware of her own slack-jawed amazement, when the bark above the knob split to reveal two dark but clearly living eyes looking across the room at her. She didn't know how she kept from screaming or fainting, but somehow she managed not to do either.

Rika swallowed, trying to get ahold of herself, to regain some semblance of composure. She didn't know who this was or what he—or she—had done to deserve this terrible fate, if indeed anything could warrant a fate like this, but she remembered the gorgaal and knew the one who had made them was surely capable of almost anything, given enough power and time. More to the point, she knew that if she didn't make a favorable impression, she might end up like this, or worse.

Rika forced herself to look away from the 'tree.' She turned from it to the golden man, slouched in his chair. The golden sheen is the visible sign of the power within, she told herself. The color of his face was the color of power, and she had plans for that power, plans for what she could do and become that required her to get used to the Jin Dara's strange appearance and terrifying strength. If she trembled and quailed before him now, she would show herself unworthy. She would not. She would be strong. She straightened, fixing her eyes on him, even as he sat there watching her.

"Do you like my pet?" he said, after what felt like a long silence had elapsed between them.

"I admire the power it required to do what you have done," Rika said, "and the strength of will. I think few men could do it, even given the requisite power."

"I agree," the man said, nodding. "Few indeed."

"And perhaps," Rika said, "even fewer women."

The Jin Dara regarded her closely. "You think you are such a woman?"

"I am such a woman."

"Then you are dangerous."

"I am," Rika said. "To some."

"But not to me?"

"How could I be dangerous to you? How can anyone be dangerous to you?"

The man smiled. "It is true. I wield great power, but I am mortal. I have the scars to prove it."

The Jin Dara raised his hand to his face, and his fingers slowly traced a line that ran down it like a long ridge, which Rika realized at last was a scar. She hadn't noticed it at first, as the golden shine of his skin almost hid it from view. She saw it now, and she wondered if he had gotten the scar before or after his assault on Barra-Dohn and his taking of a second fragment of the Golden Cord. If after, she wondered who had managed to get that close. Perhaps the man inside the tree?

"I understand why you would be wary of me," Rika said, "but I haven't come to do you any harm. I doubt I could, even if I tried."

"Then why have you come?"

"To help you."

"But you say you are from Barra-Dohn. Why would you help me after what I did there?"

"Your destruction of Barra-Dohn saved my life."

"How's that?"

"I was in the king's dungeon, awaiting execution, and—"

"You knew the king of Barra-Dohn?" the Jin Dara said, shifting in his seat, sitting up and leaning forward.

"Yes," Rika said. "I knew him."

"How?"

"I worked at the Academy of Barra-Dohn," Rika said, thinking she would omit the fact she had been Eirmon's mistress. "I was the lead researcher on his secret project, testing the pieces of Zerura he provided and looking for new ways to use them, militarily and otherwise."

"Were you now?" the Jin Dara said. "That is interesting. So if you worked for him in such an important capacity, why would he want to execute you?"

"Because he thought I was part of a plot to steal Zerura from him."

"Were you?"

"Yes."

If her honest answer surprised the Jin Dara, Rika couldn't tell. It surprised her. She hadn't necessarily planned to tell him this, but as he asked the questions, she found herself convinced that telling him the truth was the best idea. Well, mostly. She hadn't exactly been the 'lead researcher,' but giving herself a small promotion wasn't a big lie, and omitting her relationship with the King, that wasn't a lie at all, just a planned oversight.

"Why were you planning to steal from your king? And why should I trust a thief?"

"I am no more a thief than you are."

"Oh?"

"You have taken what wasn't yours because of the power it would give you, and because you could. That's what I was doing."

"Fair enough," the Jin Dara said, and something between a smile and a smirk crept onto his face. "I don't really think of myself as a thief, but I suppose that is exactly what I am."

"You are much, much more than a thief," Rika said.

"Yes, I am."

For a moment, the Jin Dara sat, watching her, and then Rika added. "So, as I have said, what you did to Barra-Dohn gives me no cause to hold a grievance with you. Far from it."

"One could love her home without loving her king."

"This is true, but I didn't really care about either."

"What do you care about?"

It was Rika's turn to smile. She couldn't help it. She just felt the smile break out on her face. She didn't try to get rid of it, but she restrained it somewhat, and after shrugging, she said. "I tried to steal Zerura from the king of Barra-Dohn at great risk to myself—does this not tell you what I care about?"

"I suppose it does," the Jin Dara said. "But it doesn't tell me why you would come to me. That I have succeeded where you failed doesn't explain why you would come."

"As I said, I have come to help you."

"All right," the Jin Dara said, leaning back and slouching again, lifting his leg back over the arm of his chair. "I will go along with you. I will act like I don't realize you still haven't told me why you're here. Instead, I will ask what 'help' you can offer me."

Rika felt the hair on her arms rise as her skin prickled at the sound of the Jin Dara's shift in tone. She had felt like things were going well, but perhaps she had overplayed her hand. She knew she couldn't afford to let this 'cooling' in his attitude toward her continue, or she'd be in trouble in a hurry.

"I traveled with the Amhuru who bears the last Southland fragment for years, all over the Southlands, and then across the Madri, and for some time after that. I know him. I know where he's been, I—"

"Of what interest is it to me where he has been?"

"Would you not like to know he has been to the island on which you were born, Dagin?"

The look on the Jin Dara's face when Rika used his proper name was something Rika could not have put into words. There was surprise, certainly, and anger, but there was something else too, something harder to name. A look that suggested she had opened a portal into his distant past, and that perhaps he was stuck at the threshold, looking back and forth between two worlds. The surprise disappeared, as did the anger, and when the Jin Dara spoke again, his voice was soft, but not weak.

"It is very bold of you to dare use my name, and while I can appreciate such boldness, I wouldn't do it again."

Rika nodded her understanding, but she did not speak.

"So, the Amhuru figured out who I am."

"They did," Rika said. "And they encountered your uncle and your creations, the gorgaal, and that taught them quite a bit about you, I think."

"It doesn't matter what it taught them," the Jin Dara said. "They cannot stop me."

"I know," Rika said. "Your victory is inevitable, but that doesn't mean it won't be hard and take time. I can help. It has taken me a while to find you, but I know where the Southland Amhuru was and where he and those with him were headed. I know where the other Northland Keepers were supposed to be hiding too. All this I will tell you."

"Why?" the Jin Dara said, leaning forward again, his voice strong and insistent. "And do not dodge my question again. Tell me why you have come."

"I have come here seeking the same thing I sought when I entered the employ of the king of Barra-Dohn. It is the same thing I sought when I agreed to help him unlock the secrets of Zerura—power."

Rika stared at the Jin Dara, letting the word hang in the air, before continuing. "And, by the way, I am an excellent researcher and scientist. I would happily continue my experiments into the usage and power of Zerura on your behalf. That isn't the main reason why I have come, but it is another thing I can offer you."

"You offer me help in the form of information," the Jin Dara probed, "in exchange for power? What power do you think I will give you?"

"I offer you myself, whatever I have or can do that will help you," Rika answered him. "And in exchange, I ask only the opportunity to be near you, to be a part of what you are doing and becoming. And if my service pleases you, perhaps I may earn a reward."

"A reward you have already picked out, no doubt," the Jin Dara said. "And what would this reward cost me?"

Rika sensed a change in the Jin Dara's disposition. He was taking her seriously. She smiled again. "Nothing you cannot afford to pay."

.   .   .

When the woman had been taken away, the Jin Dara sat pondering her. She was very bold, even beyond her willingness to call him by name. He wasn't sure whether he admired or resented it more, but he certainly felt both admiration and resentment. He looked at Devaar, standing quietly by the door. "Well?"

Devaar shrugged and said. "I believe her. I think she is who she says she is, and I think she has come to help you if she can."

"Why?"

"I could see how she looked at you," Devaar said with a grin. "Even from here."

The Jin Dara nodded. "But does she want me, or my power?"

"Both, I would imagine. She knows what you've done, and she fancies she knows you. She sees you on your way to ruling the world, and she wants to hitch a ride."

"Perhaps she tried the same thing with the king of Barra-Dohn," the Jin Dara said. "I sensed there were parts of that story that she left out."

"Perhaps," Devaar said, and then he added. "She is pretty."

The Jin Dara looked at Devaar. He had said it matter-of-factly, in the same tone he might have used to say her hair was long or her cloak was black. "You think I need a companion?"

"I don't know if you need anything," Devaar said. "I think you might enjoy one, especially one who seems so, how should I put it? Like-minded?"

"Perhaps," the Jin Dara said. "Give her a room and freedom to roam the town, but don't let her leave Krayton."

Devaar nodded. "Should I have her movements tracked?"

"Of course."

"As you wish."

In a moment, Devaar was gone and the Jin Dara was alone. He was often alone, he realized. It was something he had resigned himself to long ago. After all, how could anyone really join him on this journey he was taking? Perhaps, though, he did not need to be alone?

He would wait, and he would see. He would not kill her.

Not yet, anyway.

18

GHOST FROM THE PAST

The town of Krayton was not so very different from any number of towns Rika had visited on her journey to find the Jin Dara and her destiny. The high concentration of the soldiers in green, and also the smaller number of men in gold, was certainly distinctive. Beyond that, though, Rika figured that it felt different to her based solely on the knowledge that the man who would soon be the center of all things was here. He was here, and he had talked to her and taken her seriously.

Rika had walked all over the town, seen all there was to see, but she had no interest in going back to the small room the Jin Dara had provided for her. She had noticed an inn with a large plaza beside it full of tables where some of the soldiers and townsfolk were eating and drinking, and she made her way there. It was getting on toward dark, but lamps illuminated the plaza and a smattering of folks still sat there, enjoying the pleasant evening.

Rika settled in, removing the *swaani* and ordering a drink and some dinner. When it arrived, she found the aroma rising from the steaming bowl unusual, but the stew tasted very good and she scarfed it down, only realizing as she ate just how hungry she was. The wine was good, and she ordered another glass when the serving boy took her bowl away.

It was dark now, and the moon was just barely visible above the rooftops of the buildings across the street. She found herself wondering, and not for the first time, just why the halo effect she had noticed several times in winter didn't appear in warmer weather, and why she had never noticed it in Barra-Dohn. Perhaps Barra-Dohn just didn't get cold enough, for it was certainly true she had never experienced winters there that were anywhere near as cold as some of the weather she had endured here in the Northlands.

The serving boy returned with her wine and she sipped it, savoring its sweetness, when suddenly she had a strong, visceral feeling like she was being watched. Her hand tightened on the glass, and she looked casually around at the other patrons. Nothing of any note caught her eye, and she turned back around.

She had been under surveillance ever since leaving the Jin Dara. That much she knew. No doubt, the soldiers watching her had been given some kind of instruction to keep her from trying to leave Krayton, as if she would even contemplate leaving voluntarily. The Jin Dara would have to bind and sedate her and throw her on a transport headed out of town to make her leave. Come what may, her fate was here, with him. She might find greatness at his side, or death at his hand, but her long search for a suitable place in this world was over.

The hairs on her neck bristled, as again she felt strangely sure she was being watched. She was a scientist and a researcher who deferred to her head above her heart in nearly all things, but she had learned a long time ago that her intuition was something different from either—neither thought nor feeling, exactly. Perhaps it was a sensory process that operated at the subconscious level, but often it led her reliably even if she didn't understand it. At any rate, she trusted it now, and it was telling her that someone had taken an interest in her.

Rika reached up and started to rub her neck as though it were sore, and she turned her head as she did so, slowly scanning the tables on the plaza. Again, she didn't see anything of note, and she was about to turn around once more when she noticed a solitary figure just a couple tables away, an old man with unkempt white hair, looking her way. She hadn't noticed him before, perhaps because his table was in one of the darker patches on the plaza, but she noticed him now.

As she glanced at him, he smiled, only there was nothing friendly about it. His smile was haughty and sneering, and Rika felt certain somehow that the laughter in the old man's eyes was laughter directed at her. He wasn't very far away and no one was sitting between them, so she said, "Do I know you?"

"You once stabbed me and left me for dead—does that count?"

Rika stopped rubbing her neck. She peered through the flickering lamplight at the old man, unbelieving. There was certainly a resemblance there, but what he said was impossible. "You aren't Gamalian."

"I'm not?" the man said, the sneering look on his face now matched by the tone in his voice. "How can you be so sure?"

"Because Gamalian is dead," Rika said, adding in a hushed but insistent tone, "I killed him."

"You stabbed me and left me for dead, true," the old man said. "But as you were in a hurry to be on your way, you didn't wait around to see if I died—so how would you know if you killed me or not?"

Rika started shaking her head. She couldn't believe Gamalian had survived. She'd stabbed him, left him alone in the dark in a dungeon far beneath the palace of Barra-Dohn. The Jin Dara and his men had proceeded to destroy the city, killing everyone they found, so even if he had managed to get up the stairs to the palace, surely they would have finished what she had started if they found him.

And yet, he looked and sounded like Gamalian, sort of, and what's more, he knew what she had done down there in the darkness of Eirmon's dungeons. How could that be if he wasn't who he said he was? And it was true, she hadn't waited around to make sure the old man was dead. She had simply assumed his death—which had certainly been a reasonable inference from the situation. It was at least possible that he had survived, even if unlikely. But how in the world had he found his way across the Madri, and what was he doing in this place?

Rika stood. She walked to where the old man sat. She stared down at him from the other side of the table. He was grizzled and paler than she remembered, but in this climate that wasn't entirely suprising. It certainly looked like him, up close. "Are you going to sit down?" the man asked.

Rika pulled out a chair and sat. "How did you survive?"

"One of the Jin Dara's men found me."

"Why didn't they kill you?" Rika asked. "From what I heard, they killed everyone they found."

The old man shrugged. "Maybe they thought that if I was in Eirmon's dungeon, I was his enemy, and by extension their friend."

"That's ridiculous."

"Is it? I'm not sure it is that different from the story you came here to sell the Jin Dara."

"How do you know what I came here to do or not do?"

"Because you're predictable, Rika," the old man said. "You always were, and who you are and what you love tell me exactly why you're here. You were bound to come, sooner or later, like a whimpering dog, sniffing at a pile of worm-sakka."

Rika recoiled, bristling with rage at the insult. She was stunned, not just because she hadn't heard that Southland idiom in years, but also because she couldn't believe Gamalian had used it. It was low and vulgar, something so far beneath the honor and dignity of the former royal tutor and advisor that she couldn't believe the words had come out of his mouth. "You can't say that to me."

"I can say whatever I want," Gamalian said. "And you can't stop me."

"You're still an old man," Rika hissed, leaning across the table. "And I can finish what I started."

"How exactly will you do that?" Gamalian answered, leaning forward too. "You are unarmed and being watched, and this is the Jin Dara's world. Would you risk all you came here for?"

Rika bit her tongue. It was hard, but she did. "What do you want with me?"

"Want with you? I don't want anything with you."

"Why are you here, Gamalian?"

"Why not? I lost my home and my king. The Jin Dara's men took me in and cared for me until I had healed from my wounds. Why not travel with him? Why not come here? Do you think you are the only one who could see which direction the wind was blowing?"

Rika stared across the table as though really seeing the sneering, nasty man opposite her for the first time. "Who are you? You're nothing like the Gamalian I remember."

"Being betrayed and stabbed and left for dead can do that to you."

"I don't buy it," Rika said. "I understand why you'd hate me, but you would never accept the Jin Dara—what he has done, what he is still trying to do—not in a million years. Do you think you can stop him, or something?"

"I have no wish to stop him," Gamalian said. "The world is without honor, and whatever the Jin Dara is or isn't, once he has all the pieces of the

Golden Cord, he will be unstoppable. He will rule all things. At least then, there will be order."

"Are you going to make trouble for me here?" Rika asked.

"I have no interest in revenge," Gamalian said. "In fact, quite the opposite. I think you have a chance to do well here. I will be curious to see how you get on."

"Why?"

"Oh, well, you gave away your honor for power a long time ago, and it didn't really work out for you. Now here you are with a second chance, like me in a way. I'll be curious to see how you do. Will you succeed and become the paramour of the world's most powerful man, or will you blow this too?"

"You're disgusting."

"Really?" Gamalian said, laughing. "I'm disgusting? That's something, coming from you."

"I'm not going to listen to this or to you anymore," Rika said, standing up and pushing her chair back with a slight screech on the paving stone. "You'd better stay away from me and not interfere with my plans."

"I said I wouldn't."

"Well, you'd better not."

"Take your empty threats and go, Rika."

Rika turned and stalked away, but it galled her. Maybe because he'd been so rude and sneering. Maybe because he'd had the last word. Whatever it was, she found herself slowing as she reached the edge of the plaza full of tables. She stopped, took a deep breath, and spun around to march right back over to his table. She didn't even take a step. The table was empty.

She stared in confusion, glancing all around the plaza for some sign of him. She found none, and wondering where this ghost from the past had gone, she turned and slowly headed out into the street.

.   .   .

Rika tossed and turned all night. She drifted in and out of restless dreams where she seemed always to be running away from something or someone just out of view.

In one of these, she was fleeing through the streets of Barra-Dohn, not toward the palace, but away from it. As she navigated the deserted streets, she realized she was on her way to the Academy. She felt relief. She had spent many happy hours there, and if there was anywhere in the world where she could find refuge, perhaps the Academy was that place.

She ran up the steps toward the large front doors, which she opened with ease despite their tremendous size, and without hesitating, she dashed inside, into the dark. It was a little curious why it was so dark, since the Academy had always been lit with the latest and most impressive light technologies. But there was enough light coming in through the window slits high up on the front wall to provide sufficient illumination for Rika to survey the large main hall. It was completely empty, which was also curious, since this room was always filled with displays for the Academy's many visitors.

Rika heard laughter behind her and whirled. She saw no one there, though the room was large and the light insufficient to penetrate all the shadows. She heard laughter again, but this time it came from the far side of the main hall. She glanced around the big room nervously, then ran back to the front door. It wouldn't open.

She struggled and strained, but it was no use. It had opened easily a moment ago, but now it wouldn't open at all. One by one, she tried all the doors that led out of the main hall into other rooms and hallways in the Academy, and none of them would budge. She was trapped.

The laughter escalated, until it was so loud that it drowned out all other sounds. No matter where she ran, it followed her. Round and round the room she ran, seeking some relief, until at last, defeated, she slouched on the floor in a corner of the main hall and curled up into a ball, hands over her ears, her back to the large open room. Still the laughter echoed in the room and in her head.

When she woke, she realized she was curled up in that same ball in her bed. Her sheets were a tangled mess, and she was drenched in her own sweat. She couldn't imagine feeling less refreshed by a night's sleep, but even though she had no particular reason to get up, she couldn't countenance the thought of any more dreams and made herself get up.

A warm bath helped—a lot. She lingered until the water was cold and her skin covered in goosebumps. Then she rose from the tub, dried off and dressed, and with the awful night somewhat behind her, determined to face her day and think no more about it.

And yet, as she wrapped her *swaani* around her head and stepped out into the midmorning warmth, the orderly—and thankfully, not empty—streets of Krayton did not console her as much as she had expected.

She found herself scanning every passerby, every side street, every shop with an open door—looking for any sign of a slight, white-haired old man who was supposed to be long dead and moldering in his grave far beneath the ruin of the royal palace of Barra-Dohn.

A couple of times, she thought she'd caught a glimpse of him, but each time it turned out to be someone else. After a while, she drifted back to the same place where she had seen him the night before, half hoping he would be there so she could give him a scathing tongue-lashing he would not soon forget. He wasn't, and she took a seat and ordered lunch, feeling no small amount of relief.

By the time she had finished eating and pushed back her plate, she was slightly less jumpy, although she still scanned both openings from the plaza onto the street for any sign of a new arrival or when she noticed anyone passing by. Consequently, she noticed immediately when a familiar man entered the plaza, and she recognized him as the one who had stood off to the side through her whole interview with the Jin Dara.

He noticed her quickly also, for his eyes locked on her and he started without hesitation across the plaza to her table. Rika wondered if he'd been sent to find her, if perhaps she was about to be summoned back into the Jin Dara's presence, and a sudden, sharp sense of expectation rose inside her. She tried to hold it back, to keep calm, but when he stopped on the other side of her table, she had to drop her hands into her lap for fear that he would see that they were trembling.

"I trust that you spent a pleasant evening last night," he said and then smiled a very subdued, close-lipped smile.

"Yes, quite," she lied, unsure what else to say to this pleasantry.

"May I join you?" the man asked, motioning to the chair, not opposite her, but on the side of the table on her right.

"Of course."

"Thank you," he said as he pulled out the chair and sat down. Within moments, the serving girl appeared with a glass of wine and set it down in front of him without a word, though he nodded at her as she did so. He sipped, then said, "You are an unusual woman, Rika. Most unusual."

"Thank you," she said, accepting the statement as though it was a compliment. It certainly sounded like it had been intended as one. The man smiled that same, tight-lipped smile, and sipped his wine again. Rika decided that if she was being admired for her courage or boldness or whatever, she might as well stay in character and keep up the good work. "I'm sorry, sir. You know my name, but I don't know yours. You are …?"

"Oh, how rude of me," the man said, extending his hand to her. "My name is Devaar."

Rika took his hand, and then she said. "And what is your role in the Jin Dara's growing empire, Devaar?"

Devaar laughed, pulling his hand back to pick up his wine and drink. "You might say that I am the Jin Dara's right hand. I have been with him for a very long time."

"You are also from his island?"

Devaar's smile broadened, and yet he still managed to keep his lips from parting. He regarded her over his glass. "If you don't overplay your hand, Rika, you might just do very well for yourself here."

"What do you mean?"

"Just that. You are right to surmise that your audacity, your boldness, your nerve—that this is a quality the Jin Dara admires, as do I. And yet," and here Devaar's voice grew quieter and he leaned in over the table, "it is possible that your ambitiousness could become not so much attractive as annoying. You wouldn't want that."

The smile was gone from his face, though he didn't sound particularly angry. In fact, he was looking at her almost as a concerned friend might, though Rika couldn't remember the last time she'd had a real friend. "Yes," she said after a moment. "I see what you mean."

"Good," he said, leaning back in his seat and holding his cup up above the table at just about the level of his head. Immediately, the serving girl returned and filled it. The slight smile returned, and he took another drink.

"Now," Devaar went on, no hint of unpleasantness between them anywhere to be found in his tone. "I am glad to have this chance to chat. I would like to help you, Rika."

"Help me how?"

"You want to be the Jin Dara's companion," Devaar said, "and I think he could use one, a real one. It has been a long time since he had a woman in his life for anything more than temporary pleasure."

Rika stared at Devaar. For a moment, she had to fight the urge to deny it, but as she looked at the man beside her, who was clearly a central figure in the Jin Dara's world, she decided against the lie. "Was I that obvious?"

Devaar shrugged. "There are few things strong enough to fuel a woman to roam the world for years, cross the Madri and then leave far behind the only people in the Northlands she actually knows in order to find the man who destroyed the city she grew up in. And, since I believed you when you said you weren't here for revenge, I have crossed hatred off my list."

Devaar paused long enough to take another drink, then continued.

"That leaves love, or at least, desire—now you expressed pretty clearly your desire for the power that being close to the Jin Dara will bring, but I think you want more than to be a distant hanger-on, and that isn't necessarily a bad thing. In fact, it's one reason why you might be a good companion of a more intimate variety. You'll be as invested in his well-being as he is, since you want to share his glory."

The more Devaar talked, the more Rika struggled inside. On the one hand, his read of her motivations and plans were uncannily accurate, and that put her on her guard. She didn't know what to make of it. She didn't, as a rule, see herself as being transparent, and it bothered her that this man should see through her so easily.

On the other hand, he said he was here to offer help. So if he really could see who she was and what she wanted, and he wasn't moving to prevent her plans, then he was perhaps an invaluable ally. But could she trust him? Perhaps this was a test of some kind, designed to flush her out into the open.

Then so be it, she thought. She had come to make a play for the chance to rule beside the man who intended to conquer the world, and who might just do it. She knew when she came that it might cost her life, so that was a risk she would take.

"All right," she said. "You said you came to offer help—what help would that be?"

"For now, primarily counsel. I will advocate for you, but you must take it slow. It wouldn't do for you to be too forward, romantically speaking. The Jin Dara is a very powerful man, but he is, after all, just a man, and this man likes to be the aggressor."

"I intended to bide my time," Rika said, feeling a little annoyed that Devaar felt he had to warn her in this fashion, as though she intended to fling herself at the Jin Dara's feet. "But thank you for the advice. How else would you counsel me?"

"Prove your competence," Devaar said. "You intrigued him with the mention of the experiments you conducted in Barra-Dohn. He may begin to provide you with limited quantities of Zerura to use in experiments here. Do not disappoint him."

"I will do my best, though—"

"Your life will likely depend on doing more than your best," Devaar interrupted. "I'd produce results if I were you. Also, I could tell that your attempt at being coy and mysterious near the end of the interview intrigued him. He likes mystery in a woman. I would encourage it wherever possible, but beware, there will be a fine line between appearing evasive or non-cooperative and being mysterious. Tread lightly."

"Again, I thank you for your counsel," Rika said, and when Devaar did not continue, she decided to initiate a new topic of conversation, as much for the change of focus as for any hope of actual information. "May I ask you a question?"

"Of course."

"I met a man here, last night," Rika started, not sure exactly how to frame the question. "He says he is a man I knew back in Barra-Dohn, and he certainly looks like him, but I was fairly sure he died in the attack."

"As I am sure you know, you and those with you were not the only ones to escape the city," Devaar said. "We did not let many get away, but there were more than a few ships that did."

"Yes," Rika said, "I know we weren't the only survivors. We met others a few times during our travels in the Southlands. But, this man was injured and in the palace of Eirmon Omiir. He says soldiers from your army found him and nursed him back to health. He further says that he has traveled with your army ever since."

Devaar was silent, but his head was already shaking before Rika finished talking. "It is impossible. The palace was all but abandoned, and the few that we found alive were dispatched promptly and without ceremony."

"That is what I would have assumed," Rika said. "But he knew things he shouldn't have known about that day, and as he had suffered a serious wound, I doubt he could have escaped without help."

"Perhaps he is lying about how he escaped the city?"

"But why? And how did he get here if he didn't come with you?"

"There are many here who didn't come with us," Devaar said, now laughing. "I cannot account for them all. What I know is that we did not find anyone wounded in the palace and bring him along."

Rika sat, confused, and when Devaar spoke again, the words caught her off guard. "What is this man to you? You said you were in the dungeon of the king of Barra-Dohn awaiting execution when we came. Did you wound this man escaping?"

"Yes," Rika said, thinking it was close enough to the truth that it didn't need elaborating on.

"Describe the man."

Rika did.

"No," Devaar said. "No one like that traveled with us from Barra-Dohn. I am sure of it, and I would know."

"Thanks for the information," Rika said. "If I see him again, I'll try to get to the bottom of this."

"Be careful," Devaar said. "I would say that Krayton is fairly secure, but that's not to say we can guarantee everyone's safety at all times."

"I'm not afraid of him," Rika said.

"Ahh, but it may not be him at all," Devaar said, his slight smile creeping back onto his face. "There are many mysterious things in this world, after all."

And with that, Devaar rose, bid Rika farewell and left, leaving her to contemplate his final words to her for some time.

19

NEVER REALLY LOST

It wasn't Melaane's voice that drove Amintuu up on deck this time; it was the fury of the storm. All day it had threatened, and the ominous rolling thunder had made good its promise at last. Rain poured down and giant waves battered both vessels. A flash of lightning burst into the sky and, for a split second, Amintuu was blinded by its intensity. A second later, a wave crashed over the starboard rail, sweeping across the deck and knocking Amintuu down so that he slid sideways and up against the port rail, several feet away.

Amintuu grabbed hold of the rail and pulled himself tentatively up to his feet. He looked around, a little dazed and disoriented. The sailors under Kanns' direction were certainly scurrying around with an unusual degree of urgency. If even they seemed alarmed, perhaps Amintuu was not mistaken to regard this storm as unusually large and powerful.

More and more Amhuru were emerging on deck, drawn both by the same curiosity that had brought Amintuu out and by the desire to help if they could. They had all traveled enough to understand the fine line between being of help in a situation like this and getting in the way. The Amhuru began to move about the deck of *The Lion's Mane*, pitching in where they could.

As Amintuu turned to see what he might do, Maarta quickly approached him, his young wife trailing a little behind, clinging to his arm.

He leaned in to speak to Amintuu above the howling of the storm. "I don't think the Chief Elder should be on deck. It's too dangerous for him."

"Show me," Amintuu said, and Maarta pointed toward the stern, where Telsiin was trying to tie something down, though in the darkness between lightning flashes, Amintuu couldn't see what it was.

"I'll take care of it," Amintuu said, laying his hand on Maarta shoulder. "You should take your wife below."

The young woman bristled at that, but Maarta nodded seriously and turned to guide her back in the direction they had come. Amintuu, after watching them leave for a moment, turned to make his way down the ship's deck to the place where Telsiin was busy.

When he reached the Chief Elder, he saw that Telsiin had risen from what he was working on and was clutching the port rail as the ship rolled and lurched in the storm. Another big wave hit the starboard side, throwing water and debris across the deck. Amintuu slid up next to Telsiin and said, "Elder, you should be inside. Let the crew handle this."

"They need help," Telsiin said. "Or this storm might claim us all."

"I know," Amintuu said. "And we're helping. Leave it to us."

Amintuu looked over Telsiin's shoulder and saw a barrel rolling loose near the stern rail. Suddenly, he knew. "Elder, if you want to help with something, come give me a hand with that barrel. Then I'll see you below."

Amintuu started back along the port rail, and Telsiin followed. The ship pitched to the port side, and the barrel rolled off the stern rail and bounced across the deck, almost right at them. Amintuu got low and managed to first check its momentum and then corral it. Telsiin joined him in finding a rope and tying it tight to one of the many rings anchored here and there along the deck for just this purpose.

As they stood, Amintuu glanced around to make sure no one was watching. They were well out of the way of most of the action going on in the bow and midships, and both the crew and the other Amhuru seemed focused on matters closer at hand. The storm provided the perfect cover. Amintuu took hold of the port rail with his left hand, and he reached out for Telsiin with his right, putting his hand firmly on the Chief Elder's shoulder.

Just as he did, a wave that was bigger by far than all the others that had struck *The Lion's Mane* hit with such force that Amintuu was thrown sideways and toppled over the port rail. He managed to catch hold of the

top, and he clung to it for dear life as his body dangled above the tumultuous sea.

Telsiin was there in a second, grabbing hold of both Amintuu's arms
and pulling with surprising strength. Amintuu could feel the Chief Elder
reaching out through his fragment of the Golden Cord for the power of the
Arua, and even in his desperate straits, he felt something very much like
admiration for Telsiin's calm and ability to do so in the middle of a storm
out on the ocean. Telsiin pulled and tugged, and Amintuu lurched upward.
His feet found purchase on the side of the ship and he was able to scramble
up. Soon Amintuu had managed to get both feet on the deck, even if he was
still on the wrong side of the rail.

For a moment the two men stood there, on opposite sides of the rail,
tired and stunned and holding the rail to steady themselves. "That was
close," Telsiin said with a smile as he took deep breaths. "We almost lost
you."

"Yes," Amintuu said, "Thanks."

Amintuu held up his hand but Telsiin slid his hand all the way up and
clasped Amintuu on the forearm, right below the elbow. The Chief Elder's
grip was firm and he smiled as Amintuu swung his left leg over the rail.
Once he was straddling the rail, he glanced around one more time and
saw that his mishap had drawn no attention. He placed his large left hand
on Telsiin's back, then with a swift move slid it under his shoulder. With a
mighty heave and a pull from his right arm that jerked the Chief Elder right
up off his feet and over the rail, Amintuu launched Telsiin into the stormy
sea.

Perhaps there was a splash, but if there was, Amintuu couldn't hear it
over the cacophony of the storm. He sat, straddling the rail, gazing silently
down at the water, unable to make anything out. If Telsiin was bobbing up
and down, or calling out in any way, Amintuu couldn't see or hear it. There
was no sign of him. None at all.

When at last he was sure that the Chief Elder must be some distance
behind the ship, Amintuu turned and walked away from the rail.

·   ·   ·

Kaden lingered in the doorway of the shop. The main street was crowded,
but he could have sworn that he had seen the same man again, or perhaps
another dressed just like him.

As Kaden peered out from under the hood of his own cloak, he considered the irony of his situation. He was dressed in nondescript clothes, including this cloak and hood, as a means of hiding his golden eyes from general view. Of course he couldn't keep them from being seen by some, but that wasn't a good reason not to be discreet. Allowing a limited number to go into town, dressing alike, and staying separate, all were techniques for keeping knowledge of their true numbers hidden at any port where they stopped.

And here he was, focused on his own desire to finish what he'd been sent ashore to do and get back to the ship, but also certain he'd seen a man, a tall man, with different nondescript clothing—but nondescript nonetheless—and the same, tell-tale golden eyes hidden beneath a generous hood. Meeting other Amhuru wouldn't be a problem; in fact, it would be welcome, especially if they could get news of the larger world and what might be going on in it. But of course, with the Jin Dara and his Najin in the Northlands, Kaden didn't know for sure that this was an Amhuru, and if it wasn't, he needed to be sure.

Kaden scanned the street. He didn't see the man, and that worried him. He had hoped to figure out how to handle this situation on his own, but he thought perhaps the best thing to do would be to head straight back to *The Sorry Rogue*—taking care not to be followed, of course—and he would see what Tchinchura counseled.

He stepped out from the doorway and made his way along the outskirts of the crowded street, keeping the people going both directions along the street always on his left. As he passed along, he'd glance inside an open storefront or down a side lane just to be sure he didn't see the man, and then he would continue forward quickly, keeping a good pace.

Kaden knew that he was almost running, knew that if he moved any faster he would be running and that this would attract attention. Still, he found his legs churning away beneath him, almost with a mind of their own, eager to get out of the center of the town and to be away. He knew he should take a deep breath and slow down, so he did.

He was rattled. They all were. Losing Telsiin in the massive storm they'd passed through ten days ago had unsettled them all. When they'd realized in the morning that the Chief Elder must have gone overboard during the night, they had circled back around, searching the part of the sea they thought he might have been washed out into for two full days before giving it up as hopeless, though of course it had been hopeless from the beginning. There was no way of knowing just where he'd gone over, or how far the current had taken him, or in what direction, and the odds of finding him at all were miniscule, let alone finding him alive.

Still, they had gone back and looked, largely at the insistence of Amintuu, who seemed especially distraught over Telsiin's loss. Kaden hadn't noticed any particular closeness between the men, but then again the Amhuru were notoriously careful in their displays of emotion. Besides, as Amintuu was the only Northland Amhuru with them who bore an original fragment, he no doubt felt the weight of being looked to for guidance now that Telsiin was gone, and in days like these, that weight would have hung heavily on any man, of that Kaden was sure.

As Kaden kept going, walking quickly but not running, he reminded himself that, while it was easy to see Telsiin's loss as a sign of the larger unraveling of the world around them, it was a mistake to read too much into it. The Chief Elder had been old, the storm ferocious, and the work on the decks that night unsafe. As Captain D'Sarza had said many times, the sea was majestic and beautiful but also capable of remarkable destruction. It was a mistake to take it personally or to dwell too much on it. The loss was an accident that had come at a difficult time, but they would endure and figure out what was next. All of them, together.

Kaden reached the corner where he would at last leave the main street behind, and he paused, glancing around quickly for any sign of the man, before turning away down the street that would lead to the quay. It was a fairly small port, but almost a dozen ships were in at the moment, so there had been room for only one of theirs to dock. As a result, *The Lion's Mane* had moored at the dock, while *The Sorry Rogue* had dropped anchor further out in the harbor. Kaden had come in on a longboat and would head back the same way, along with the water and other supplies he had helped to secure. Hopefully, with their business concluded, they could be on their way shortly after dawn.

With no sign of the man anywhere in the street behind him, Kaden turned the corner and headed down the short, wide street that earlier in the morning had been full of carts bringing goods for trade up from the quay. It was late afternoon now, though, and the street was almost empty, which is why it was easy for Kaden to spot the tall man in the brown cloak standing not very far away, regarding him closely.

Kaden's hand dropped to his side, instinctively preparing to draw his axe, when the man took a step closer. "Is that any way to greet a friend?" the man said. "A brother?"

Kaden heard the voice and knew it, but he didn't believe what he was hearing. He raised his hand from his axe, though, and pulled down his hood. The tall man did the same. Sure enough, it was Zangira.

"I can't believe it," Kaden said, rushing to Zangira and throwing his arms around him in a great hug. "I never thought I'd see you again."

"The way has been long and dark," Zangira said, returning Kaden's warm embrace and then stepping back to regard him. "But I have come, I and all the Southland Amhuru I could gather."

"I'm so glad," Kaden said. "And I know Tchinchura will rejoice to see you."

"Then he is here," Zangira said quietly, looking past Kaden at the harbor beyond them. "I thought that was *The Sorry Rogue* anchored out there, and when I saw it, I hoped to find him here, but of course, so much time has passed, I couldn't be sure."

"He's here," Kaden said. "The same as ever. Whatever else might change, Tchinchura doesn't, does he?"

"Na," Zangira said with a smile. "I guess he doesn't."

"Na," Kaden said, "listen to you, Northlander."

"Sa," Zangira laughed, "we've been above the Madri some time now, long enough to begin to adapt, anyway."

"I'm headed back to the ship now," Kaden said. "You must come with me."

"I believe I will," Zangira said. "There is much to talk about, but we must make a stop first."

They started away, and then Kaden stopped. "You're limping, Zangira. What happened?"

"Of that," Zangira said, "and of many other things, we will talk later."

•   •   •

Deslo had spent so much time over the years on *The Sorry Rogue*, that he no longer found it suprising how much rope there was to coil or how often he was called upon to coil it. So, as they waited for the small expedition that included his father to return from purchasing their supplies, he had agreed quite readily to work on some of the ropes that Captain D'Sarza had indicated were in need of coiling.

He was almost done when the longboat returned, and had he thought anything unusual was going on, he might have left his current job not quite finished and gone over to see what was happening. But he did not suspect any such thing, so after duly noting the return of the longboat, he kept right on, coiling length after length of rope. He was quite focused on the job, so much so that he did not notice either of the two figures approach until their shadows fell right across his face.

He looked up just as she said hello, and between the musical quality of her voice and the perfection of her face, framed as it was by the late afternoon sunlight, he almost dropped the armful of rope he had worked hard to coil so well. "Shaline?"

"Sa, Deslo," Shaline said with a smile. "It's me, and Trabor, of course."

Deslo glanced at the tall, strong young man behind Shaline and couldn't believe it was Trabor. He had changed enormously, it seemed, while she hadn't changed at all. He looked back at her, immediately realizing that wasn't true. She had changed, in at least two ways that he could see. Her hair was a little darker than he remembered, which would make sense if they'd been traveling well above the Madri for a while, farther from warmer climes. And her face, though smiling, had been marked by sadness, he thought. She looked less carefree than she had before, and if their road had been anything like his, he didn't blame her.

Deslo might have gone on staring at them both for some time, so dazed was he by their sudden appearance, but Trabor stepped forward. "Are you just going to stare at us, old friend, or can we have a hug?"

Trabor grinned, opening his muscular arms wide, and the spell on Deslo was broken. He stepped forward, wrapping Trabor in his own strong, if shorter, arms and giving him a bear hug that was half greeting, half test of strength. Trabor responded in kind, also hugging Deslo tight, so that both men were reminded of their brief but real youthful friendship while also managing to test the other's powerful grip. They stepped back after a moment, looking both pleased and satisfied at the meeting.

"It's my turn now, Deslo," Shaline said coyly as she opened her arms for a hug too, "but if you hug me as tightly as you did my brother, you might break me."

"I would never do that," Deslo said, but his words came out in a soft rush that was barely more than a whisper, and he wrapped his arms around Shaline in a much more tender embrace.

They were brother and sister, they were both his friends, and yet words could not describe for Deslo just how different it felt to hug Shaline again. He had hugged her beneath the talathorne trees of Azandalir by the lagoon, as he and his family had prepared to leave. He had believed that he loved her, and that more than likely he would never see her again. Of that moment and that hug, he had dreamed more than a few times over the years.

Now here she was, standing in front of him, her arms wrapped around him, the sweet fragrance of her hair once more reaching his nostrils and filling him with memories and feelings he'd believed lost long ago. There was a momentary hesitation as he thought of Olli, flicking back her short blond hair and laughing, but Deslo pushed that thought away. Olli was lost to him, married to Maarta now, and besides, Olli had encouraged him not to give up hope of seeing Shaline again. And now, here she was.

"Easy, Deslo," Trabor laughed, making as if he had to separate them for fear Deslo might hurt Shaline by hugging her too hard. Deslo let go, reluctantly, and it seemed that Shaline, for her part, was just as reluctant to let go of him.

"We've got plenty of time to get reacquainted, now that we've found you all," Trabor said, then added with a smirk. "There's no need to rush anything, you two."

"Having grown almost as large as Yadi," Shaline said, taking a moment to send Trabor a look that was quite clearly a warning shot across his bow, "Trabor seems to have forgotten he's my little brother."

"As large," Trabor said, and when both Deslo and Shaline looked at him curiously, he added. "You said almost as large as Yadi, but as large would be the way of it. I've definitely caught up."

"That's lovely, my dear," Shaline said. "Now I'm asking you to grow up as well, all right?"

Before Trabor could respond in any way, either good or bad, Deslo stepped between them. "I see that whatever else has changed, you two still have the sweetest brother-sister relationship I've ever seen. Oh, how I've missed being a witness to it."

He laughed, and soon they were laughing too. Moments later, the unfinished coil of rope long forgotten, Deslo found himself sitting with

Shaline and Trabor on the deck of *The Sorry Rogue*, the ship that had taken him away from them, hearing all about what had passed since last he'd seen them.

.   .   .

Kaden and Deslo stood together at the rail, looking at the moonlight dance across the water. It was very late, long after midnight, but even so, Zangira and his children had only just recently left, as had Amintuu and some of the other Northland Amhuru. They were still planning to head out early in the morning, only there were five ships going now, not two.

There had been some discussions about that, specifically about the likelihood that five ships together would attract more attention than two, especially if anyone noticed just how many Amhuru these five ships contained. Still, they had known that it was necessary, and reasonable precautions had been put in place about how they would deal with the next port, and those could be further refined as needed.

"So," Deslo said as they stood there together. "Tchinchura is now the Chief Elder of the Southland Amhuru."

"Sa," Kaden said. "It appears that way."

"There seemed to be something unusual about the process by which he became Chief Elder," Deslo added. "Did you understand what they were talking about when that came up?"

"I think so," Kaden said. "Normally, the Chief Elder is simply the oldest Amhuru, unless he, for reasons of infirmity or something else, passes on the position. And while there are, among the survivors from Azandalir, a couple of older Amhuru than Tchinchura, it appears that they have unanimously voted that he should be the one to wear the title."

"And bear the burden."

"Sa," Kaden agreed. "And bear the burden."

"I'm glad for our sakes," Deslo said after a moment, "but I feel for Tchinchura. I wouldn't want to be in charge just now."

"Na," Kaden said emphatically. "Nor would I."

For a while they stood there, the soft rhythmic sound of lapping water coming up from below. Laughter echoed quietly from across the deck, as some of the crew were sitting and smoking their pipes. Deslo thought perhaps the time for sleep had come, but he was reluctant to go in just yet. Just like that, Shaline had reappeared in his life, and he'd been so caught up in the fact of her presence all evening, that he hadn't really had time to figure out just what he thought about it. He knew two things for sure.

First, he had genuinely cared about Shaline and been heartbroken about saying goodbye. Second, since then, he had genuinely cared about Olli, for a longer time and, he felt, in a deeper way, and then he had been heartbroken about losing her too. Now that Shaline was back, things would appear to have become clearer, simpler, but somehow it didn't actually feel that way.

"It's curious, you know," Kaden said suddenly, and Deslo turned to look at his Yadi.

"What is?"

"Life, I suppose," Kaden anwered. "When Telsiin was washed overboard, it felt like we'd lost more than one Amhuru, more than a Chief Elder even."

"Sa," Deslo said. "It did."

"It felt like we'd lost hope itself," Kaden continued. "And yet, here we are, just ten days removed from that, and with Zangira's appearance, I feel as though the hope we lost has been found."

"Maybe it has been."

"Or," Kaden said, "maybe Kalos is trying to tell us that it was never really lost in the first place."

"Who can say?" Deslo said.

"Not I," Kaden admitted, turning from the rail. "Now I suppose we should both get to bed, or we'll be useless in the morning."

"Good night, Yadi," Deslo said.

"Good night, Deslo," Kaden said, and he smiled at his son as he walked away from the rail. Deslo watched Kaden go, thought about following him, but in the end he lingered outside in the moonlight, late into the night.

20

TERRIBLE THINGS

Behind the Jin Dara's house was a walled garden, though there weren't many flowers in it. The garden was mostly beds of decorative rocks, with some green lawn in the middle and some scraggly bushes by the walls themselves. Nevertheless, it had become the Jin Dara's favorite place to be while he was in Krayton, and on this particular morning, he was seated on a stone bench in the sunlight, staring at another one of his experiments.

In a patch of almost completely bare earth there was a large clover. The bluish-purple flower bud rose well above the cluster of five rounded leaves, and it was at these five leaves that the Jin Dara stared. The anomalies he had been working on extended out well beyond the furthest edge of the leaves on all five, and he wanted to see how well they would work now.

He summoned a wriggling earthworm from its cool place in the dirt well below the warm surface of the bare patch of ground, and it broke through into the open some little distance away from the clover. It started to wriggle toward the shade the clover offered, almost on instinct, so the Jin Dara didn't have to push that direction very hard at all. As it drew nearer, though, it started to slow, almost as if it sensed its danger, and then the Jin Dara compelled it to go on, none too gently.

When it slid under the first of the leaves, the reaction of the clover was immediate and ruthless. It plunged down, driving the long stinger at the end of the leaf through the soft body of the worm, over and over. As the worm wriggled and coiled and tried to pull away, the other leaves got in on the action, bending and contorting in dramatic ways, driven by their lust to stab the worm too. Soon the worm had been torn to pieces, and tiny bits of it were strewn about on the dirt beneath the clover.

The Jin Dara smiled. He had completed and perfected this project in just a few days. His power over plants and animals, to bend and shape them, had grown exponentially with the addition of the third fragment of the Golden Cord. He already felt like there was nothing he could not do with his power, and he could not even imagine what it might mean that he was only halfway home. To bear six fragments and to wield that much power—it was beyond him to envision.

The sound of footsteps crunching across the rock garden announced Devaar's arrival. The Jin Dara did not turn around, but he motioned to the chair next to him, and Devaar came and sat down.

"And?"

"And everything I've found," Devaar said, "confirms what we already thought."

"Tanisaan?"

"Tanisaan," Devaar echoed. "It appears to be almost universally considered the strongest and most advanced city of the Northlands. It is as close to—what was your phrase?"

"A crown jewel," the Jin Dara said.

"Yes, it is as close to 'a crown jewel' of the Northlands as we are going to get, I think."

"I just wanted to be sure."

"I know," Devaar said.

"Any place might work," the Jin Dara said, "but I don't want to do what I am about to do in just any place."

"I know," Devaar repeated, as though perhaps trying to ward off the conversation they had already had so many times.

"The things I am going to do," the Jin Dara said, closing his eyes and peeking once more into the dark places, the wonderful places, hidden deep inside his own mind. "Terrible things, they will break the city—Tanisaan, or wherever—but they will do more than just that. They will break the mind and will of all who hear about them, and they will draw the Amhuru out of their hiding, for I know them, Devaar."

At that point, the Jin Dara opened his eyes again and turned to face Devaar. "I know them and their 'honor.' They will not be able to skulk and hide while such things as these are being done in the world. They will have to come to me, to try to stop me, and when they do, they will bring the other fragments to me. Then I will take them, and my quest will be over."

The Jin Dara rose, took a step, and crushed the clover under the heel of his boot. It was probably an illusion, but he imagined he could feel it, squirming to avoid the fatal blow, even as he ground it into nothing. He walked on until he stood in the middle of the open space where he glanced up to look at the thick white clouds moving lazily across the blue sky.

"You still intend to go as soon as possible?" Devaar asked.

"I do, and we will take every Najin from the most experienced who have traveled with us since the Southlands to the most raw recruit, as well as any skilled laborer vital for our support. We will leave no one behind."

"The preparations are already underway."

"Good," the Jin Dara said, turning to look at Devaar in his seat. "How long before we are ready?"

"Within the month, I would say?"

"And it is two months, more or less, to Tanisaan?"

"Yes, if we make good time."

"We will make good time," the Jin Dara smiled. "I assure you, the weather conditions for our voyage will be favorable."

Devaar smiled and nodded, but he did not excuse himself, though normally he left the Jin Dara to his quiet reveries out here. "Is there something else, Devaar?"

"There is," he said. "I told you yesterday morning that a somewhat notorious group of brothers arrived in Krayton, seeking to join your Najin?"

"You did," the Jin Dara said. "What of it? Many come now, seeking to join my Najin."

"I have done a little investigating, and I think I rather understated their notoriety," Devaar said, almost apologetically. "I am sorry, but even after having been here a few years, there are still things I don't understand like a Northlander would."

"What are you talking about, Devaar?" the Jin Dara said, taking a step closer to the still seated man. "Out with it."

"These men, the Jaen brothers, they run a notorious band of mercenaries called 'the JaenSing,' who are both known and feared across the length and breadth of the Northlands."

The Jin Dara stood, hands clasped behind his back, staring at Devaar. "Go on."

"In fact, one man said to me last night when asked about them, 'Meldriic Jaen is the only name that causes more fear and trembling around these parts than the Jin Dara.'"

"Did he?" the Jin Dara said, and Devaar could hear that his voice had grown cold.

"Yes, he did," Devaar said, "though of course he immediately started to backtrack, no doubt aware of the foolishness of such a statement, saying that people just didn't know any better yet, that you would show them, and that you were much more fearsome than Meldriic Jaen, etc."

"Of course I am," the Jin Dara said, almost spitting with rage. "What is the point of this, Devaar?"

"The point is that this man and a number of others have made it very clear to me, that these Jaen brothers are not just another batch of recruits; they are a tool we can use."

"Yes," the Jin Dara said, calming down. "I see what you mean."

"When the Northlands hear that the JaenSing have come to you, have bowed the knee and sworn their service, it will only enhance your growing reputation and make easier what we intend to do."

"We are sure that this is what they have come to do?"

"They asked for an audience with you," Devaar said, "and when asked what it was for, that is exactly what they said."

"Good, then you should bring them over today."

"They are already here," Devaar anwered. "I thought you would want to see them immediately."

"I do," the Jin Dara said. "You have my curiosity aroused."

"There is, though, one other thing you should know about them," Devaar said as he rose from his seat.

"What is that?"

"Almost all the men I talked to, who knew anything about the JaenSing other than their formidable reputation—they all said the Jaens hate the Amhuru."

"So they hate the Amhuru, eh?" the Jin Dara said, and he smiled a broad, open smile. "Now I am really curious."

·   ·   ·

Meldriic Jaen wasn't exactly nervous. He didn't really get nervous. Nevertheless, he was uncomfortable. So much about coming here, to Krayton, reminded him of his own base of operations, of the small world he presided over as though a king, and yet he was the visitor here, the stranger. He wasn't used to simply walking into another man's domain, and more than that, to coming as a supplicant. That he did not like, there was no doubt about it.

They had all been shown into a room that this Jin Dara obviously used for receiving visitors. On his right, near the large set of windows, a bizarre tree grew inside the room. Meldriic noted it but turned his attention to the golden man on his 'throne,' or whatever he would have called the ornate wooden chair he sat on. His eyes and skin were golden, and his shiny appearance answered at least one of Meldriic's questions about the affects of wearing multiple fragments.

What struck him, arresting his attention the moment he saw it, was the thin line of Zerura that wrapped around the man's golden head. The Jin Dara had the *cadeen*. There could be no other conclusion.

The Amhuru, Draagan, had spoken of two Southland fragments in the Jin Dara's possession, but the *cadeen* was a Northland fragment. This meant that the Jin Dara had three originals. At least three. The game had changed.

"You are fascinated by my appearance."

"I have seen the affects of Zerura on the men who wear it before," Meldriic replied. The Jin Dara was looking right at him, so he knew the question was meant for him and not one of his younger brothers.

"No doubt," the Jin Dara said. "But probably never quite like this."

"That is true. Never quite like this."

"You are Meldriic Jaen?" the Jin Dara asked, and then motioned toward the others with his outstretched hand, "And these are your brothers?"

"Sa," Meldriic said, acknowledging the truth of it. Then he turned a little to the side and introduced his brothers in descending order of age. "They are Petaar, Renoud, Traliin and Vaall, and we are all at your service."

"For that I thank you," the Jin Dara said good-naturedly. "I am always looking for good men to join my Najin, and from what I have heard, you are very good men."

The Jin Dara abruptly rose and stepped down from the slightly raised dais on which his chair sat in the far corner of the room. He stepped closer to Meldriic, and even though the Jin Dara was shorter, there was no mistaking the aura of power that he cast with his golden sheen and bright golden eyes, but Meldriic held his ground and did not flinch as he moved closer.

"In fact," the Jin Dara said. "From the little I've been told, you and your brothers are extremely good men."

He was now only three or four feet away. He hesitated, then started to circle around Meldriic, and Petaar, the nearest of his brothers, stepped out of his way to give him a clean pathway to walk all the way around Meldriic. He did so, without saying another word. He only looked, regarding Meldriic closely, and once he was back around front, Meldriic met his eyes and did not look away, matching the Jin Dara stare for stare.

"You will have to forgive me, for I am still something of a stranger to the Northlands, and I had not heard of the JaenSing before. I have now, and what I have heard raises in me the fairly simple, logical question—why would you come to me? You are not the type to serve any man. I see it in your defiant eyes."

"Na, I am not the type to serve anyone," Meldriic said simply.

"Then why come? Why offer me your service?"

"Many months ago now, we received a visitor," Meldriic said. "An Amhuru."

"I was told that you hate the Amhuru. Why would one of them come to you?"

"We do hate the Amhuru," Meldriic began, but before he could continue, the Jin Dara interrupted him.

"We'll come back to your story in a moment," he said. "I want to know about this hatred of the Amhuru. Where does it come from? Why do you hate them?"

"My grandfather was an Amhuru, and he was wrongly—"

"You're ex-Amhuru?" the Jin Dara exclaimed. "I've never heard of such a thing. I didn't know Amhuru could leave."

"I can'na say if it has happened before. I'm not aware of other examples where they have," Meldriic said. "But my father and his two brothers and their families all left, rather than live with the disgrace of the false accusations that—"

"Did they take their Zerura with them?"

Meldriic had to grit his teeth to avoid showing his irritation. He was never interrupted, ever, and certainly not sentence after sentence while he spoke about something that was obviously personal and delicate. Still, he was no fool, and showing his irritation to the Jin Dara would not help him in any way.

"Na, they left their fragments behind."

"But still, your family went from being Amhuru to, apparently, the most feared band of mercenaries in the Northlands. That's quite a change."

"It is," Meldriic said. "We were good at the art of war, very good, and we started fighting for hire to earn our keep. Before long, we had earned a reputation and were sought after all over the Northlands. Men who weren't part of our family joined us, and we grew, and that is how we became the JaenSing."

"I see," the Jin Dara said. "Now this Amhuru, the one who visited you?"

"There were actually two," Meldriic said. "I spoke to only one, but two came to see us."

"No matter," the Jin Dara said, waving away the discrepancy with a flip of his hand. "Surely given their history with you and you with them, this was most unusual, for any Amhuru to come to you."

"Most unusual," Meldriic said. "But the Amhuru who spoke to me is an audacious man. He said you would remember him, perhaps, as he gave you those scars."

Whether the casual, almost light-hearted manner of the interview up until that point had been feigned or not, Meldriic didn't know. What he did know was that the Jin Dara's mood changed immediately. His face grew hard and the golden eyes seemed to burn with an intense hatred and fire that almost made Meldriic step back. Almost.

"What is his name?" the Jin Dara finally asked.

"Draagan."

"Draagan almost killed me," the Jin Dara said, and his voice rasped in a low, growling tone, "but he failed, and he will live to be very sorry that he failed. Why would he come to you?"

"Even though I don't really know him, his family and my family were friends, long ago."

"What did he want?"

"He wanted help."

"Help with what?"

"Killing you."

The Jin Dara stared at Meldriic, and Meldriic stared back. For a long time the two men stood, just a few feet apart, staring. At last, the Jin Dara broke the silence. "I don't understand. It is common knowledge that you hate the Amhuru?"

"Sa."

"Then why would this Draagan come to you and ask for your help?"

"He thinks that we, my brothers and I, that deep down we want a way to go back, to become Amhuru again."

"Do you?"

"Na."

"Then why would he think that?"

"Because he's Amhuru," Meldriic shrugged. "Of course he thinks that. What we did was inconceivable to an Amhuru, so of course it is inconceivable that we wouldn't want to undo it."

"And that's why he asked?"

"That, and because he assumed we still felt some loyalty to the mission of the Amhuru, to protect the Golden Cord and keep it separate."

"Do you?"

"Na," Meldriic said. "At least, not like he thinks. We wouldn't mind getting our hands on some, but we have no interest in the mission of the Amhuru."

"Have any of you ever worn Zerura?"

"Na," Meldriic said. "None of us had yet been born when my grandfather left. But, we grew up hearing stories about wearing and using Zerura."

"I see," the Jin Dara said, and still he stared at Meldriic. "Why are you telling me all this?"

"Because you asked," Meldriic said. "And because it is what happened."

"You're not worried that I'll suspect you?"

"You would suspect us anyway."

"Why would I suspect you?" the Jin Dara asked, and the somewhat lighter tone was back, at least for the moment.

"Because you can see that we are capable, powerful men," Meldriic said. "And powerful men always suspect other powerful men."

"Then why come, if you knew I would suspect you?"

"For two reasons."

"Which are?"

"You know them both already," Meldriic said. "First, we hate the Amhuru, and obviously, if you succeed, the Amhuru will be destroyed. We'd like to help."

"And second?"

"Wearing and using Zerura is our birthright, and it has been denied us for a very long time. We are ready to wear it again, even if it means serving someone else."

"How very ironic," the Jin Dara smiled. "The Amhuru take away your right to wear Zerura, and now you've come to me to get it back."

"Sa, we have," Meldriic said.

The Jin Dara turned around and walked back to his chair. Once he sat down, he said, "I will need to think about this."

"Of course," Meldriic replied.

"But if I say yes, you will need to do more than swear to me," the Jin Dara said. "You will need to kneel. Can you kneel, Meldriic Jaen? Is it possible for you?"

"Sa," Meldriic said. "I can do it right now if you'd like."

Again the Jin Dara made his waving gesture, dismissing the idea. "There will be time for that later. What I have in mind for now is something a little different."

Here the Jin Dara paused, only just for a moment, and then he added, "What do you think of my tree?"

The question was so unexpected, so disconnected from the conversation they had been having, that for a moment, Meldriic almost didn't understand that the Jin Dara was speaking of the tree by the window. When he did understand, he looked over at the tree, and then back at the Jin Dara. "It is an odd tree, in an odd place."

"Yes indeed," the Jin Dara laughed. "It is a very odd tree. In fact, we could truly say it is a one-of-a-kind tree."

Meldriic didn't know if the Jin Dara expected him to say anything to this, but he figured it would be best just to stay quiet. So, he waited, and a moment later the Jin Dara said, "I saw you admiring my headwear, earlier."

As he said this, the Jin Dara ran his fingers lightly along the line of the *cadeen* as it ran back from his face, around his head. Again, Meldriic wasn't quite sure what to say, so in the end he only said, "Sa, I noticed it."

"Well, the fellow I took this from," the Jin Dara said, sliding his fingers forward and off the *cadeen* as he did, "is the fellow I turned into that tree."

Meldriic heard the words, understood what they were suggesting, but still he turned to stare at the tree in disbelief. Gradually, the faint outline of a body began to appear, somehow inside or underneath the bark of the tree. Could anyone do such a thing, even with the power of multiple fragments of the Golden Cord?

"Here's the thing," the Jin Dara said, rising again from his seat. "I have grown weary of this … this tree, and would like to be rid of it now. I thought that you, perhaps, given your ancient animosity for the Amhuru, might be willing to kill it for me?"

Meldriic turned to look at the Jin Dara. "You want me to kill this tree?"

"Yes, I do."

"How?"

In answer, the Jin Dara said nothing, but a second later Meldriic heard a cracking sound and, turning to look at the tree, noticed that a section of bark near the top had split to the side and was still pulling back. Underneath was a dark sap of some kind, but Meldriic soon realized that something beneath the sap was pulsating in and out.

"All you need do is plunge a knife into that opening, and I assure you, the tree will die."

Meldriic was still staring at the tree, for now, two more small holes in the bark had opened further up, and two gleaming eyes peered out at him. He shivered, for though he was staring at a tree, he seemed certain that this tree had somehow heard what the Jin Dara had said and understood what was going on.

Meldriic did not hesitate. He extended his hand. "We left our weapons outside."

"Devaar."

The man behind them came forward and placed a knife with a long, narrow blade in Meldriic's hand. It occurred to him that the Jin Dara was a very confident man to put a knife in Meldriic Jaen's hand at such close quarters, but it also occurred to him that the Jin Dara was probably testing him. With multiple fragments of the Golden Cord on the Jin Dara's person and ready to be used, Meldriic probably wouldn't get anywhere close to him if he attacked him. So, Meldriic did the only thing there was to do. He stepped over to the tree and drove the blade into the pulsating black object just beneath the dark sap.

A wretched sound broke free from the tree as he did so, like wood ripping or like boards being smashed with a sledgehammer. The tree convulsed, the various odd branches rippled in the air, and the few ugly leaves that hung on them detached from those branches and floated in drifting patterns to the ground. After a few seconds, the tree sagged forward, the branches dipped lower, and the room was once more silent.

"Well done, Meldriic," the Jin Dara said. "It must have felt good to kill not just any Amhuru, but one of their Keepers. I will do similar and worse to Draagan when I catch him, I assure you."

Meldriic remained quiet, gazing at the silent, sagging tree. He still couldn't quite believe that what had just happened had really happened. And then, a moment later, the Jin Dara was speaking again, dismissing them, but Meldriic missed the first part of what he said, "… for now, go with Devaar, and he will show you all to your rooms. For the time being, enjoy the hospitality of Krayton."

"Thank you," Meldriic said, and turned to leave. The man named Devaar, who had handed him the knife, took it back now and walked to the door to open it for them. They were all about to head out when the Jin Dara spoke again. They stopped immediately.

"Oh, Meldriic."

"Sa?" Meldriic said. He turned, still a little dazed and unsure of how to officially address the Jin Dara.

"Perhaps you could weigh in on a debate we've been having."

"I will, if I have anything to add."

"Good," the Jin Dara said. "If I asked you to pick one city that is a symbol of the might and power and glory of the Northlands, a strong city, an advanced city, a city that seems like it is somehow beyond tragedy and disaster—what city would you pick?"

Meldriic stood and thought for a moment. There were many strong cities in the Northlands, but the more he considered the question, the more there seemed to be one that fit the description better than the others. "Tanisaan."

"Thank you, Meldriic," the Jin Dara said with a smile. He nodded to Devaar, and the man led them out of the room a moment later.

21

THE SOLDIERS AND THE SCIENTIST

Meldriic Jaen wasn't trembling—he never trembled. The slight shaking in his fingers that he felt as he lifted his wine cup to his mouth, then, must have come from something else. The breeze coming in through the window was markedly chilly, so that might have been it. He considered closing the window but decided against it. It was good to have a window open in all weather but the unbearably cold, or so his father had always maintained.

"You don't think that tree was once human, do you, Meldriic?"

"I don't know, Petaar," Meldriic said, but in truth, he thought he did know. He just didn't want to admit it out loud.

"It was, I'm sure of it," Traliin said. "I could see it, even before he told Meldriic to stab it, and then there were the eyes—"

"Traliin," Meldriic said firmly, but kindly. "Enough. I agree with you, but in the end, none of us can be completely sure about what we just saw or what I just did."

"He has the *cadeen*," Renoud said. "I'm sure of that."

"Yes," Meldriic said, turning and looking at Renoud. "That we do know."

"It couldn't be a replica?" Vaall asked.

"No, Vaall," Meldriic said. "The Amhuru would never duplicate the *cadeen*. Never. Not for any reason. That law is inviolate. Nor do I think there is anything anyone could do to force an Amhuru to duplicate it. If it has been duplicated, then the Jin Dara has done it. Either way, whether he wears the original—which I assume he does—or a duplicate, he must have the *cadeen*."

"The Jin Dara said the tree was the Amhuru Keeper from whom he took the *cadeen*," Renoud said, looking at Meldriic with concern. "You doing all right with what just happened, Meldriic?"

"Whoever it was," Meldriic said. "I saw those eyes when they opened, and I could have sworn they were pleading with me."

"It's not your fault—" Renoud started.

"Na, he wasn't pleading with me to let him live," Meldriic said. "He was pleading with me to kill him. I think I did him a favor."

"I wouldn't want to be a tree," Petaar said and grunted. "Not if I would somehow know I was a tree and be conscious of the world around me like that. Would be like prison."

The others grunted too, nodding, and they all seemed taken for a moment with trying to imagine what kind of life that Amhuru had been living for who knew how long.

"Draagan said the Jin Dara had two of the Southland fragments," Traliin said after a moment, breaking the spell. "He didn't say anything about the Jin Dara having the *cadeen*."

"He must not have known," Meldriic said. "I assume the Jin Dara has come into possession of the *cadeen* since Dragaan's encounter with him."

"You sure about that?" Petaar said. "Maybe he sent us here on a suicide mission. Maybe he saw in the Jin Dara a chance to finally settle the score between the Amhuru and the Jaens."

"No," Meldriic said emphatically. "Draagan wouldn't have done that."

"You don't actually know him, Meldriic," Petaar replied. "How can you be so sure?"

"I haven't known him a long time," Meldriic said, "and I don't know him as well as I know some people, but I know him."

"You'd bet our lives on that?"

"I would, actually," Meldriic said, looking hard at his next oldest brother. Petaar seemed to feel it was his job to challenge him as often as possible, since so few others dared do it at all. "But that isn't the point here."

Meldriic turned and walked back across the room to the table. He refilled his cup. "Aside from the fact that I stand by my assessment of both Draagan and his offer from the moment we first discussed it, it would make no sense for Draagan to go out of his way, risk his life to come among us, to set us up in such a needlessly complex and indirect way."

Petaar opened his mouth but Meldriic held up his hand to forestall him "Besides, while my ego is plenty big, I don't think for a second that Draagan or any Amhuru would see the Jin Dara as their chance to deal with us, as though we were the real problem. You saw him, Petaar, glowing all golden like that. You saw what he's capable of with that 'tree' monstrosity. You really think we're the ones that Draagan is worried about?"

Meldriic paused, but Petaar didn't rush to step into the space left by his silence. In fact, none of the brothers seemed eager to fill that space, so in the end he filled it himself. "You know, as I stood there, in his presence—I finally understood why Draagan had come to us. Despite Draagan's attempt to explain it, it just didn't sit right with me, you know? I couldn't ever imagine something driving me to them for help. But if I were Draagan, entrusted with protecting what he bears, and if I had encountered the Jin Dara? Well, then I might do just about anything—even go to the dreaded Jaens—if I thought it might help me deal with him."

"We should have killed him tonight, while we had the chance—"

Traliin cut off once he saw the furious glare Meldriic directed his way. When he did, Meldriic walked quickly to the door and opened it, checking the hallway. There was no one there, but that didn't stop him from scolding Traliin as he closed it again and telling him to keep his voice down.

"We had him," Traliin said, his voice now barely louder than a whisper. "He had only the one guy in there with us."

"We wouldn't have gotten anywhere near him," Meldriic said, and this time, rather than challenging him, Petaar nodded his head in agreement.

"Sa," Petaar said. "You think a guy who can change a man into tree can't defend himself?"

"All five of us were there," Traliin protested. "He couldn't have stopped us all, could he?"

"I think he very well could," Meldriic said.

"Then why'd we even come?" Vaall asked. "If we were no match for him tonight, why would we think we ever would be?"

"I'm not saying we aren't a match for him," Meldriic said, "I am saying he was on his guard tonight. He is probably on his guard whenever he receives anyone in that room, and with five men like us, even more so."

"We need to earn his trust, see if we can get him off his guard," Renoud said.

"That's exactly right," Meldriic agreed. "And it is precisely what we are going to do."

"You still planning to try to do this?" Traliin asked. "Even knowing he must have at least three fragments? Even knowing he might turn us into trees?"

Meldriic stood, surveying his brothers. All four were looking to him now for wisdom. They would turn back if he said they should turn back, and as good as the Jin Dara's soldiers might be, he didn't think there was an army in the world that could keep the Jaen brothers in a town that they wanted to leave.

What's more, leaving might well have been by far the most sensible thing to do. Traliin was right. Draagan had seen something in his encounter with the Jin Dara that had driven him to seek out the Jaens, and then the Jin Dara had possessed only two fragments. What must his power be like now? Even if they could earn his trust, why should they think they would ever be able to get close enough to kill the Jin Dara—if the Jin Dara could even be killed? It was anyone's guess what wearing all that Zerura was doing to the Jin Dara's physiology—that glowing skin might be more than a merely cosmetic change.

But Meldriic knew they weren't going to leave. If the Jin Dara had gotten harder to kill when he obtained his third fragment, it had also become more imperative that he be killed. And while he didn't want to die doing it, Meldriic knew that few men would stand as good a chance as they did of pulling it off.

"I understand and feel your apprehension," Meldriic said. "But he has to be stopped. We knew that when we agreed to come, and it hasn't changed. We also knew we might die trying to do it. That's why we agreed that we would all come. If we go down, we go down together."

Renoud nodded at this, and slowly the others did too.

"So we're agreed?"

"We're agreed."

"All right then," Meldriic said. "We will kill him if we can, and we will recover the missing fragments if we can."

"And if we do get them back?" Petaar asked. "Does the fact that he has three—or more—change anything?"

"Probably."

"So you've decided if we're going to keep them or give them back to the Amhuru, then?" Petaar pressed.

"No," Meldriic said. "That, I have not decided."

.   .   .

The Jin Dara gazed out his window at the steady procession of supply wagons gliding down the street and the mighty oxen that pulled them. In the town where he'd taken the third fragment, and in the surrounding towns, teams of horses had been used to pull wagons like these. Some of those teams got as large as six or even eight horses, held together by means of an elaborate harness system. Two of these oxen, though, could pull wagons that were almost as big as the biggest of those wagons, and when four were hooked onto the same load, the wagons they could pull were simply enormous.

Even so, the Jin Dara couldn't help but feel like he was gazing at something archaic and primitive. Many larger cities and towns in the Northlands had carts and transports that capitalized on the power of meridium beyond its ability to suspend a load above the ground on the surface of the Arua. Many used some form of corness for fuel, though not all did. Even so, he thought of places like Alaxundra and Barra-Dohn, and the remarkable array of technologies he had encountered there, and he couldn't help but feel that relying on animals for locomotion was unforgiveably backward.

He would have to see to this, perhaps introduce a common transport system and make universal the very best means of propulsion for both power and speed. That was another thing she might be good at, and he tucked it away on his growing and already surprisingly long list of things she might be uniquely suited to manage for him.

The door opened and Devaar crossed the room to stand beside him. The Jin Dara turned from the window. "All seems to be going well."

"Yes," Devaar said. "By this time tomorrow, Krayton will be all but empty."

"Two weeks to the coast, you said?"

"That's right. And then six to eight weeks to a port that's a couple days removed from Tanisaan."

"Six, you mean," the Jin Dara said. "I keep telling you, Devaar, the weather will be most cooperative."

"Six weeks, then, by ship," Devaar said. "Meldriic Jaen says there's a large garrison of Tanisaan troops just inland from the port. They will be our first skirmish."

"Meldriic Jaen," the Jin Dara repeated. "And how is the training going for him and his brothers?"

"They're the best soldiers we have," Devaar replied. "That's how it's going."

"The best of the recruits, you mean?"

"No," Devaar said, and the normally calm man was quite emphatic. "The best soldiers, period."

The Jin Dara frowned. "Surely they are no match for some of the Najin who have borne the fragments for years. A month of training could not replace all that experience."

"I'm not saying they've mastered use of the fragments, and yes, there are plenty of Najin who can manipulate the Arua field better and do things the Jaens cannot," Devaar said.

"Nevertheless," he continued. "They are the best soldiers we have. Their skill with weapons, any weapon, their reflexes, their ability to see the battle unfold and anticipate the strategy of their enemy—it is unlike anything I have seen, and all of your commanders agree. They may not have experience with the fragments, but they draw on their own experience, a kind that none of our men can equal."

The Jin Dara nodded. "Well, if they really do fight for us, then I supposed I will see this for myself."

"If? You doubt their story?"

"Not necessarily," the Jin Dara said. "I simply don't think they've told me all of it."

"That doesn't mean they won't fight for you."

"No, it doesn't," the Jin Dara said. "On the other hand—"

A knock at the door interrupted them, and Devaar went to see who it was. When he returned, all he said was, "She's here."

"Show her in," the Jin Dara said, and Devaar nodded and left the room. The Jin Dara crossed the room and took his seat.

A moment later, Devaar was back and she was with him. She was clearly both nervous and excited, but she was doing an admirable job of maintaining at least the façade of a woman in control.

"Are you packed?" he said.

"I am," she said. "But that's not saying much, since I don't have much to pack."

"Do you know where we're going?"

"I've heard that we are headed farther north, to a great city called Tanisaan."

"That is true," the Jin Dara said. "And do you know why we're going there?"

"Na," Rika shook her head. "I can only assume you think one of the remaining fragments is there."

"I suppose it might be," the Jin Dara said. "And while that would be fortuitous for us, I'm not counting on it."

"Then I have no idea."

"I have picked Tanisaan," the Jin Dara said, "as a prominent and powerful city, to be the site of a great demonstration of my power, and even more than that, of my will to use it."

"You're sending a message to the Northlands," Rika said, and the Jin Dara could see her trying to work out the puzzle. "As a warning against helping or harboring the Amhuru?"

He smiled. It wasn't a bad guess. She had a quick mind. "Not exactly. The message I am sending is to the Amhuru themselves."

She didn't have anything to say to that, at least not immediately, so he continued. "I will do things at Tanisaan, terrible things, things the world has never seen before or even imagined. Then I will wait for the Amhuru to hear of them, and to come to stop me."

"You're sure they'll come?"

"I think so," the Jin Dara said, "but if they don't, I will pick another city, and I will devise worse things. And this will continue until either I have laid the world bare, or they come out of their hiding spots to face me."

Rika nodded. "Having traveled with the bearer of the last Southland fragment, I think it will work. I just can't say if it will work right away.

When they hear of Tanisaan, they will debate if it is a trap, and whether they should go, or even if they should send some to help while others hide the originals—but even if they don't come to you at Tanisaan, they will at some point come to you. They won't be able to watch you destroy the world from a comfortable distance."

"I am glad you think it is a good plan," the Jin Dara said, with only a hint of irony in his voice. "But, whether it works or not, my days of chasing the Amhuru and running all over the world are finished. I will do as I please, and if they don't like it, they can try to stop me."

Rika looked at him for a moment, and then she bowed before him, even if only slightly. Lowering her head toward the floor and looking down, she acknowledged his implicit claim to be the master of all things.

"I have summoned you to tell you why you are coming with us," the Jin Dara said. "When we arrive in Tanisaan, you will have complete authority to assemble the best minds of the city, in whatever manner you see fit—voluntarily or involuntarily. I will then make available to you ample space and a supply of Zerura with which to begin again your experiments from Barra-Dohn."

"I am honored that you—"

"There will, of course," the Jin Dara said, speaking over her, "be no question of stealing from me, as something quite worse than death awaits anyone who betrays me."

Rika looked at him, and he was impressed to see anger more than fear in her eyes. "There is no need to threaten me, I assure you. I will serve you the best I can, for as long as you allow it."

"Good," the Jin Dara said. "But I needed to be clear. And in that vein, let me be clear about something else. You will be free to experiment on better lights and ovens, on superior meridium sleds and transports, better weapons and many more such things as those you have worked on before. However, I also have some ideas of my own that may require some, shall we say, less conventional kinds of experiments."

"I will do as you direct."

"I am sure you will," the Jin Dara said. "This line of experiments will require fairly regular contact with me, since you will want access to my expertise and I will want to know what you discover."

"All the better," Rika said, and when the Jin Dara looked into her eyes now, the heat behind them was from something other than anger altogether.

"Very well, then," the Jin Dara said. "We have both come a long way to reach this place, Rika, and the journey doesn't end here. Devaar will answer any questions you might have about your travel arrangements, and may I suggest you take advantage of the next few months before we reach Tanisaan to dream up a few creative lines of research of your own?"

"Happily," Rika said, and again she bowed as Devaar stepped forward to lead her out.

The Jin Dara watched the door close, then shut his own eyes. For a long time he sat there, lost in his own thoughts, which were increasingly a jumble of seemingly random musings about his new soldiers and his scientist, before he fell asleep.

.   .   .

Rika gathered her things from her room, knowing she'd be early, but she was too excited to wait any longer. Her mind was spinning with questions. What unorthodox experiments did the Jin Dara have in mind? What experiments of her own could she come up with, and if they piqued his interest, might the time they spent together working on them be the doorway to her hopes and dreams?

As she walked down the streets of Krayton, preparing to say farewell to it, other questions came to her too. What happened to the tree that so dominated the Jin Dara's room the last time? A chair now sat where the tree had been—was it there just to cover up the hole in the floor?

And what about Gamalian? She hadn't seen him again after that first time, but she refused to second-guess herself. He had been there, or at least someone posing as Gamalian had been. But how could Devaar know nothing about him? And how could she not have seen him again since? Krayton just wasn't that large.

She reached the transport depot and pushed all her questions aside. Her plan had worked. Despite all the setbacks she had endured since running afoul of Eirmon, here she was, being entrusted with a position of responsibility by the Jin Dara.

And if she had come this far, there was no reason why she might not hope to go still farther, and to that end she would concentrate all of her considerable abilities.

22

FIELD CAPTAIN

Deslo had fled his home of Barra-Dohn with two Amhuru, and he had traveled most of the next three years with just one Amhuru. Since crossing the Madri and entering the Northlands, he had spent a good deal of time in the company of many Amhuru. Now, though, he was part of an envoy of five ships comprised mainly of Amhuru, and that was something he never would have imagined to see, let alone be a part of. Whatever else you said about life, Deslo thought, it was certainly curiously surprising at times.

Something Deslo had learned in his time among the Amhuru was this: when a job needed doing, you didn't have to draw straws or make vague threats or offer crazy incentives—you just had to ask and you would have more volunteers than you needed. It was just the way Amhuru were.

Consequently, when the five ships put down their anchors along a secluded coastline where a large creek emptied into the ocean and men were sought to go ashore from each ship and see that ample supplies of fresh water were obtained, it was no wonder to Deslo that when he, Trabor and Shaline went ashore, they found that all five landing parties were significantly larger than necessary. Of course, since they were cautious about letting too many Amhuru ashore when they docked at ports either large or small, the extra large landing parties here were partially a function of folks wanting to get ashore and stretch their legs a bit.

With more than enough volunteers to gather and carry the water, many of the other Amhuru offered to spread out through the woods and establish a perimeter around the creek, just to make sure that they weren't being spied upon by anyone, though the remote location made this a rather unlikely possibility. Still, Deslo and Shaline and Trabor happily offered to go up the beach a ways and then into the woods as part of this effort.

While they were walking along the rocky shoreline, a call from behind caught their attention, and they turned to see Olli and Maarta jogging to catch up. Deslo tried not to show his disappointment that they were coming, as Olli looked so happy to have the opportunity to go with them and spend some time together, but he really wished she wasn't there. It wasn't that he felt awkward being with both Olli and Shaline—it had already happened a few times since Shaline returned, and though it wasn't great, it was bearable—it was more that he just didn't like seeing how happy Olli and Maarta appeared to be.

Once those two caught up, the five of them walked along together, but there was something strangely amiss. The day was overcast and a little drizzly, but more than clouds hung over them. Olli happily reminisced about a variety of things, but no one else was talking. Maarta occasionally chimed in with a question, trying to help her out as he could see she was struggling to get everyone talking, but as he hadn't been there during the time the four of them had spent together at Azandalir, his ability to help Olli carry the conversation was limited.

Why Shaline and Trabor were quiet, Deslo didn't know, but he thought he could guess. Those memories were happy memories, but given that the Jin Dara had come not long after they left, and given that their mother had died when he came—well, it wasn't hard for Deslo to figure out that the shine had come off those memories for those two a little bit. He wondered if Olli just couldn't see it, if perhaps the happy filter through which she saw the world these days just didn't allow her to.

For Deslo's part, he did find it awkward listening to Olli talk about a time in his life when he had been infatuated with Shaline, even if being around the two of them wasn't itself the issue. It just felt odd for the girl he had fallen for, and fallen hard for in the years since leaving Shaline, should be talking so happily about the time he had spent with them both so many years ago. It was a swirl of confusion that added to the perplexity he already felt, and he just wanted Olli to be quiet or for someone to change the subject.

In the end, it was Olli who changed the subject. They eventually reached the bend in the coast where they had agreed to cut inland, and they did so, leaving the shore behind and heading into the thick wood. As they moved through the trees in a tight, single file, Olli said, "Remember that day we were out hunting, and we ran into the bear, Deslo?"

"Yes," Deslo said, and that was all the encouragement Olli needed to launch into a full version of that story, as though Shaline and Trabor needed to be informed of this exciting adventure. Maarta had already heard this story, in fact more than once, so he just politely listened as Olli told the tale.

Just about the time Olli was drawing to the climax of her story, they found themselves stepping from the thick wood into a small glade, and suddenly Trabor, perhaps moved by Olli's story, leapt onto the Arua field and threw his axe at a tree across the glade, where it struck with a loud 'thwack!' He summoned it back into his hand, and in a flash he whirled back to face the others and said, "Come on, someone play a game with me. We'll see who's the fastest and most accurate with his axe."

"I was telling a story," Olli protested at this strange interruption.

"Don't do it," Shaline said, glancing at the others. "All he does is practice."

"Don't listen to her," Trabor said. "What do you say? Deslo? Olli? Maarta?"

"I guess I'm done with my story," Olli grumbled.

"I don't think so, Trabor," Deslo said, feeling pretty sure he'd only get humiliated if he ended up matched against Trabor in a contest of Amhuru skills and not sure if there was anything he desired less at this particular moment in this particular company.

"What about you, Maarta?" Trabor pointed his axe at Maarta, who was trying to soothe Olli's hurt feelings by rubbing his hand gently on her back. "Care to represent the Northlands in a little contest of skills? Nothing too serious, of course, only the honor of our respective hemispheres riding on the outcome."

Maarta smiled good-naturedly, though Deslo could tell that he wasn't entirely comfortable with the situation either. "I'm sure that there are many better candidates to represent the honor of the Northlands."

"Perhaps so," Trabor said, hurling the axe in his hand at a smaller tree even further away. Again the blade struck with a 'thwack!' and again he summoned it back into his hand in a flash. "But they're not here. Come now, play a game with me, or have the leisures of marriage made you soft?"

"Trabor, that's not—"

Maarta squeezed Olli gently on the shoulder and she stopped her rebuke in mid-sentence. Then Maarta said. "I am sure you are very skilled, Trabor, and I'm sure we'd all enjoy a demonstration of that skill. But I don't think any of us are in the mood to join you just now."

And then it happened.

Though Maarta was careful with his words and tone, a cloud of anger rolled across Trabor's face. His other hand, the one not holding his axe, drew a small knife and flicked it directly at Maarta, who saw it coming and dove backwards to avoid it, just as Trabor halted its momentum so that the knife hung as still as could be on the Arua field. And then, as a stunned and shaken Maarta picked himself up off the ground, covered with leaves and dirt, Trabor summoned the knife back into his hand and laughed.

"How dare you!" Olli cried out, once the momentary shock of what had happened had passed. Her face was red with rage, and Deslo thought she might explode. "How could you draw a knife on a friend? Let alone throw it? What if you'd let it fly just a little too far?"

"I don't make mistakes with my weapons," Trabor answered, his voice cold and unapologetic. "Ever."

He stepped down off the Arua field and stood at a distance from the others. Shaline strode up to him and slapped him in the face. As she started to withdraw he grabbed her wrist.

Deslo had seen enough and stepped in between them, grabbing Trabor's forearm and trying to gently pull them apart. At first Trabor resisted, and Deslo was amazed at his strength. He quickly realized that if Trabor didn't want to let go, he wasn't going to be able to make him.

But Trabor did relent, and with a glare at both Shaline and Deslo, he let go of his sister and started walking across the glade, away from them all. When he reached the far side he turned and said. "The Jin Dara is out there, and he's going to exterminate us all if we don't get a whole lot tougher."

With that he turned back around and disappeared into the wood. Deslo stood and watched him go, not really sure what to do now. Shaline, for her part, had turned toward Olli and Maarta. Olli had turned her back on Trabor and was holding Maarta tightly, as though it had just occurred to her that perhaps, one day, she might lose him. All the while, Maarta was stroking her hair and whispering that everything was all right.

"I don't know what to say, Olli," Shaline said. "There's no excuse for him. I'm so sorry."

Olli nodded, but she didn't answer. She just looked up at Maarta and said, "Can we go back now?"

"Of course."

They started back the way they had come, and Shaline started to follow. Deslo could see that she was looking for something to say, something that might diffuse the awkwardness or perhaps even mitigate her brother's inexcusable behavior, but he knew that whatever there might be to say, now was not the time. He reached out as Shaline stepped past him and took her arm, but gently, knowing that having just had Trabor grab her, she might be sensitive about being held.

When he did, she stopped and turned toward him. He simply shook his head, as though to say, 'Not now.' Shaline looked back through the trees at the retreating figures of Maarta and Olli, then back at Deslo. She nodded.

Soon they were alone in the glade. Trabor had disappeared heading one way, Olli and Maarta the other, and Deslo didn't much want to follow either of them. He motioned to a place where a tree was down, and he and Shaline walked over and sat on it.

"What do you think got into Trabor?" Deslo asked after a little while.

"I don't know," Shaline said quietly, and she didn't look at Deslo when she did. "Sometimes, he gets in these really intense moods. It can be a little scary."

"Do you think it's about your mother?"

"Of course it's about my mother," Shaline snapped, and Deslo was taken aback. She had never spoken to him that way.

As soon as she did, though, she seemed to regret it. She turned to him with tears in her eyes. "I'm sorry, Deslo. I didn't mean that."

"It's all right," he said. "I didn't mean to reopen old wounds."

"You didn't reopen them," Shaline said. "I'm not sure they've ever closed, not for either of us, perhaps, but certainly not for Trabor. He never talks about it, and he acts like it's just a fact that we all need to get over, but I think it eats him up."

"And all the practicing with his weapons?"

"Revenge," Shaline whispered. "He's obsessed with it. I think he day-dreams that somehow, one day, he'll come face to face with the Jin Dara, and that on that day, his incredible skills will save him, and more, give him a chance to avenge her."

Deslo nodded. "Well, I guess if you're going to be obsessed with something, that's as good an obsession as any."

Shaline didn't answer. She sat shaking her head, gently but persistently.

"What?" Deslo asked. "You can't blame him for that. We'd all like to kill the Jin Dara, and he has more cause than most."

"I don't blame him for wanting it," Shaline said. "I'm just not sure I like what it's doing to him."

"Maybe he just needs some time," Deslo said, unsure what else to say.

"Maybe," Shaline said, but Deslo was pretty sure she said it more out of politeness than agreement.

They sat side by side on the fallen tree, and between the thick canopy of leaves and the overcast sky, the day seemed to darken around them, even though Deslo was pretty sure it wasn't yet noon. He was just about to suggest they head back and see how close to being finished the men gathering the fresh water were, when Shaline spoke again.

"You're in love with Olli, aren't you?"

He grew very still. She had framed it like a question, but it wasn't a question. Shaline, staring straight ahead, made the observation like she might have observed that the sky was cloudy or the log they were sitting on was damp—matter-of-fact, emotionless.

"No," Deslo protested, perhaps more vigorously than he intended. "Of course not, she's married."

"Deslo, I can, I don't know, not see it exactly, but sense it."

"Shaline," Deslo said, and it was suddenly very important to him to persuade her that she was wrong. "Olli and I have traveled together a long time and been through a lot. We did get very close. And yes, when Maarta came along and that whole thing happened between them, it was weird. Maybe it still is. Maybe that's what you see or sense. But that doesn't mean I love her."

For a long time Shaline didn't answer. She sat beside him, staring either at the ground or straight ahead. And then, without any words or warning, she leaned over and kissed him on his cheek, then rose to walk away, heading back the way Olli and Maarta had headed just a few moments ago.

Deslo rose to follow her, wondering if Shaline believed him at all and, more to the point, wondering why, if he did love Olli, the ground was suddenly unsteady beneath his feet in the wake of Shaline's tender kiss.

·   ·   ·

Meldriic Jaen lay on his back with his eyes closed, a small stack of cushions under his legs. Three skirmishes with the army of Tanisaan in the last three days had taken their toll. He was tired and sore, and for some reason this position had always been his favorite way to unwind and rest after battle.

There had been no surprises so far. The Tanisaan commanders were competent, their men well trained. They fought well but yielded ground rather than face large losses. They were stalling for time, slowing the advance of the Jin Dara and his army so that those behind them could prepare the defenses of the city.

They were out of time now, though, and tomorrow when both armies took the field, it would be with the mighty walls of Tanisaan within view. When the Jin Dara threw the full force of the Najin and their power against the enemy, and when the battle got out of hand—as Meldriic Jaen knew absolutely that it would—there would be nowhere to retreat. They would have to stand, and they would be slaughtered.

His brothers understood this too, and they were unusually quiet tonight. Soldiers since birth, they had seen many battles. They did not sit around at night, after a day in the field, overly concerned with what they had done. It wasn't in their nature. And yet, Meldriic knew they were struggling, both with the things they had already done the last few days, and also with what they knew they would do in the morning.

Of course it was Renoud, though, who had the courage to give voice to it. "I don't like it, Meldriic. It's not a fair fight."

"Give me an unfair fight any time," Meldriic answered, not moving or opening his eyes. "As long as the odds are in my favor."

"I'm not talking about odds, or strategy, or anything like that," Renoud said. "I'm talking about the fact that we wield a kind of power the world has never seen before, a kind of power no man should have."

"I know," Meldriic answered.

He said this, fully aware of not only his own apprehension about the two fragments of Zerura that he wore, but also his growing attachment to them and how they made him feel. Even now he felt them, pulsing with his heartbeat. They felt like life. He wondered even as he focused on them what it would feel like to take them off, or even if he could.

"Meldriic," Renoud said, and Meldriic could tell that Renoud had moved closer, was perhaps even squatting not far away in the tent, "What are we going to do tomorrow?"

"We're mercenaries, Renoud," Meldriic said. "We'll do what we always do."

"Don't act like tomorrow is a battle like any other," Petaar said, chiming in. "Not when we're fighting for him."

"No," Meldriic agreed, finally opening his eyes and looking at his brothers. "It isn't a battle like any other. It's more important than any we've ever fought. And that's why tomorrow we're going to pay the butcher's bill, and pay it well, so the Jin Dara can learn, if he hasn't already, that we're the best he's got. We're the men he needs."

His brothers were quiet, and Traliin even nodded in agreement. Meldriic knew the matter was settled, but he added, "The Najin are capable men, but we're a breed apart. I think the Jin Dara's captains have already seen this, but tomorrow will be our best chance to make sure they do."

There was no further discussion of the matter, and eventually Meldriic closed his eyes again. He thought he could probably go to sleep if he wished, but if he did, he would miss dinner. He didn't like skipping dinner the night before a big battle. He would need his strength.

Still, he must have drifted off, for the next thing he knew, Renoud was shaking him awake. Devaar had come for Meldriic. Tonight he was going to dine with the Jin Dara. Meldriic, once aware of what was happening, rose and followed Devaar into the evening air.

The Jin Dara's tent was spacious, but it was not especially luxurious. Certainly, Meldriic had fought for men who required much fancier accommodations, even on a battlefield. Perhaps it said something about the Jin Dara that his tent was large but simple, though perhaps all it said was that he was confident he wouldn't need it for very long.

Meldriic joined the Jin Dara and Devaar for dinner. It was only the three of them, and the food was good if unspectacular. It was simple fare, no doubt regarded as adequate for the time being while they waited to enter the city in triumph after their presumed victory the following day.

The Jin Dara didn't waste much time on small talk. As soon as Meldriic arrived and they were served, the Jin Dara started plying him with questions—questions about the city's defenses and weapons and strategies. Most of these things they had talked about before, but Meldriic understood and appreciated the Jin Dara's thoroughness that on the eve of battle, he would go back over this well-traveled ground.

"Explain how these garrows work again?"

"The garrows are large, stretchy bands—basically very large slingshots," Meldriic said. "Both on the walls and on the ground outside the walls, there are networks of posts, strategically placed. The teams that man a garrow can slip the ends over two of these posts, load an explosive, pull it back, and launch it in mere seconds."

"Why add the extra step?" Devaar asked. "Why not just have several already set up at fixed intervals?"

"Flexibility and speed," Meldriic said. "There are literally hundreds of posts, especially on the ground, so that the garrow can be lined up to face almost any direction from almost any angle. If the enemy advances from multiple directions, the team doesn't have to move from fixed position to fixed position to attack them. They just slip the end of the garrow off one post and swing around until they're facing the enemy and slip it on another."

"I like it," the Jin Dara said as he nodded. "It won't save them, but I like it."

They talked a little more about Tanisaan, its weapons, and strategies, but soon the Jin Dara took the conversation a different direction. "I have to say, Meldriic, that I was skeptical of the lofty reputation of the Jaens, but everything I have seen so far has borne witness to the truth of it. You and your brothers are remarkable soldiers."

"Thank you, sir," Meldriic said.

"Consequently," the Jin Dara continued. "I'd like you to serve as my Field Captain tomorrow. Lead the attack."

"I'm not sure about that," Meldriic said, hesitating at the unexpected offer.

"Why not? Have you not led an army before? Have you only fought in one?"

"I have led many attacks of various sizes and commanded many men," Meldriic said. "But soldiers are hierarchical, sir, and you have commanders who know your men better and have served you far longer. They may not appreciate an outsider in that role. I'm not sure it's my place."

"Well, I am," the Jin Dara said, "and it is my decision. I assure you, Meldriic, my commanders will accept my decision without dissension. Besides, they know what I know, that you are the right man for the job."

"I will do my best then," Meldriic said, understanding that the matter was decided.

"I know you will," the Jin Dara said.

They sat, eating for a moment, and then the Jin Dara smiled. "Just think, Devaar, when the soldiers and captains of Tanisaan hear that the notorious Meldriic Jaen is here, serving as the Field Captain of the Jin Dara, they will tremble with despair."

"That they will," Devaar said with a grin of his own.

"And then we will kill them all."

23

TANISAAN

Vaall came into view, and Meldriic felt a surge of pride as he watched his youngest brother dealing death with fury and vengeance. All of his brothers were close by, and while they were wearing the gold of the Najin, they also wore black bands wound tightly on their right forearms. The black band was the mark of the Jaen, and it was borne in battle, not only by the Jaen brothers, but by all the mercenaries who served them in the JaenSing.

Meldriic would have liked to have more of his own men here, but that had been out of the question. They would have come if he had asked, but this job was for him and his brothers alone. They would succeed, or fail, alone.

Again he scanned the far side of the battlefield, where most of the army of Tanisaan was now concentrated, having been forced by the long morning to yield most of the battlefield to Meldriic Jaen and the army of the Jin Dara. Again he wondered why the garrows hadn't been more active. They had managed to do some damage throughout the battle, but he had expected much worse.

That the Jin Dara had interfered with their usage from afar was certain, and Meldriic would have loved to know how he had done so, but his attention had been given to matters closer at hand most of the day. Now, though, as he led the Najin forward across the center of the field toward

Tanisaan itself, closing the noose around the throat of the enemy, he was especially mindful of the situation at the foot of the city's walls.

He saw nothing that gave him pause from preparing to signal the advance, and he trusted that whatever the Jin Dara had done so far to protect his men, he would continue to do. For his own part, Meldriic could feel his battle fatigue beginning to pull him from the battle frenzy he had been in throughout the long morning. Now that the worst was over, it would be tempting to let that frenzy slip away, but he never liked letting go until a fight was finished.

He needed to stoke the fire.

He was the incarnation of rage, a storm of wrath no man could resist. When his winds blew hot, a deluge of blood always followed, soaking the earth and leaving behind the mark of his coming. Though he wore the gold of the Najin, his clothes were dark with blood like the ground beneath his feet.

He was Meldriic Jaen, Field Captain of the Jin Dara.

He was the right hand of death, and he wore the black band of the Jaen around his right forearm to serve as a visible reminder of this. He had reached out from the grave to take hold of many a man of Tanisaan today, and he had pulled them down into the darkness from which there is no return.

He was Meldriic Jaen, Field Captain of the Jin Dara.

He was pestilence and plague, a silent killer that came unbidden and struck down untold hundreds and thousands in the prime of life. In sunshine and in rain, by day or by night he came, and there was no way to predict or escape the hour of his coming.

He was Meldriic Jaen.

He could feel the frenzy deepen, and the fatigue seemed to fall away. It was time to move, time to finish the enemy.

He gave the command to advance.

·　　·　　·

Gil Danning had served in the army of Tanisaan for almost forty years. He was the oldest man to command a garrow squad, a position usually held by men almost half his age. And yet, while he lacked the reflexes and speed usually sought after to be in charge of a garrow, he made impeccable decisions in the field and maintained one of the most efficient and effective teams in the entire army.

Even so, for all his experience and ability, Gil Danning had never seen anything like the things he had seen today. He had kept his squad alive in the worst of it, though, and that was saying something. Most of the other garrow squads were down, dead or disabled. He had no idea how their enemy had done the things they had done, but he knew that against that kind of power, there was probably nothing he could do. Nevertheless, if he could guide his men to some of the garrow posts on top of the wall and do just a little bit of damage before the end, well, then Gil Danning could die, not a happy man, but a contented man.

He had managed to get his garrow team into the city before the enemy advance reached the base of the walls, but that had been harder than it should have been. Everywhere Danning looked there was chaos and disorder, two words which had never, at any point, characterized his life in the Tanisaan military. Any other day he would have been furious at the men who were supposed to be operating the gate for the delays there had been in getting his men inside, but today, he was simply grateful that there were still men trying to do their duty and that they were able to help before he and his squad also got pinned against the city walls by the enemy's men.

He didn't know who this Jin Dara was, but Danning didn't really need to. He knew two things that were enough for him to realize that Tanisaan was lost and that his was a suicide mission. The first was that the man leading this attack for the Jin Dara was the notorious Meldriic Jaen. Meldriic Jaen was almost as old and grizzled as Danning, only the Jaen brother was an elite soldier with a legendary reputation and Danning was just a squad leader.

The second thing that Danning knew was that there was someone—or perhaps many someones—wielding a power over the Arua field that was like what an Amhuru could exert, only greater. They were wielding power that made the impossible possible, for Danning had seen it with his own eyes.

It had started early that morning, when his garrow squad had been deployed at the base of the city wall, facing south, waiting for the command to launch their first attack at the enemy army as it moved out onto the field. Eventually, that order did come, and he moved his squad into position and set up the garrow to begin, as did dozens of other garrow squads around him.

Suddenly, vibrant yellow-green blades of grass began to grow out of the ground all around them. It grew where the ground had been bare from the trampling of many feet, and it grew where there was already grass, coming up in the midst of it. And as it grew, the yellow-green grass bent ever toward the feet and legs of the soldiers operating the garrows, and then these new blades climbed up over shoes and slipped inside the pants of the men and stung them repeatedly with a painful, deadly sting.

All this Danning saw and only partially understood at first. He and his squad survived because he had the sense to move as soon as he saw the impossible happening—yellow-green grass suddenly bursting out of the ground all around him. He did not wait to see anymore, did not assume that, even if odd, it was only grass and couldn't harm him. He moved his men as far as he needed to move them to get away from the strange phenomena, and consequently both he and they survived when many of the soldiers trained to use the garrows did not.

The second bizarre thing Danning had seen had been an attack, not on the garrow squads in particular, but on the initial wave of infantry soldiers dispatched by the captains to march out to meet the enemy in the field. Moving on the city's fastest transports, they zoomed out of the gates, racing across the surface of the Arua to get into position. As they spread out, though, several gaping holes in the ground had opened and out of these holes massive clouds of what looked like bats had flown up into the sky.

These bats exploded out of the ground in a dense cloud but very quickly spread out across the field, flying directly at the faces of the soldiers from Tanisaan. They would swoop down, attach themselves to the face and wrap what appeared to be, from where Danning was standing, their long and sticky wings around the heads of the men. They seemed then to squeeze and push their own bodies into the mouths of the men and down their throats, apparently to suffocate their victims. Many men choked and collapsed on their transports, while others simply tumbled off so that the now unmanned transports careened across the field at crazy speeds, often crashing into other men who were fighting to keep the odd black creatures off their faces.

Meanwhile, the enemy soldiers across the field stood and watched all this calmly. Not one of these bat creatures flew in their direction or attached themselves to any of their faces. Danning did not see any patches of the yellow-green grass on their side of the field either, nor any other strange aberrations of nature. An enemy had come who could manipulate not only the grass beneath their feet but even animals who inhabited subterranean chambers far beneath that.

And if that hadn't been enough, there was of course the lightning. The sky had started mostly clear of clouds, but strange clouds had come, blown by a strange wind, and from those clouds lightning had fallen at regular intervals, generally on any spot where the forces of Tanisaan seemed to be having success. Not only so, but the lightning had fried more than one large transport bringing ranged weapons to men in good position or ammunition to garrow squads who had survived the earlier attacks. The lightning seemed quite strategic, falling wherever the army of Tanisaan was most concentrated and vulnerable or where equipment of some value was seen on the field. Wherever it fell, men and more were fried in an instant, leaving behind only their singed corpses.

All this Danning had seen while trying to command his garrow and do his duty. He had seen, and he had accepted his doom and the doom of his city.

Of course, accepting his doom and doing nothing to avoid it were not the same thing, hence his attempt to get his garrow squad into position. As they reached the top of the Tanisaan walls, he led them steadily but carefully along until he had the position he wanted, a place where he could see most of the field below him at the base of the wall and also the center of the enemy reserve line out beyond, in the middle of the battlefield.

He squatted, as did his squad, so they weren't easily visible to any of the men down below, and he watched over the edge of the wall, looking for one, good, clear target. If he was going to die from some impossible, nature-run-amok attack, he wanted to take something or someone of value with him. Perhaps he could take Meldriic Jaen. That would be something, Danning thought, to be the guy who took down the mighty Meldriic Jaen.

As he was daydreaming about this, though, he saw something that was almost as unusual as the yellow-green grass, the cloud of bats, and the strategic lightning. Out there in the middle of the field, far behind the bulk of the enemy army which had advanced right up to the Tanisaan walls, was a figure who—there was only one way to describe him—glowed with a brilliant, golden glow. For a moment, Danning simply stared at the strange, glowing figure, but then he turned to his men and whispered directions.

They slipped the garrow over the garrow posts that afforded the best angle on the part of the field where the golden man walked. Gil Danning personally selected the largest explosive that they had, a projectile big enough to take out a three-hundred-man transport. It would blow up everything within at least a fifty foot radius, and he would be sure to put it right on the man in gold. He had operated a garrow his entire life, and he would aim and take this shot personally. He loaded the explosive, measured the angle, and pulled back the garrow with help from his second. When he was sure of the shot, he nodded and they released the garrow, watching the explosive fly.

As soon as the garrow shot forward, thrusting the projectile out over the wall in a long, high arc, Danning knew that the shot was perfect, or very nearly perfect. If it didn't hit the golden man, it would hit very near to him, and it would blow him into the sky. At the same time, as soon as the garrow shot forward, a terrible rending sound broke through the mid-afternoon air, and Danning looked in disbelief as the ground between the city and the man in gold opened up and a great, shooting vine flew up into the air.

The vine rose at a terrific speed, and it rose directly between the golden man and the projectile that Danning had just launched. He watched in disbelief as the vine intercepted the projectile, wrapping around it as it bent backward so as to gently catch it without setting it off through impact, and then, after flowing backward further and further with the explosive wrapped tighter and tighter in its grip, the vine lashed forward, hurling the projectile straight toward the city gates.

The projectile that Danning had launched at the man in gold struck the gates of Tanisaan a moment later, exploding on impact, as the gates did not gently intercept and give way before it as the vine had. Danning felt the impact, knew that the gates had been blown to pieces by the weapon he had launched at the golden man, and felt utterly helpless in his rage.

He looked back over the field, and once more was overwhelmed with disbelief at what he saw. The end of the vine was transforming in front of his very eyes. The head of an enormous serpent was breaking through the pulpy vine stem, its red, gleaming eyes peering out of two long thin slits and looking straight at Danning and his crew on the city wall.

He rose and ordered his men to run, but it was already too late. The serpent head was flying toward them in a similarly high, sweeping arc to that of the projectile they had just launched with the garrow at the golden man, and it was gaining speed as it flew their way. As it came, a great gaping mouth, filled with a double row of long jagged teeth, opened wide to greet them.

Danning had tried. Danning had failed. They all had. Tanisaan had fallen, and the golden man was coming.

·   ·   ·

Meldriic Jaen peeled off the last of his clothes and dropped them on the rest. He bent over and picked up all of his garments, both outer and inner, and he crumpled them into as tight a ball as he could. The blood that had soaked them was largely dry, though here and there he felt some parts of the fabric were still slick with it. He tossed the clothes into the large open fireplace where a good strong fire was burning. Clothes like these would not be fit to be worn again, and he liked to burn them personally when a battle or campaign was finished. It marked for him the end of the fighting, at least for a time.

He walked to the washbasin and took up the cloth, washing himself as best he could. There were places where he would really need to scrub to get the bloodstains off, but he did not have time right now. He had already been summoned, and so he focused on his face and arms that would be visible even after putting on a new tunic and trousers. When he had achieved all that a few minutes could do, he dressed and exited into the hallway, where a pair of soldiers were waiting to take him to the Jin Dara.

He followed the guards through the wide hallway. The royal palace of Tanisaan was a large structure, but it wasn't especially ornate. Meldriic thought it communicated power and grandeur more than most such buildings, and far less luxury and softness. He appreciated it for those reasons, but it was odd to see it nearly empty as it was now.

Nearly empty, but not empty. As they walked down the hall, they approached a strange sight that would have disturbed Meldriic more if he hadn't seen its like before. A woman, or what had certainly been a woman, was off to the side of the hall. One leg was still a leg, and it seemed to be convinced it could take a step and kept moving as though to do so. The other leg, though, was no longer a leg, and it had punched down through the stone floor, sending roots in all directions at once.

Likewise, one of her arms had become quite clearly a branch, or something like a branch, but it too had extended out to the side and broken through the near wall, anchoring her there. Her other arm was bent up over her head at an awkward angle, and little shoots were even now appearing out of it, showing tiny buds that Meldriic didn't doubt would soon blossom, though into what exactly he had no idea. Perhaps on the way back he would find out.

The woman's head was largely still unaffected by the transformation, though the long strands of hair that hung down over her face had a distinctly mossy look. Her face was largely hidden by her hair, but as he approached, he could hear her weeping and moaning, and as he passed, the inarticulate groans became words. "Please, sir, can't you help me?"

Meldriic Jaen walked by without a word. It was a harder thing to do than he would have expected. And yet, he knew that the Jin Dara was just getting started here. He had promised terrible things, and terrible things he would do.

Soon, the soldiers had shown Meldriic into the Jin Dara's presence. He was in a large, comfortable room with Devaar and a few other officers from the Najin. When Meldriic entered, the officers and Devaar congratulated him on the successful attack, and then shortly after that the officers left. The Jin Dara, for his part, had stood, watching him as he came in, never moving or speaking until the officers were gone.

"The attack was masterful," the Jin Dara said now, handing him a cup full of wine so Meldriic could join in a toast. "To Meldriic and the Jaens."

"Hear, hear," Devaar echoed, and they each one drank.

"Thank you, sir," Meldriic said when he was finished taking his drink. "Though of course, we both know that it would have been much harder going today without all your help."

"Well," the Jin Dara said with a wry smile, "I try to do my part."

He walked over to a small table and motioned for Meldriic to come and join him. A large wooden box sat in the middle of the table, and when Meldriic took his place beside him, the Jin Dara reached down and opened it. Inside lay several long fragments of Zerura.

"You know what these are?"

"I believe so."

"They are replicas of my third original," the Jin Dara said, and his hand strayed to his head, lightly touching the Zerura that rested there. "You're to take one for yourself, and one for each of your brothers."

Meldriic stared at the golden bars in the box. These weren't just fragments of Zerura, they were replicas of the *cadeen*. They should never have been made, and in a way, they were symbolic of just how much of an abomination the Jin Dara was. And yet, even as part of Meldriic was repelled by what he saw, part of him was drawn to them. He had felt with wonder the joy of wearing Zerura, and the thought of having a third fragment was more than a little appealing. Not to mention, if he had three pieces, he would not be so very far below the Jin Dara in the power he could muster and control. He would be one step closer to feeling able to do what he had come to do.

"It will take some time for what we have done here to reach the ears of the Amhuru," the Jin Dara was saying. "And even when it does, there may well be deliberation and indecision about what to do. Nevertheless, they will come, or at least some of them will come. I am sure of it.

"I want you and your brothers to take these and train. Train yourselves and train my Najin. Be ready to deal with the Amhuru. Then, we will both get what we want. You will get the revenge you have long desired, and I will get the rest of the Cord."

"Yes, I will see to it." Meldriic reached down into the box, selecting five of the slender, golden rods. They seemed to hum and vibrate under his touch, and he couldn't wait to get back to his room to have the fragment sync with his heart and the other fragments, to feel it join with him and know what three fragments felt like.

He was suddenly aware of the Jin Dara's golden eyes staring at him, and he felt a quiet chill. There was no hostility in the look, no hint of suspicion, but there was something else, something that made Meldriic uneasy. He had spent his life in the company of powerful, dangerous men, but none of them had been anything like the Jin Dara, who was power incarnate.

He bowed, took the fragments, and headed out to find his brothers.

24

THE WISE WOMAN

Rika reached up and poured some more corness into the lamp. The strong, bright yellow glow began to emanate from it once more, and Rika had to shade her eyes until they got used to the dazzling brilliance of the light. She grumbled to herself again and felt homesick for the softer bluish hues of the lights she and the other Academy scientists had crafted for use back in Barra-Dohn.

She wondered what exactly it was that made this lamp—and most of the other lights she had observed so far in Tanisaan—glow with this ridiculously overdone, bright yellow light? She doubted it was the corness, though she couldn't say what differences substituting something like the sage oil of Barra-Dohn might have made. It probably had more to do with the particular alloy of the meridium core, how it was mixed, or even the material it was encased in inside the lamp. Whatever it was, she wasn't a fan, though admittedly, once it had faded a bit from its obnoxiously bright starting point, the yellow light wasn't all that bad.

Thinking of the lights from home made Rika remember the wall lights they had developed not long before the Jin Dara came. She found herself wishing she had some of those here. They were no doubt all destroyed in the Jin Dara's attack, or even in the Academy collapse right before that. Unfortunately, she hadn't spent much time on that project, so she wasn't sure she could replicate them, or at least not right away. Still, she thought that might be a good project to have her new team work on, since she hadn't seen anything like it in her travels and she would like to present the Jin Dara with something he'd never seen before—even if it was only a hand-activated wall light.

Of course, to have her new team working on it, she would need to finish selecting her new team. She shuffled through the pages of notes she had taken over the last four days. Most of the candidates had been woefully inadequate, desperate people who had somehow heard about the woman that had come with the golden man and was looking for scientists and re-searchers. And these desperate people, knowing what was happening to the citizens of Tanisaan right in the middle of their streets and all around them, stopped any soldier they could find and made the case that they were just the person she needed for her project, whatever it might be.

Fortunately, Rika had gotten some help from among the Jin Dara's people, specifically some logistically-minded officers who had a good nose for personnel. They had been put to work screening candidates, so a large number of those who had absolutely nothing to offer had been turned away before they even reached her. Even so, many of those who made it through this initial screening had second or third rate minds at most, whatever their credentials, and Rika would accept only the best. She'd rather her team be small than have any weak links.

As Rika looked through her sheets of notes, she saw a hastily scrib-bled note she'd made for herself the previous morning. It said, "wise woman—north." She set the paper down and thought about the woman with short grey hair she had been interviewing when she jotted down that note. The woman, much older than Rika, perhaps in her mid- to late-fifties, had been quite shifty—literally she shifted back and forth in her seat con-stantly. She was probably aware that she'd been lucky to get through the screening and meet with Rika at all. At any rate, she'd kept trying to tell Rika that if it was true knowledge Rika wanted, she had to go see the wise woman who lived north of Tanisaan, at the base of the mountain that lay just a few hours away.

This wise woman, or so the nervous candidate had insisted, knew just about everything. She had traveled all over the Northlands, had even lived among the 'Graymir'—the shifty woman had whispered this part of her story to Rika as though sharing a great secret, even though Rika didn't have the slightest idea what it might mean—and if Rika wanted an introduction to the wise woman, the woman with the short grey hair kept assuring her that she would be only too happy to take her there and give her one.

Rika stretched, yawned and rose from her desk. She had done all she was going to do here for now. She had been told that the Jin Dara wanted an update, and now she intended to go and give him one. And yet, even as she headed out to the transport to get a ride to where the Jin Dara was doing his work, she found her mind drifting back to the things this woman had been whispering about the 'wise woman.' They were the kinds of things she would have dismissed out of hand in her youth. Superstitious things about secret knowledge and insights, hidden wisdom and all that—but now that she was older and had seen some of the things she had seen, she didn't dismiss anything too quickly.

The wise woman was probably some glorified purveyor of herbs, home remedies and folklore, but it might be worth a visit just to see if there might be something to it. After all, if there was such a woman and she did have some special insight or knowledge that would help Rika and by extension the Jin Dara, she would risk wasting a day to go see her. In fact, she would be willing to risk a great deal more than that.

The soldier driving the transport waited for her, and once Rika had adjusted her *swaani*, she indicated she was ready to go. He took off, flying down the wide main street of Tanisaan and, just a moment later, out of its open gates. The Jin Dara had left his 'decorations' periodically along the roads and elsewhere, so occasionally the soldier had to zig-zag around them, which created the feeling for Rika of careening wildly even if the maneuvers were precise and perfectly executed.

They were almost an hour out of Tanisaan when the transport finally came upon the Jin Dara and his little entourage of soldiers. Rika doubted he needed protecting, doubted there was much he couldn't do to save himself from just about any kind of attack, but she understood the retinue all the same. It made the soldiers feel better—and their commanders—for the Jin Dara not to be out somewhere like this alone. And the Jin Dara, for his part, humored them. Or maybe it was more than that. Back in Krayton, she had gathered that the Jin Dara had had some kind of near miss when hunting one of the Amhuru who possessed an original fragment. She wondered if that memory lingered with him.

The transport pulled over and Rika hopped out. She walked toward the Jin Dara, marveling at his work. He was sitting, as he often did when he worked, and in front of him a man and woman stood on their hands, their bodies pushed up as high off the ground as their hands could push. And while their bodies rose straight off the ground, their legs were arched gently backward so that their feet touched at the top of the arch.

Of course, as with all of the Jin Dara's creations, the hands had become something quite more than hands, sinking into the soil with deep, anchoring roots. The arms were stiff and barky, though not quite wood. Their legs were likewise stiff, now that they were bent in the position the Jin Dara wanted them preserved in, and though she couldn't see any means by which they were attached, Rika felt sure something had connected the feet to one another so that they would not easily be disconnected again.

What made this particular piece, though, was the small child dangling upside down from the arch. The child's legs beneath the knees were both curved unnaturally, like long, wooden hooks, and these hooks fit just perfectly over the conjoined legs of the adults. From the knees up the child still looked rather like a child, though from the angle of the outstretched arms and hands, Rika suspected those would never move again. The child had a shock of red hair that was hanging in what seemed a fairly natural way from her head, but as the face of the girl was pointing the other direction, Rika couldn't see if she was alert or aware of what was going on.

As Rika watched, the child convulsed and shook, and out of both hands grew a vine, green and curly, which immediately started to wind back up the two outstretched arms. The vines grew to about the armpit, where they wrapped one final time around the arms and then sprouted delicate white flowers.

Nothing new happened for the next few minutes, and then a small gust of wind blew along the road. The girl started rocking back and forth like a creaky wooden sign hanging from a pole outside an inn, but the child's hook-legs never slipped off the adult legs from which she dangled. Soon the wind died down. Rika felt strangely sure the Jin Dara had called the wind just to see if the little girl would be blown off the arch he'd made for her.

The Jin Dara rose a moment later and brushed the dirt from his pants as he stretched and looked around. Rika was flattered to see that once he noticed her, he stopped his non-chalant perusal of the world around him and came straight to her. It made her feel important, and she wondered, not for the first time, if he possibly might desire her. She tried not to let that idea get too far. After all, it made sense that he would come to talk to her since he had asked her to come and report.

"You like my work?" the Jin Dara asked as he stopped before her, indicating the girl dangling from the upside-down-people arch.

"I wouldn't want it in my living room," Rika said, "but I understand its purpose and approve."

"O come now," the Jin Dara said, turning to admire his handiwork. "Don't I deserve a more enthusiastic review than that? For that little girl and her parents, I've literally turned their lives upside down."

The Jin Dara seemed very amused with his joke, and Rika felt constrained to smile at it too, even if she didn't find it especially funny. It wasn't that she felt much, if anything, for the upside-down people or their daughter—she neither knew who they were nor cared—but she'd never been a fan of humor that involved puns.

Fortunately, the Jin Dara seemed eager to move on to business, saying as he turned back around, "How does your search go?"

"Good," Rika answered. "My team won't be large, at least not at first, but it will be very good."

"Excellent. You've found some worthy candidates, then?"

"Yes," Rika said. "There are a handful who are top notch, excellent minds with extensive backgrounds. And then, there's another handful who lack the experience but have the potential. I think collectively, we will be able to do valuable work."

"Glad to hear it," the Jin Dara said. "I've told Devaar to keep his eye out for spaces that might work for you. So, check with him when you get back to Tanisaan, and when you're ready, have him show you what he's come up with."

"Happily," Rika said. She hadn't yet given thought to where she would work with her team, and given all the Jin Dara had on his plate, she was impressed that he had.

"Is there anything else you need to report?" he asked.

"Not really," Rika said, but she paused.

"But?"

"But there is one thing," Rika started, feeling a little foolish for bringing this up. "One woman, not a great candidate herself, mentioned something about a 'wise woman' living north of the city, at the base of the mountain a few hours away. And, well, it's probably nothing, but she had some interesting things to say about her. I'd like to go meet her, if I might."

"Of course," the Jin Dara said. "As you see fit. Take a few of my soldiers along, as an escort, and use a quick transport so it doesn't take all day."

"Thank you," Rika said, almost surprised that the Jin Dara had accepted her odd request and approved it so readily. "I look forward to getting my research under way, my lord."

"As do I," the Jin Dara said. Then he turned and walked back toward his entourage. Rika watched him for a moment, then returned to her transport and headed back to Tanisaan.

. . .

The hut of the wise woman was unimpressive from the outside, to say the least. It was small, and Rika suspected much of the wood it was made from was rotting. The thatched roof looked wholly inadequate to keep rain or any other weather elements out. But it was the woman and not the house that Rika had come to see, so she walked briskly to the door and knocked.

It had taken her five days to put this expedition together, much to her surprise. As it turned out, finding the grey-haired woman who had put herself forward for Rika's research team had proved beyond Rika's ability. No one seemed to have written down her name, and inquiries at all the places that might have some knowledge of her had yielded nothing. Rika had quietly concluded after three days of searching Tanisaan for her that she must have been selected for one of the Jin Dara's decorations and that no one would ever see her again—at least, not as she had been.

So, Rika had been forced to seek for the whereabouts of the wise woman in other ways, and concrete information about either her or her location had been surprisingly difficult to come by. Oddly, this difficulty hadn't diminished her interest in the trip out here at all. Quite the opposite, her anticipation of what she might find once she did get here had grown with each passing day, so that she was now enormously curious and hoped it hadn't all been a complete waste of time.

The wizened creature who opened the door in response to Rika's knocking must have been the ugliest person she had ever seen. Small, bent with the weight of far more years than Rika could imagine, she had thin wisps of white hair that covered her head—but barely. The pink outline of the skull showed through the scant hair clearly, and Rika almost shuddered, the sight of her was so unpleasant.

The wise woman, having opened the door, peered up at Rika with shockingly bright eyes. They were a pale, luminescent blue and were covered with a white, milky film that added to the strangeness of their appearance. "Well, you took your time, didn't you?"

Rika was taken aback. Both the words and the familiar manner surprised her. "I beg your pardon?"

"Tanisaan fell almost a month ago," the wise woman said, shuffling away from the door into the shadowy interior of her house, which was one reasonable-sized open room.

A lone chair sat in front of a large, open fireplace, and the wise woman sat down in it. She did not motion to Rika to follow or suggest anything further about what Rika should do now, so Rika closed the door and walked over until she stood beside the fireplace and could see the wise woman's face, illuminated as it was by the light of the fire.

"I have heard that you are wise," Rika said. "That you have answers."

"I have seen more than a hundred winters," the wise woman said. "Anyone who lives this long ought to be wise and have answers. Is there something in particular that you want to know?"

"Sa, there is."

"You should say 'yes' and not 'sa,' since you are not a Northlander," the wise woman said. "And pull down that *swaani* so I can see your face clearly."

Rika reached up and pulled down the *swaani* so that it hung about her neck. She felt oddly exposed before the wise woman, but she stood silently, letting the old woman look her over. "Well," the wise woman said after she had done so. "What is it you wish to know?"

"I have been given an important charge," Rika said. "By the man who conquered Tanisaan. He is a great man, and I do not want to disappoint him."

"Great men come and go," the wise woman said. "It is the way of things."

"Perhaps," Rika said. "But this man is very great. He possesses three original fragments of the Golden Cord, and he means to take them all."

"Does he now?" the wise woman said, but she was not looking at Rika. She had turned away from her and was staring into the fire. "Why would he want to do that?"

"Perhaps to have unimaginable power?" Rika said, wondering if the wise woman was joking, or testing her for some reason. "To be able to rule the world?"

The wise woman laughed. "You speak as though having unimaginable power and ruling the world are things to be desired."

"Are they not?"

"And if he succeeds," the wise woman said, as though Rika had not responded to her. "What will there be left to desire, I wonder?"

"I'm sure he'll think of something," Rika said, regarding the woman's question as completely missing the point.

"Perhaps he will," the wise woman said, "but I can see you are not interested in my doubts. What is this charge that you have been given?"

"I am researching the properties of Zerura," Rika said, standing tall. "Exploring its potential uses and applications."

"You think you can plumb the depths of Zerura, the living matter that generates the Arua field and governs the ecological systems of the world?"

"Why not?" Rika said. "I already have experience working with a team on this very matter in a great Southland city. We made good use of what we learned. Why would it be unreasonable to think we can learn more?"

"We can always learn more, my dear," the wise woman said. "But what is the point of learning more when we don't learn the lessons we should have learned the first time?"

"I don't understand what you're saying."

"How did it work out the first time?" the wise woman replied. "This research of yours in this great Southland city? How did it go?"

"We developed many things," Rika said. "Including many powerful weapons."

"So the city is prospering?"

"The city doesn't exist anymore," Rika said quietly, but then hastened to add. "But that is because my current master destroyed it."

"And how do you know he was not the pawn of a higher power?"

"Higher power?" Rika scoffed. "What higher power?"

"There are more than one," the wise woman said, and now she looked full upon Rika, and her face showed a strange intensity in the firelight. "Kalos and Nekron are the greatest of them, but you cannot serve them both. You must make your choice."

"Kalos and Nekron?" Rika said. Of Nekron, she had never heard anything, and of Kalos, she had heard too much. Convinced now that she had wasted her time in coming here, she said, "Bedtime stories for children."

"I think not," the wise woman said. She rose from her chair and shuffled to the small pile of wood beside the fireplace, took a small log and gently tossed it into the fire.

"I have devoted my life to Nekron," she continued as she returned to her seat. "And I can assure you, he is closer than you think."

"I'm sorry," Rika said, turning to leave. "I have wasted your time."

"You are no longer interested in information about the nature of Zerura?"

Rika hesitated, halfway to the door. "Information, yes, but not jibberish, philosophy, or myths."

Rika continued to the door and had put her hand on the handle to open it and leave before it registered with her what the wise woman had just whispered. Her hand dropped from the handle and she turned to look at the wise woman, who had her back to Rika and was still staring into the fire. "What did you say?"

"I said, did anyone on your team try ingesting Zerura?"

Rika's mind raced. The first image that came to her was of picking up one of the bars of Zerura Eirmon had provided for the Academy and trying to take a big bite of it. It would have been painful, for sure, but then she thought of the powdery dust that sometimes lay like a film in the workshop where they cut and manipulated the Zerura for mixing with meridium and other things. That dust could be mixed in water or some other drink and ingested, easily.

And what would Zerura do inside you? In your very bloodstream? Would it even do anything? She understood from her time among the Amhuru that their command of the Arua field was very different when they were over water, as opposed to their control on land. So would Zerura in blood be mediated differently than Zerura on the skin? Or was that a silly analogy? If Zerura worn on the skin turned your eyes and hair gold—and possibly more, thinking about the Jin Dara—what would ingesting Zerura do to you?

Rika was suddenly aware that she had been oblivious to all else except her questions and musings and had walked slowly forward toward the fire, where she now stood, feeling its warmth. Her back was to the wise woman, though, and she didn't like that thought. She turned, and as she had suspected, those bright blue, luminescent eyes were staring at her.

"Why did you ask me that?"

"Far from here, there is a wild place that is home to a wild people, the Graymir."

"The Graymir," Rika echoed, almost as though in a trance, thinking of the grey-haired woman who had mentioned that word when she told her of the wise woman.

"They also serve Nekron, and I lived among them for a time," the wise woman said. "They have long experimented with ingesting Zerura, and they have done remarkable things this way. They have broken down the barrier between human and animal, molding and remaking themselves, as well as molding and remaking many of the living things in the world around them to suit their own purposes."

"By ingesting Zerura?"

"Yes, and by practicing some rituals of Nekron, which you could also learn if you were so inclined."

"I," Rika started, and she faltered. She suddenly felt a little flushed by the fire, and at the same time knew it was time to go. "I may wish to speak with you about this further at some point, but I need to go now."

The wise woman did not speak. She merely sat in her chair and watched Rika step away from the fire and pull up her *swaani* to prepare for going outside. "I thank you for your hospitality and may, perhaps, be back. If you ever wish to see me, ask for Rika Elandras when you get to Tanisaan."

Rika walked quickly to the door, almost threw it open, and stepped outside into the fresh air with a gasp. She gathered herself, closing the door more carefully than she had opened it, but she felt weak and almost overcome. If this were true, and there was a people out there who had manipulated the Arua field by ingesting Zerura, just as there was a people who had done so by wearing it, what might be accomplished if these two approaches were combined by the Jin Dara and his Najin?

The thought was intoxicating, and if there was anything to it, anything at all, she would give the Jin Dara a lot more than hand-activated lights.

25

THE PUPPETEER

Rika walked alone along the streets of Tanisaan. The lights that illuminated the streets had the same yellowish tint as the lamp on her desk, but fortunately she had never noticed the same overpowering brightness in these streetlights as what glowed from her lamp whenever she added corness. These lights, unlike those in Barra-Dohn, were dependent on people adding corness each night in order to work, so that couldn't account for the difference from her desklamp. Maybe the lamplighters simply filled them early enough each day that the initial brilliance of the lights was muted by the failing daylight.

Rika didn't know, and her attention now was bent toward more important things, namely her time with the wise woman and the striking suggestion she had heard there about experimenting with ingesting Zerura. It was certainly intriguing on many levels, but Rika wasn't sure what to make of it, given that the wise woman had also spoken with obvious sincerity about Kalos and this Nekron of hers—as though she believed both were real beings. Could she trust anything this woman might say? Did her belief in Kalos and Nekron undermine her credibility so severely that everything she said should be ignored?

Her whole life Rika had ridiculed the idea of a god, an invisible superbeing with incredible power. She didn't find the idea any more plausible now, but she understood better where it might have come from. Zerura, and to a lesser degree meridium, were powerful things and could be combined with the Arua field to work seeming wonders. That some would see or experience these things and turn to the mystical to explain it was understandable. So, she could see where the notion of Kalos had come from, but she just didn't understand why it persisted in an age where science had helped push back the boundaries of mystery so far and to explain the previously unexplainable.

As for Nekron, Rika was much more hazy about exactly who he was supposed to be. She had never heard that name, but she did have some vague recollections of a being that Kalos had made and who had turned against his maker. She didn't know for sure if that was the way the story had gone, or even if the being in the story had been this Nekron. Either way, it was a ridiculous story that only served to further illustrate the absurdity of the whole idea. If Kalos really did exist and if he had really made this other being, why would the lesser creation turn against his all-powerful master? That didn't make any sense to Rika, but then again, not much in the myths about Kalos did.

But, as Rika considered her current situation, she didn't think she had to dismiss everything the wise woman said just because she wasn't so wise in her superstitious beliefs. She might well have traveled the Northlands and might well have lived among these Graymir, and if they somehow had a supply of Zerura—which was itself a mystery, now that Rika thought about it—then perhaps she really had observed what they had done through ingesting it.

There really were no doubts in her mind. It would have to be tried. She would have to convince the Jin Dara of the absolute necessity of doing this, and more than that, that it was the highest priority. If he balked at it or hesitated to supply the Zerura necessary for any reason, she would have to persuade him. The possibilities were too great, too exciting, not to undertake with zeal this avenue of research.

Of course, ingesting Zerura would constitute, essentially, experiments on people, not just objects. There would be an inherent danger for anyone who tried it. She had no idea what amounts of Zerura needed to be ingested to have an affect, knew nothing about whether Zerura in large quantities or small could be harmful to the person ingesting it. What's more, she had no idea if it mattered if the person ingesting the Zerura also wore it. There were, in fact, many unknowns. She'd need subjects who wore fragments and subjects who didn't. She'd need lots of controls to try to isolate as quickly as possible the ideal quantity to take and how frequently.

Rika felt a chill, because she knew what else she was going to ask the Jin Dara—she had to be one of those who participated in the experiment. She had known this since she'd left the wise woman's house. All the time she'd spent with the Amhuru, and she'd never worn Zerura. (She tried not to think about her failed attempt to take Tchinchura's fragment off him after passing through the Madri.) And now, traveling with the Najin who wore multiple fragments, she was once more surrounded with men who were literally clothed in power. She had always wanted some for herself, and it had always been close by but beyond her grasp. Now, though, there appeared to be a way that she too could lay hold of it.

A gust of wind blew down the street, and Rika paused in her aimless wandering to draw her cloak tighter. By day or by night, these streets were usually pretty empty. Early on, more Najin had been in the city, since many residents of the city had taken to hiding when it became known what the Jin Dara was doing with them. By now, though, most if not all of those had been located after days and days of going from building to building and searching, so now most of the Najin slept in their tents out by the traing grounds. Some lived in the city and could be seen out at night, but it was not uncommon for Rika to find herself out walking essentially alone, and she quite enjoyed it.

There was a quiet peacefulness to the city at night. She'd always loved both the darkness of nighttime and being able to go for solitary walks, and so now, after all the years of being confined onboard a ship, she treasured her freedom to move about at night. But even so, a sudden chill that had nothing to do with the gust of wind that had just passed by swept over her, snapping her out of the reverie that she had been lost in. A misty fogginess lay low on the street so that her feet were almost lost in it. As she looked around, she realized she was not alone. A solitary figure watched her from the mouth of the alley just ahead of her.

She started walking again, reassuring herself it was just one of the Jin Dara's men, but as she drew closer and prepared to bid him good evening, she felt her pulse quicken. The sneer on the old man's face was unmistakable. "But," Rika said, dumbfounded. "You can't be here."

"That again," the old man snorted in disdain. "Tell me we're not going to rehash the same old ground."

"You're not Gamalian," Rika said, pointing at him demonstratively. "I don't know who or what you are, but you aren't him. The Jin Dara's army didn't take someone in from Eirmon's palace. You didn't cross the Madri with them or travel with them to Krayton. I don't know how you got there or how you knew who I am—or how you even look like him, for that matter—but you're not him."

"I may not have told you the whole truth, before," the old man said. "But if I'm not Gamalian, you have yourself a little predicament. That I can do what I do and look how I look doesn't seem to fit in any of your categories, Rika, now does it?"

"What are you talking about?"

"You know what I'm talking about," the old man said. "I'm proof of a world you've never wanted to believe in, but it is time to accept it. I have a plan for you, a great plan, but you need to open your eyes."

Rika took a step back. "I don't have time for this or for you. I have things I need to attend to."

She tried to turn and go, when the old man who looked both like and unlike Gamalian suddenly pounced—there was no other word for it. He crossed the gap between them in an instant, and his hand shot out with lightning quick speed, grabbing her throat. The grip that closed upon her neck was like iron, and he lifted her from the ground with ease. She hung in the air, choking, gasping for air, wondering how someone who looked so frail could be so strong.

"Let's get something clear, Rika," the old man said, and his eyes burned as they stared into hers. "I am not the puppet. I am the puppeteer, and soon, the whole world will dance to my strings."

He set her down and relaxed his grip. She gasped, reaching up to massage her sore neck even as she eagerly sucked in the air that had been denied her momentarily. She looked up at him, feeling a deep, unsettling fear like nothing she had ever felt before. The old man smiled, and from just a few feet away, she could see his teeth were half-rotten and black, and she felt revolted.

He stepped closer, and she smelled foulness when he opened his mouth to speak. "You must go to him with what you learned today."

Rika stepped backwards, shaking her head in disbelief. How did he know? He couldn't know. The old man's strong hand shot out once more and grabbed her by the wrist as he pulled her toward him. "It is not only a means to help him to greatness, but it is your best chance to secure his interest and achieve your goal of becoming his paramour—a goal I very much want you to be successful in achieving."

"Who are you?" Rika said, but her words came out barely loud enough to be a whisper. "What are you?"

The old man smiled, and Rika noticed that the misty fog that had been lying about her legs was now rising, swirling all around her. She felt woozy and faint, and the next thing she knew, she was falling.

.   .   .

The Jin Dara looked down at Rika's unconscious form. The soldier that had brought her in had laid her on a couch, and now he was standing nearby while the Jin Dara tried to decide if he should rouse her or not.

"She was just passed out on the ground, you say?"

"Yes," the soldier said. "There was so much fog, we—I was with some friends, you see—we didn't see her until we were right on top of her, almost tripped over her in fact."

"Fog?" the Jin Dara said. "I hadn't noticed any fog tonight."

"Yes," the soldier said. "It was odd. We hadn't noticed any either, until we were on the street where we found her. It must have just started to roll in."

The Jin Dara nodded, looking back down at Rika. "You may go," he said, and then added. "On your way out, tell the guard at the door to summon Devaar."

As the Jin Dara waited for Devaar, he left Rika and walked to the fireplace. The girl was breathing and didn't seem to have suffered any physical harm, whatever had happened. He was inclined to let her sleep, although he wanted to check with Devaar to see what he thought. He stood before the fire, staring into the flames, until at last the knock announcing Devaar's presence echoed from his door.

It did not take long to update Devaar on what had transpired, or for Devaar to concur with the Jin Dara's instinct to let the girl be, at least for the time being. If it got too much later, they'd try to rouse her so that she could be escorted back to her own rooms.

"As long as you're here," the Jin Dara said. "Perhaps you could tell me how it is going, rounding up more people for my work."

"All the houses and farms within a day of Tanisaan are completely deserted," Devaar said. "Either we've already taken the people who lived there or they have fled. We have moved on to the smaller towns that lie farther out, and we are moving systematically through them, but we are finding that, even there, word of your experiments has gone before us and most have moved on."

"Spread the nets as far as you need to," the Jin Dara said. "At the rate that I'm going, I'll have used up all the residents of Tanisaan that we currently have under lock and key in a week or so, and I want to decorate every road that leads to Tanisaan, every town along that road, every junction and crossroad for as far as we possibly can. I will cover the land with these displays of my power and my will to use it, and word of what I have done and am doing will spread."

"It is certainly spreading," Devaar said, "there is no doubt about that. Spreading so fast that your men are hard pressed keeping up with it."

The Jin Dara nodded. "It was inevitable that the day would come when we'd have to go farther out on raids to take people and bring them back for the work to continue. Just be sure to keep the flow coming steadily in."

"The men know what is required of them," Devaar said, "and they are working tirelessly. The advance teams go farther and farther each time."

"Good," the Jin Dara started, but he didn't finish his thought, for a groan from the girl behind him on the couch drew his attention back to her. "It looks like the sleeper is finally awake."

Rika was indeed awake. She sat up and rubbed the sleep from her eyes. Her gaze moved from the Jin Dara to Devaar and back with puzzlement, but before she could ask any questions, the Jin Dara provided the answer. "You were found in the street, about an hour ago. You had collapsed there."

"Yes," Rika said. She sounded groggy. "I remember falling."

"Are you feeling ill?" Devaar asked. "Would you like us to send for some food, perhaps?"

"No thank you," Rika said. "I'm all right. I don't know why I fainted. The fog was rising, and there was the strange man from Krayton again, and—"

"Strange man? Krayton?" the Jin Dara asked. "What do you mean?"

Rika stole a furtive glance at Devaar, and the Jin Dara saw that this was something they had discussed before. "Devaar? Do you know something about this?"

"Yes," Devaar said. "Shortly after she came to you in Krayton the first time, Rika had an encounter, I guess you would call it, with an old man claiming to be someone she believed had died in the fall of Barra-Dohn. A man who claimed to have been rescued by us and to have accompanied us ever since."

"What?" the Jin Dara said. "Why have I not heard anything about this?"

"When the man never appeared again," Devaar said, "it seemed like some kind of mistake, not the kind of thing to bother you with, given all that was going on."

"And you say you've seen him again? Here?" the Jin Dara asked, walking over so that he stood right in front of Rika.

She nodded. "It isn't him, though. It can't be. But he knows things, things he shouldn't be able to know."

The Jin Dara frowned. What she was saying didn't make sense. Tani-saan had been scoured about as thoroughly as any city this size could be, and any and all people who weren't with his own forces had been rounded up. He didn't see how anyone could be out there loose, and certainly not an old man who claimed to have followed him or her from Barra-Dohn.

"Devaar, any thoughts on who this mystery man could be?"

"No idea," Devaar said, shaking his head. "But perhaps, in the light of his reappearance, an escort should be provided for Rika wherever she goes?"

"No," Rika said, shaking her head. "That's not necessary."

"It's a good idea," the Jin Dara said. "I have high hopes for your work and don't want to endanger it."

She nodded, but the Jin Dara could tell that something in what he had said had prompted a thought in her mind, something entirely different than this mystery man. "What is it?" he asked.

"Well, speaking of my work," Rika said, and he saw that she was looking for the right words.

"It's late, Rika," the Jin Dara said. "Just say it."

"I went to see the wise woman," she said after his prompt. "She suggested we try experiments that involve ingesting Zerura."

"Ingesting it?" the Jin Dara wondered, but it was more of a statement than a question. He smiled. "Why have I never thought of that before?"

"I never thought of it either," Rika said, showing her own excitement at the idea now that he had shown his. "She said a people far from here, called the Graymir, have done this."

"Graymir," the Jin Dara said, echoing her. "We've heard tales of them before, haven't we, Devaar?"

"Yes," he said, nodding, "we have."

"But nothing about ingesting Zerura," the Jin Dara found his mind wanting to follow many different threads at once. "We'll have to go and visit these Graymir once we've dealt with the Amhuru, I think."

"Yes, we could—"

"But in the meantime," the Jin Dara continued, cutting Devaar off. "We will need to experiment with this on our own, see what we can learn, see what we can use. What do we need to get started?"

"Well," Rika said. "I only just learned of this possibility. I think we'll need to consider carefully whom we select and how we do it. We should have some who are currently wearing Zerura, and some who aren't. We'll need to play around with how much they take, and how often, and of course, we'll need to monitor all of this carefully."

"Of course."

"And," Rika added, immediately, "I can't guarantee that ingesting Zerura won't harm any or all of those who participate. This is completely uncharted territory. There will be risks."

"Everything I have achieved," the Jin Dara said, "has come with risks. I have no problem with that."

"Good, I'm—"

"Let me take some time to consider what you've said. I will think about some candidates for the research, and I will get back to you, soon. I don't want to wait too long to get it started."

"That's great," Rika said. "I will have my team start working on some other things, and I will start working on a possible protocol to use—but I will of course wait to hear from you before I start doing anything with this."

The Jin Dara nodded. As he looked at Rika and noticed how she was looking at him, he knew once more that there was something else. "Will you never learn to speak when you have something to say?"

"I ..." she said, but hesitated before going on. "I would like to participate in this experiment myself—be one of the subjects."

He looked hard at her. "You said yourself that there are risks."

"There are," she said. "But, as you said, great things are achieved only with risk."

"True," he said, and then he nodded. "I will not deny you a place in this study, if you so desire it. It may be easier for you to guide the experiments if you are a part of them."

"This is true," Rika said.

"But," the Jin Dara said. "I don't want you to be first. We'll find some others to take the first few doses, make sure this isn't a trap, a lie spread with the intent of doing harm to myself or those close to me."

"Fair enough," Rika said. "I can do that."

"And who knows," the Jin Dara said. "Depending on what you find, I might soon join the study myself."

"My Lord," Devaar started, but the Jin Dara merely held up his hand and the man fell silent.

"I will take no needless risks," the Jin Dara said. "But if ingesting Zerura proves effective, I will try it. I suspect that I will know quickly if it is helping or harming, and I doubt that taking only a little bit could harm me very much."

He looked at Rika, who was gazing up at him with something very much like adoration. On impulse, he reached down with his hand curled and lightly caressed her cheek with the outside of his fingers. Her eyes fluttered shut and a look of sheer ecstasy passed over her normally impassive face.

When he removed his hands, her eyes opened again, and the look of adoration wasn't gone exactly, but a deeper, more passionate look of desire had superseded it. He could almost feel the heat radiating from her eyes as she looked at him.

"Do you feel able to make your way back to you rooms?" he asked a moment later, breaking the silence.

"Yes," she said, rising, and he was impressed with her self-possession to transition so readily from their intimate moment to dismissal. "I am."

"Good," he said. "But you will, of course, allow two of my men to escort you."

"As you wish," she said, and she turned to go. Devaar saw her out, giving instructions to the guards at the door to secure the escort.

When he returned, the Jin Dara said, "Devaar, I think you may have been right about her."

"Oh?" Devaar said.

"Perhaps I have been alone too long."

26

GOODBYE, MY LOVE

Kaden adjusted Kiki on his shoulders, where she sat, babbling away, happily chatting about whatever came into her pretty little head. Ordinarily, Kaden enjoyed nothing more than to listen to this babble, which was more like music to his heart than babble anyway. Today, though, he was struggling to focus on what his daughter was saying.

Nara had not been well the past few days, and though she had downplayed it as nothing, she looked pale and gaunt. He couldn't remember ever, in all the years he'd known her, seeing her like this. He was growing worried. He couldn't shake the feeling this was serious, despite her protests to the contrary.

Fortunately, Amintuu has assured them that today would be the day. They would finally arrive at the location chosen by Telsiin five years ago—when Kaden and his companions had crossed the Madri—to be the site where the Amhuru gathered if the Jin Dara had not been dealt with.

The Jin Dara had not been dealt with. In fact, Kaden had begun to wonder if the Jin Dara ever would be. The problem he posed seemed intractable. And yet, Kaden did not speak his fears out loud. He did not want Nara or Kiki to hear his despair, and so he tried to be optimistic for their sakes.

Around Deslo, he could be a little more free with his fears, but even with him he had to be careful. Deslo was eighteen now, and very much a man, but still Kaden had to remind himself that, for better or for worse, he had a lot of power to shape how Deslo saw things. Deslo had grown harder, which was perhaps inevitable, but there was such a thing as becoming too hard—even in a world as dangerously close to the abyss as this one.

"Kiki," Kaden interrupted. "I'm going to set you down now."

"Awww, Yadi," Kiki complained.

"I'm sorry, darling," Kaden said, lifting her up over his head and setting her gently down. "You're getting so big. I just can'na carry you for as long as I used to. Besides, you need to stretch your legs and walk a while."

Kiki was downcast, but she nodded. "Can I go catch up to Delo and Shaline and Trabor and walk with them?"

"Sa," Kaden said. "Just be sure your brother doesn't get so far ahead that Noni and Yadi can'na see you."

Kiki barely hesitated long enough to nod her acceptance of these terms before she dashed off down the winding path to catch up to Deslo and the others who were far below them in the descent into the valley. Kaden watched her go for a moment, then turned to see if Nara needed a hand.

Nara was coming slowly behind, her hand on her hip as though she was winded. Kaden extended her a hand and she took it gladly, giving him a wan smile. They proceeded down the winding path, through the smattering of large trees, and every so often Kaden would pause to point out a large rock or root to make sure Nara stepped over it.

"What would I do without you," she said, again smiling, just after Kaden had pointed out another possible impediment to her.

"Fall flat on your face," Kaden answered, giving her hand a squeeze.

She squeezed his hand too, and the gentle pressure of her delicate fingers brought tears to the corners of his eyes. That there had ever been a day when he had not treasured the feel of these fingers and the delight of this hand was shameful, but he did not focus on the shame. Instead, he considered the surprising mercy of the collapse of Barra-Dohn.

What if the Amhuru had never come? If the Jin Dara had never come? What if Kaden's life had continued along the trajectory it had been on, and then everything collapsed around him?

He would have been a King, ruler of an empire that spanned a continent. He would also have been hated and reviled by most of the people he ruled, and he would have been miserable. And how could he know of this? Because he had been miserable most of his life up to that point, and he wasn't sure why it would have changed without the radical shake-up that had come to him.

So, if he had lost a throne and an empire and a life of relative easy and luxury, so be it. He had found purpose and love, and he would not exchange them now for all the thrones in the world.

They rounded a corner in the path, and there far below he saw Deslo, holding Kiki's hand, waiting with Shaline and Trabor. Once he and Nara were clearly within view, they started forward again. Kaden smiled to think of Kiki loudly reminding her big brother, her beloved 'Delo' that Yadi didn't want them out of sight.

"I wish I knew what was going on there."

"Where?" Kaden said, absently.

"With Deslo and Shaline," Nara said, as though this should have been obvious.

"Ah."

"I thought at first that her return might help," Nara said. "You know, with Deslo's sadness. But I'm not sure it has."

"Sa," Kaden agreed. "They spend a lot of time together, but it doesn't feel entirely natural, does it."

"Na, not like when we were all together before."

"They were so much younger then, though, weren't they?"

"Sa, they were," Nara said. "But that isn't it, and we know it. It's Deslo that's changed, not Shaline."

"Olli," Kaden said as they walked along together, carefully descending an especially steep portion of the path.

"Olli," Nara said, agreeing. "It's just so hard for him. In anything like a normal situation, Deslo would be able to leave, to go somewhere and get away from her. But there's no escaping. She married Maarta what, eighteen months ago? More?"

"Something like that."

"He can't let it go. She's always so close."

"Sa, it's a tough situation to be in," Kaden said. "Any ideas about what we should do?"

Nara shook her head. "I wish I knew."

They rounded another bend, and up ahead the path was clear of the trees that were scattered on the landscape, so that suddenly the view of the valley below became much clearer. Kaden drew his breath. The green valley floor was dotted with brilliant flecks of blue, and from this vantage point it was beautiful to behold.

"It's so lovely," he said, turning toward Nara. "Don't you—"

As he turned, Nara's hand suddenly let go of his. He saw her eyes roll back in her head, and she started to fall. He reached out for her but couldn't grab her in time. She collapsed beside the path on some loose rocks and started to slide downhill. He moved in front of her and arrested her downward motion, but he could see that she was clearly unconscious.

"Nara! Nara!" he called as he dropped to his knees beside her. He took up her hand. It was warm but unresponsive. He called down the slope for help. "Deslo! Come back! Deslo!"

He saw Deslo, who must have heard his first cry for Nara to respond, already running back up the path, and he turned back to his wife. "Hang on, darling, I'm going to get you some help."

.   .   .

Kaden ran both hands through his golden hair. Owenn quietly reached over and put his massive hand gently on Kaden's shoulder, while Marlo said, "I'm sorry this is happening, Kaden."

"Sa," Kaden said, acknowledging his friend's attempt to comfort him. "But what is this? What's going on with her?"

Marlo and Owenn remained quiet. Kaden knew they didn't have the answer any more than he did. He and Deslo had gotten Nara down the rest of the way to the valley, and with help, they'd carried her to the tent city the Amhuru who were converging here from all over the Northlands had erected. Now Nara lay in a large tent with a couple older Amhuru women examining her, but still Kaden had no idea what was wrong.

A moment later one of the Amhuru women emerged. She had no news, but she said Nara was awake and encouraged Kaden to go to her. Kaden slipped inside the tent, and the other Amhuru nodded to him as she left. He sat down beside Nara and took up her hand in his.

"How are you feeling?"

"Awful," Nara said, trying to muster a smile. Her voice was weak. "I'm so tired."

"Maybe you should try to sleep?" Kaden suggested, though he feared that rest alone couldn't fix what ailed her.

"In a little bit," she said. She stroked his hand with her fingers and said, "Darling, I am sorry I didn't tell you this sooner."

"Tell me what?"

"I think I'm pregnant again," she said. "But I wanted to wait until I was sure."

"Are you sure now?" Kaden said, feeling a rush of hope. Pregnancy might explain her fatigue and her fainting. Certainly, at their age, it was possible. And they'd been on foot the last few weeks since disembarking from *The Sorry Rogue* to head inland.

"No," Nara said, and a look of sadness came over her face. "And if I am, there's something very wrong. With me, or with the baby, or both."

"How do you know?"

"I can feel it."

"And the Amhuru," Kaden said, glancing back toward the tent flaps as though to indicate the recently departed women. "What do they say?"

"They don't know what's wrong with me," Nara said. "But I can see in their faces that they think it is serious."

"Well, did they do anything for you? Are they going to help in some way?"

"I'm sure they'll help in whatever way they can," Nara said, "But you can't just expect them to snap their fingers and make me well. They're not immortal, and neither am I."

"I know that," Kaden said.

He was going to speak further but Nara squeezed his hand and said, "Please, darling, I'm very tired, and there's something I want to tell you before I rest."

He swallowed what he had been about to say and nodded. "All right, I'm listening."

"I just wanted to tell you how happy I've been these last eight years, how happy you've made me. I never thought that—"

"No, Nara," Kaden said, shaking his head adamantly. "No goodbyes. We're not saying goodbye, because you're not going anywhere."

"I hope not," Nara said. "But that isn't up to me. Or you."

"Nara, I won't—"

"Please," Nara pleaded.

Kaden bit his tongue and nodded again.

"Maybe I'll be fine, but if I'm not, I want you to know how much I love you, how happy I am we finally found each other. And, I want you to know that if something does happen to me, I know you're ready to take care of Kiki and Deslo. You're a great father."

By the end, her voice was strained and very soft, so Deslo reached down with his free hand and brushed her hair back from her face. "All right, Nara, I've heard you, now we're not going to talk about this anymore. You're going to rest, and we'll talk more when you wake up. All right?"

"All right," she said, closing her eyes.

"Try to sleep."

She nodded her head gently, her only reply.

Kaden sat holding her hand, watching her try to sleep. Even long after he knew she was asleep, he sat, watching.

How strange life was. For years now, the world had been teetering closer and closer to the brink of disaster, but all the while, his own world had been fine—more than fine, it had been better than it had ever been before. How quickly that had changed. In the blink of an eye the troubles of the world as a whole had become completely inconsequential. What happened to the Jin Dara or the Amhuru, to the Northlands or the Southlands—what was that to him?

If he lost Nara, though, what would he do?

.   .   .

Kaden sat in darkness, just a few feet from the entrance to the tent where Nara slept. The Amhuru women were back in with her, and Tchinchura and Zangira were sitting with him, keeping him company.

It was very late, and Kaden was cold, but he would not get up and walk the fifty feet to the nearest campfire. He wanted to be close to her. More than that, he needed to be close to her. He would have been inside with her except that the women had shooed him out, since he kept getting in their way.

"Zangira," Kaden said. "Do you remember when we took Tchinchura down from the wall at Barra-Dohn, the day the city fell?"

"Of course."

"Do you remember what I asked you?"

Zangira shook his head. Even in the darkness, Kaden could see it. "I'm sorry, Kaden, I don't remember."

"I asked if there was something you could do for Tchinchura's wounds, with the power of Zerura—do you remember what you said to me?"

"I vaguely remember this, now," Zangira said after a moment. "But I don't remember the details, though I can imagine what I said, more or less."

"You said that some things Zerura does to you automatically when you wear it. Some other things that you can do with it are permitted, a gift of sorts to the Amhuru who bear it and pay a price to do so. And you also said some things that Zerura can do are forbidden."

"Sa, Kaden," Zangira said. "All these things are true."

"I gathered from what you said that there might have been something you could do to heal Tchinchura that you weren't prepared to do, that you felt was forbidden you. Is that right?"

"Kaden, I'm not sure—"

"Is it true?" Kaden reiterated, more insistently.

"I trusted Tchinchura into the hands of Kalos," Zangira said. "And you should trust Nara into those same hands."

"I'm not asking you to do anything you don't feel you should," Kaden said, plaintively. "But maybe you could show me how to use Zerura to heal. I could do something for her, maybe, and then if I cross some kind of moral line, Kalos can be mad with me, not you."

"The women will have done anything that is permissible with Zerura already," Tchinchura said, finally joining in the conversation. "It is hard, my friend, but her life is not in our hands."

"Neither of you have answered my question," Kaden said, and he could feel the anger rising. "I'm not an apprentice anymore, so if there's anything that wearing Zerura can help me do for her, I want to do it. I don't care about the consequences."

"Not caring about the consequences of his actions was your father's habit," Zangira said, quietly but firmly. "I would have thought that you had learned the danger of living this way, since we are all still paying the price for it."

"He's got nothing to do with this," Kaden said, almost shouting, but then, remembering that his wife was lying ill not far away, he added, in an angry but hushed whisper. "You have no right to bring him into this discussion."

"No right?" Zangira said, and Kaden thought he could hear anger in Zangira's voice too. "Think about that day on the wall, Kaden. If Eirmon doesn't betray us, we probably defeat the Jin Dara. If we defeat the Jin Dara, he never comes to Azandalir. If he never comes to Azandalir, my wife is probably still alive and well today. I think, Kaden, you should not tell me I have no right to bring your father into this discussion."

"You're blaming me for my father's treachery?" Kaden said. "You're going to let my wife die because my father's folly and wickedness led indirectly to your wife's death?"

"Peace," Tchinchura said, reaching out his hands and motioning to the both of them to settle down. "None of this will help Nara, and if you two keep going, you will both say more things that you will only regret."

Kaden glared at Zangira in the dark, and Zangira met his glare with a hard stare of his own. For a moment they sat silently, eyes locked like this, until Tchinchura continued. "You are not to blame for your father's actions, Kaden, and Zangira knows this. At the same time, you must understand that both Zangira and I have lost women we loved, and we would never violate the commands of Kalos or the traditions of our people to misuse the Cord on their behalf. Death cannot be cheated. All men—and women—must someday die."

The flap to the tent was suddenly thrown open, and one of the Amhuru women called to Kaden. "You should come. Now."

Kaden didn't argue or speak. He merely moved swiftly into the tent. A candle was burning now beside Nara, and its light showed her face, as white and pale as the awful gorgaal had been. Kaden's heart sank at the sight of her, but he moved to her side and took her hand in his.

She opened her eyes and looked at him. Recognition showed there, but not much more. She moved her lips, but the words were almost inaudible. He bent over until his ear was right above her mouth. She tried again, but all she could muster was, "I'm sorry, darling, I think I have to go now."

"No, no, no," Kaden said, squeezing her hand forcefully, tears flowing freely down his face. "Don't go, Nara. Don't go."

"Tell Deslo I'm proud," she said. "Tell them both, and how much I love them."

"No," Kaden reiterated, his voice suddenly hoarse as the word cracked coming out of his mouth. "Ellenara, what will I do without you?"

"See," she said, raising her hand the few inches necessary to touch the tears on his face. "You ended up loving me after all."

Kaden wept. There were no words to say. Her hand dropped onto her chest. Her eyes fluttered shut, and soon Kaden realized the hand he held was limp.

"Don't go," he sobbed. "Don't go."

For a long time he clung to her and cried. When at last the tears had stopped, and when he was finally ready to let go of her hand, he placed it gently down beside the other one, leaned over her face, kissed her forehead and whispered. "Goodbye, my love."

27

COMING APART

Deslo thought the place where they buried his mother was beautiful. He believed Nara would have approved. They had traveled all over the world, but few places were as striking as this small, hidden valley, remote and tucked away up high and protected on all sides by daunting alpine ridges. The floor of the valley was covered with thousands and thousands of small blue wildflowers that mingled with the green of the grass, carpeting the ground as far as the eye could see. And running through the valley, not quite in the middle, was a lovely stream. Not far from this stream, underneath one of the few trees that grew here, they had buried Nara, almost ten days ago.

As they had stood over the grave, Deslo turned to his father, his Yadi, and he handed him the small red statue Kaden had given him on his thirteenth birthday. He nodded toward the grave to indicate his willingness for Kaden to drop it in. Kaden held the statue, stroked the smooth red marble with his finger for a moment, then handed it back. "This should stay with you. Think of her when you hold it; think of home."

Every day since, Deslo had walked to the grave with Kiki and Shaline. They talked some as they walked there and back again each day, though Kiki had grown quieter, Deslo thought, since Nara's death. At the grave itself, though, none of them talked. There might be tears, but there were no words. Perhaps, if on the first or second visit, one of them had said something, it might not have been impossible to speak there later. But by now, after so many days, it had become an unspoken rule among them to observe silence for the duration of their visit and to speak only when they were once more on their way back to the tents.

They were returning now, so talking among them was no longer taboo. Shaline was holding Kiki's hand and talking about the small chain of wildflowers they had made together and left behind on Nara's grave. Deslo looked over his sister's bobbing head and smiled gratefully at Shaline. She smiled back, and again Deslo felt it.

He couldn't have described just exactly what 'it' was, but it was a connection of sorts. Ever since Nara's death, the empty space that had been growing between them since Shaline and her family had joined them in the Northlands disappeared. They shared a bond now, having both lost mothers. Shaline didn't even have to say anything to be a comfort to Deslo. In fact, she was quite often a comfort to him precisely because she knew when not to say anything. She seemed to know instinctively when just being there with him was enough.

And now, as he watched her with Kiki, he wondered what he would have done these past ten days without her. Kaden had seemed all right at first, but after they buried Nara, he had disappeared into his tent for longer and longer stretches, so that he now was almost never outside it. Deslo had tried talking to him, had tried leaving him alone, had tried everything he could think of, but Kaden had been almost non-responsive for several days. The council was tonight, with the fate of the world at stake, but Deslo was consumed with what to do about his Yadi.

When they reached the tents, Deslo said to Shaline. "Would you mind taking Kiki and getting her something to eat?"

"Sure," Shaline said. "Would you like that, Kiki?"

"Sa," Kiki said, nodding.

Shaline looked at Deslo and motioned in the direction of Kaden's tent. Deslo nodded, and he knew Shaline understood. She took Kiki by the hand and turned to go in the other direction.

Deslo looked at the sea of tents, sighed, and started to make his way through, wondering as he went what he would be able to accomplish today, having failed with Kaden so many times already. Perhaps if he didn't respond to him this time, he would slap him in the face, try to shock him out of his withdrawal. He felt like doing it, anyway. Deslo had lost his mother, and he shouldn't have to be doing this.

But when he arrived at Kaden's tent, his verbal knock was greeted not with silence but with a clear invitation to come in. And, when he opened the flap to step inside, he saw Kaden was not lying down, curled up in the dark, as he had been so often before. Rather, he was seated, facing the tent flaps, and he nodded to Deslo as he entered.

"It's good to see you up," Deslo said, truthfully.

Again Kaden nodded. "I'm sorry, Deslo. I know I've worried you."

Deslo shrugged. It was true, so he couldn't really deny it. He sat down beside Kaden.

"Come," Kaden continued, reaching over and putting his hand on Deslo's shoulder. "Much of the days that have passed since your Noni died are lost to me. I have been plagued by bad dreams, and for a while there, I didn't know where reality ended and the dreams began. It was almost like passing through the Madri again, only this time, I preferred the nightmares to being awake."

Deslo felt he understood what Kaden was telling him, but he did not speak. "I know you came often," Kaden continued, "and that you tried to draw me out of myself, but I don't remember much more than that about your visits. What news is there of the other Keepers? Have they come yet? Has a day been set for the council?"

"The council is today."

"Today?" Kaden said. "Then they have come?"

"One of them has come," Deslo said.

"One of them," Kaden echoed him, and Deslo could hear his disappointment. "And they are meeting tonight. Does this mean they have given up on the other?"

"I don't think they've given up on him," Deslo said. "But I do think they suspect he has been killed and his fragment taken."

"Tell me," Kaden said. "Tell me what has happened."

"The Elders were already nervous that Maccado had not come—he's the Keeper who is still missing. He is, I gather, not the kind to be late for something like this. Still, they knew that any number of things could have detained him, and the mood of the camp was fairly positive.

"Then yesterday," Deslo continued, "the other Keeper came. His name is Draagan, and he met alone with the Elders for a long time. When they were finished, word began to circulate throughout the camp that the council would be tonight. Along with it, there spread a quiet fear that whatever

Draagan has told the Elders, they no longer held out much hope that Maccado would come."

"Maccado is the name of the one who has the *cadeen*, isn't it?"

"Sa," Deslo said. "And I think the prospect that the Jin Dara might now have three has cast a pall over the camp."

"Three," Kaden said, shaking his head. "If he has three, how can we beat him?"

"I don't know," Deslo said. "I guess that's one of the questions the council will have to discuss."

"They can discuss it all they like," Kaden started, but as Deslo looked at him, he seemed to think better of what he was going to say and grew silent. A moment later, though, he spoke again. "I guess it's a good thing I've returned to the land of the living today, if the council is tonight."

"It's a good thing, regardless of what's happening tonight, Yadi."

"Sa, Deslo, it is good," Kaden said. "I know you have just lost your Noni, and I am sorry to have failed you and Kiki so egregiously, I should have—"

"Yadi," Deslo said. "Don't. You don't have to apologize to me. I'm just glad you're back."

"I am back."

"Do you want to come get some lunch?"

"Sa," Kaden said, and then he laughed. "I'm really hungry."

.   .   .

The Amhuru gathered in the large open field beside the city of tents. Torches on poles surrounded them, creating ample light for the assembly. Kaden was greeted warmly and kindly by many of the other Amhuru, but he drifted to the back with Deslo, Kiki, and Shaline. Trabor stayed with them awhile but then moved with Zangira further up through the gathering.

Marlo and Owenn had found them in the crowd, and they too stayed near the back. Kaden looked at his children and the two Kalosenes, and he felt the pang in his gut again. Rika had left them years ago, and now Nara was dead. The few exiles from Barra-Dohn that had fled together from the collapse of the city had dwindled even more. Such a small remnant already, and now further dimished. Not for the first time he wondered how much longer any of them would last and if the Jin Dara could possibly be stopped.

He was not left alone with his doubt for long, though, as Amintuu began the council. He said a few words at the start, during which he called Tchinchura to stand and introduced him as the Chief Elder of the Southland Amhuru for any of the Northland Amhuru who might not have met him yet. Kaden could see and hear the Northland Amhuru murmuring quietly where they sat, greeting him each in their own way. Then Amintuu summoned Draagan, and he came to address the crowd.

Kaden listened, fascinated, as the Northland Keeper told the story of his encounter with the Jin Dara. It was a remarkable tale, and he felt a curious mix of emotions as the story ended. On the one hand, he was of course disappointed that Draagan had come so close to killing the Jin Dara, only to fail, but he was also strangely heartened. If Draagan, with only one fragment and a clever plan could almost take down the Jin Dara when he was wearing two, then perhaps the Jin Dara wasn't invincible after all. Perhaps there was hope.

There wasn't much time to think about that, though, for Draagan moved quickly on to tell of the rumors he had heard on his way to the council. The reports spoke of the Jin Dara conquering Tanisaan, one of the stronger cities of the Northlands. More than that, the tales told of abominations the Jin Dara was creating there, taking the people of the city and many who lived close to the city, and warping them, changing them, transforming them into horrible things that were in most cases more plant or tree than human.

The descriptions Draagan gave of some of these things made Kaden shudder. If he hadn't seen the gorgaal with his own eyes and if he hadn't been forced to reckon with the Jin Dara's power to mutate and transform, he wasn't sure he would have believed what Draagan was saying. But he did, and he shook his head at the thought of the population of a whole city being mangled by the Jin Dara.

He was just starting to ask himself why the Jin Dara would do this, what he hoped to accomplish with it, when Draagan said. "I believe he is sending us a message. He is daring us to come, to try to stop him."

As soon as Draagan said it, Kaden knew that this was true. It was exactly the kind of thing the Jin Dara would do. He had probably grown tired of traveling all over the Northlands, trying to track down the remaining original fragments one by one. Or, perhaps, having almost been killed by Draagan, he simply had second thoughts about the wisdom of letting the Amhuru pick whatever strong place they wanted to defend and then going to them there. Whatever the Jin Dara's reasoning, Kaden had no trouble seeing the plausibility of Draagan's theory.

Neither, apparently, did any of the other Amhuru. Angry murmuring had been growing as Draagan had described what the Jin Dara had been doing since taking Tanisaan. Those angry murmurs were now turning into something Kaden would have called outrage, and soon Amintuu returned to the front and motioned to the assembled Amhuru to quiet down. When they had, Amintuu spoke.

"You have heard what Draagan told the Elders yesterday," Amintuu said. "And you should know that while we cannot say for sure that these things the Jin Dara has done required possession of a third fragment of the Cord, we believe he has it. We think this is why Maccado is not yet here, that the Jin Dara has the *cadeen*."

If the assembly had been outraged before, they were even more so now. Kaden felt the Amhuru feeding on the growing rage passing among them, and as he looked at Amintuu, who stood watching this reaction, he realized that creating outrage was Amintuu's goal. He had only calmed their earlier reaction so he could throw more fuel on it.

"Brothers," Amintuu called out, now motioning to them to hush their voices, at least enough that he could be heard. "I believe the time to run and hide has passed. The time has come to fight, to reclaim what the Jin Dara has stolen."

There were murmurs of agreement, but not all who reacted to Amintuu approved this sentiment. An Amhuru closer to the front cried out. "How can we defeat him when he wields the power of three fragments?"

"Exactly!" Amintuu said, seizing this moment eagerly. "We cannot defeat him as long as we bear one and he bears three. That is why we must also combine fragments, meet him strength for strength, three against three. Then we can win this war, once and for all."

What happened next was as close to chaos as anything Kaden had ever witnessed during his many years among the Amhuru. People cried out, both in favor of and also clearly in objection to this proposal. Amhuru all over the assembly started loudly arguing with their neighbors, and Kaden began to think that the meeting had gotten away from Amintuu entirely. But he managed to amplify his voice enough to start to draw the crowd back to him. It took him some time, but when the place had settled down, he continued.

"It is important that you all know what I am proposing. Replicas of the three fragments still under our control must be combined, and we must use them to defeat the Jin Dara. Then they must be separated, never to be combined again. This is only to be done this one time, so that we may go to Tanisaan and stop the abominations that the Jin Dara is doing there, so that we may stop him."

This time, the reactions to Amintuu's words were not so vehement, and it seemed to Kaden that they were also more favorable. Couched as a one-time exception, not a change in Amhuru tradition, Kaden felt Amintuu stood a much better chance of gaining support for his proposal. It was with growing curiosity, then, that Kaden watched Tchinchura rise and move to the front.

Amintuu yielded his place at the front freely. Kaden thought that Amintuu moved aside as though he had been expecting this and waiting for it. Tchinchura had little difficulty getting the assembly to quiet down, as his authority as the Chief Elder of the Southland Amhuru and their curiosity about what he would say both worked in his favor.

"There is a certain logic in what Amintuu says," Tchinchura opened, and Kaden thought he saw surprise in Amintuu's reaction. "It makes sense to meet the Jin Dara, strength for strength, force against force. Certainly, I would feel safer going to meet him on the field of battle if I wore three fragments and had the kind of control over the Arua that they would give me."

More murmurs of approval rippled through the crowd. Kaden was surprised. He thought for sure Tchinchura would oppose combining fragments. And yet, here he was, talking the gathered assembly of Amhuru into it.

"However," Tchinchura said, "I cannot wear three fragments, nor can I condone that anyone else do so. I believe that Kalos asks us to be faithful to his commands—that alone is what we can control. His command is not that we defeat the Jin Dara, it is that we obey his words—the rest is up to him. We have kept the fragments and their replicas separate for a thousand years, and we should keep doing that. Whether we stand or fall, we must be faithful."

For the first time since Draagan started telling his tale about the Jin Dara, the crowd was almost completely silent. Kaden gazed around them, amazed by how well Tchinchura had handled the emotions of the crowd, how well he had touched them by acknowledging the appeal of Amintuu's proposal before opposing it. He wondered what Amintuu's next play would be, and he didn't have to wait long to find out.

"How well that sounds," Amintuu said, coming forward so that he stood just in front of Tchinchura as he spoke, half to the crowd, half to Tchinchura. "How noble, too. Much comfort it will be when the Jin Dara has killed every Amhuru man, woman and child—or perhaps, when he has turned us all into shrubs and trees and planted us in the ground for his own amusement!"

Some of the murmurs were back, and Kaden heard much of the support and approval, as well as much of the anger from before. Amintuu had some of them back in his hand, at least.

"Oh yes, how comforting it will be," Amintuu continued. "To know that when we died, predictably, inevitably, that we did it the right way. That we died having stuck rigidly to a rule about combining replicas, when the command Kalos gave our forefathers was about combining originals. Yes, we will know that we didn't even get close to violating this law, even as we didn't even get close to stopping the madman who cared nothing for it or us, and so wiped us out and covered the world with darkness and terror."

The mild irony in Amintuu's voice at the beginning had become full-blown sarcasm, and Kaden couldn't help but feel outraged that he would dare talk to Tchinchura that way. He knew he was really talking to the crowd, trying to sway them to his side, but it was still wrong. He clenched his jaw, feeling his helplessness to do anything but watch this drama play out.

And then, surprisingly, a third player entered the conversation. Draagan appeared between Amintuu and Tchinchura, and there, side by side by side, the three stood. Two were Keepers of original fragments and the third had once been one too but now wore a heavier burden of authority. The crowd once more grew silent.

"I am not here to tell you what to think of Amintuu's proposal," Draagan said, "nor what to think of Tchinchura's opposition to it. Perhaps that moment will come. There is, though, something else you need to know."

He paused, then continued. "After my brush with the Jin Dara, I took the liberty to make what was, I think you will agree, a daring move. I went to the Jaens."

Kaden had no idea who the Jaens were, but you would have thought Draagan had said he went to have dinner with the Jin Dara. There was plenty of angry shouting, and the vehemence of some in the crowd was unsettling. He wished he understood what was going on. He turned and looked at Deslo and then at Marlo and Owenn, but they all looked as confused as he did.

When Draagan finally regained some modicum of cooperation from the crowd, he continued. "I solicited help from Meldriic Jaen."

More shouts, though they were more quickly hushed as the crowd seemed compelled to want to hear where this was going. "I asked him to go and join with the Jin Dara, to try to get inside his Najin, and to try to assassinate the Jin Dara from within."

A hush fell over the crowd again. They seemed stunned, unsure what to do with this statement. "And before I left him, Meldriic said that he and his brothers would go, that they would try to do this."

Still the hush, and Kaden looked around, curious, wondering what exactly this meant. "So," Draagan went on, "this is my suggestion. Let's give Meldriic and his brothers a chance to do this. In the meantime, I propose we head north, far north. I say we go to the Cura-Katane and seek their aid."

That didn't get as strong a reaction as mentioning the Jaens had, but it got a strong one, nonetheless. "Amintuu is at least right about this," Draagan plowed on. "The time to confront the Jin Dara has come. We must do it now, before we are weakened any further, and I suggest we do it on ground of our choosing, with what allies we can convince to join us—and the Cura-Katane will help. If the Jaens fail, we can send for the Jin Dara and he can come to us there, and there we will make our stand."

The confusion that ensued was made worse by the fact that some sort of exchange, heated but not violently so, had broken out among the three Amhuru up front. It wound down, after a moment, and Amintuu returned to the front.

"Without calling a separate meeting to confer with the Elders, I am a little at a loss to speak to the issue of the Jaens," Amintuu said. "Personally, I have serious questions about bringing them into this, and I am not sure if I am hoping for their success or not, as the thought of the Jaens having three original fragments of the Golden Cord might be more disturbing than that the Jin Dara has them."

More than a few Amhuru seemed to agree with this, as the nodding of many heads and the murmurs of assent revealed. "However," Amintuu said, "regardless of what any of us might think about the Jaens, the fact is that we must prepare for war, and I still say, that any plan for war that does not include our combining fragments and training with them to be ready for the Jin Dara and his Najin is folly. We can stand with the Cura-Katane on any battlefield you like—but if the Jin Dara and the Najin bear three fragments each and we all bear one, we are going to fail. That's a fact."

"So," Amintuu pushed on, before interruptions from either the crowd or the other two could derail him, "this is what I say. We will put it to a vote—Draagan's plan against mine. Only, I would ask both Tchinchura and Draagan to agree—and Zangira as well, since he bears the remaining Southland fragment—that if the will of the majority of the Amhuru is to follow my proposal, that they will not withhold their fragments for the creation of the necessary replicas. I say that no man shall be made to do what I ask in violation of his conscience, but that no man should be prevented from doing it if his conscience leaves him free to do so."

Murmurs of assent again rippled through the crowd. Tchinchura stepped forward and announced, "If the will of the majority is behind Amintuu's plan, I will make the last Southland fragment that Zangira bears available for duplication, so that the necessary replicas may be made."

Draagan nodded and added his agreement.

"We are agreed then," Amintuu said. "The people will decide. Consult with each other as you are able, and in a little while, the Elders will pass among you to gather your votes and know your will."

In the time that followed, Kaden spoke earnestly but quietly with those around him. He admitted, "I have no idea who these Jaens are, or who the Cura-Katane are, but I have to say, I like this Draagan's style. Anyone who could almost take down the Jin Dara single-handedly gets my vote."

"He gets your vote because he is with Tchinchura," Deslo said.

"That too," Kaden agreed with a smile.

They talked for some time about the options, and what they had just witnessed, all of them agreeing that this level of emotional reaction from a crowd of Amhuru was extremely strange. None of them knew just what to make of it, and they all acknowledged that they were fascinated with how it would work out.

Eventually, one of the Elders made it back to them, and he spoke separately and quietly with both Deslo and Kaden. The Kalosenes made no attempt to vote, though Kaden thought he could see that Marlo was disappointed not to have even been asked. A few minutes later, the Elders returned to the front of the assembly, and they talked briefly with the three Keepers.

After the Elders had conferred with the Keepers, Amintuu returned to the front. "The decision has been made. Most of you have agreed with me that we must combine the replicas to meet the Jin Dara on the field of battle. Tchinchura and Draagan have agreed that work should begin right away to make all the replicas that will be needed."

Kaden's thoughts whirled. He had been curious about who would win, but now that Amintuu had won, he wasn't sure what he thought of it. He really was with Tchinchura and Draagan on this. Amintuu continued, "I need everyone of you who is even remotely open to doing this to consider joining us. Even with three fragments, there need to be enough of us to match his army. In the morning, come back out to the field if you are willing to start training with me, and we will build an army to match the Jin Dara's own."

There were many cheers, and Kaden felt that the tenor of the gathering had moved from outrage to excitement. He could understand it, as he saw hope on many faces, and it had been a while since hope had been within reach. He also understood it, because many people around him were soon to feel what it was like to wear three fragments—and that had a lure all its own.

"Brothers," Draagan called, and those who had started to disperse stopped, turning to afford Draagan the respect he deserved. "While those who choose to go with Amintuu to Tanisaan begin to train, Tchinchura and I will make preparations to head north to the Cura-Katane. Any Amhuru who wants to come with us will be welcome."

And with that, the council was over.

For some time, Kaden stayed where he had been, watching the ebb and flow of the Amhuru leaving the field to go back to the city of tents. Some were clearly excited, talking to one another with animation about the coming day. Others left sadly, shaking their heads.

Kaden watched them go, and a deep sadness came over him. Sadness and uncertainty. It felt like he had just watched a great rift form right through the heart of the Amhuru community—the most stable thing left in his world, and possibly in the world as a whole.

Nara was dead. She lay buried in this very valley. And now, the unity of the Amhuru was broken. It lay in pieces here in this field, just as surely as

Nara lay below it. At some point, the two groups of Amhuru on either side of the rift would leave this valley and head away in two different directions, following two very different plans.

The world was coming apart beneath his feet, and there was nothing Kaden could do about it.

28

THE DEEPER CUT

When Kaden awoke the next morning, he felt surprisingly eager for the day. Nara was still gone, and he felt her absence physically, an ache that never dissipated. The Amhuru were still divided, and the ones that he best knew and respected were in the minority of that division. And of course, still hovering like a shadow over all of this was the sense that both factions saw what was coming as a final stand with victory far from assured.

But still he rose in better spirits than he had any day since Nara died, and when he examined himself to try to understand why, he was a little surprised to realize that much of it boiled down to simple curiosity. He was fascinated by the little he had heard about Draagan, and he looked forward to traveling with him on their way north. He was curious to learn what the commotion had been about when these Jaens were mentioned, and to learn who the Cura-Katane were that Draagan wanted to ally with. It was as if he had—for the first time since leaving the Graymere behind—finally risen to face a day that contained more than traveling for the sake of traveling and trying not to be found. In short, Kaden felt the invigorating throb of purpose, and it agreed with him.

What put a little bit of a damper on his good mood was the realization that Deslo was quiet and had clearly withdrawn from him. Kaden couldn't blame him, exactly, as Deslo had lost his mother and then watched

his father slip into an almost totally unresponsive state. He could understand Deslo's grievance, and he had no problem giving him space until he
wanted to talk about it.

So Kaden took Kiki with him everywhere he went in the camp, giving
Deslo free range to do as he pleased, while he focused on reassuring his little girl that he was back and that he was all right. Kiki didn't talk about the
days that Kaden hadn't been all right, but she did hold tightly onto his hand
wherever they walked, as though she was afraid that, if she let go, he might
go back to his tent. Kaden just held on tightly right back, and he tried to
treasure every moment and savor every word that came from Kiki's mouth.

Losing Nara like that, so suddenly, as well as preparing to march to
what might be an unwinnable battle had made Kaden painfully aware of
the uncertainties of life. He did not want to take anything for granted—not
Deslo, not Kiki, not anything. Anyone and everyone could be lost at any
time, and the time they had together was a gift. A gift he meant to enjoy as
much as possible, every day, from now until he joined Nara in the grave.

In the afternoon, he caught up for a little while with Marlo and
Owenn, who had been as curious as he was about some of the mysterious
aspects of the council the night before. They hadn't learned much about
the Cura-Katane, but they had learned a great deal about the JaenSing, as
the band of mercenaries that followed Meldriic Jaen and his brothers were
called. What's more, they had learned a bit of the Jaen history, and once
Kaden knew that history—knew of their estrangement from the Amhuru
and the deep grievance between them—he understood Amintuu's reaction
a bit more.

Kaden thought of the Five Cities that Barra-Dohn had governed, and
more particularly of the representatives of those cities who had hated Eirmon. He knew it wasn't a perfect analogy—after all, they had good cause
to hate Eirmon, but he didn't know if the Jaens had good cause to hate the
Amhuru—but nonetheless, it was an apt analogy because there was deep
bitterness if not hatred there. He wondered if he could have gone to any of
them for help as Draagan had gone to the Jaens, and more to the point, he
wondered if he could have trusted them to give that help even if they said
they would.

In the end, Kaden decided that since he didn't know the Jaens, he
would have to reserve judgement about the wisdom of the deed until he
knew Draagan better. The man was not a fool, that much he could see, so

he wouldn't assume he had behaved foolishly—as some of the Northland Amhuru obviously did—until he had good reason to think he had.

When Kaden parted from the Kalosenes, they agreed that their next priority was to learn something about the Cura-Katane, but when Kaden went to bed that night, he didn't know anything about them he hadn't known when he woke up. He was disappointed about that, but with Kiki curled up in his arms, fast asleep and breathing lightly on his neck, Kaden couldn't consider the day anything but a success.

Kaden didn't see much of Deslo the next day, or the day after that for that matter, but he did eventually learn something about the Cura-Katane. He learned it from Zangira, in the end, as Tchinchura was very busy, having assumed a kind of co-command with Draagan of the expedition that would go north and not to Tanisaan. Zangira was busy too, for now that he was back, Tchinchura consulted with him often and relied on him always, but he took time to share with Kaden what he knew.

Essentially, what he had learned was that the Cura-Katane were a tough people who lived in a rugged land that for a large chunk of the year was brutally cold and almost perpetually dark. In fact, Zangira explained, they might find that it was light for only a few hours a day when they got there, and this concept was stunning to Kaden. Not to mention, when Zangira explained just how cold it could get, he found himself shivering almost uncontrollably. He had grown up in the bright, hot world of Barra-Dohn, and this place that Zangira pictured sounded too fantastic to believe.

After hearing the description of the place and the people, Kaden asked Zangira. "What makes Draagan think they can help with the Jin Dara?"

Zangira shrugged. "Draagan believes their chief attribute is that, given the nature of the world they live in every day, their perpetually hostile environment, they will be undaunted by the Jin Dara."

"They have no special weapons? Or power?"

"Not that I know of."

Kaden's heart sank. "It will take more than courage to beat the Jin Dara."

"True," Zangira said. "But we won't beat him without it."

On the fourth day after the council, Kaden was eating lunch with Kiki and the Kalosenes, talking about heading north with Tchinchura and Zangira, when Marlo asked, "I wonder how many miles we have traveled together since we fled Barra-Dohn on *The Sorry Rogue*?"

"A staggering amount," Kaden said. "I don't think that I would even want to know how many. It makes me tired just thinking about it."

"I wonder how many more miles lie ahead?" Marlo said.

"Not that many," Owenn said, "if we don't find a way to kill the Jin Dara."

Marlo leaned over and pretended to whisper to Kaden. "He's been saying lots of cheery things like that since the council."

"Do you think Amintuu was right?" Kaden asked, looking at Owenn. The big Kalosene was no longer quite the enigma he had been when they first set sail from Barra-Dohn all those years go, but that didn't mean Kaden was going to pass on getting an insight into what might be going on in his brain when the opportunity presented itself.

"No," Owenn said. "Tchinchura was right."

"At the same time," Marlo continued, when Owenn didn't say anything more. "We both feel the frustration of suspecting that Amintuu was right too."

"How do you mean?"

"That we can't win without combining fragments," Marlo said, "which we can't do—hence the frustration."

"I don't trust Amintuu," Owenn volunteered, after a few moments.

"Why not?" Kaden asked.

"I don't know," Owenn said. "But I don't."

"You know what I wonder," Kaden said. "I wonder what we'll all say if Amintuu succeeds. After all, defeating the Jin Dara is the goal, isn't it? And if it works, will it mean he was right?"

"Of course not," Marlo said, and he was uncharacteristically sharp when he said it.

"Why not?" Kaden said, perhaps a little defensively.

"Did your father's plan against Garranmere work?"

"Yes," Kaden said, a little sheepishly.

"And the Jin Dara's plan against Barra-Dohn? And Azandalir? And this Tanisaan and lots of places inbetween?"

"Point taken," Kaden said, raising his hands and motioning for Marlo's onslaught of examples to stop. "Achieving your goal isn't proof that it was a good goal, or that it was pursued the right way."

"It certainly isn't," Marlo agreed.

"Then will we ever know who was right here?" Kaden asked. "If success can't prove Amintuu right, then failure can't prove him wrong—so whatever the outcome, will we ever know?"

"That's a different question," Marlo said. "And short of Kalos revealing the answer, I don't know if we will. We must do our best to understand what Kalos has commanded—and what he hasn't—and then we must do our best to obey him. That is all we can do."

"You sound like Nara," Kaden said.

Marlo smiled, but the sadness in his eyes belied the smile, and the conversation drifted on to other things. Eventually, Kaden and Kiki parted from the Kalosenes, and they passed the midday by walking to Nara's grave and spending time together there.

Darkness came, and Kaden had just put Kiki to bed and was considering going to bed himself, when Deslo stopped by the tent. Deslo asked if they could talk for a few minutes, and as it was the first time Deslo had come looking for Kaden since the afternoon before the council, Kaden quickly agreed. He stepped out into the cool night air, and they walked a short distance away from the tent to have a little privacy.

"Deslo," Kaden started, wanting to have the first say. "I just want to say again how sorry I am that I disappeared on you like that after your Noni died. You needed me, and I failed you."

"Yadi," Deslo said, and Kaden thought Deslo looked caught off guard and uncomfortable. "You don't need to keep apologizing for that. I was worried about you, but I'm not angry."

Kaden was a little surprised. If that wasn't the reason for the distance and withdrawal, then what was? But Deslo didn't add anything, and Kaden decided he'd fill the space while Deslo worked up the nerve to say whatever it was he'd come to say.

"I don't know what you've learned so far about these Cura-Katane that Draagan and Tchinchura are going to take us to," Kaden said. "But it sounds like the place where they live is so cold we might all freeze to death on the way. I'm not sure how we Southlanders will handle that kind of weather—"

"I'm not going," Deslo said.

"What?"

"I said I'm not going."

"Of course you're going," Kaden said, frowning, and feeling a little confused. "All the Amhuru who aren't going with Amintuu are going—"

"I am going with Amintuu."

Kaden's mouth hung open. He gawked at Deslo, struggling to comprehend what his son was saying. He wasn't suggesting he was doing something apart from the rest of those who disagreed with Amintuu, he was suggesting he agreed with Amintuu—a possibility Kaden had never considered.

"I don't understand," he said, and his voice was cracked and quiet.

"Trabor decided first," Deslo said. "And Shaline has been torn, since Zangira is going with Tchinchura, but she's decided to go with Trabor—I don't know that she supports Amintuu, exactly, but she doesn't want Trabor to go alone. I've thought about it, and I want to go too."

"I know Shaline is important to you," Kaden started.

"It's not about Shaline," Deslo said. "Not just about her anyway. The Jin Dara has to be stopped, and if this is our best chance, we need to take it. We need to do whatever it takes."

"Whatever it takes?" Kaden said, his voice rising. "You would do that, whatever it takes?"

"I would, yes," Deslo said.

"We need to do this right," Kaden said, "and I trust Tchinchura when he says Amintuu's plan isn't right."

Deslo stared at Kaden, and for a long moment he didn't say anything. Then he said, "Why do you care so much about a 'God' who has forgotten us?"

"What?"

"Barra-Dohn, your home and mine, is destroyed," Deslo said. "And now, Noni is dead. How can you actually care about some ancient rule that may or may not even apply to this situation—let alone the distant, uncaring being who gave us this rule?"

Kaden still felt stunned. His mind was running in lots of different directions at once. There was so much that he could say to this—so much of it based on things Nara had said to him over the years when he had his own questions—and yet he could see a hardness in Deslo's face. He knew arguing this point wouldn't change Deslo's mind, and Kaden needed to change his mind. He decided in that moment to try a new approach.

"Deslo, we need to keep the family together."

Kaden could see right away this had been the right call. For the first time since he'd come to Kaden's tent, he could see Deslo waver. This was why he had hesitated to join Amintuu's cause sooner. This was why he had withdrawn.

"I don't want to leave you and Kiki—"

"Then don't!"

"But if the Jin Dara isn't defeated," Deslo hurried quickly on, "it won't matter if we are together or not. We will all eventually be crushed, and you know it."

Kaden couldn't say anything. He'd betrayed his own doubts and skepticism too often to Deslo. He knew any denials now wouldn't ring true. Kaden did feel the situation was all but hopeless, and Deslo knew it.

"It is better that we be apart, for a time," Deslo said, "if it leads to the Jin Dara's downfall. Isn't it?"

"And if it doesn't?" Kaden asked.

"Then we're all in trouble."

"No, Deslo," Kaden said, and the tears that had been threatening since he realized Deslo might not be coming north started to fall. "I won't allow it."

"It's not your decision, Yadi," Deslo said, but he wasn't defiant when he said it. In fact, he was surprisingly gentle. "I'm a man, and a full-fledged Amhuru in my own right. The decision is mine to make."

"Sa, you're right," Kaden said, stepping closer to his son. "But I'm begging you. Don't go."

"I am going," Deslo said, and Kaden knew he had lost.

Deslo turned to go but Kaden reached out and grabbed his son. He pulled him closer and threw his arms around him, hugging him tight. The tears flowed freely, and when at last he eased up on his grip, he pulled Deslo's head down so that he could kiss his golden hair.

"I love you, Deslo," he whispered.

"I know, Yadi," Deslo said. "I love you too."

And then Deslo walked away into the darkness.

Kaden watched him go, disappearing among the tents. There was no reason to think he wouldn't see Deslo again, probably several times, before he left with Tchinchura and the others to head north, but as he watched his son go, something broke inside him.

He was struck with a strong memory of a young Deslo, perhaps six or seven, trying so very hard to impress his father, even just to get his attention.

But Kaden didn't give the attention desired. He felt cut off, a million miles away from both Deslo and Nara. He tried to picture Nara in the memory, but her face eluded him. All he felt was the distance he had created between himself and his family.

That wound had been a wound of his own making, and thankfully, that wound, though deep, had been healed. This wound, this parting, this loss—after tasting all the joy a loving family could provide, and after losing Nara so suddenly, so unexpectedly—this wound was the deeper cut.

And, he suspected, it might well be beyond healing.

Part 3

THE COLDER MOON

29

ALL YOU DESIRE

R ika walked through the large hall, admiring the work going on throughout. Several teams of researchers were working simultaneously on a
wide array of projects. Most involved work on ordinary domestic items,
like lights, ovens, and lamps, or innovations for travel and locomotion, but
a few were clearly more militaristic.

She'd had greater ambitions on this front at the start, but after one of
her researchers took a weapon he had been developing and tried to get past
the Najin and use it on the Jin Dara, she'd been forced to reevaluate her
plans. She'd feared for her life when it happened, but fortunately, the Jin
Dara had never even appeared to question her loyalty or blame her for the
incident.

Instead, as they conferred about the event, both had agreed that the
wisdom of recruiting top minds from the conquered populace of Tanisaan
and having them help develop weapons might have been a little unwise.
To help ensure that none of the rest harbored mutinous dreams, the Jin
Dara had selected, with Rika's help, a couple of the researchers she thought
rather expendable, and turned them into a complex, intertwined display in
the center of the hall where they worked. There they still grew, a tangled
mess of limbs and vines, a living reminder of the Jin Dara's power.

Even so, Rika had redirected most of the teams to work on more
peaceful applications of Zerura, while just a few hand-picked researchers

under strict supervision of several members of the Najin continued working on the weapons projects. It was to a demonstration of one of these
projects that Rika was headed now.

She passed outside the hall, and her usual escort of two Najin moved
ahead of her as they walked to the transport. The driver asked no questions, for he already knew where they were headed, and once all three had
boarded, they zoomed away.

They started toward the mountain north of the city, though well before they would have reached the area where the wise woman dwelled, the
transport left the road and traveled east to a quarry where the people of
Tanisaan had long mined stone for their buildings. Rika disembarked and
followed the Najin down the winding path that descended into the quarry.
There she found the team of researchers to whom she had entrusted this
project waiting, along with their Najin supervisors.

A sturdy wooden table stood in the open, and on the table was a small
chest. Rika walked over to the chest and opened it, and there, sitting packed
in straw, were about a dozen small meridium spheres about the size of a fist
wrapped in soft linen cloth. She picked one up and unwrapped it, so she
could feel the cold meridium in her hand. It was smooth to the touch, and
the veins of golden Zerura running through it vibrated under her fingers.
She smiled at that feeling, and what it meant.

She took the orb to one of the Najin standing nearby. She handed it to
him and said, "Show me."

He nodded and turned to face the quarry wall about a hundred fifty
feet away. He reared back and threw the orb, and though it lost some alti-
tude at first, it seemed to settle in on the Arua surface and glide along until
it struck the wall and exploded. Rika nodded approvingly. Designing explosives patterned after those made to destroy Garranmere, only smaller,
had been the goal. At least, it had been part of it.

"And your directional control?" Rika asked.

The Najin walked over to the chest and removed another sphere. He
walked back to where he had stood to throw the first one, only he pivoted
to the side, so he was facing parallel to the quarry wall instead of facing
it directly. He reared back again, and he threw the meridium ball. It flew
once more along the surface of the Arua, only this time, once it had traveled thirty yards or so, the Najin motioned with his hand as though he were
throwing a knife, and the ball was redirected on almost a ninety degree

angle toward the quarry wall, hardly losing any velocity. It struck the wall and, like the first, exploded.

"Excellent," Rika said. "It is coming along quite well, I'd say."

She turned to the five researchers who had been watching the demonstration silently. "You have done great work; thank you."

The relief on their faces was visible, and she added with a smile. "If you keep it up, I am sure that you will be rewarded for your efforts."

She lingered only long enough for the members of the team to express their profound gratitude for her trust and the opportunity to serve the Jin Dara—the kind of thing that she had heard a lot of in the last six months—and then she was on her way. Back in the transport, though, the memory of the demonstration faded pretty quickly and her mind strayed to her own ongoing experiment.

Returning to her new academy, as she referred to it in her own mind, she passed again through the main hall and then up the winding, narrow stair that led to her private office. It was large and had a lovely balcony that overlooked the city. It made her think sometimes of Eirmon's office in the palace of Barra-Dohn, and when it did, she couldn't help but smile at the thought that he was long dead and she was still going—and going strong.

Inside her office, in the corner was a table with another chest on it, much like the one in the quarry, only this one had a heavy duty lock to which only she had the key. She walked over to the chest and inserted the key. Once unlocked, she opened it and pulled out the sack that contained the precious Zerura powder.

She poured a large cup of water, measured out the usual generous portion of powder and began to stir. When as much of the Zerura had dissolved as was likely too, and while a small cloud of the golden flakes still swirled around in the tiny whirlpool she had created, she lifted the cup and drank the mixture down, swallowing repeatedly and being careful not to let a drop escape her mouth.

The water drained down her throat, and she felt the infusion of Zerura like a freezing man might feel an infusion of hot, steaming jonda. For six months she had been taking these doses of Zerura, and they had not disappointed. It had taken a month or more for her to become aware, through them, of the Arua field and her ability to feel and influence it, but once she had, she progressed quickly. Now she could reach out and touch it, and in limited ways, work through it to affect the world around her.

She knew from her time on the island where the Jin Dara had grown up that he had started learning his mastery of the Arua through experiments in which he mixed the elements of various living things, both plant and animal, and so she had begun her own similar experiments. She walked over to the small tank she kept under a cloth, pulled the cover off, and gazed on her handywork. The tail of the rat she had trapped under her desk was now very much like a growing vine, though her attempts to make the tip of the tail blossom into a flower had so far failed. She would keep working on that today, as she had each day this week. Perhaps today would be the day.

She dropped some scraps into the tank, and the rat scurried toward them and started eating. Rika reached out for the Arua and, through it, for the rat. It squealed as she took hold.

.   .   .

A single petal. It was all Rika had managed, but still she was elated. The viney tail she had given the rat had produced a yellow petal—slender, delicate, small—just like the petal of the flower she kept in a small vase on the table by the tank. Studying it, even taking it up to hold it and to probe and examine it physically as well as through the Arua field had seemed to help her. One day, no doubt, she wouldn't need such help—certainly the Jin Dara no longer did. But, for now, she didn't mind relying on it, so long as she continued to grow in her ability.

Rika watched the rat sniff the new appendage on his tail, but its expression was inscrutable. Curious? Afraid? What did it feel? And what would she do, she wondered, if she felt herself seized through the Arua field, felt an outside force tampering with her body, transforming her? What would she do if she looked down and suddenly her arm or leg were a branch, and at the end of the branch, a cluster of leaves?

She shuddered at the thought, realizing that precisely this and much, much worse had gone on continuously since their arrival. The entire city of Tanisaan, all the roads and approaches to the city for miles in every direction, every neighboring town and even some that weren't so neighboring—all of it was filled with the Jin Dara's creations, and all those creations had come to pass in just this way.

Rika certainly understood intellectually that most would expect her to be aghast that what she was doing as a clearly cruel experiment with a single rat, the Jin Dara was doing openly and callously with an entire population of human beings. And yet, that wasn't how Rika saw it. The obvious lesson here, she thought, was that in life, you should do everything you can possibly do to make sure you are never in the position of the rat.

That's what Rika was doing, she thought as she rose from her seat at the table, taking up the linen cloth and draping it back over the tank that housed the rat. She was doing everything in her power to make sure she didn't end up like all those twisted experiments dotting the landscape. This was what smart people did, what survivors did. They did whatever the situation required of them, and if possible, they did it in such a way as to enjoy themselves as well. In that, Rika had done quite well for herself.

She stretched as she turned from the table and looked through the glass windows at her large balcony. She was a little surprised to see how dark it was outside. She had noticed, of course, the fading light, and so she had lit the lamp and proceeded with her work. However, it was now completely dark and obviously much later than she had thought it was, a fact confirmed by the growling of her stomach. She'd not eaten since breakfast and her body complained mightily about its mistreatment, as it often did at the end of one of her long days.

Rika walked to the interior room of her office and placed the key to the chest with the Zerura powder in its secret spot. She sat at her desk and scribbled a short note in her journal about her progress with the rat, and then she rose and walked back out into the main room.

She was shocked to see the glass door to the balcony open and a man standing in the doorway, leaning against the frame. Not just any man, of course; it was the mysterious Gamalian look-alike, for Rika had settled in her own mind after the last time she had seen him that whoever—or whatever—this man was, it was not Gamalian.

It required only a moment to take him in, and in that moment Rika realized that his appearance was deteriorating. She'd been surprised by the rotting teeth in his mouth the last time, but as he stood, grinning a foul and disgusting smirk at her, those same teeth looked far worse, where there were any teeth at all. His wispy hair was greasy and stringy, and the wrinkled flesh on his face was spotted and blotchy.

But still those eyes were dark and cold and sinister, and if she had shuddered before when thinking of the unpleasant prospect of being manipulated like she was doing with the rat, she also shuddered now just to be in close proximity to this creature who stood once more before her. Instinctively she reached out through the Arua to take hold of him, almost before she could really think about what she was doing.

The pseudo-Gamalian laughed as her attempt to seize hold of him completely failed. It wasn't so much that she couldn't take hold of him as it was that in a sense, she couldn't find him. Her eyes told her he was there, just across the room in the doorway, but as she reached through the Arua to seize him, she felt nothing there, except for maybe a deep coldness, and that made no sense.

"You can't hurt me," he said, still laughing. "Not like that. Not with your paltry skills, no matter how dear they are to you or how proud you are of them."

Rika's mind reeled, trying to make sense of what she had experienced. All living things were affected by the Arua; it regulated them and more, governing the life-cycle and ecology of the entire world. That she might not comprehend what it was she could touch, or be able to change or control what she touched—that she could understand. That she would fail to touch what was right in front of her, that she could not grasp.

"Who are you?" she said. "What are you?"

"Don't you recognize me anymore, Rika?" he said. "I'm your old pal."

"Gamalian was never my pal," Rika said. "And whatever you are, you aren't him."

"Fair enough," the man said, and as he took a step into the room, Rika stepped back. "The time draws near when I will tell you who I am, but for now, it is not important."

"I want answers," Rika started.

"I don't care what you want," the man said, his voice now a low growl. "At least, I don't care what you want from me. What you want from the Jin Dara, on the other hand, about that I care a great deal."

This frank admission surprised her. "Why do you care about that?" she said, then added when she'd had a moment to think more carefully about what he said. "And what is it exactly that you think I want from him?"

"You want many things," the man said. "But there is something that you want more than anything else. You wanted it before you started your experiments, but now that you have begun them, now that you have started to have success, you desire it even more. It is your heart's desire, and I believe the time is very close when you shall have it."

Her heart rose in her chest. She felt, intuitively, that he knew. Somehow he knew. She'd never whispered a word out loud about this, but this man knew. She didn't know how, and the fact that he knew only confirmed her growing suspicion that he wasn't actually a man, but what he was, she couldn't have guessed. Still, her curiosity got the better of her. "How do you know it is going to happen?"

"I don't know," he said. "But I have worked very hard to orchestrate events in just such a way that this moment would come. Keep up the work you have been doing to prepare him, and then be ready when the moment comes to seize it. Then you will indeed have all you desire and more."

And with that, the man walked through the door and disappeared into the darkness. For a moment, she stayed where she was, reluctant to follow him. Then she got up the nerve and walked out the door onto the balcony. He was nowhere to be seen, and peering over the rail, she could see no sign of him down below either.

For a long time she stood there, and despite the curious manner of the man's disappearance, where he had gone was not one of the questions on her mind. Rather, the two questions she couldn't push away were who was this 'man,' and was what he said true? Was the dream that she harbored deep down inside her finally going to come true?

30

IT'S TIME

Meldriic ran along the surface of the Arua. The sun had slipped below the horizon and the dusky half-light of evening was fading. It was all right, though, as his sight was remarkable, like all of his Zerura-enhanced senses. Of course, his brothers had the same sensory enhancements, so he was not overconfident.

He was approaching a large abandoned farmhouse on his right. There were several secondary buildings clustered beyond it too—a silo for grain, a smaller shed that probably housed the now-unused farming equipment, and a barn that had probably once been the home of the farm's livestock.

Several tall trees were also clustered near the farmhouse and around the other tightly grouped structures. They represented some unique opportunities, but they also posed some possible threats, and he would need to be wary as he passed through.

He heard a slight whistle and immediately veered hard right, diving and rolling across the surface of the Arua. When he came up out of his roll, he was facing the direction in which the whistle had come from, and with a motion of his hand he had redirected the blunt thrown at him so that it hit the hard siding of farmhouse and bounced off harmlessly.

In a moment, he had a blunt in his own hand. The haft of the blunt felt just like that of a knife, but the rounded, smooth metal protruding from it wouldn't hurt anyone if it hit them—at least, not seriously. It was heavy enough to give you quite a headache if you took it to the head, but that was still a good bit better than the alternative.

Meldriic had learned early on when training the Najin in the use of three fragments, that the power they all possessed was too great and their control of that power too tenuous to train with actual weapons. Several Najin had been hurt, one almost fatally, and even though he had survived, his fighting days were over.

This had prompted a meeting between Meldriic and the Jin Dara, in which they discussed how to proceed. Meldriic had advised scaling back the live training with weapons, suggesting instead that they could focus on experimenting with their new power over the Arua and separately work on more standard weapons training. The Jin Dara had been reluctant to accept this proposal, though, since the battle that was coming would not be against stationary targets but the Amhuru, who were more than capable of holding their own in battle.

Meldriic knew this, and secretly he agreed, but he had hoped to slow down the progress the Najin were making, lest he and his brothers fail and he provide too much help to the Jin Dara's fight against the Amhuru. However, he knew that if he himself was to succeed, he had to continue to convince the Jin Dara that he was doing his best in his service, so when it became apparent that live training would continue in some form, he had advocated for the use of the blunts.

The blunts approximated the weight and feel of an actual knife without the same lethal ability to penetrate when they struck their target, and Meldriic thought that in a week, enough could be made to equip all the Najin with multiple blunts for their training to continue. The Jin Dara loved the idea, and by week's end, he had provided Meldriic enough blunts to equip several armies. The live training had then resumed.

Just about every day since then, after the Najin were dismissed to return to their other duties, Meldriic and his brothers remained behind and trained on their own, playing their own kind of war game. Today was no different, and while it was just a game, you were not a Jaen if you didn't take things like this seriously. Very seriously.

Meldriic scanned the area from which the blunt had come and, not surprisingly, he didn't see anyone. The silo, he thought. That was where one of his brothers was hidden, or possibly two. Vaall and Petaar were out, but Renoud and Traliin could be working together.

No sooner had that thought crossed his mind than a flash of movement beside him drew his attention and he wheeled, ready to throw his blunt. It wasn't one of his brothers, though, but one of the tall trees beside the farmhouse that had moved. It was bending toward him and one of its outstretched branches was whipping down toward Meldriic with incredible speed.

He could feel the strength of his brother—whichever one it was—bending his control of the Arua toward the tree, and he reached out through the three fragments he also wore to try to challenge his brother's mastery and control. At the same time, he tried to dodge the limb, but he wasn't quite fast enough. The end wrapped around his ankle, as the branch was not hard and inflexible as it should have been but pliable like rope, and it squeezed tightly as it took hold.

The next thing Meldriic knew he was flying. The branch, having secured his ankle in a vise-like grip, shot upward to its full height and then let go. Meldriic launched upward, suddenly soaring high above the farmhouse and all the other buildings that surrounded it.

Meldriic watched the ground and trees and buildings spin as he rotated upward to the top of the arc on which he'd been thrown, then he reached out through the Arua himself and focused on a smaller tree that he had seen between the barn and silo. He took hold of the tree and commanded it to run. It pulled its roots up out of the soil in a spray of dirt and grass, and as the roots rolled up into knobby feet, it began to lumber across the farmyard toward the door to the silo.

Meldriic started to fall, and as he fell, he tried to maneuver himself so that he could watch the base of the silo as the tree he had sent that way got into position by the door. He wasn't worried about hitting the ground, as he knew he would be able to use the Arua to break his fall. He concentrated on the field itself, or rather, on the field's connection to himself, and he used it to slow his momentum as he neared it, enough that he came to rest on top of the Arua almost gently.

He rolled over, knowing things would happen quickly. Sure enough, the door to the silo burst open and Renoud and Traliin both leapt out, blunts in hand. Meldriic directed the tree to move, and it did, swooping in and seizing both brothers tightly in its branches.

The tree was overmatched with two to control, and Meldriic knew it, but he didn't need much time. The blunt was out of his hand in mere seconds as he sprinted toward the silo. He bent his will toward using the tree to keep Renoud still, and Traliin broke free, but not before the blunt took him in the side, knocking him out of the game.

As Meldriic closed the distance between himself and the scene playing out beside the silo, the blunt flew back into his hand. Renoud was fighting back with fury against his control of the tree, and Meldriic strained to hold him back. Renoud was the strongest of the others, which was why Meldriic had taken out Traliin first. He continually sought to measure himself against the best, and of his brothers, that was Renoud.

He held on, resisting Renoud's counterattack in the intense battle of will and determination playing out invisibly for mastery of the tree, and then he ran. He would not throw the blunt. He would make contact with Renoud directly, get within arm's reach and win the game up close.

A loud, cracking sound rent the evening as the tree broke into a dozen large shards of wood, flying all over the farmyard. The tension of so much power fighting for control had been too much for it, and the tree had broken under the strain in spectacular fashion.

Meldriic had no time to observe the spectacle of the flying fragments, for Renoud, suddenly free of the tree's grip was moving to the side in an attempt to dive behind the silo before Meldriic could reach him. Forced to adapt to the new circumstances, Meldriic abandoned both his pride and his plan to touch Renoud personally, and he threw his blunt as hard as he could throw, knowing as he did that it would be tough to hit Renoud before he disappeared behind the silo.

Sure enough, Renoud passed out of sight before the blunt could hit him. So Meldriic redirected the blunt once it passed the curved side of the silo, but he was doing so blind. He had no idea where exactly Renoud was around the other side. Even so, he had gotten pretty good at throwing around a blind corner these past several months, and he gambled on the probability that Renoud would be hugging the silo wall as closely as he could.

A grunt confirmed the hit, even before Renoud called out to acknowledge it. Traliin, who had been standing where he could see both brothers on different sides of the silo, clapped his hands and said. "Well done, Meldriic. That was quite a throw."

"Forget the throw," Renoud said, coming back around from behind the silo to join his brothers. "That tree wasn't right outside the silo door when we went in, Meldriic."

"Neat trick, huh?" Meldriic said, and he grinned as he caught his breath.

"Sa," Renoud said, sarcastically. "It was great."

"Come now," Meldriic said. "Petaar is the sore loser in our family, Renoud. We don't need another."

"Fair enough," Renoud conceded. "But surely you can sympathize with us, Meldriic. Even though you are the oldest, it is still hard for the rest of us to lose to you all the time."

"All the time?" Meldriic said. "I don't win even half the time."

"Meldriic," Traliin chimed in, "There are five of us, you know. Almost half the time is domination, and you know it."

"Maybe it is," Meldriic said, "but look at it this way. With four such talented little brothers who have always measured themselves against me and made everything a competition, I've had to work really hard to keep my edge. Have I not?"

"Sa, it's true," Renoud conceded. "You work harder than anyone I've ever known, at everything you do."

"Come," Meldriic said as they started away from the silo together, "Petaar and Vaall will wonder what has become of us."

"That's their problem for getting knocked out so early," Traliin said.

"True," Meldriic said. "But still, tomorrow it may be you, or me, so let's not keep them waiting."

.   .   .

Meldriic sat with a cup of water in his hand, but he was not relaxed. He never relaxed anymore, not that he'd ever been very prone to it before. All of life now was divided into states of comparative alertness, and he knew that if this was true of him, how much more must it be so of the Jin Dara?

It was almost inescapable with so much Zerura on his body. He found that it not only heightened his senses, though that in itself was remarkable, but his awareness in general seemed razor sharp, all the time. Without trying, he sensed and saw details of what was going on around him, and when he actually concentrated and focused, it was scary how much he noticed.

He glanced around the table at his brothers, and he finally broached the subject they had been avoiding for far too long. "We have to make a decision."

There was no need to be more specific, for they all knew what he was talking about. Petaar looked at him. "Has something happened?"

"Na," Meldriic said, shaking his head. "But we all know it is true. We've delayed too long, put this off too long. We must decide."

"I agree," Renoud said. "But the same things that have led to our delays, they remain true. Do you have something new to propose that would help us see the road ahead more clearly?"

"I don't," Meldriic said. "I have only my gut, which tells me increasingly that waiting for the Amhuru to come is risky."

"It's all risky," Petaar said.

"True," Meldriic said, a little annoyed. "I know that. But the premise of waiting for battle with the Amhuru was that it might provide cover for our attempt on the Jin Dara, but the more I train with the fragments the more I doubt that."

"Why?" Renoud asked.

"You know what it is like when we train, when we play our game," Meldriic answered. "I have never felt so alert, so aware, and if that is true for us who have only had six months to train with replicas, how much more do you think it is true of him, who bears the originals? Do you not think it unlikely that in the heat of battle, when he is most alert, that we could ever surprise him?"

"But if he is focused on the Amhuru, on their movements and their actions," Vaall said, "perhaps he will not be focused on us?"

"I think that's Meldriic's point," Traliin said. "He doesn't need to be. He will be alert to any threat, and when we move against him, he will be ready to strike back."

Meldriic nodded. "That is my fear, that he will be ready to counterattack against any move we might make, if for no other reason than the fact that Draagan almost got to him once, and he will be determined that no Amhuru—or anyone—will ever get to him again."

"And there's another thing," Renoud said. "The more we train the Najin, the more we help assure the Jin Dara's success against the Amhuru if we fail."

"I'm not sure why we care if the Amhuru do fail," Traliin said. "The Jin Dara might do the world a favor by destroying them."

"Don't be a fool," Petaar snapped. "I feel no love for the Amhuru either, but if we fail, they are the only ones who have a chance to stop the Jin Dara."

"And we've all seen what it would mean if they don't," Meldriic said. "Our grievance with the Amhuru has nothing to do with this. Whatever wrong they've done us, there's no question who must win that battle if it comes, and Renoud is right. By stalling so long, we've served only to make the Najin stronger by training them."

"Then we need to make our move," Renoud said.

"Sa," Meldriic agreed. "It's time. We need to make our move."

"When?" Petaar asked.

"I say we go tonight," Meldriic said. "We wait until the middle of the night, hope that he is asleep, and we go."

Meldriic looked at his brothers, but if his suggestion caught them off guard or provoked fear, it wasn't evident. They each looked thoughtful, but none of them looked hesitant or afraid.

"What do you think?" he asked after a moment.

"I think that if you say we should go tonight, we should go tonight."

The others nodded their heads in agreement with Renoud, but Meldriic wanted to be sure. "Petaar?"

"Why not?" he said. "It's as good as any other time."

"Traliin?"

"Sure," Traliin said. "If we're not waiting for the Amhuru to come, we should get on with it."

"Vaall?"

Vaall shrugged. "It's what we came to do, isn't it?"

"Good," Meldriic said. "Then we're agreed."

"What time do you think we should go?" Petaar asked.

"I think we should wait until just a few hours before dawn," Meldriic said. "From what we've been able to learn about the Jin Dara, he's more prone to staying up late than getting up early, so I think it would be safer to wait until then."

"I think the trickiest part will be getting to his chambers without having to use the Arua to incapacitate or kill any Najin who might be guarding him," Renoud said. "If we have to seize the Arua before we get to him, I think he'll know."

"I agree," Meldriic said. "It would be like triggering an alarm, even if he is asleep. We must do all we can to get to him without doing that, which means killing every Najin we encounter between here and there by means of stealth is all-important."

"And we might want to consider splitting up for at least part of the way from here to there," Petaar said. "If all five of us are seen moving together out on the streets, it will arouse suspicion."

"We move together all the time," Traliin said.

"Not in the middle of the night," Meldriic countered. "I think Petaar is right. We should go over our route again, consider where we're most likely to encounter Najin, and plan the formations we take in every street and hallway between here and the Jin Dara's bed."

"Then let's get to it," Renoud said. "I'd love to get an hour or two of sleep before we go, if possible."

"I agree," Meldriic said. "We plan, then we sleep."

"Then we go."

"Sa, then we go."

31

THE WILL OF MELDRIIC JAEN

The house in Tanisaan that the Jin Dara had given the Jaens to live in shortly after he entrusted them to guide the work of training the Najin in the use of their three fragments wasn't far from the city's main gate. The gate, of course, was always guarded, so the first concern of the Jaens in getting to the Tanisaan palace where the Jin Dara had his rooms was that they not bump into a patrol going to or coming from the gate.

Meldriic stepped out of the house and started down the street. He was not alone, but to the casual observer—if there was one—he would look alone. Petaar and Vaall, and Renoud and Traliin had slipped out of the back door at separate times, and by now both pairs had reached their appointed places. They would shadow him and, if he had trouble of any kind, come to his aid, but they didn't expect trouble. Not yet, anyway.

They had been with the Jin Dara less than a year, but Meldriic's reputation had preceded him. What's more, nothing that had happened since had done anything to lessen it. The Jin Dara was unquestionably feared more, but that didn't mean that Meldriic didn't inspire his own kind of awe and fear. It seemed unlikely anyone but the Jin Dara himself, or perhaps his right hand man Devaar, would dare to interfere with Meldriic as he walked alone through Tanisaan.

When they came to the palace, though, all bets would be off. It might be that Devaar was able to come and go freely from there without being summoned by the Jin Dara, Meldriic didn't really know, but certainly Meldriic didn't go to the palace unless he was sent for. So whatever they assumed about Meldriic not being challenged on the street, they did not make any assumptions about the palace.

Meldriic walked along the street, which unsurprisingly was empty at this early morning hour. The air was brisk, so much so that he could see his breath in small misty puffs. Meldriic gazed up at the moon and stars shining in the cold night, and it occurred to him that he didn't mind dying today nearly as much as he might have thought he would.

That he was going to die today, Meldriic found entirely likely. It wasn't that he assumed they would fail, although that was a real possibility of course. Success was no guarantee of survival, though, and that Meldriic understood full well. Even if they managed to kill the Jin Dara, they would be in the heart of Tanisaan, surrounded on all sides by the Najin, who would almost certainly do everything they could to avenge their fallen leader.

It was strange, how his own heart and motives had changed during this past year, but especially during the six months since the Jin Dara had taken Tanisaan. He had accepted Draagan's proposal, in part because he agreed that the Jin Dara needed to be stopped, but just as much because the allure of wearing Zerura and possibly getting his hands on some of the original fragments of the Golden Cord was hard for him to turn down.

His brothers, especially the younger two, still talked about the dilemma they would face once they killed the Jin Dara and escaped with the three original pieces. They seemed to take for granted that if they could kill the Jin Dara and gain the pieces of the Cord, then no one would be able to stop them from getting away. Meldriic wasn't so sure, and he had almost been surprised to learn some time ago that he didn't care. Getting his hands on those fragments no longer had any attraction for him. For him, all that mattered was killing the Jin Dara, and for Meldriic's part, there was no dilemma about what to do with the fragments if they got them and somehow survived.

They must be returned. It was the order of things, and he no longer disputed that.

And so, as he walked alone through the streets of Tanisaan, he felt completely calm. He had known battle, had been a hair's breadth from death many times, and he was not afraid. The only trepidation he felt was that they might fail, and the whole world might fall under the sway of the

Jin Dara. That thought and that thought alone had the power to make him tremble.

Meldriic continued on his way, and the streets continued to be empty. This was certainly what the Jaens had hoped for, and it made complete sense that no one would be out and about at this time. Even so, the quiet felt suspicious and unnatural, and Meldriic wasn't sure if he liked it.

At last he came to the street that ran perpendicular to the large open courtyard in front of the Tanisaan palace, and he slid up next to the building that provided cover between him and the large front entrance to the palace in the distance. Meldriic peeked around the corner, and there in front of the palace entrance stood not one, not two, but three Najin chatting together in the circle of light that illuminated the entrance.

Seeing the guards comforted Meldriic. They were the first Najin he had seen, and seeing them standing guard at the front of the palace felt right. The Jin Dara might be the most powerful man in the world, but Meldriic had also come to see him as a strange mixture of complete confidence and deep paranoia, so multiple guards at his front door made perfect sense.

He moved back along the front of the building he had been shadowing and started through the side lanes that he and his brothers had picked for him to use in getting to the small side entrance of the palace that they felt was their best bet for a quiet way in. They expected it to be guarded, but it presented the easiest opportunity to approach undetected and hopefully kill the guards without use of the Zerura they bore.

In fact, the longer Meldriic walked without feeling anyone manipulate the Arua, the more hopeful he felt. If all went to plan, Renoud and Traliin would already have killed any Najin by the side door and hidden their bodies out of sight by the time Meldriic and his own guardians, Petaar and Vaall, arrived.

Sure enough, when Meldriic reached the place from which he could see the small side door, there were no guards there, and there certainly should have been. More to the point, the small white stone sitting next to the door indicated that Renoud and Traliin had been there and the guards had been dispatched. Meldriic crossed quickly over toward the door but hid in the shadows up against the palace wall just far enough away from the actual door that the light above it did not reveal him.

Darting across the open space to grab a share of the shadow beside him, right on cue, were Petaar and Vaall. Meldriic nodded as they joined him, and then he turned to look past the doorway. Sure enough, Traliin and

Renoud came around the corner from behind the palace, jogging along beside the wall until they reached the side door. He saw dark blotches on their hands, and he knew it was the blood of the men who had been positioned here just a few moments ago.

None of the Jaens spoke. They had been over the plan enough and weren't so foolish as to speak out loud and endanger everything. When Meldriic opened this door, all would happen very quickly.

There was a short hall to the back stair, which they would take up to the third floor. The stair opened up on the far end of a long, wide hallway, with several nice apartments on either side. In the middle, the main floor of the former king of Tanisaan's apartment lay, on the other side of a pair of ornate, double doors. They would proceed through those doors into that apartment, but the Jin Dara would not be in that room.

His room was above, on the fourth floor, but you couldn't get there any other way than by means of a spiral staircase in the middle of the third floor room they were heading for. They'd go to the spiral stair, then up, and then hope to find the Jin Dara asleep in his bed. Meldriic had never been up the spiral stairs, but he figured they would find the bed easily enough.

For all this to work, an equal premium would need to be placed on both speed and stealth. Meldriic thought that from the side door they would use to enter the palace to the bed, it would take them only about a minute, depending on whether they encountered resistance anywhere along the way. A minute, he thought, his heart racing, and then he reached for the handle and opened the door.

Meldriic was in and jogging down the hallway in seconds. It was empty, like the streets had been, and once more, while he was grateful for his good fortune, he was also suspicious of it. He didn't trust good fortune very much. Perhaps he'd had too many good plans go awry to be comfortable when they didn't.

His brothers moved in silently behind him, but as quiet as they were, his heightened senses heard the door softly click shut behind him. He certainly hoped there weren't any Najin awake, close enough to notice, but there was no time to wonder about that. He had already reached the bottom of the back stairs, and without hesitation, he started up.

He ran up past the door to the second floor and on upward until he reached the door to the third floor hallway. He stopped there, waiting just a moment for the other four to join him on the landing. The door was closed, so he couldn't see down the hall, but he did not expect this hallway to be empty. He'd never been here without seeing a guard at the Jin Dara's door, and he fully expected there to be one there now.

Slowly, Meldriic cracked open the door so he could peek down the hall. It was reasonably well lit by several lamps hung from both walls. In the middle of the hallway, right next to the double doors that led into the main floor of the Jin Dara's apartment, a guard stood. Or rather, he leaned, as he was somewhat slumped back against the wall on this side of the doors. His head nodded down and then jerked back up suddenly, but then it began immediately to nod again. The man was either sleeping or trying to sleep, right there on his feet.

Meldriic acted decisively. He pushed the door open firmly but quietly and started running as fast as he could down the hall, while at the same time stepping as lightly on the plush carpeting as he knew how. The soldier by the door never knew what hit him, for barely had Meldriic covered half the distance to the doorway when he had his knife in hand, and a few more strides only and the knife was on its way.

It took the guard in the neck, sinking all the way in up to the hilt. The man started slowly to tilt and then slide away from Meldriic, but before he could hit the floor, Meldriic was there, catching him by the torso and then guiding him gently the rest of the way down. He would have blocked the doorway if left where he fell, so Meldriic pulled him all the way across, and when he stood back up, his brothers were already there beside him.

Again they didn't say a word, and again Meldriic didn't hesitate. He opened the door and they slipped into the large open room on the other side. Across from the doors was the large glass window that overlooked the city, and through that window came a faint glow from the city lights and the bright moon in the night sky. It was more than enough for the Jaens to make out the furniture in the room and find their way quietly to the foot of the spiral stair in the middle of the room. Once at the bottom, they started noiselessly up without hesitation.

It did not take Meldriic long to spot the large canopied bed, and motioning to his brothers, they spread out and moved toward it. They had it fairly surrounded in just a moment, and all had their weapons out. They had reached their goal, and it had all gone smoothly. It was time to do the deed. Meldriic threw the canopy back and moved to strike.

The bed was empty.

There was just a moment of hesitation as Meldriic processed the empty bed before him, and then he was whirling, knife raised, having leapt immediately to the conclusion that they had walked into a trap. The Jin Dara had known they were coming. How he had known, Meldriic didn't know, but he suddenly knew with an eerie certainty that he had known.

Lights flared all around the once dark chamber, and a dozen Najin, dressed in black instead of the normal gold, stepped forward from their hiding spots along the walls and in corners. Out of the corner of his eye, Meldriic saw the Jin Dara himself, sparkling gold in the sudden flood of light.

The battle was immediate and intense, as the five Jaens reached out in concert for the Arua, as did the Jin Dara and his Najin. Everyone had a weapon in his hand, but the real weapon was the invisible power both sides fought to control. Meldriic turned so that he faced the Jin Dara, who was already focused upon him.

Meldriic locked his eyes on his foe, giving silent vent to all the hatred and rage he felt toward the 'man' before him. A part of him was glad it had come to this, glad he could stare his enemy in the eye, even if it did cost him his life. If he was going to die, so be it. At least he would show the Jin Dara that there was a man left in the world who did not fear him.

The struggle was incredible. Meldriic didn't think the Najin alone could overpower the Jaens, as so much of a man's success when wielding the power of Zerura had to do with his own inner strength, and none among the Najin could match the Jaens for that. But with the Jin Dara there, who was so strong, so very strong, Meldriic felt the tide of the battle turning against them. He felt his brothers pushing, as he was, so valiantly and so hard, but he also felt fatigue—in himself and in them. If it continued as a stalemate for too much longer, the Jin Dara would surely win.

Meldriic knew that their only hope was for the Jin Dara to fall, and fall now. What's more, he knew the only way that would happen would be if he, personally, broke through the invisible impasse and took hold of the Jin Dara just long enough to get himself or his knife across the room and take him down. To do that, though, would require an act of the will of monumental proportions.

Meldriic Jaen smiled. If anything marked his family, if any quality stood out about them, it was defiant acts of the will. From his grandfather and father to himself and his brothers and his own sons whom he had left behind to manage the JaenSing, sheer will was something no Jaen lacked, least of all himself. He reached inside and gathered himself for the push, and then he reached out through the three fragments of Zerura he wore and struck with a power that shocked even himself.

For a moment, just a moment, indeed the very briefest of moments, he broke through the Jin Dara's hold of the Arua, broke through and took hold of the Jin Dara himself. Shock and dismay and something not unlike fear registered on the golden face across the room. Meldriic Jaen stepped forward, knowing he could not hold his enemy long, and he threw his knife, straight and true.

Meldriic only needed to hold him still for a second, but it was a second too much. The Jin Dara struck back, breaking the hold Meldriic had taken on him, and he moved to the side. The knife missed his heart and hit the Jin Dara's arm. The Jin Dara then struck out at Meldriic, who was exhausted from the force it had taken to break through. He could not stop the Jin Dara's counterstroke. He was seized and gripped and controlled as completely as if he had been wrapped with a thousand cables and tied to a post.

He was finished, and he knew it.

.   .   .

The battle was over; the Jin Dara knew that. His Najin controlled the four Jaen brothers, and he held Meldriic personally. Still, the shock that had just now registered when for a moment Meldriic had pushed through and taken hold of him still dominated him, though pain from his wound and anger and rage were rising inside too. He pulled the knife out of his arm and tossed it behind him, and then he walked forward until he stood eye to eye with his enemy.

"How did you do that?" the Jin Dara asked. "How could you, even for a moment, do that?"

Though he could have spoken if he wanted to, Meldriic remained silent, and the Jin Dara knew that the look of smug defiance and hatred in the man's eyes said all he was ever going to say on the matter. The Jin Dara saw the look, but rather than be angered or annoyed by it, he couldn't help but like and admire Meldriic Jaen. He had always done so, even as he had always mistrusted him.

The seething turmoil of shock and indignation, of rage and anger, calmed inside him. It calmed, because the Jin Dara forced it to calm. He seized control of his own emotional state, even as he had seized control of Meldriic. He would not be mastered by anything or anyone, not even his own passions.

"You know," the Jin Dara said, much more calmly than he had spoken just a moment ago, "I distrusted you from the first, although I can't say why. Your story, it sounded so plausible, so real, that I didn't know why I shouldn't trust you. Still, there was something not quite right about you."

The Jin Dara turned his back on Meldriic, a silent slap in his enemy's face, as he wanted him to know that he was so much in control he didn't need to even bother keeping an eye on him. Then he continued.

"I don't doubt that much of your story is true, of course. I have learned enough of the Northlands to know you really do have a grievance with the Amhuru, and I saw enough in my own encounter with the Amhuru, Draagan, to understand that going to you with the request that you come and try to kill me is just the kind of unconventional, bold move he might make."

Images of Draagan stabbing him flashed in front of the Jin Dara's eyes. He heard the mocking words, *the kitchen knife is king, until it meets the sharper blade.* He clenched his jaw in seething hatred. The debt he owed that particular Amhuru kept growing, and he would see it paid.

"Still," the Jin Dara continued, turning to look at Meldriic again, "I didn't buy it. All I could think of to explain my mistrust—besides the vague notion of intuition—is that you're just not the kind of man to kneel. Coming to me, offering service, all of that, it was logical in a way, but I don't know if all the logic in the world could ever have persuaded you, of all men, to do it."

The Jin Dara glanced at the Najin on either side of him and nodded. They moved forward and started to remove all the replicas of Zerura that Meldriic and his brothers wore, as well as the weapons that they carried. Then the Najin escorted the five Jaens down the spiral stair and into the large open main floor of the Jin Dara's apartment. The Jin Dara watched silently, as the Najin arranged the five brothers so that the four younger ones stood like the four corners of a square with Meldriic in the middle.

Then the Najin took over with the now-easy task of holding the Jaens still, and the Jin Dara went to work on the four younger Jaens. Their bodies started to twist and change, each in its own special way, though for each of them, he changed their necks into growing vines that stretched up and up, right over Meldriic's head until they met high above him but below the ceiling. There the Jin Dara twisted the four neck-vines together into a complex kind of knot, so that the knobby and now mostly wooden heads of the four younger Jaens hung like ripe pumpkins awkwardly to the side, with looks of pain and horror now frozen on what remained of their faces. And, all the while as he worked, the Jin Dara stood and stared at the angry but helpless face of Meldriic Jaen.

"I suppose it can't hurt now to tell you how I knew you were coming," the Jin Dara said. "But the story really goes back quite a long way.

"Not long after I had taken the second fragment of the Golden Cord and started wearing it," he continued. "I realized that the connection between myself and those few that I trusted at first to wear replicas of both originals was far stronger than I had expected. I explored that connection, only to discover that within a certain range, if I concentrated, I could tell where they were. I got to the point where I could identify their precise locations up to several miles away, and beyond that, I could still get a general sense of direction when they moved.

"So when I got my third original, I was of course curious to know if my connection to those who wore all three replicas would grow still stronger, and I was not disappointed. In fact, I discovered that I could actually hear what anyone wearing the replicas was saying. At first it was difficult to control, and the constant babble was frustrating until I learned to tune out what I didn't want to hear and focus on what I did. And, again, there were limits in terms of distance, but ever since I learned to control the ability, it has come in quite handy.

"As I said before, I mistrusted you from the start, so giving you three fragments wasn't so much an act of trust as it was an act of mistrust, a way of keeping tabs on you. It was a fairly easy decision to focus on listening to you and your brothers as much as possible. That's why I gave you all your own house, so you would have enough privacy to feel comfortable to speak to one another freely, which you did, and I was not disappointed.

"So," the Jin Dara continued, smiling as he saw the fury written on every inch of Meldriic Jaen's face. "I've known for some time that you intended to make an attempt on my life, but you were doing such a good job training my Najin, I didn't want to stop you. I took a calculated risk, letting you proceed, but thanks to the forewarning you gave me tonight, I was able to prepare this little reception for you. Thanks for letting me know."

"You knew," Meldriic Jaen said, speaking for the first time. "And you had us outnumbered, and we still almost beat you."

"Almost," the Jin Dara said, stepping up so close that he was nose to nose with Meldriic. He could feel the other man's hot breath on his face. "Though I can't imagine you will find much consolation from this fact in the days and years to come, as you suffer the perpetual agonies I've pre-pared for you and your brothers."

The Jin Dara stepped back and smiled again as he stared at Meldriic standing beneath the spectacular four-cornered arch he had made from the other Jaen brothers. "Maybe it will *almost* comfort you, though."

He reached out for Meldriic and went to work.

32

THIS IS GOODBYE

Kaden used to think he had experienced real cold during his many years of traveling after fleeing the collapse of Barra-Dohn. He learned quickly during the last month that this was not the case. What's more, he also learned to stop saying to himself on any given day that surely this must be as cold as it gets, for it seemed like every time he convinced himself that this was true, a colder day lay directly ahead.

He had also come to understand why the Northlanders referred to the bright full moon surrounded by the grey, misty halo as a 'cold moon.' It did seem as though on the particularly cold nights, when he gazed up into the nighttime sky, that the moon was likely to have the strange grey ring around it. He didn't understand the connection between the temperature and the phenomenon, necessarily, but he understood why people had made it.

Ahead of Kaden, Kiki walked hand in hand with Olli along the road. Kaden's chief concern as the climate grew less and less hospitable was for Kiki, but another thing he had learned on this journey was that his little girl tolerated the cold far better than he did. No wonder, he thought to himself, as she had spent her whole life in the Northlands. Or perhaps it was simply a function of the surprising resilience and durability of children. Whatever it was, he was glad that she appeared more or less unfazed by the deepening cold.

He was also glad, and increasingly so, for the presence of Olli and Maarta on this journey. He didn't doubt that he could have taken care of Kiki without Olli, but he was glad he didn't have to. There were simply times when both Kiki and Kaden needed a break from one another, and Olli stepped into these gaps with a seamless ease. She appeared somehow just to know when to come by and offer to take Kiki for a while, and since Kiki had known Olli her whole life, she was perhaps the only person in this whole group that Kiki accepted in anything like a maternal role—not that Olli ever presumed to mother her. She simply took upon herself the role of an older, caring female who was there for Kiki at any time, whatever the situation.

And Maarta, for his part, never complained or showed any annoyance at having Kiki join him and his wife, sometimes just for a meal, sometimes for the better part of a day. Kaden had expressed his gratitude to them both on more than one occasion, but both had insisted that he say nothing more about it. They loved Kiki, they said, and knew it was hard for both Kiki and Kaden without Nara. They were happy to do it.

Still, as Kaden watched Olli and Kiki walking, watched Kiki chatting merrily away, he couldn't shake the feeling that there was something Olli wasn't telling him. She had seemed at times to be sad and distant when he talked to her. At first, he'd assumed that was all about Nara, as the two had been very close ever since they'd rescued Olli from the island of dreadful daylight.

But Kaden wasn't so sure anymore. He knew he wasn't the most astute observer when it cames to things like this, but Olli at times acted guilty around him. But what she could possibly be guilty of or feel guilty for, he couldn't imagine. She'd been unfailingly gracious to him and to Nara from the first, and since Nara died, she'd been superb. He determined that when they set up camp for the night, he would talk to her and find out, once and for all, what was going on.

This proved to be easier said than done. The ebb and flow of the activity within the camp seemed to conspire against him, and it was only long after Kiki was down for the night that he was able to make his way to the campfire where Olli and Maarta were keeping warm and ask her for a moment to talk together.

Olli excused herself, and Kaden promised Maarta that he would bring her right back. They walked off through the crisp evening until they were standing in a small hollow just down a slight embankment from the main camp. Olli followed Kaden without a word, and when he stopped, she watched him warily as though she was afraid of what was going to come next.

"Olli," Kaden started, realizing he didn't know exactly how to put this. "I know something is bothering you. I see it in your eyes and your body language at times—like now. I hear it in your tone, a kind of sadness, or a sense of regret maybe, and it seems to have something to do with me. Am I crazy? Or is there something perhaps that we need to talk about?"

Olli didn't say anything. She looked away. Not at the camp, but over the open field beyond the hollow. Kaden waited, but when Olli still didn't say anything, he continued.

"Olli," he coaxed, trying to sound as gentle and encouraging as he could. "You can say it, whatever it is. You're like family to me."

Olli burst into tears. She raised her hands to cover her face, and Kaden stood, watching her weep, horrified. He didn't know what to say or do, so he reached out his hand, awkwardly, and placed it gently on her shoulder, hoping to comfort her. Olli responded to this by turning toward him and putting her arms around him while she buried her tearful face against his chest.

"It's my fault he's gone," she said as she sobbed. And then she said, over and over. "It's my fault."

Kaden had no idea what was going on, but he tried his best to comfort and quiet her. After a moment, the sobbing slowed, although the tears continued to fall as Olli wiped them from her eyes with her sleeve. When it looked as though she had regained her composure, Kaden said. "Olli, I don't know what we're talking about."

"Deslo," she whispered. "We're talking about Deslo."

Realization washed over Kaden suddenly, and he understood. At least, he understood that Olli was implying it was her fault Deslo had chosen to go with Amintuu's faction of the Amhuru, instead of coming north with them to find the Cura-Katane. But why she would think this, he had no idea.

"Olli," Kaden said. "Are you saying it's your fault Deslo chose to go with Amintuu?"

Olli nodded.

"Why do you think it is your fault?"

Olli took a deep breath, then she said. "He came to me a few days after the council. He asked if we could talk, and I said sure."

Again Olli raised her arm and used her sleeve to wipe her eyes, and when she continued, her voice was steadier. "He said he didn't blame me for not loving him, but that he couldn't bear to be around me anymore, couldn't bear to watch me and Maarta together. He wanted to know what we were planning on doing …"

Her voice faltered then, and she looked up at Kaden, as though trying to gauge his reaction—perhaps to see if he was upset with her. He tried to smile, to encourage her to go on, but he could feel a knot forming in his own gut as she talked.

"I told him we were going with Draagan and Tchinchura, of course," she said. "And I told him it was the right thing to do, and that he should come too. I said we could work something out, but he just said he couldn't, that he had to go."

She started to cry again and started shaking her head as she cried. "I'm so sorry, Kaden. I tried to tell him not to go. I tried, but he wouldn't listen to me."

"Olli," Kaden said, taking her shoulders firmly. "You need to listen to me. Whatever Deslo has done, it is not your fault."

Olli stared up at him, but what she was feeling, he couldn't tell. He continued. "Do you understand what I'm telling you? It wasn't your fault. As Deslo told me when we talked about his decision, he is a man and he made his own choice."

"But I'm the reason for that choice," Olli moaned, and Kaden could hear the agony in her voice.

"Maybe," Kaden said. "I don't doubt that you are part of it, but I don't think you were all of it. Not at all."

Olli sniffed. "You don't?"

"I don't," Kaden said. "I think Deslo wants to see the Jin Dara pay for what he did to Barra-Dohn. I also think he feels loyalty to Trabor and Shaline, and that he wants to help avenge their mother's death. And I think he honestly believes that Amintuu might be right, that unless we combine the fragments we have, we can't beat the Jin Dara.

"So even if you were a part of his decision, you were only a part," Kaden said. "And you are certainly not to blame, not even a little bit, for that part. It isn't your fault how he feels about you. You have dealt honorably with him. It's just an unfortunate situation, is all."

"You're not upset with me?"

"Na, Olli," Kaden said. "But I am sad that you've carried this so long when you didn't need to. You need to lay it down."

Olli leaned back in, putting her head against Kaden's chest. When she spoke, her voice was faint and very quiet. "I'm so worried that something will happen to him, that I'll never see him again."

"Me too," Kaden admitted. "But we can't help him now, can we?"

"Na," Olli said. "We can't."

"All we can do now," Kaden said as Olli stepped back and looked up at him, "is move forward with what we have before us, and trust Deslo and the other Amhuru to Kalos."

"But if Draagan and Tchinchura are right, then what Amintuu and the others are doing is wrong. How can we trust him to Kalos if he's disobeying Kalos?"

"I don't know, Olli," Kaden said quietly. "But it is the only answer I have."

Kaden didn't know if he had managed to help Olli set her feelings of guilt aside completely, but it certainly appeared as though after their talk, the clouds had lifted a good bit. At least, he didn't notice in her the same signs as before. So life went on, much as before, as she continued to spend a great deal of time with Kiki, only without the weirdness when Kaden was around, and for that, he was grateful.

For his part, though, Kaden couldn't help but wonder just how significant a part of Deslo's decision Olli had been. He believed what he had told her, both that Deslo's decision wasn't her fault and that there had been other factors, but he did wonder what Deslo would have done if Olli had said she was going with Amintuu? Would that have been enough to convince him to stay with Kaden and Kiki and to go with Draagan and Tchinchura's group?

He told himself that it didn't matter, that what was done was done, but for some reason, the question bothered him. He didn't share Deslo's convictions, but he thought his son had acted because of them. The thought that Deslo had gone with Amintuu, quite possibly to his death, to avoid the heartache of seeing Olli—well, it just felt pointless.

Of course, Kaden knew they might all be marching to their death. Nothing Draagan or Tchinchura had said at the council or since suggested that doing what they believed to be right was any kind of guarantee that they would survive. In fact, Tchinchura had been quite pointed that he didn't think that. As he had said at the council and reiterated since, he believed the Amhuru were called to be faithful, even if they fell—and fall they just might, every one of them. Kaden tried not to lose hope that he would see his son again, but at times he felt that Deslo was as lost to him as Nara.

One evening, almost a week after his talk with Olli, as Kaden was finishing setting up his camping spot for the evening and preparing to get dinner for himself and Kiki, Marlo and Owenn came to find him. They asked if they might have a word, and Kaden said of course. Marlo looked at Kiki, and then back at Kaden, and Kaden understood.

"Kiki," Kaden said, "Why don't you go find Olli and see if you can eat dinner with her while I talk to Marlo and Owenn. I'll come find you when I'm finished, all right?"

"Sa," Kiki said, then she ran off through the Amhuru to find Olli.

"Well," Kaden said, as he looked at the Kalosenes. "What is it?"

Marlo looked at Kaden, then reached out his hand, which Kaden took in some confusion. "We've traveled together a long time," Marlo said. "We didn't want to leave without saying goodbye."

"Leave?" Kaden asked. "What do you mean?"

"We're going in the morning, before first light," Marlo said. "Kalos has given us a task to do."

"But we're going to the Cura-Katane," Kaden said, looking around and gesturing almost helplessly as he sought for something that would deter his friends from going. The Kalosenes had been so good to him, and he had lost so much already. He couldn't bear the thought of losing them as well. "The Jin Dara ... we have to stop him."

"Kaden," Marlo said, stepping closer and putting both hands on Kaden's shoulders. "I have to go where Kalos sends me."

"Where's he sending you?"

Marlo looked at Owenn, who nodded, and Marlo looked back at Kaden. "Even farther north than the Cura-Katane, on the very edge of a frozen waste, there is a remote hermitage in a cave by a cold, cold sea. I have seen it several times in my dreams. Kalos is sending us there."

"But why?"

Marlo shook his head. "I don't know exactly, but there is something we're meant to find. Beyond that, there is something we're meant to do. For after."

"After?"

"Kaden," Marlo said again, and a look of deep sadness was etched on his face. "Something terrible is coming, and soon. There is no escaping it, but it will not be the end."

"How do you know?"

"Do you remember the prophecy I received when we were still on *The Sorry Rogue*, in the Southlands?"

"Sa," Kaden said. "When you became a Guardian of Truth."

"Sa," Marlo said, "That's right. But do you remember the words?"

Kaden thought back, but in the end he said. "That was a long time ago."

"It was," Marlo agreed, "but I memorized it. This is what the prophecy said:

From the many, one. Only he will return.
Dark is the way, and long—
The rest will fall.
He who made the lesser sun will eclipse the greater;
He brings judgement, yet shall he be judged.
The tool of Him he mocks.
Victory will come from defeat, and defeat will come from victory—
My own will betray me.
What was scattered will be brought together, then scattered again,
Beneath the colder moon.
The world will lose what long it had,
That it may find what long was lost.
And in the long dark, two families share one fate,
Two sons bound by hate,
Only one can live.
He will find what has been lost
Restore what was torn apart
Return what was given
Rebuild what was destroyed.
Then the days of judgement will pass,
A new dawn for all shall rise—
A second chance to remember
What should never have been forgotten.

When Marlo stopped, the words of the prophecy hung in the air between them like a tangible thing, but Kaden's mind, struggling to process the news that the Kalosenes were leaving, didn't understand what Marlo was trying to tell him. "I don't understand, Marlo."

"Look up, Kaden."

Kaden stared upward at the bright, gleaming moon, surrounded by the odd grey ring. "Beneath the colder moon," Kaden whispered.

"Beneath the colder moon," Marlo echoed. "Just before that phrase, the prophecy says that what was scattered will be brought together, then scattered again. We think it means the fragments of the Golden Cord. Two of them are here, three are with the Jin Dara—and quite possibly, he might soon have four."

"You think he's going to come, going to bring them all together?"

"I think so," Marlo said, "though I don't know for sure. The prophecy then says what was scattered will be scattered again, which would give me hope, except the next line speaks of the world losing what long it had, and that doesn't sound so good."

Kaden shook his head, agreeing.

"There's much after that I don't understand, Marlo said, "But a few lines later, it speaks of a long dark. I think the long dark is coming, Kaden, and Kalos has a job for us to do to prepare for the long dark."

"Are you sure?" Kaden asked, but his heart wasn't in it. Part of him already knew that Marlo was right. He felt it too. The long dark was coming.

"I think so," Marlo said. "And Tchinchura told me just before that whole episode with the Graymir that Telsiin had heard a prophecy when he was a boy, that one day the sun would rise beneath the colder moon, and then our doom will come. I don't know what that means, or how it fits with the prophecy Kalos gave me, but Telsiin and Tchinchura both believed that time was coming, and with it, our doom."

"Then this is goodbye," Kaden said.

"Sa, this is goodbye," Marlo said. "I suspect that if we live to see each other again, the world as we know it will be gone."

Kaden stepped forward and took Marlo in a great hug, holding his friend fast. And when they separated, he took the massive Owenn in a hug too, though the big man's grip almost crushed him. When they were finished, they each shook hands one more time.

"You've been very good to me," Kaden said, choking back the emotion. "I'm glad to have known you both."

"Sa," Marlo said with a smile. "So are we. May Kalos smile upon you."

"And also on you," Kaden said, having long ago learned the proper Kalosene response.

Marlo smiled again at that, a warmer smile, and then he and Owenn turned and walked away. They disappeared into the darkness, and Kaden could hear the words of the prophecy echoing in the cold nighttime air, *the long dark* was coming.

33

KISS THE EARTH

Kaden slid closer to the fire, until its heat radiated on his face and hands. He was doing his fire dance again, and he knew that in a moment, he wouldn't able to bear being this close and would have to scoot back. Then, once back from the fire, he would gradually cool down until his face and hands were too cold again, making him creep closer, starting the whole process over.

When he was close to the fire, though, he could close his eyes, feel the heat on his face, and almost imagine that he was back home in Barra-Dohn, soaking in the hot desert sun instead of a crackling campfire. It was a pleasant illusion, and he tried to enhance it by imagining his feet sinking deep into warm sand, but this was harder to do as his feet were more than a little damp and bundled inside multiple pairs of socks.

Kaden kept his eyes closed and tried to ignore the growing feeling of heat on his face that usually preceded the inevitable slide back away from the fire. He tried to keep the lovely image of standing in the sun pleasant and nondescript, but his mind kept trying to fill in the missing pieces and bring forward into his consciousness a very specific day. Kaden, for his part, tried to keep it out.

It was no use, though, and a clear, strong memory of the day they had fled Barra-Dohn on *The Sorry Rogue* filled his mind. He could see the quay teeming with people, all looking for a way out of the city. He could see

D'Sarza's crew moving back and forth on the deck of the ship with purpose as they sailed out into the harbor. He could see the awful wind-ray and feel it grab hold of the ship. And, wondrous still to him, to this very day, he could see a soaked, dripping, and exhausted Zangira leaning against the rail of the ship after stabbing the eye of the wind-ray and getting it to let go.

As *The Sorry Rogue* had sailed out of the Barra-Dohn harbor and made for the open sea, there had been so many mixed emotions among the passengers. On the one hand, there was gratitude, relief, and excitement at having escaped the collapse of the city and the grip of the wind-ray. But, there was also anger, sadness, and fear over the loss of their home and the uncertainty of the road ahead. All those same emotions washed back over Kaden as the memories flashed through his mind's eye.

Kaden opened his eyes and gazed at the fire. Melancholy pushed away the momentary lightness he had felt when imagining his feet in the sand and the sun on his face. Instead he thought about how many faces from those memories were gone now.

Nara was dead, so she was really gone. She was so gone, in fact, that sometimes at night, when Kaden tried to picture her face, he couldn't do it. He'd figured out a trick to get her back, though, and that was to try to re-call a specific memory that had her in it. When he did that—concentrating on recollecting the memory in general and not trying to think about her in particular—he often found that he could see her after all. Still, she was gone, buried in a valley Kaden had left behind, probably for good, so he would never even see her grave again.

And of course, it wasn't just Nara. Deslo was gone, and it hurt deeply for Kaden to think about that, so he didn't. Rika was gone, had been for several years. One night she just up and left. Kaden had sometimes won-dered where she'd gone, even thinking at times that maybe she'd dared the Madri crossing again to venture back down into the Southlands. Wherever she is, he thought, I hope she's safe and well.

And the Kalosenes, they were gone now too. They'd been gone for only a week, but he felt their absence keenly. They'd traveled together for the better part of a decade, gone through so much together, shared so much, and now they felt almost as lost to him as Nara. He hoped he would see them again some day, but with the shadow of the Jin Dara looming over all things, Kaden doubted that he would.

Of course, the two Amhuru that they'd picked up at Azandalir, Calamin and Trajax, they were still here, and Tchinchura and Zangira weren't gone either, and that was something. Tchinchura was still Tchinchura—solid and steady and seemingly unshakeable even in the most dire of circumstances. Zangira, well, he wasn't quite so unshakeable. Of course, he'd been in Azandalir when the Jin Dara came, had lost his wife then. He'd lost Trabor and Shaline to Amintuu's cause, just like Kaden had lost Deslo. So Kaden sympathized with Zangira's hardships and understood if his old friend wasn't quite himself these days.

And if there had been loss, Kaden told himself as he finally pushed himself back from the fire to give relief to his uncomfortably hot face, there had also been gain. They'd picked up Olli along the way, and even more importantly—at least to him—Kiki. What life would be like without Kiki, Kaden couldn't imagine. He would feel completely alone if not for her. But she was here, the light in his life, and he was glad. Still, despite the precious addition of Kiki, and others like Olli, it felt like the core that had escaped Barra-Dohn was no more. They had been so different, but they had shared a common fate and embraced a common purpose, and those things had bound them together. Not anymore. They had broken apart and their fellowship had been lost.

Suddenly, Kaden felt a chill, and it had nothing to do with the slight cold of being farther away from the fire. The prophecy that Marlo had quoted to Kaden the night he said goodbye, something in it popped into his mind, though he wasn't entirely sure why. Before the part about what was scattered coming together, there was a part that talked about someone returning, and then it went on to say something like "Dark is the way, and long—the rest will fall."

The old Kalosene—the one who had prophesied against Barra-Dohn and been executed by his father for it—he had said something about the city lying in ruins for seventy years while a remnant wandered. Kaden had spoken some with Tchinchura and Zangira about this, and they believed their group was at least part of that remnant. Did Marlo's prophecy somehow connect to that other, older prophecy? Was the one who would return a member of their remnant? Was Nara's death and the breaking apart of the group a fulfillment of sorts of "the rest will fall"?

And suddenly, hope and excitement rose in Kaden. If the two prophecies were connected, and if one of the exiles would survive and return, might it not be Deslo? He had been only ten when Barra-Dohn fell, and if the exile was really going to be seventy years, he would be eighty when it ended—old, but not impossibly old. Kaden was too old to be the one who survived, but Deslo wasn't. Maybe he would survive whatever 'long dark' Marlo had been talking about and one day go back to what was left of Barra-Dohn?

Kaden savored that thought, even if he knew he was making quite leap to get there. He had no idea if the lines from Marlo's prophecy had anything to do with one of the exiles from Barra-Dohn returning to it, and what's more, no reason to think that even though they were exiles from the city that they were the only ones. In fact, he knew they weren't. But as a father on the brink of despondency, desperately missing his son and deeply afraid that he might never see him again, Kaden wasn't above making some pretty large leaps of logic if that was what it took to feel hope, even for a moment.

Kaden sighed, curled up and lay by the fire. He didn't know if he could sleep, but he figured he needed to try. Hope, even false hope, had a way of occupying the mind when it got lodged inside. He thought maybe it would hang around a while.

He wasn't wrong.

.   .   .

The next few weeks for Kaden were a strange vascillation between the very depths of depression—where he trudged silent and withdrawn through an increasingly bleak and barren landscape, so cold he could barely feel what little skin he dared leave exposed—and the pinnacle of an unreasoned euphoria that simply broke through the darkness from time to time like the sun suddenly emerging through deep fog. He knew the hope that would bubble up and burst out of him was based on nothing more than his crazy notion that the words of both Kalosene prophecies might somehow be tied to his little group of exiles and wanderers, but he held onto it anyway.

Kiki must have been confused by her father's extreme mood swings, but she bore with him admirably. When he was silent and almost unresponsive to anything but her most insistent attempts to get a reply from him, she would scoot up close and take his hand and simply walk alongside him. When he was talkative and gushing almost on a par with her own remarkable verbal output, she would embrace it as though it were not a sudden effusion of words that came out of him without any visible warning or explanation. And Kaden, when he considered all this in the quiet of the night, treasured his little golden-haired girl all the more.

One day, as Kaden was deep in the silent funk of despair, something large and black moving in the distance caught his eye. It was far away, but given the white, snowy landscape, anything that size and that dark, even at a great distance, was easy to see. He watched with fascination as the dark shape, which he realized was actually moving very quickly, drew nearer.

Soon he could make out that, much to his surprise, the shape was really several objects moving in a tight formation, and they had large, slender sails. Having grown up around sandships in Barra-Dohn, this perhaps shouldn't have surprised him, but having now traveled much of the world, he had discovered that this design was relatively rare. To see something very similar so far away from home was striking, and the black objects were immediately christened by him to be 'snowships.'

There were five snowships, and as they drew closer, Kaden could see that the ships themselves, not just their sails, were sleek and narrow. The winds here in the far Northlands could be very strong, so he imagined that while these snowships might be both very maneuverable and capable of great speeds, they might also be very delicate to handle, depending on the conditions.

The column of Amhuru stayed where they were, but Kaden could see a small party that included Draagan, Tchinchura and Zangira jogging out on top of the Arua field to meet the snowships, which slowed to a halt a short distance away. And, as a small party disembarked from the foremost snowship, Kaden got his first look at some of the Cura-Katane.

His immediate and dominant impression was 'blue.' Not their clothes, so much, but their faces and their hair were dominated by blue. He was too far away to be sure, but it certainly looked like their faces were painted blue, and while he could make out many different hair colors, all of them had streaks of blue dye in them. What that was about, he had no idea, but the meeting of the two parties—the one gold, the other blue—was visually striking against the white and black backdrop of the snow and snowships.

The convocation between the Amhuru and the Cura-Katane was short, and not long after, Kaden found himself carrying Kiki on his shoulders as he followed the Amhuru across the snowscape toward the snowships. All five ships took on Amhuru, and they were still crowded, but the Cura-Katane crew on the ship Kaden boarded was polite and friendly, welcoming the Amhuru as honored guests. And all of them, to a person, took time to greet Kiki in particular when they passed. Soon the snowships were underway, and while it had been a long time, Kaden thought they were indeed moving much faster than any sandship he'd ever been on.

Kaden held Kiki close as they sped across the snow. The ships seemed to turn and swing in a wide arc as though going around something, which Kaden didn't quite understand, as he could see nothing in front of them. But before long, they had come upon a series of rocky ridges rising from the ground like sharp, stone teeth. They were narrow but jagged, and topped out at perhaps 150 feet tall. Kaden saw no opening in the ring of ridges, but the snowships maneuvered deftly until they found a long narrow channel that led through them into a very large, open clearing inside.

Clearing wasn't really the word, Kaden thought, as there was an enormous, open plain before him, across which the snowships sped. Kaden could now see that his first impression of this place as a circle of rocky ridges wasn't quite right. Dead ahead lay a small mountain. The sharp, rocky ridges now looked even more like teeth to him, as they extended out in a long arc on either side from the mountain, almost coming together at the end but falling just far enough short to leave the channel through which the snowships had entered this place.

Nestled at the foot of the small mountain was a sea of neat, little stone houses. They were laid out in a surprisingly symmetrical way, with some larger buildings and a long, low stone wall between them and the field. Here in the plain, the snowships came to a halt, and Kaden disembarked with the rest of the Amhuru, having come at last to the home of the Cura-Katane.

As they passed beyond the stone wall and were walking among the houses and other buildings, the whole community of the Cura-Katane came out to meet them, men, women, and children. Soon Kaden and Kiki found themselves surrounded by a small sea of blue-faced children and many of their blue-faced mothers. Kaden wondered if Kiki would be scared by their strange appearance, but Kiki mingled among them with apparent ease and happiness.

For their part, the adults were very friendly, smiling and greeting him and the other Amhuru warmly. He learned that a small delegation of the Amhuru was already meeting with the Aiden—which he gathered was something like the Elders of the Amhuru—to discuss this auspicious event. The Cura-Katane rarely received visits from the Amhuru—not surprisingly, given their remote location—and they were filled with wonder that so many had come all at once.

The sun had already sunk below the rocky ridge to the west, though, so the crowd of Cura-Katane did not linger outside with the Amhuru. Rather, they began instead to organize housing for their guests. Each Amhuru individual or family was assigned a host, who took responsibility to see that their guests received food and shelter for the evening. A Cura-Katane couple with a little girl not much older than Kiki came up to Kaden and excitedly informed him that they would be their hosts.

As Kaden and Kiki walked with this couple through the sea of stone houses, the husband introduced himself and his family. "My name is Guuntir," he said, indicating himself, and then he motioned to his wife and daughter, saying, "and this is Markiit and Sanjoot, but we just call her Joot."

"My name is Kaden, and my daughter's full name is Sonakita, but we call her Kiki."

"Kiki," Guuntir said with a broad smile as he looked at Kiki. "I like that very much. Don't you, Joot?"

"Sa, Yadi," she said, and little Joot smiled that same, broad, inviting smile, which softened a bit her wild appearance—the striking blue paint covering her face and the strong blue streaks running through her raven black hair.

"Kiki is such a lovely name," Markiit said, and Kaden was struck by the melodious sound of her voice. "We're so glad you will be staying with us, Kiki. We will have a fine rabbit stew tonight in your honor. Would you like that?"

"Sa," Kiki said, and Kaden could hear genuine enthusiasm in her voice. Their meals had been less than remarkable of late, as their supplies had dwindled considerably, and the farther north they had gone the more difficult the hunting had been.

True to her word, Markiit, with Kiki's and Joot's help, made a fine rabbit stew, which they all enjoyed a great deal. After dinner, Guuntir brought Kaden a fresh, steaming hot cup of jonda, and the two settled in for a chat. Guuntir was careful to avoid pressing Kaden too much for the reason the Amhuru had come, and Kaden divined it would have been considered a breach of hospitality to ask such things. So Guuntir asked instead about Kaden's home. When he learned that Kaden came from the Southlands, he was astonished, and the rest of the evening he asked questions about life on the other side of the Madri—climate, geography, customs, flora and fauna, anything he could think of.

It was late, and Kiki and Joot had long since been asleep, curled up together beneath a blanket on a fur laid out before the large open fire, when Markiit placed a hand gently on her husband's shoulder. "You are wise to seek knowledge from one who can give it, my darling, but you should let our visitor get some sleep."

"Sa, sa," Guuntir said, rising. "We will talk more tomorrow."

Kaden stretched out on another fur before the fire, not far from Kiki and Joot, and as he lay there, enjoying the fire's warmth, he thought about how lovely it was not to be either in a tent or in the open. The house was small, but it was cozy, and the stone walls kept the fierce wind out and the fire's warmth in. It had been a long time since he had been so physically comfortable, and soon he drifted off to sleep, in which he dreamed of Nara and living with her in a pretty stone house in a place that reminded him an awful lot of Azandalir.

When Kaden awoke in the morning, he noticed that Joot and Kiki were already up and helping Markiit as she prepared a light breakfast. When Kaden rose and stretched, Guuntir greeted him kindly and asked him how he had slept, as Markiit brought the girls over. Kaden said he had slept quite well, and Guuntir said he was glad. Then he walked to the door and opened it.

A gust of cold air blew in, and Kaden felt it keenly. Guuntir stepped outside, and then Markiit and the girls followed her. Kaden, unsure what exactly was going on but realizing this was something he should do too, stepped outside as well. Guuntir knelt down, as did Markiit and the girls, so Kaden knelt too. Guuntir bent forward and kissed the bare ground, and this also the others did.

When Guuntir straightened, he said, "Kalos, we kiss the earth, and we ask that if today is the day for her to receive our bodies in her cold embrace, that you keep our souls in your mighty hand."

Markiit and Joot began to repeat what Guuntir had said, and Kaden found himself also whispering along with them, though Kiki just watched and listened. When they had finished echoing Guuntir's statement, he smiled as he stood. "Now let's go back inside where it is warm and have some jonda with our breakfast."

Not long after breakfast, word came to the house that the Aiden had called for the Cura-Katane to gather, and soon Kaden and Kiki were making their way with Guuntir's family to one of the large buildings they had passed the previous night. Again, Kaden surveyed the odd assembly of gold and blue, mingled together in the large open place before the building, and while there were maybe three times as many blue heads as gold, they weren't so vast an assembly that he thought they could take on the Jin Dara and his forces. Sleeping in a stone house had been comfortable, and this location was certainly more defensible than most, but all the comfort and natural defenses in the world couldn't save them now, he thought gloomily.

The large building before them had two stories, and a door on the second story opened onto a small balcony. An older Cura-Katane man came out onto the balcony, followed by Draagan and Tchinchura, but the three of them were all the balcony could hold. It was certainly nothing like the large stone balcony from which Eirmon had addressed the people of Barra-Dohn the day the Kalosene had come, Kaden thought, his mind straying to that event for a moment.

"That is Chaarnir," Guuntir said, leaning over and whispering to Kaden. "He guides the Aiden."

Chaarnir raised his hand, and whatever quiet talking was going on throughout the assembly stopped immediately. Then he lowered his hand and spoke, and in just a few minutes he had introduced Draagan and Tchinchura and outlined for the rest of the Cura-Katane the story of the rise of the Jin Dara and his play for all the fragments of the Golden Cord. He was matter-of-fact in his descriptions, and Kaden heard little or no reactions from the assembly. He finished by telling of Amintuu's plan to confront the Jin Dara at Tanisaan, and it was obvious that he shared Draagan's and Tchinchura's disapproval of that plan.

"There are no safe places for the Amhuru anymore, and the time to hide is past," Chaarnir said. "They have asked if we would stand with them against the Jin Dara, and I have said that we would."

Again Kaden heard no audible reaction to Chaarnir's words, but when he looked at Guuntir to see how his host was reacting, Kaden saw a look of grim but fierce determination on his face. When Guuntir saw Kaden looking at him, he nodded, and Kaden felt his silent support for their cause.

"We will discuss how best to prepare the moljiir and our other defenses as we ready our hands for war," Chaarnir continued. "But for now, let us kneel and kiss the earth together, for her long, cold embrace awaits us all."

34

HAUNTED DREAMS

Deslo jogged along beside Trabor and Shaline as part of the Amhuru scouting party. His eyes searched not just the road ahead, but also the ground to the right of the steadily inclining road, whose shoulders sloped steeply downward before falling away entirely. He didn't think the area provided many good spots for an ambush, but no one was willing to presume anything with the Jin Dara out there.

Despite the fact he had been wearing three fragments for months, not only the fragment of the Golden Cord that he had worn for years on his left bicep, but the replicas on his right forearm and left leg just above the knee, scouting was still a remarkable experience. His senses functioned at an extraordinary level. But even so, he neither saw nor heard anything unusual up ahead.

Around the bend in the road, though, he saw in the distance another of the Jin Dara's horrific creations. This one looked fairly extensive, as it covered just about the whole road from side to side. He glanced left at Shaline and Trabor, and they looked at him too. He was reasonably sure that they, like he, were wondering what this one would be like, but none of them spoke as they jogged on. They would all see soon enough.

As they drew nearer, Deslo saw that while most of the ones they had encountered so far had a plant or tree 'theme'—for lack of a better word, they had fallen into thinking of these things as the Jin Dara's twisted artwork, each with its own theme—this one had a clear bird theme to it. A large circle of people—and again, Deslo used the word in his mind loosely—sat smack in the middle of the road. From out of the pants of each one, a pair of stark, skinny bird legs descended, ending in very bird-like feet.

This Deslo noticed only as he drew closer to them, but what was visible even from quite a distance were what looked to be pairs of wings that extended from each person to meet the tip of the neighbor's wing. It was almost as if the people the Jin Dara had used here had been made to stand with arms extended, fingertip to fingertip, before he did his monstrous work, transforming them into these horrible things.

The heads were half human, half bird, with tufts of feathers intermingled with human hair in very surreal fashion. The faces had long, curved beaks right above very human looking mouths and just below some beady black eyes. All told, in the entire circle, there were maybe twenty-five or thirty of them, and Deslo wondered why in the world the Jin Dara had gone to all the work of hauling them up here to this place just to do this to them.

"Look at how small they are," Shaline said as they came to a stop some thirty feet from the circle, while the rest of the scouting party moved silently past the circle on either side.

Deslo had thought the people in the circle were short when looking at them from a distance, but now he could see what Shaline had already noticed. "They're children."

"Sa," Trabor said, his voice as calm and cold as ever.

"How far is Tanisaan beyond these mountains?" Deslo asked, still staring at the silent, terrible ring in front of him.

"About eighty or ninety miles, southeast," Trabor said.

"And we've been seeing these things along the road for what, the last fifty miles?"

"Sa, and in the abandoned towns we've passed through too," Shaline added.

"He's mad," Deslo said. "Completely insane."

"Na," Trabor said, shaking his head as he disagreed. "He's not mad. He is sending us a message. Maybe sending the whole world a message."

"And judging by how widespread the stories we've already heard about him were," Shaline said, "and by how great the fear was, as well as how abandoned everything is for hundreds of miles, I'd say the message has been delivered."

There was nothing more to say, so they moved around the silent circle to the right, and Deslo tried not to look at the little children and bird faces as they passed. But it was hard not to, for as awful as these things always were, they were still strangely compelling. It was almost impossible not to look.

The scouting party passed several more examples of the Jin Dara's handiwork, but none of them were as extensive as the circle of bird-children. When it was completely dark, the scouting party stopped for the night, camping on the side of the road with the steep mountain slope behind them. Still, they did not make a fire and they made sure they always had at least two members of the party on watch.

When another member of the scouting party woke Deslo for his watch, he rose eagerly. He had been dreaming about being alone in a large room with a great, high ceiling and huge wooden rafters overhead. Fluttering around the rafters were large black birds with human faces. Deslo found the birds disturbing, but in the strange, twisted logic of a dream, it never occurred to him that they were unnatural or that he should, perhaps, leave the room. So, when he was finally rescued from the dream by being awoken, he didn't mind one bit.

His watch was uneventful, and when it was over, he woke Trabor to relieve him, curled back up, and promptly went right back to sleep. This time he had no odd dreams, for which he was grateful when he awoke in the morning. The scouting party ate a quick and simple breakfast, and long before most people would have thought it light enough to continue up a winding mountain road, they were on their way.

Along towards midday, the rise in the road began to level out, and the space between the edge of the road and the drop-off widened. They slowed as the terrain changed, and soon they stopped altogether, moving silently off to the side of the road to huddle in a group. Up ahead, they could see some small buildings beside the road. It appeared they had come to the distant outskirts of a small town.

They had encountered many towns both large and small, though none since starting their ascent up this mountain, but it had been well over a week since they'd seen a person in any of them—at least, a person who wasn't part of one of the Jin Dara's decorations. Still, their task was to scout the town, make sure it was really empty and not a trap of some kind, then send word back to the main body of the Amhuru force a few days behind them about what they had found.

As the scouting party approached the small town, Deslo crept cautiously along on the Arua beside Trabor and Shaline, who had spread out to his left to cover the whole road. He knew without looking that most of the rest of the scouting party had spread out to either side of the town and all of them would converge on it from different directions at more or less the same time. For his part, Deslo kept his eyes trained on the small buildings up ahead that demarcated the transition from mountain road to mountain town.

The buildings and the town beyond them looked just as empty and deserted as the other towns they had recently passed through, but Deslo felt a knot in his stomach forming as they drew near. He had grown so attuned to the Arua field that he had also learned to trust his intuition when he felt that something was 'not quite right' with it. He glanced left past Shaline at Trabor, and Deslo saw that he too was on edge. They all had their axes out, and Deslo tightened the grip on his.

As he stepped forward, Trabor thrust out his hand to the side and called, quietly but clearly, "Stop!"

Shaline and Deslo both looked at Trabor, whose eyes were still trained on the buildings straight ahead. "The doors, they're all shut tight. And the windows, they all have shutters, and all the shutters are shut tight too."

Deslo scanned the buildings in front of him, and then those farther back in the town that he could see, and it was true—every building was shut up tight. It wasn't the haphazard look of the deserted towns they had seen so far. Not at all.

Suddenly, someone—or more likely, many someones—beyond the town on the far side reached for the Arua and took hold. All at once, the doors and shutters burst open, and great black clouds of flies came flooding out of all the buildings, the tiny sound of their individual buzzing made a great din by their vast numbers. They swarmed with purpose directly at the Amhuru—not just Trabor, Shaline, and Deslo, but all the scouts approaching the town from multiple sides at once.

As they swirled toward Deslo, he waved his axe in a futile effort to keep them away. The thought 'they are only flies' died the instant he felt one of them bite his exposed hand. The bite was sharp and strong and surprisingly painful. He swung his axe more forcefully and started moving toward the building straight ahead as though to take refuge inside it.

No sooner had he stepped toward the open door of the building some thirty yards in front of him, when a great, black mastiff appeared in the doorway. It darted out of the building and started to close the gap between itself and Deslo in a hurry, while he braced to defend himself against the new threat as the dog drew closer. He felt more bites on his hands and arms and face, but his attention was fully directed to the black shape moving toward him beyond the swirling cloud of flies.

And then the mastiff stopped, maybe twenty feet away. It crouched and opened its enormous mouth, dropping its jaw farther than Deslo would have thought possible. Out of that mouth came a tongue that flew across the space between them and wrapped around Deslo's left wrist. He had seen a frog do just the same thing to a fly, but to see a much larger tongue come out of the mastiff's much larger mouth and grab him from twenty feet away shocked him.

But Deslo had traveled the Graymere and, shock or no shock, his reflexes were quick and battle-tested. Hardly had the mastiff's tongue grabbed his wrist and started to pull when Deslo's right hand chopped down with his axe and severed the tongue, so that a good foot of it dangled from Deslo's wrist as the rest flew back into the mastiff's mouth, and the creature howled in pain and anger.

Deslo's axe flew after the tongue toward the mastiff's head, but the creature saw it coming and dodged to the side. It couldn't get completely out of the way in time, though, and the axe took it in the shoulder. Again the dog howled as Deslo summoned the axe back into his hand and turned, trying to keep his eye on the mastiff as the swirling cloud of flies swarmed around his head.

Then Deslo felt Trabor grab the Arua with great strength—it had to be Trabor, for he excelled in the manipulation of the Arua as he did in all other Amhuru skills—and a mighty wind blew up and drove the swarm of flies back into the town. It was sudden and striking in its power, and even Deslo had to struggle to keep his feet and not be blown back. The injured mastiff, for its part, did not keep its feet and rolled backward until it hit the side of the building out of which it had come.

Deslo did not waste time watching its futile efforts to escape the power of the wind, but he followed after. And no sooner had it struck the wall than Deslo's axe struck it in the side. The mastiff struggled to its feet, but the wounds it received had rendered it unable to pose a serious threat to the Amhuru. Still, it staggered closer to Deslo, trying to growl, and Deslo dispatched it once and for all a moment later.

For the first time since the swarm of flies had erupted out of the buildings, Deslo had a moment to take stock of their situation. The mastiff he had killed was not the only one that had come out after the flies. There were several more engaged with Amhuru around the town, and Deslo even saw that there was one lying dead on the road near Shaline and Trabor.

Fortunately, the encounters seemed to have gone well pretty much all around, though Deslo could see one Amhuru had been bitten by one of the mastiffs, as another Amhuru was there, helping to tend the bite wound. Deslo felt bad for the Amhuru who had been bitten, but mostly he just felt glad that the massive jaws that had opened to shoot that dexterous tongue at him had never bitten him.

Deslo examined his hands, where he saw several nasty, discolored welts from the bites the flies had given him. He reached through the power of the three fragments he bore and probed his wounds, soothing them, and reordering his skin to make the bites go away. The pain and itching that he had felt in them began to subside, and the welts began to look less angry. Most of his training with three fragments had been focused on the art of war, including manipulating his surroundings in a fight, but he was grateful that some of it at least had been focused on how the power of fragments could be used for healing. He suspected they might need this skill more and more the closer they came to Tanisaan.

Movement in the distance caught his well-trained eye, and Deslo was instantly alert to potential danger. He crouched where he was and scanned the road beyond the town, where he had seen something move. Sure enough, almost so far ahead that the downward slope of the road beyond the town hid them, a couple of men—they were dressed like Najin—were getting onto a meridium transport of some kind and gliding away. They soon disappeared from sight.

He looked at Trabor and Shaline nearby, and they looked back and nodded. They had seen them too. Again, they didn't need to speak to understand each other, for Deslo knew that they too hoped this encounter was over.

The quaking ground a moment later told them that it wasn't.

"What was that?" Deslo said as he turned to Shaline and Trabor once more. "You felt that, right?"

"Sa," they both said, and Shaline added, "I sure did."

The ground shook again, and it was clear by now that all the Amhuru had felt it. All around the outskirts of the small town, the Amhuru who had been advancing before the flies and mastiffs engaged them, were now backing slowly away. Deslo, Shaline, and Trabor also started backing slowly away.

A large, furry brown head appeared over the same horizon beyond which the two Najin had disappeared a moment ago, and as the lumbering beast came closer, the two, massive forelegs also appeared and then the haunches. Deslo stared in disbelief at what he was seeing. He had seen a creature like this once before; in fact, one had chased him and Olli several years ago. But that bear had been much smaller than this, and it had moved with speed and agility, not just power. This thing moved awkwardly, as though not quite accustomed to its enormous frame, which Deslo thought might be the case. It was at least three times the size of the bear he had encountered before, and though he knew little about bears, he doubted this one had achieved its great size naturally.

Then, all at once, the Amhuru acted in concert, reaching out through the Arua to seize the behemoth bear as it shambled into the town. Deslo joined in, lending what strength he had to their collective effort to at least arrest the bear's movement. They slowed and then stopped him, but the bear fought against their control with surprising force and determination.

Trabor ran forward along the surface of the Arua, and Deslo and Shaline followed along behind, but Deslo did not let go of the Arua as they ran. As they got closer to the bear, Trabor veered off to the side and paused at the entrance to a building there. He turned to Shaline and Deslo, "Don't follow me. Just stay back."

He ducked into the building and disappeared. A moment later he appeared again at the window of the building out of which a great flood of flies had come just moments ago. Crouching in the window, he stopped to take stock of the distance between the building and the bear. Then he leapt.

Trabor hit the right front foreleg of the bear and grabbed on, his arms almost disappearing into the dark brown fur. He started to slip and then stopped, his grip securing him to the side of the bear's arm. Then, hand over hand, he worked the rest of the way up until he had climbed onto the bear's enormous shoulder.

Deslo could feel the bear trying to break free of the Amhuru's hold, trying to at least pull his head free so he could turn it toward Trabor as he scrambled up onto its back. But Deslo and the other Amhuru held on, and they held on dearly. Trabor moved on back behind the bear's head, so that even if it did break free, it couldn't turn far enough to reach him.

Trabor's axe rose and fell, then rose and fell again. It took several strokes, and by the time he was finished, the axe was covered with the bear's blood, but finally he succeeded in severing the bear's spinal cord. Deslo could feel the life of the bear slipping away as it slowly stopped resisting the control of the Amhuru.

Trabor, meanwhile, slid part of the way down from the bear's back on the same leg he had climbed up and then dropped the rest of the way to the ground. When he hit the ground he rolled and ran to be sure he was clear, and then the Amhuru let go of their hold of the bear. It tilted, slowly at first, and then more quickly, falling until it slammed into the side of the same house that Trabor had used to get up onto its arm. The wall took the full force of the weight of the bear admirably, though Deslo saw several of the stones around the window collapse inward, and gradually the creature slid down until it rested against the base of the house.

It took some time for the Amhuru to feel sure the encounter with the town's various surprises was really over, but when they were, the scouting party met in the middle of the town and conferred. The first order of business was to discuss the significance of what had just happened, as this was the first time they'd come to a deserted town with actual traps left for them instead of just twisted examples of the Jin Dara's artwork.

In the end, it was Shaline who said, "I think these things—the swarm of biting flies, the mastiffs with tongues like reptiles, and the enormous bear—I think they have been left with the same purpose as the Jin Dara's less dangerous creations. They're not here to stop us but to frighten us."

"Sa, he wants them haunting our dreams," Deslo said, agreeing with her. What she said made perfect sense. The stories of the strange doings on the day the Jin Dara had taken Tanisaan—grass that stung, bats that attached to the face and suffocated a man, and lightning that attacked the defenders of the city—were just as widespread as the stories of the terrible decorations the Jin Dara had littered the towns and roads around Tanisaan with. The Jin Dara was waging a silent war with them, a war they couldn't let him win.

Many if not all of the other Amhuru nodded, and quickly the conversation moved to what to do next. There was some talk of the possibility of going on as planned and sending messengers back to the main body of the Amhuru, but they felt this incident warranted a more cautious approach.

They decided to pull back from the town to the point where the road had not yet leveled out and the ground beside it hadn't either. There they would camp and wait for the others, and when they came, they would tell of what they had found and see how the rest of the Amintuu wanted to proceed.

.   .   .

The night sky was full of bright stars, and in the midst of it all, the cold moon shone. Amintuu lay on his back, staring up at it. As he rarely slept anymore, he had spent many hours gazing up at the night sky.

He had thought that throwing Telsiin overboard, into the sea, would satisfy his daughter's restless spirit, and that perhaps she might stop haunting him. And for a time it had been so. But after barely a week of peace, she had returned to trouble his sleep and steal his dreams.

She did not come every night, but when she did come, he trembled at her presence. She had changed, for though she still sounded like his little girl, she looked less and less like her. Now, she looked as he imagined a body would look that had moldered in the grave a few days, and the sight and smell of the decay on her was more than Amintuu could take.

So these days, Amintuu dreaded the dark. He would lie down and wait, wait for the little voice that called to him, "Yadi, I'm so thirsty." And when it came, it generally came with some kind of pleading for him to hurry, for him to move faster, for him to finish what he had started. "You must get to Tanisaan," the voice would say, or something like it, "you must stop the Jin Dara."

Amintuu took a deep breath. The sun had gone down long ago. There were probably only a few hours until daylight. Perhaps, tonight, she would not come.

He closed his eyes, only to hear the accursed words begin. "Yadi, I'm so thirsty …"

35

DAY OF RECKONING

Deslo stared across the large open field at the walls of Tanisaan. The gate was open, like an invitation, daring the Amhuru army to come across the field and try to get in. Or perhaps the gate was open like an insult, suggesting that the Jin Dara knew they had come and felt no need for ordinary defenses.

Whatever the message, the Amhuru had come to answer it, and they were eager to do so. Deslo felt it in the air, felt it inside himself, felt the tingling and the excitement. A day of reckoning had come. The Jin Dara would die today, or the majority of the Amhuru left in the world would die trying to kill him. No quarter would be sought or granted on either side, and the sun would set on a very different world, a world either saved from unimaginable darkness or condemned to it.

The eagerness he felt, the eagerness they all felt, had a lot to do with the road they had taken to get here. All those terrible decorations made from the mangled bodies of people who had done nothing to deserve their fate other than to be readily available as a target for the Jin Dara's cruelty, and all the bizarre creatures left along the way to attack and harass the Amhuru—these things had increased the loathing and hatred that Deslo and the other Amhuru felt for the Jin Dara. To be sure, the Jin Dara had earned that loathing and hatred before the Amhuru had ever left to come here, but the nightmarish road had confirmed and deepened it by a wide margin.

There was hatred, but there was also relief, fueling the eagerness Deslo felt to fight this battle today. He was so glad to be finished with the journey that he didn't have words to express it. If he had thought the sporadic encounters they'd started having before the mountains were bad, the frequent encounters they had after them were terrible. These last twenty miles or so, they could hardly go fifty yards without coming across yet another piece of the Jin Dara's handiwork, and some of them were so large that they must have been made up of almost a hundred people.

No more. If they succeeded in killing the Jin Dara, he would never take another man, woman, or child and warp them into some strange hybrid plant or animal. He would never take a family or a group of friends or a selection of total strangers and twist them beyond all recognition. He would never take a whole town and plant them like an awful orchard in the grassy field beside the houses that had been their homes. And if they failed to kill the Jin Dara today, at least Deslo would never have to see any of this again. That was a consolation in a way, too.

That thought—that they might fail and that he might die—was very hard for Deslo to take seriously as he wore three pieces of Zerura. He felt so strong, so unimaginably strong, that the prospect of an Amhuru defeat was almost absurd. He had to remind himself that the Jin Dara and his Najin also wore three fragments of the Cord, and no doubt they also felt unstoppable. Soon, two armies wielding what felt like irresistible force would clash. Something would have to give, but what? Deslo shuddered at the thought, for if there was something out there strong enough to stop them, he didn't want to see it.

And then, just like that, the signal was sent for them to move forward. Deslo advanced out onto the field, his eyes fixed on the open gates of Tanisaan.

.   .   .

The first attack against the Amhuru came from the garrows high up on the city walls. Deslo and the other Amhuru had scouted Tanisaan from afar, and more than one source had told them of the garrows and their use, so to see teams use the garrows to launch projectiles against them was not a surprise.

There was at least some surprise when those projectiles began to explode, throwing up massive sprays of dirt and grass wherever they hit the field. Deslo was taken back to his childhood, and every boom and reverberation reminded him of Garranmere. These projectiles were smaller, and perhaps not quite as powerful as those had been, but Deslo wondered who in Tanisaan had unlocked whatever secret combination of ingredients that had made the army of Barra-Dohn so formidable.

Fortunately, the projectiles could be manipulated mid-flight, and while both the Najin on the walls and the Amhuru in the fields sought to control them, neither side quite got what they wanted. The Najin couldn't overpower the Amhuru enough to have them land in their midst, at least not consistently. Here and there the enemy scored a direct hit, but not often, and the Amhuru had their successes too.

Some of the explosives were seized and hurled back against the city walls, and these did some real damage. But more than just damaging the walls, on at least a couple of occasions, whoever seized hold of the projectile was able to direct it back against the very men who had launched them. Deslo watched an explosion rock the top of the wall, watched the men in gold fly up and back off the wall and presumably fall to their death below, if they weren't dead already.

The struggle to control the projectiles raged on, and Deslo could feel it ebb and flow through his fragments. Out of the corner of his eye, he saw one of the shiny meridium orbs rocketing in his direction. He dove to the side even as he reached out through the Arua to contest its control and perhaps alter its trajectory. He was barely able to interfere and divert the orb to the side, and it hit the ground not twenty feet away, showering him with dirt and rock, though thankfully leaving him uninjured.

"You all right?" Shaline said, darting up beside him. Trabor followed close behind her.

"Sa," Deslo said, nodding, and Shaline helped him up. He glanced around at the Amhuru, separated into pockets all over the field, trying not to cluster together too much and make for easy targets. "I wonder how long this dance at a distance will last?"

"Who knows?" Shaline said. "They've had a long time to stockpile those explosives, so they might be able to keep this up a while."

"Have you felt any attempt to do something unusual with the Arua?" Trabor asked. "Something other than just redirect an explosive your way?"

"Na," Deslo said, shaking his head. "I haven't."

"Neither have I," Trabor said. "And that worries me. All the strange stuff we've seen. All the strange stuff he did when he took the city. What is he up to, I wonder?"

"Maybe he knows we're ready to counter him," Shaline offered, hopefully.

"Maybe," Trabor said, though he sounded doubtful.

"Father always said a good commander doesn't do what his enemy expects," Shaline said, further expounding her point. "With all that we've heard about the Jin Dara, and all we've seen with our own eyes, he probably knew we'd expect to be attacked from above and below, by flora and by fauna, and he probably knew we'd have a plan for it."

"Which we do," Deslo said.

"That's right," Shaline said. "So, he's not doing what we expect."

"Then what is he doing?" Trabor asked, reiterating his earlier question. "What does he know that we don't? What does he have that we don't?"

His question lingered in the silence, and they all realized, at just about the same time, that it was silent. No explosions rocked the ground, and as Deslo scanned the walls, he saw the garrow teams were either gone or going. It seemed like whatever was going to come next was going to come now.

And then the floodgate opened. Out of the open gate of the city poured the Najin, making the gate look as they poured outward for all the world like a dam that has been breached, allowing a golden river to disgorge its waters into the green field. Deslo looked in wide-eyed astonishment as more and more Najin came out of the city. They came out on foot, they came out on speeding transports, but out they came, until the flowing river of gold reached flood tide.

"What do they have, you ask?" Deslo said, turning to Trabor. "Numbers."

.   .   .

Deslo fought for his life. Everywhere around him the sea of gold surged and swelled, and the sheer force of it threatened to wash him away. He defended against knife and axe, against smaller versions of the same explosives the enemy had launched from the city walls by the garrows, versions so small they could be held in the hand and thrown. He defended against attack on all sides, all the time.

And, in the midst of his constant defense, he attacked whenever he could manipulate an opening. He threw his own knife or axe when he thought a target was close enough and unaware, but the Najin were hard to surprise. Indeed, they were every bit as good with their weapons and every bit as strong and savvy with their fragments of the Cord as Deslo was, and indeed, as almost all the Amhuru were.

Whatever gap they had expected to exist in their skill levels since most of the Amhuru had grown up wearing Zerura and working with the Arua field, that gap had been closed. Perhaps it had closed because of the greater amount of time the Najin had enjoyed to train with three fragments, or perhaps—Deslo grew cold at the thought—perhaps this Meldriic Jaen that Draagan had asked to help assassinate the Jin Dara really had betrayed them.

For most of the way to Tanisaan, Meldriic Jaen had been the subject of much conversation among the Amhuru. Deslo had learned everything he had ever wanted to know about Meldriic Jaen and more. And then, as they drew close to the boundary between the still-inhabited towns and those left empty and desolate, and more and more stories reached their ears about the Jin Dara, the more they heard about how Meldriic Jaen had helped lead the assault on Tanisaan.

This fact alone didn't mean that the Jaens had betrayed Draagan and the Amhuru, for as many of the Amhuru pointed out, Meldriic could have been helping the Jin Dara to gain his trust. Nevertheless, it was enough for those who hated Meldriic and his brothers to be sure that he had betrayed them, and that Draagan had been a fool to trust him. By all accounts, Meldriic Jaen was a warrior among warriors, and if he had joined the Jin Dara and trained his men, then the surprising skill and ability that Deslo was seeing right now made perfect sense.

Whatever it was that had enabled the Najin to become so good with the Arua and their weapons, Deslo felt his hope for victory slip away. Their enemy had superior numbers, and their own hope had been in superior skill if not strength, which they did not have. Their defeat now seemed inevitable. It was just math. If the Amhuru were no stronger or better than the Najin, and if there were way more Najin than Amhuru, then the victory of the Najin was assured.

The feeling of being invicible as he stood on the edge of the battlefield just that morning was a distant memory for Deslo, as was the hope of killing the Jin Dara. Now all that mattered to him was selling his life dearly and helping Shaline and Trabor for as long as he could before he succumbed and was overwhelmed.

Shaline was doing well, in fact far better than Deslo, who was barely holding his own. She was skilled all around, but especially so with the Arua field, and she always had been. Deslo watched her work and thought, she really is Zangira's daughter. Trabor, though, was more than just skilled. He was a warrior without parallel, at least on this battlefield. Whereas Deslo struggled to defend himself against attack and to create an opportunity to attack in return, Trabor whirled like a raging storm, turning back every move against him and striking out like lightning in all directions, seemingly at once. He was, at least in Deslo's eyes, fury incarnate.

Being near him and his remarkable abilities was both a blessing and a curse. On the one hand, he tended to draw the attention of all the Najin in the area, as he was so clearly powerful and deadly. That sometimes provided moments of respite for those nearby, like Deslo and Shaline. On the other hand, he drew the attention of Najin not so nearby too, and that just meant the flow of Najin to their part of the battlefield never slowed down. He was a magnet for the enemy, and they just kept on coming.

Trabor's strength was magnificent, but even he couldn't hold back the flood, and Deslo felt the tide turning against them. The sea of gold was deepening all around them, but it wasn't in their physical presence that he felt them start to submerge, to go under. It was in the invisible battle for control of the Arua. He could feel the concerted effort of the Najin. They knew they had to stop Trabor, that he was in many ways an epicenter of the Amhuru resistance to their complete control of the battlefield.

Deslo knew their time was slipping away, and he drew near to Shaline, to stand with her and with Trabor as they fell. He reached through the Arua to turn away a knife, redirecting it toward a Najin moving in on Trabor. Another Najin saw and deflected it away, the story of the day so far for Deslo. Just too many Najin eyes to watch him and counter his moves and too great a Najin presence for him to make any headway.

"It won't be long now," he said as Shaline moved so close to him that he could hear her panting from the exertion of the fight.

"Sa," Shaline said. "Not long."

For a moment they said nothing, focused as they were on the fight and on staying as close to Trabor as possible. Then Shaline said, "I'm glad you came, Deslo. Dying isn't so bad with you here."

Before Deslo could respond to her, an explosion from very close to the exact place where Trabor had been standing rocked them all, pitching Deslo and Shaline sideways. Deslo knew immediately that the explosion had seriously hurt or killed Trabor, for his strong presence in the war for control of the Arua was suddenly and completely gone, blinking out like a lamp that has run out of fuel.

Even as Deslo struggled to keep his feet, he felt warm blood trickling down the side of his face and knew that something had cut him on the head, but in all the confusion he didn't know if it had come from the explosion or something else. He felt dazed and exhausted, and everywhere around him there were so many men in gold. He tried to turn and find Shaline, to see if she was all right, but he couldn't see her. He felt his invisible hold on the Arua being taken from him. It slipped away like sand through his fingers, and when he felt the Arua again, it was like feeling invisible cords being wrapped around him. He tried to fight it, but he couldn't.

He felt the Arua squeeze around him tighter and tighter, until his fingers involuntarily opened and he dropped his axe. It fell to the ground. He saw it lying there, motionless and only just below his feet, but he couldn't do anything to get it back. Still the cords tightened until he could barely breathe. His breath grew short, and darkness came over him as he collapsed.

'Goodbye, Shaline,' he thought as he slipped away, 'my first love.'

36

TIPPING POINT

Deslo wasn't dead. The thought came to him with a tiny feeling of relief, a feeling that quickly disappeared, replaced at the same moment with something that could only be called despair.

He couldn't feel the rhythmic pulsing of Zerura against his skin. This pulse was the tell-tale sign that you were wearing a piece of living matter. Tchinchura had once called it the heartbeat of all creation, and to Deslo its lack was like missing a limb.

Indeed, Deslo felt naked without it. For six years now, ever since he first became an apprentice on his thirteenth birthday, he had never been without the feel of Zerura. He felt it first thing when he got up in the morning, felt it pulsing as he drifted off to sleep at night. It was a source of comfort in difficult times and gave a sense of peace in the midst of turbulence. As he opened his eyes and began to apprehend his surroundings, he knew he would need both comfort and peace now.

He was in a very large room, not physically bound, but held in the same invisible cords that had wrapped around him when he passed out on the battlefield. Around him were many other Amhuru, so he was not the only one that had been taken captive rather than killed. It surprised him that the Najin would take any of them captive, as he hadn't expected that, but he realized now that it probably shouldn't have surprised him. No doubt the Jin Dara wanted to make a show of the defeated Amhuru, and

Deslo felt suddenly sure that he was shortly going to become a part of one of his enemy's twisted decorations.

His eyes had adjusted fully to the light now, and Deslo tried to see if he could find Trabor or Shaline among the other Amhuru in the room. He was near the front and had to twist his head around to see what was behind him. His neck was stiff, but the cords that held him didn't restrict the motion of his head even if his arms were clamped tightly against his side. He turned right but couldn't see either Trabor or Shaline that way, so he turned back to the left. At first he didn't see them in that direction either, but then he caught a glimpse of Shaline's long golden hair, her head bowed, just a few people away, almost directly behind him.

He felt mixed emotions at the prospect of her survival. He was glad she wasn't dead, very glad, but he didn't want her to end up in one of the Jin Dara's artworks any more than he did himself. He had no idea how aware he would be of the world around him or even of himself, but being aware at all as one of those things sounded bad. It seemed to him that being dead would be better than being trapped in the living death he had witnessed over and over on their way here. Certainly, he didn't want that for Shaline.

As for Trabor, there was no sign of him, and Deslo felt sure he was dead. The more he thought about it, the more he believed this. The explosion had been so close, had been strong enough to knock both Deslo and Shaline off their feet—how could Trabor have survived it? He would miss Trabor, who had become like a brother, but Deslo hoped that Trabor really was dead. If he was right and the Amhuru were going to pay generally for their opposition to the Jin Dara, he could well imagine that Trabor might be a special object of wrath given his exploits on the battlefield.

A door opened near the front of the room and a group of people entered, but Deslo really saw only one—the Jin Dara. His bright golden sheen left no doubt about who he was (although the way he carried himself probably would have been enough to tell Deslo even without it). He strode across the room until he stood in front of the captive Amhuru, and there he stopped and stared.

Only then did Deslo notice what was in his hands. In one, he held a squirming piece of Zerura, which Deslo could only surmise was the original fragment that Amintuu had worn. This seemed certain since, in the other hand, dangling by his golden hair, was Amintuu's severed head.

"Your friend told me I'd have to pry the original fragment he bore off his dead body," the Jin Dara said as he set Amintuu's head down on a table facing the other Amhuru. "So, I did."

Amintuu's head began to shake. His nose began to expand and flatten, while two tusk-like protusions pushed out of his face on either side of it. It was very odd for Deslo to know the Arua was being forcefully manipulated and not be able to feel it at all, but he couldn't, and all he could do was watch in horror. He had seen boar in some of the places he had visited in his many travels, and Amintuu's face now had a distinct boar-like aspect, but what the Jin Dara did next was not in keeping with that theme at all.

A soft ripping or cracking sound echoed in the room, and a thick, prickly stem of sorts poked up out of Amintuu's head, quickly branching out in several directions. The branches were prickly too, but from the end of each small branch a delicate white blossom appeared. All in all, Amintuu's transformed skull looked like it had come from a boar-man with thorny antlers, adorned with flowers. Deslo, sickened, turned away.

"He should have come to me on bended knee," the Jin Dara said, gazing at the captive Amhuru. "Instead of thinking he could challenge me."

The Jin Dara, who had been a little back from the table where he had placed Amintuu's head, came forward and now stood within reach of the frontmost Amhuru. "I thought you all might like to see this moment, to bear witness to the tipping point, when I go from being the one who controls half of the Golden Cord, to being the one who controls two thirds of it. If you had any hope before, you certainly have none now."

Without saying another word, the Jin Dara pulled off the shirt he was wearing, and just as readily, slipped off his pants. He stood before them, shiny and golden in his undergarments, holding out his hand and watching the Golden Cord dance in the air above it. For a long moment he stared at the fragment, clearly savoring his triumph at having obtained it. Then he lay down.

He set the wriggling Zerura on his chest, and Deslo watched as the fragment of the Cord shivered and gyrated there, remembering what it had been like to feel Zerura do that against his own skin. Then the fragment began to crawl down his torso and across the top of the Jin Dara's left thigh until it was just above his knee. There it stretched out until it had gone all the way around and secured itself.

The Jin Dara's whole body began to convulse and shake, and Deslo watched in fascination. He couldn't help it. A moment later the Jin Dara began to rise above the floor, floating upward several feet, until he lay stretched out above the ground. The glow of his golden skin seemed brighter. Deslo could see all the muscles in his arms and legs flex at once, saw his hands clasp and his toes curl up, and he wondered what the power running through the Jin Dara must feel like.

For a moment he felt something not unlike envy. He'd felt the power of three replicas—felt it and then lost it. He could not imagine the power of four originals, the invigorating vitality of having them pulsing against his skin in tune with his heartbeat. He hated the Jin Dara for having them, and in that moment he wanted them for himself.

Deslo looked down, ashamed. For the first time in his life, perhaps, he thought he understood, at least a little bit, what it must have felt like for his grandfather when he both conspired to take and then keep an original fragment of the Golden Cord. Since learning of what Eirmon had done, Deslo had always judged him harshly, but he saw in his own brief flirtation with desire just how strong it could be.

The Jin Dara sat upright in the air and lowered his feet until they touched the ground. He laughed, still clenching his fists so that his biceps and other muscles bulged as he stood before them. "I am so strong. You cannot understand or even imagine."

Deslo could hear in the Jin Dara's voice that he wasn't gloating. This wasn't boasting; it was rapture. He was excited, and he had to express that excitement in words. Deslo heard those words, and he believed them. He could neither understand or imagine.

"The last two original fragments aren't here among you," the Jin Dara continued, and while the euphoria was still on his face and in his voice, Deslo heard a hardness there too, a cold malice that frightened him. "And as much as I will enjoy wearing replicas until I get them, I want the originals."

The Jin Dara turned toward the cluster of people behind him, back closer to the door, and he motioned. Two of them came forward, a man and a woman. As they drew nearer, Deslo realized he recognized the woman, but he couldn't believe what he was seeing.

Rika.

The man leaned in to talk to the Jin Dara, and Rika just stopped and stood nearby at a respectful distance. Deslo glared at her, anger rising inside him. He didn't know how she had gotten here, but it didn't matter. She was clearly with the Jin Dara, in his counsels, on his side. Rage flooded him.

Rika had been there when the Jin Dara destroyed their home. She had been with them for years after the fall of Barra-Dohn, been with them on their quest both to learn about his origins and to find and stop him. She had shared in their counsels, had been one of their number. To find her here, obviously aligned with their enemy, it was a betrayal of staggering proportions, and Deslo wanted nothing more than to break free of the bonds that held him and to throttle her.

Just then Rika looked his way, and recognition of her own dawned on her face. She looked at him for a moment, and then she took a few steps toward him until she was only perhaps ten feet away. She stopped and smiled at him, and then she said, "I know this one. I think he might be able to help us."

The Jin Dara and the other man stopped talking. Both turned to look at Rika. The Jin Dara walked up beside Rika. "Which one do you know?"

Rika strode forward until she was right in front of him. She reached out and pointed, "This one."

The Jin Dara walked forward until he too stood right in front of him. His eyes searched Deslo's face. Deslo felt their intensity and was afraid.

"You know," Rika said, turning to the Jin Dara. "It really is a small world. This is Deslo, the grandson of the King of Barra-Dohn whom you killed on the day you destroyed the city. He was the royal brat I had to tutor."

Rika turned back to him and stepped in closer, gazing into his eyes with a cold malicious stare all her own. "And now, here he is, just like his grandfather—in your hands and at your mercy."

The Jin Dara, still staring at Deslo, simply said, "Where are the other two fragments? Tell me, boy."

"They're not hiding from you anymore," Deslo said, and it took all his courage to do so. "They said they would send a message to you, telling you where to find them."

"Did they?" the Jin Dara said, and the hardness was there in force now. "You know, your leader here"—and with that, he gestured toward the head of Amintuu behind him on the table—"said much the same thing."

"It's true," Deslo said, hoping that was the end of it.

Rika stared at him during the silence that followed his brief exchange with the Jin Dara. She even moved closer to look at him more carefully. "You know more than that, don't you? You know where they are."

She turned excitedly to the Jin Dara. "There's something he isn't telling you, I know it. I've known him since he was a little boy, and he's hiding something. I guarantee it."

"Are you hiding something?" the Jin Dara asked.

Deslo didn't know for sure that Draagan or Tchinchura would have wanted him to hide the fact that they had set out in search of the Cura-Katane. After all, they said they intended to face the Jin Dara there if need be, they only wanted to do it on ground of their own choosing. So Deslo had no idea if it would be wrong to tell the Jin Dara what they eventually intended to tell him, but he just couldn't bring himself to do it, not if it meant jeopardizing them. What if they weren't there yet? Or what if they weren't finished preparing their defenses?

"You think you can keep your secret from me, boy?" the Jin Dara asked. "I can do things you wouldn't believe."

"I saw lots of your handiwork on my way here," Deslo said. "I know what you can do."

"Do you, Deslo?" the Jin Dara said, smirking as he said his name. "Do you really know what I can do?"

"I know you can turn me into a tree or bird, or even a boar," Deslo said, glancing past the Jin Dara at Amintuu's head, "but I won't tell you anything I don't want to tell you."

The Jin Dara grinned. As he did, Rika suddenly looked past Deslo, and then she walked past him too. "I know this one, also," she said, "and I think she is precious to the boy."

Deslo panicked. Shaline. He had completely forgotten about Shaline, forgotten that Rika had been on Azandalir with them and had seen them together. Forgotten that Rika could recognize Shaline and link them together. The little bit of courage he had mustered disappeared.

"Release her," the Jin Dara said as he walked past Deslo, and for a brief but awful moment he couldn't see what either of them were doing. Then they reappeared, leading Shaline between them. She looked terrified, but Deslo could see she was trying to look as though she wasn't.

"Oh," Rika said, and there was inexpressible delight in her face, "I think that whatever he says about keeping his secrets, if you start working your magic on her, he'll tell you whatever it is you want to know."

"Leave her alone," Deslo said, knowing even as he said it that he wasn't helping and he couldn't stop what was about to happen. They dragged her out into the middle of the floor.

Shaline started screaming.

.   .   .

Rika walked with bounce in her step. She had meant to head straight back to her room, but she was too excited, had too much energy, so she'd decided to stroll around Tanisaan for a while first. The stars sparkled in the night sky, and she thought this might just be the most beautiful, wonderful night imaginable.

She slid her hand into her pocket and pulled out the flask. She had filled it before leaving her room, but it was almost empty again, another reminder that her rate of consumption of the Zerura-powder solution had substantially increased even since she had started to carry some with her all the time just a couple months ago. None of the others who were being tested with ingesting the powder were taking nearly as much as she was.

She didn't know what it felt like to wear Zerura, but she did know what it felt like to have it coursing through her veins, and the feeling was magical. She couldn't imagine going back to what it had been like before. She couldn't even bear now to think about the feeling she had experienced in the early days of her testing when several hours had passed after a dose and the effects were beginning to diminish. Of course, this was why she had eventually decided to abandon her timetable for regular doses and simple carry pre-made solution with her to take as desired. As it turned out, she desired it a lot.

But maybe she wouldn't have experienced what she had tonight if she hadn't been taking so much for so long. Maybe she would have just been an observer in that room, only able to see what was happening, instead of being something much more like a participant, feeling and absorbing what was going on in a much more tangible way.

To be sure, as her connection to the Arua had grown stronger over time, her ability to sense the Jin Dara's own powerful connection had grown. She sometimes felt a slight tingling when he wielded his power in her presence, and that was exciting enough, but tonight. Tonight! When he put that fourth fragment on, when he rose up off the ground, just hovering in the air! Well, there had been a surge of life—Rika didn't know what else to call it—and it had emanated from him, had radiated throughout the room, and she had felt it ripple through her own body.

She had felt it. She had almost seen it, visibly; it was that strong. And while it had diminished somewhat after the initial surge, it never disappeared. As long as she was in that room with him, she'd been able to detect the raw, unrestrained power and virility that emanated from him, and it was an aphrodisiac of staggering proportions.

Consequently, it was both wonderful and terrible to have to leave. On the one hand, she couldn't bear the thought of going away and losing her proximity to it, to him, but on the other hand, it was equally unbearable to be in his presence and not be able to touch him, to act on the desires he prompted in her. She wondered, candidly, how she was going to be able to manage being in his presence, going forward, if this was what it would now feel like all the time. She wasn't sure she could long endure it.

She stepped inside the building where she lodged, right next door to where her little Tanisaan Academy conducted most of its research, and she started up the stairs. She hadn't even reached the first landing before she realized something was going on inside her. By the time she passed that landing and was nearing the top of the stairs she could feel the goosebumps all over her body. That emanation of power and virility that she had been walking all over Tanisaan dreaming about—it was here, in her building. He was here, in her building.

She walked quietly and calmly down her hallway. The feeling grew stronger and stronger, and she took a deep breath with every step. She touched her hair involuntarily and straightened her dress. Then, almost without thinking, she stopped, pulled out the flask and drained the last few drops of the solution inside. She dropped the flask and it bounced on the carpeted floor without making a sound.

She took the final few steps to her door, reached out, turned the handle and pushed. The door swung gently open, and she searched the room hungrily from the hallway. When she saw that he wasn't in her sitting room, she entered and closed the main door behind her. Then she crossed to the interior door, which was already open. There she stood in the doorway, her eyes transfixed by the Jin Dara, who stood not more than ten feet away, inside, watching her.

For some time, neither spoke. They stood, staring at one another, and Rika, for her part at least, soaked in the feeling of power and virility again, letting the aphrodisiac do its work on her some more. Finally, she spoke. "You have come, at last."

"I have come," he said, and then he added, "I want to tell you, to explain what this is like, but I don't know how."

"Show me."

"I will."

She unfastened her dress.

"I am a god," he said as it dropped to the floor. "Or if I am not yet, I soon will be."

"I know," she said. Then, she went to him.

37

RIKA'S DREAMS

Rika lay alone in the dark. The Jin Dara had gone. Thirty minutes ago? An hour? More? She could no longer feel the life-giving connection to the emanation of power and vitality she had felt in his presence as it had gradually receded and then gone. And, adding to the sense of emptiness and fatigue that had overtaken her, she felt well past due for some more Zerura-powder solution.

Usually, if she fell asleep before feeling this sense of lack, when she woke up in the morning the thirst for more wasn't overwhelming. But, when she ran low while awake, the desire to consume more could grow almost out of control. Now, as she lay in her bed, she thought of the empty flask in the hallway where she had dropped it, and she wondered if she should get up and go next door and fill it, or try to get to sleep before her desire compelled her. She thought she could see the first faint traces of daylight outside her window, and if she wanted even a few hours of sleep, she wasn't sure she should delay trying.

But Rika neither got up to go next door nor did she make a serious attempt at going to sleep. Rather, she allowed her mind to return to the matter of the Jin Dara. She had achieved her goal of becoming his lover, but what that would mean going forward was not clear to her. He had made her no promises and offered no insights or clues to what was going on inside him, so she had no idea what his thoughts or intentions with regard to her were.

She was certainly aware of at least the faint possibility that she might be in a worse position today than she had been yesterday. She had sensed his growing interest and even attachment to her, but she knew that last night could have changed that. Whatever she was to him today, she was less mysterious and might then be less desireable. She didn't know, and she would simply have to wait to see how he reacted.

Rika, of course, hoped that the Jin Dara would see this as just the start of something new and perhaps permanent between them, but even if he didn't, she thought she had established her usefulness to him sufficiently to at least guarantee her safety. She had proven, both through the work of her Academy and through her help with Deslo to be a resource worth having.

And, though she didn't especially like thinking about whatever or whoever had been impersonating Gamalian, the things that 'being' had said to her suggested that what had transpired last night was something that he desired as well. Whether or not her liaison with the Jin Dara had produced the other thing Rika had been hoping for—and apparently the false Gamalian as well—she still did not know and wouldn't know for some time.

She threw her covers off decisively and rose from her bed. The thirst for more of the solution was growing stronger, and though she did want at least a few hours sleep, she did not think she'd get them until her desire for more was satisfied. She dressed and slipped out of her rooms, picking up the flask where it still lay in the hall before going to her office next door.

After she had taken a dose of the solution in her office, and then filled the flask to the top, she returned to her building. The grey light of morning was definitely upon the city, and in just an hour or so, Tanisaan would awaken. She opened the door to her rooms, and for the second time in the last day she found that someone was waiting there for her.

"Why are you here?" she asked as she stepped in and closed the door behind her.

"I have come to congratulate you, of course," the false Gamalian said. "You have done well, on multiple fronts, no less."

"What do you mean?"

"Well, first of all, you did a beautiful job exposing that young man who used to be your charge and helping the Jin Dara discover through him the plans of the remnant of the Amhuru. You seemed to really enjoy be-traying that boy—was he really such a burden to you?"

Rika thought of Deslo's distress as the Jin Dara tortured and trans-formed Shaline, and she shrugged her shoulders. "He wasn't so bad. My grievance is with his family, mostly, more so than the boy himself."

"Interesting," the false Gamalian said. "Another thing you have in common with the Jin Dara, I see. A willingness to carry out vengeance on the descendants of the people who have actually hurt you."

He smirked when he said this, and his voice had a mocking tone, but Rika didn't take the bait. She had decided after the last time he visited, that the next time—if there was a next time—she would take the approach of a supplicant. She would make no demands and ask no questions. At least, she had decided she would try to do this, as she'd already asked a few questions. No more, she told herself, and she waited.

"And of course," the false Gamalian continued when it became clear Rika wasn't going to say anything. "The really big thing is that you and the Jin Dara have finally consummated your relationship."

"How do you know these things?" Rika asked, despite her promise to herself that she wouldn't ask any more questions.

"And the good news," he continued, ignoring her question with some obvious enjoyment of the fact that he was doing so, "is that I think you will discover that among its many other attributes, the solution you've been drinking with such zest has a quite potent effect on a woman's fertility."

She felt a shiver run down her spine, and both her eyes and hands strayed involuntarily to her smooth stomach.

.   .   .

Deslo sat in the dark, his knees drawn up against his chest with his arms around them, hugging them tight. His forehead rested on one knee, and his eyes were closed, trying to shut out the painful memories of what the Jin Dara had done to Shaline. Deslo had told them everything he knew that they might want to know. He had even told them things that didn't matter to anyone, as he had babbled on and on in the vain hope the Jin Dara would stop what he was doing, stop and leave Shaline alone.

Of course, the Jin Dara didn't stop. In fact, when he finished twisting and mangling her, he went to work on some of the other Amhuru in the room as Deslo sat and wept, broken and desolate. And though he waited for his turn to be manipulated and transformed by the Jin Dara, it never came. After some time, he was led from the room to this dark place. His feet were chained, and he was left alone.

A long time had passed since that had happened. He didn't know how long, as there was no light from the outside to provide clues to the passage of time. He thought it had been a good while, though, as strong hunger had come and gone inside him more than a few times. The desire for food ebbed and flowed, and right now it was at a low ebb, but the desire for a drink was strong and getting stronger. His body cried out for water, but his mouth was so dry he didn't think he could literally cry out, even if he tried.

So, Deslo sat in the dark, alone with his hate. If he had hated the Jin Dara before, he really hated him now. He had spent much of his time here in his dark prison fantasizing about escape and about coming upon a sleeping or otherwise unsuspecting Jin Dara, and of slitting his throat with a knife or burying his axe in his forehead.

But as much as he hated the Jin Dara and as deep as it ran, Deslo thought his hatred for Rika might just run deeper. When he thought of the Jin Dara, he felt hatred, but also fear and despair. When he thought of Rika, all he felt was anger and hate. It was pure and unalloyed. She had enjoyed turning Shaline over to the Jin Dara, enjoyed watching him suffer as she suffered. She was, in her own way, worse than the Jin Dara, and Deslo wanted to kill her too.

The door opened and light flooded into the small room from the hall. A woman stood silhouetted in the doorway, and perhaps because he had just been thinking about her, Deslo knew who it was before she even spoke. She said, "I have brought water for you, and food."

Rika motioned to someone in the hall that Deslo could not see, and then a man came in and brought him water. He drank eagerly, until the water spilled out of his mouth and he tipped up the cup to keep from pouring it down his front. He swallowed and felt the cool water wash down his throat. Relief. He took up the cup and drank some more.

All the while, as he drank greedily as much as they would let him drink, Rika stood back from him in the darkness of the room. Now she lit a small lamp on a table across from him and sat down while the man who had brought the water set a plate with bread and a bowl of stew beside Deslo. The man left the room, closing the door behind him and leaving the two of them alone.

"Aren't you going to thank me?" Rika said, as he started to devour the food.

"Get out."

"My, my," she said. "You are a rude one."

"Get out!"

"You don't tell me what to do, boy," Rika hissed, leaning forward and almost coming up out of her chair. "I'm the only reason why you aren't a mangled mess of vines and branches on display in the Jin Dara's little museum of horrors, and don't you forget it."

"I didn't ask you for any favors," Deslo said. "I'm not afraid to die."

"Maybe you aren't," Rika said, settling back in to her seat. When she spoke again, her voice was no longer angry, but Deslo could hear an unmistakably cruel gloating in it. "But you wouldn't die, would you? He would leave you very much alive, and aware, trapped inside a living tomb. Oh yes, to die would be much, much better than that."

"How can you help him? How can you be a part of it?"

Rika shrugged. "It's all about picking the winner. I picked the Jin Dara for the same reasons that I picked your grandfather. It's the smart play."

"Smart?" Deslo said, incredulous. Now it was his turn to mock. "Joining with the Jin Dara is smart? Getting involved with my grandfather wasn't so smart, was it? Didn't you end up in a prison cell awaiting execution?"

"You were a child," Rika said. "You know nothing about it."

"I know what Gamalian would say about the folly of not learning from the past."

"Gamalian? Gamalian!" Rika said, almost shrieking and sounding agitated and borderline hysterical at the mention of his name. "Let me tell you something about Gamalian and folly."

Rika did rise from her seat now and walk closer, stooping in the dark so that she was only a few feet away from him. When she spoke again, her voice was calm and controlled and barely more audible than a whisper.

"Your precious Gamalian knew that I had betrayed your grandfather. He knew that I had been plotting to steal some of Eirmon's stockpiled Zerura and run, to make my fortune with it. He knew that I had set up three innocent researchers at the Academy to take the fall for this, to die for my crime. He knew that when I was confronted by your grandfather that I had turned on my accomplice without hesitation and suggested it was all his idea. Gamalian knew all this about me, and you know what? I still talked him into coming down to the cells where we were held captive and letting me out."

Rika paused in her story, paused to watch Deslo's reaction to what she was saying, and then she continued.

"And yet, knowing that I was dangerous, a viper who wasn't afraid to bite anything and anyone, he not only let me out, he gave me a weapon to defend myself against the Jin Dara's soldiers who were on the verge of entering the city. He handed me the weapon himself, Deslo. And do you want to know what I did with it? I killed him. I killed him right there. I drove the knife he gave me home into his old, fragile body, ending his life, just so he couldn't set my accomplice free. I couldn't have that, you see, as he was a man who had good cause to want to hurt me.

"So," Rika said, rising and walking back to her seat. "That's what happened to your wise Gamalian. He died by my hand. So much for his counsel about the folly of not learning from the past, as he learned nothing from it himself, and it got him killed."

"You, you ... " Deslo didn't know what word to call her. There was no word foul enough to describe her. So he finished the sentence blandly, with the only word that came to mind, "... traitor. I hate you."

"I don't care if you hate me, Deslo," she said. "You are of no consequence. The Amhuru cause is doomed, and as long as you cling to it, you are a fool."

Now she rose again but did not approach him. She stepped toward the door and then turned. "You know, it may not have occurred to you, but you do have options. You could always consider changing your allegiance. The Jin Dara would be skeptical, of course, but I could, perhaps, intercede for you."

"Never," Deslo said, and then he said it again, louder. "Never."

"I didn't think so," Rika said with a sigh. "You never really were very bright. Of course, after you watch the Jin Dara destroy the few remaining Amhuru in the north, perhaps you'll change your mind—though of course, even if you do, it'll be too late by then."

Deslo didn't respond to her goading, but as he considered what she said, he realized that she was implying that he would be taken with the Jin Dara's army when they headed out. "I'm to go north?"

"I believe so," Rika said, matter-of-factly, and not as though she'd given anything of any importance away.

"I'm not to be twisted and mangled into something awful for the Jin Dara's amusement?"

"Well, you may yet be, to be sure," Rika said. "But not now. I've suggested that you might prove useful in some way when we encounter the rest of the Amhuru."

Now she did walk back toward him and stoop once more. She stared into his eyes and he saw in her look the same cold malice he had seen there before. "And besides," she said, "I assume your parents are with the group in the north, and it would be a dream come true to bring you all back together—so I can watch you watch each other be, as you put it, twisted and mangled into something awful."

She stood, extinguished the lamp, and then walked to the door. She opened it so the light from the hallway illuminated her from the side, but she hesitated there in the open doorway before going out. She turned to him with a vengeful smile. "And that little sister of yours, Deslo, won't she just add some real charm to whatever the Jin Dara makes with you all? Yes, I am sure your reunion will be most enjoyable to see."

38

THE MOLJIIR

Marlo trudged through the deep snow. Owenn waited up ahead patiently, as he so often had to. Even with the big man going ahead and blazing the trail, Marlo found it difficult to keep up. All the layers in the world couldn't keep the cold at bay up here, it seemed, and he was so tired that he just didn't know how much farther he could go.

He reached Owenn at last, and they paused together for a moment before pushing on up toward the ridge. The wind was even stronger up here, so close to the top, and fortunately for now it was at their back. It was bearable then, but those times when they had to head straight into it—Marlo shuddered at the thought. As a child of the desert, he had learned to appreciate the power of the wind and the danger it represented, so it did not surprise him that in the very cold places of the world, as in the very hot, the presence of the wind and how strong it might be could make all the difference.

"Let's go," Marlo said, and Owenn nodded in reply and turned back upslope. They pressed on through the late afternoon, and though Marlo had been skeptical that they would make the ridge before nightfall, they did. There they stood, scanning the world beyond. Separated from them by a steep descent down the other side of the ridge was a large white plain that terminated at the edge of a very large and very dark body of water that extended as far as the eye could see and stretched across the horizon.

"The Lonely Sea," Marlo said, and again Owenn nodded his silent acknowledgement that he had heard Marlo. "It's beautiful."

"Sa," Owenn said, and Marlo smiled. Owenn had never spoken very much, but since crossing the Madri he had developed a seeming fondness for the Northland word for 'yes.' Perhaps it was preferable to the Southland word because it was a whole letter shorter?

"So," Marlo said, "we head for the edge of the sea and then east. Somewhere beyond that bend over there we should come across the hermit's cove and find entrance into the cave."

"But first we look for the shelter the old man at the village told us about."

"Sa," Marlo agreed. "First we look for the shelter."

The shelter in question was supposed to be a little way down from the ridge on the north face, built on a wide ledge for the use of any villagers or even the rare Northlander from elsewhere who might have cause to cross this ridge and need refuge overnight. It was a harsh world up here, so close to the top of the world, but this reality had only increased the tendency of those they encountered to be hospitable. This made sense to Marlo, for in the desert you gave shelter and water when you were in a position to do so, because you knew there might be a day when you would need those things yourself and would be at the mercy of others.

Owenn looked back and forth along the ridge, and then after a moment, pointed down to the right from where they were standing. Marlo followed his finger, but at first he couldn't see it. Then, after a moment, he did—a strip of blue cloth fastened to a pole, whipping in the wind.

"I see it now," Marlo said. "Lead on."

Owenn started down from the ridge, and Marlo followed behind. They would, hopefully, spend the night in the relative protection of the shelter, and then tomorrow they would push on to the Lonely Sea. If all went well, by the end of the day tomorrow or perhaps the day after, they would be making their way along the shore in search of the hermit's cove and the end of their journey.

·   ·   ·

The snowships were preparing to return with those who weren't going to stay and fight here against the Jin Dara. For the last few days, the whole community of Amhuru and Cura-Katane had worked on the moljiir and prepared the defenses, but there were several elderly Cura-Katane and some of the mothers with very young children who were going to return to the corral with all the children too young to fight, and there they would wait for the outcome.

Kaden knew that they couldn't really be kept out of the fight, for if things went poorly here, then the Cura-Katane and Amhuru who survived would fall back to the outer walls of the corral and defend them for as long as they could. Nevertheless, Maarta was working hard to convince Olli she should take Kiki and go back on the snowship. She might, he insisted, be able to find a way to hide and survive if things went badly.

"You're a survivor," he said as he stroked her blond hair. "You survived the gorgaal, didn't you?"

"I was rescued, you mean," she said.

"Well, you kept yourself alive long enough to be rescued," Maarta countered. "Look, Olli, I need to know that if we fail, there's at least a chance you will survive."

"And I need to die knowing that I stood beside you and did all I could to keep you alive."

"Olli," Maarta said, putting his hands on her shoulders and leaning down until his forehead rested gently on hers. "This is the longest of long shots. We both know it. The odds say neither of us will see tomorrow. Please, take Kiki and go back. I will do all I can to live long enough to fall back to the corral with the others."

Olli put her arms around him and whispered something Kaden couldn't hear into his ear, and then Maarta answered her, "Sa, me too."

When they let go of each other at last, Olli turned to Kaden and held out her arms, and he handed her Kiki. "Thank you, Olli."

She nodded, tears silently running down her cheeks. "Are you ready to head back, Kiki?"

Kiki hesitated, looking back at Kaden and extending her arms for him to take her back again. Instead, Kaden stepped up next to her and gently kissed her brow. "Yadi has to stay and fight. You need to go with the others—Joot will be there, remember. Olli will take good care of you until Yadi can come back."

There was no time for more. Olli boarded the snowship with the rest of those who were returning to the corral and then sped away across the open, snowy plain, and Kaden stood with Maarta, watching it go. He wondered if

he would ever see Kiki again, wondered if today they would both join Nara and Deslo in the grave?

Most likely, he thought, but if possible, he would help the Amhuru who remained and the Cura-Katane to take the Jin Dara with him. The Jin Dara had killed his father and destroyed his home. He had sent them out into exile, and it was entirely possible that the difficulties of that wandering had cost Kaden his wife. And with the coming of the Jin Dara here, there could be no doubt that Amintuu's attempt on Tanisaan had failed. That the Amhuru who had gone with Amintuu had fallen, no one doubted, which meant that Deslo too had been taken from him by this man.

It was time for him to die.

·   ·   ·

Kaden squatted by the thick rope that was tied to the moljiir, holding it down. He looked at the massive stone lashed to the top of the moljiir with a fair bit of skepticism, but Guuntir assured him they would work. He certainly hoped so, for it had been a colossal project getting them all out here and set up in the week since word had reached them that the Jin Dara was already on his way.

There were about a hundred moljiir lined up a good distance in both directions from where Kaden was seated, and each of them had an Amhuru like Kaden stationed there to protect, not just the moljiir, but the small team of Cura-Katane who were to work it. Guuntir and Markiit were in Kaden's team, and he was glad. In the months that he and Kiki had shared their home, he had come to think very highly of them. If he was going to die today, he would gladly do so while trying to hold the enemy back while Guuntir and Markiit did their work.

Guuntir walked over and squatted next to him. He extended a blue hand with a cup of hot jonda in it, and Kaden took it gratefully. He sipped the jonda and said to Guuntir, "I think today might actually be the day, Guuntir."

"The day the earth receives our bodies in her cold embrace?"

"Sa, that day," Kaden smiled, wryly. They had discussed more than once the Cura-Katane morning ritual of kissing the earth and asking that if this be the day that the earth received them in her cold embrace, that Kalos would hold their souls in his mighty hand. Kaden didn't object to the ritual, necessarily, but like any number of cultural rituals that he hadn't been rasied with but had encountered during his travels, it struck him as odd—and more than a little bit morbid.

"Any day might be that day, Kaden," Guuntir said with a twinkle in his eye. This, of course, was the whole point of the ritual. The Cura-Katane lived a hard life in a hard place, and they didn't take life for granted.

"True," Kaden agreed. "Any day might be that day, but today seems like a better candidate than most."

"Sa," Guuntir said, laughing. "It is that. All the more reason to have some more of Markiit's excellent jonda. If I'm going to die today, at least I'll have had my fill."

He slapped Kaden on the back and rose, taking his empty cup back to the small fire Markiit was tending behind the moljiir. Kaden watched as she served him some more jonda, and as he bent over and kissed her forehead tenderly.

Kaden turned away and gazed out over the expanse of white snow beyond the line of moljiir—all lined up and waiting for their enemy. Guuntir and Markiit seemed so nonchalant about the possibility that today was the day that not only they but possibly all the Cura-Katane might fall. In all the time Kaden had been in their home, they had expressed no resentment or anger that the Amhuru had come to them and asked them to get involved, when either reaction would have seemed perfectly natural to him.

From what Kaden could see, they were by no means unusual in this. The Cura-Katane to a person had all appeared to accept as ample reason to risk everything the fact that the Jin Dara had taken several fragments of the Golden Cord, done terrible things with them, and was even now trying to get those that remained. It was as though once they saw the course they were preparing to take as the right one, the cost, even if devastating, no longer mattered. Kaden found this remarkable, and he wished it were so easy for him to make his peace with the possibility of meeting his end today.

He was not afraid to die, but he was afraid of dying and leaving Kiki behind, alone, even if only for the amount of time it would take for the Jin Dara to move on from the combatants and the battlefield to kill the elderly and the children. And if he was honest, Kaden had to admit that his greatest fear was not that Kiki would be alone until she died, it was that the Jin Dara would take her and the other children and that she would live on, without her Yadi to protect her.

He pushed that thought from his mind. There were always, throughout life, terrible possibilities looming around the corner, over which one had no control—but like the Cura-Katane, Kaden understood that the only way to live was to decide on a course that seemed right and pursue it. Once you did that, Kaden thought, you could let the chips fall where they may, for you had done all that you knew how to do.

.   .   .

Deslo stretched his legs. It was quite enjoyable to be walking again, even if it was across this cold and treacherous terrain.

For several weeks now, he had been riding in a transport, his hands tied tightly together, as well as his feet. Of course, when the meridium transports had reached the shore of this enormous, frozen lake, they had been forced to dismount since the Arua above even frozen water didn't behave quite as it did above the ground.

From the little he could pick up from the Najin in charge of guarding him, Deslo had gathered that the frozen lake had provoked quite a bit of discussion among the Najin. Some said it was a large, natural phenomenon near the home of the Cura-Katane and that it didn't mean anything. Others, though, suggested that the Cura-Katane and Amhuru with them had set up on the other side of the lake because they intended to engage the Jin Dara and Najin on top of it in the hopes that the frozen water might mitigate the enormous power over the Arua that the Jin Dara had.

Deslo wasn't quite sure what to think. He doubted that Tchinchura and the others really thought this would slow down the Jin Dara very much, as he now had such enormous power. Kaden had told him about a conversation he once had with Tchinchura on *The Sorry Rogue* many years ago, concerning what Tchinchura could do with the Arua while at sea if pressed. He imagined that a simple frozen lake would not pose much of a threat to the Jin Dara's ability to do almost anything with the Arua he wanted.

It did occur to Deslo that perhaps there might be something else about fighting on the lake that could make it appealing for the Amhuru and Cura-Katane, but if so, he couldn't figure out what it was. He had dismounted at the place where they left the transports behind, and so he had walked from the shore onto the lake and felt no real difference at all. The snow was hard packed on both surfaces and his feet didn't push all the way down until they touched ground or ice on either one. So it didn't seem like fighting on the lake would actually feel all that different than fighting on solid ground.

Whatever their reasoning for setting up on the far side of the lake at the base of a series of large, jagged stones, this was what the Amhuru and Cura-Katane had done. Deslo could see them as the Najin passed out onto the lake and started to advance across it. He couldn't see them as clearly as he would have if he still wore Zerura, and he did miss his heightened senses. Nevertheless, he saw them well enough to see that the Cura-Katane were every bit as blue as the stories he had heard about them on the way had said, and that they were waiting in the midst of a long line of odd-looking war machines.

From where Deslo stood, they looked something like catapults—long, sturdy poles with big rocks on the end, tied back horizontally to the ground. He looked at these things and his heart sank. He certainly hoped that his father and the last remnant of the Amhuru had a better plan to resist the Jin Dara than to throw big rocks at him. He thought that the time had long since passed when a big rock might be enough to solve their problems.

They continued to advance across the lake, but the Amhuru and Cura-Katane waiting on the other side did not move, nor did they fire the catapults. Deslo looked at them and frowned, wondering why they had set up in front of the jagged rocks where they were exposed, rather than behind them, as the rocks seemed like an excellent natural defense.

And then the front lines of the Najin began to throw their hand-held explosives, lobbing them toward the Amhuru and Cura-Katane and using the Arua to guide them. He could not feel the battle for control of the Arua, but he knew it must have already started. Some of the explosives found their mark, or nearly, but some were redirected and crashed into the ground where they blew snow and chunks of ice high into the air.

Deslo was glad to see that the Amhuru were putting up a fight, but he despaired as he remembered how strong the Najin had been on the day he had helped to attack Tanisaan. He had worn three fragments of Zerura, as had the others with him, and they had not been strong enough. There were fewer Amhuru here, and they were wearing one fragment. He just didn't see how they could hold out very long.

And then, all along the line of the Amhuru and the Cura-Katane, there was movement. He heard the sound of many cords snapping, and he saw the great war engines he had taken for catapults suddenly launch upward very fast. Up they went and then over, picking up speed. Suddenly, they were all swinging down very fast, and one after another they smashed into the ground with a giant 'thwack!'

There was motion now along the enemy line, as teams of the blue men and women started cranking the war machines, raising the long arms up and backward again. As they did, Deslo heard a loud rending, cracking sound that was much bigger and louder than the noise any machine could make. It took a moment to realize what it was, but when he did, his jaw dropped and he stared at the machines he had mistakenly taken to be catapults.

The thick ice down beneath the snow beneath his feet was shaking, and he could tell that for the Najin much farther up, it was doing more than that. The surface of the lake was cracking into hundreds, no, thousands of chunks of ice, and as the Najin could not just hop up onto the Arua to avoid it, some were in danger of losing their footing and sliding down into the freezing water that here and there was starting to bubble up through layers of ice and snow.

Deslo smiled as several of the machines—those first few that had been cranked at least far enough up to be able to gain some momentum on their way back down again—crashed once more onto the surface of the lake.

They weren't catapults after all. They were hammers.

39

COLD EMBRACE

The world around Kaden was a swirling mess of chaos and confusion. Behind him, the Cura-Katane worked together furiously to crank the moljiir, to raise it to at least the ninety degree point so they could slam it back down again and continue their assault on the icy lake. Before him, the thick ice was splintering more and more into smaller and smaller shards, and already many of the foremost Najin had slipped down into the freezing water and were struggling to find their way out.

He could feel the Najin struggling to take hold of the Arua in some way that would help, in some way that might save them. He could feel it, and again he wondered what the Jin Dara was doing in the face of what was taking place here. That the Jin Dara had held back as his Najin crossed the lake, Kaden understood. He had probably wanted to wait until the Amhuru tipped their hand and moved, and then he would counterattack. And, just as Draagan had predicted, he did not seem to have conceived that their assault would not involve the Arua.

"I taught him a lesson once about not underestimating the creative use of far more ordinary means than Zerura and meridium," Draagan had said with a smile, "but I suspect he might still have something to learn about that."

So it seemed, for not only had the Jin Dara not foreseen what the moljiir might be or do, but he had allowed his Najin to throw their explosives.

Whatever use they might ordinarily have, and even whatever damage they might have succeeded in doing today, did their enemy not understand that they were on a frozen lake? Could they really not see the danger those explosives might pose to their own safety, or did the Jin Dara see but not care?

Whatever the Jin Dara thought, or the men who had thrown the explosives, Kaden gave thanks that they had done so. He had helped the Amhuru protecting the moljiir to redirect the explosives so that they struck all along the edge of the lake, up and down the shoreline, softening up the ice for what was coming next. He didn't necessarily think the moljiir would have failed to shatter the ice without them; he just thought it had been crushed more completely because of the softening that had already taken place.

The moljiir beside him reached ninety degrees and the Cura-Katane working the crank let it go. It flew downward, striking the shattered ice out in front of them with a thunderous crack. Great chunks of ice with water flew in every direction, and immediately the team behind him set to work, cranking it back up again.

They never got the moljiir more than a few feet up off the water, for the counterstroke from the Jin Dara that Kaden had been waiting for finally came. A sudden, incredibly strong gust of wind came sweeping, not from the lake, but along the shore, right in front of the jagged rocks and parallel to the water. Many of the great moljiir, in fact most of them, including the one Kaden had been protecting, tottered and then fell over on their side.

Kaden lost his feet in the fury of the gale too, and he tumbled backward until he slammed up against the wooden beam of the moljiir next to the one he had been stationed with. He grabbed onto the thick wooden beam and held on as the wind kept blowing, whipping snow and ice relentlessly along the shore. Even as Kaden struggled to hold on, he knew that the work of the moljiir today was basically done. They were far too heavy for the small teams operating them to lift back up.

The wind died down and Kaden felt the Jin Dara redirect his efforts toward the ice and water of the lake itself. He couldn't really follow what the Jin Dara was doing, but Kaden knew that he was working with a level of mastery of the Arua that was far beyond him. The link between the Arua and living things was fairly direct, even if animals had wills which could, for a time at least, be used against the one who wielded the power of the Arua. The link between the Arua and the ecological elements that affected those living things—things like weather, wind and water—was more subtle, and it took a more practiced touch to affect those things well. At least, that had been Kaden's experience.

What the Jin Dara did now was not subtle. All around Kaden, the broken fragments of the ice on the surface of the lake began to solidify and come back together. Kaden didn't know if the Jin Dara was somehow reversing what the moljiir had done, or if he was refreezing the water between the floating shards of ice, but what was clear was that the bobbing pieces of ice were becoming once more a solid surface—only with many of the Najin who had already gone into the water now trapped underneath.

Kaden wasn't prone to sympathy toward anyone who served the Jin Dara, but he felt at least a little horror, even if involuntarily, for those now trapped below the rapidly resealing ice. He couldn't imagine the terror of first finding the ice beneath your feet to be shattering, only then to discover that you were sliding through a crack into the freezing water, and then worst of all, to find in all your thrashing that those same cracks—now your only way out—were rapidly disappearing and being replaced with a thick, solid sheet of ice above you.

Kaden staggered to his feet. There was no time to think about the unpleasant fate of the Najin trapped below the ice, for a great many more were on top of it and their way forward had been opened up again. The Jin Dara and his army were still coming, and the Amhuru and Cura-Katane had done all that they could do here. It was time to fall back and begin the retreat to the corral of the Cura-Katane.

.   .   .

The walls of the corral were almost within reach, but the Amhuru numbers were now so small and the enemy so close that Kaden doubted they would reach them. He and the other Amhuru who remained, including Zangira and Maarta, had circled around Draagan and Tchinchura to provide what defense they could for them and the final two fragments of the Golden Cord.

Kaden didn't think many of the Cura-Katane were left, though he felt quite sure that they wouldn't have made it this far without them. The archers they had placed among the jagged rocks had held back the Najin from the opening through the rocks long enough for the Amhuru to get a good head start across the open plain. And then, once those had fallen, the Cura-Katane on snowships had managed to harass the Najin too—until the snowships also had been dealt with.

Kaden had seen one of them get torn apart by a great vine that suddenly broke up through the snow and punched through the hull of the ship. It then proceeded to rip the ship to splinters from the inside. All the while, the Cura-Katane on the ship either continued to fire their arrows at the Najin out on the plain, or else tried to fight the vine itself, though to no avail.

He hadn't seen Guuntir or Markiit since passing through the opening in the jagged rocks and forming lines with the other Amhuru to fall back together to the corral. He hoped they were still alive, but he knew better than to deceive himself with too much hope. It seemed more than likely that they had gone to the cold embrace of the earth, and as he surveyed the scene around himself, he though it more than likely that he would join them soon.

A muffled cry from a few feet away was the only warning he had before Maarta tumbled from the surface of the Arua with an axe planted firmly in his back. His face and head went straight down into the snow, and he didn't move or try to get back up. Kaden felt the pang as he watched his friend fall, and he wanted to stop and help, but he knew he couldn't. There was nothing to be done for him now. Besides, the only thing that mattered any more was protecting the Golden Cord if they could, so on they ran, trying to make the corral.

The walls were just up ahead, maybe twenty yards away. The plan was to get back inside and then make a final stand there. There were so few of them, though, Kaden didn't know what kind of stand they could make. He just hoped—

Something sharp pierced his side. It drove in, deep. He stumbled, losing his footing on the Arua. He tried to keep his balance, but couldn't. He fell, hands outstretched to break his fall. He hit the snow, shoulder first, driving down through the hard-packed coldness as it arrested his momentum. The other Amhuru kept going, and soon he was lying in the snow, all alone.

His hand reached down to his side, feeling the warm blood seep out through his cloak and into the snow. "Kiki," he murmured. He felt light-headed, like he might pass out. "Deslo."

His eyes drooped and then closed. "Nara, I'm coming."

·   ·   ·

The few Amhuru that had lived long enough to make it back to the walls of the Cura-Katane settlement had been stripped of their Zerura by the Najin. They were now bound and sitting with the rest of the captives, awaiting their fate, outside the big building with the large open courtyard before it.

The Jin Dara was inside this building, and he had not yet taken up the final two fragments of the Golden Cord, entrusting them instead, for the moment at least, into the care of Devaar, who held them lovingly and respectfully. The Jin Dara had waited so very long to take them, that it was hard to wait much longer, but he would not now grab and grasp after them like a beggar after scraps of food. He would take them to himself when the time was right.

That time was soon, but first he had some unfinished business with the two Amhuru who had, until just an hour or so ago, possessed the final fragments of the Golden Cord. One of these, the one called Zangira, many years ago had almost stopped him from carrying out his family's long-awaited vengeance on the city of Barra-Dohn. And, if he had, the Jin Dara would not only have failed to repay his family's ancient grievance, he would never have taken the second fragment of the Golden Cord nor discovered his true destiny.

He had met the other one, Draagan, more recently, and the man had very nearly killed him. He had failed, of course, but not before giving him the scar on his face that still remained—though it was now nearly invisible to the naked eye in the almost solid gold appearance of his entire body. He knew it was there, though, and he touched it every day with his fingertips to remind himself of the one who had given it to him, even as he dreamed of this very moment, when Draagan would stand captive and powerless before him at last.

The kitchen knife is king, until it meets a sharper blade.

The thought of those words now made the Jin Dara smile, and he walked over to Draagan where he stood and stopped before him. "I think you now know who the sharper blade is."

"Do I?" Draagan answered, and the Jin Dara found his tone insolent and his refusal to lower his eyes infuriating.

He had special plans for Draagan, but not until after, not until his power was complete, so he did not want to kill him now. However, that didn't mean he couldn't have a little fun. He would just have to make sure he didn't get carried away.

He walked over to a small mirror hanging on the wall, took it down and shattered it on the floor. He bent over the shards and picked up a long, jagged-looking one, and then walked back to Draagan. Holding the shard firmly in his hand, he took the narrow end and dug it into Draagan's cheek, just below his right eye, and then he carefully cut down across the fleshy part of the cheek until the fragment passed just below the corner of his mouth. When he reached the point of his chin, he pulled the fragment out.

Blood was now seeping out of the wound he had cut on Draagan's face, but the Amhuru did not cry or call out. His cheek twitched involuntarily from the pain, but otherwise the man simply stood and took, quietly, what the Jin Dara had done. The Jin Dara tossed the mirror shard away. "That's for the scar you gave me. Of course, when I'm through with you later, neither you nor your new scar will be recognizable, so you won't have to endure it for long. Still, I wanted you to know what it felt like before I transformed you into something not so easily cut."

The Jin Dara started to turn away from Draagan, but then he turned back and said. "By the way, even though you sent him to kill me, I thank you for sending Meldriic Jaen to me. He proved useful before his failed assassination attempt. He didn't get quite as close to killing me as you did, but he tried his best."

"I am sure he died with honor," Draagan said simply.

"Oh, he didn't die, Draagan," the Jin Dara said, smiling widely. "I imagine he lives still in the palace of Tanisaan, though admittedly you wouldn't recognize him unless I pointed him out to you."

Now the Jin Dara turned from Draagan to Zangira, who, through all of this, had stood silent and still, staring straight ahead. The Jin Dara stepped over so he was directly in front of him, and only then did the Amhuru look him in the eye. "We have met before, you and I, though not face to face."

"We have," Zangira said simply.

"Do you think about that day much?" the Jin Dara asked. "How you almost had me and the fragment I bore in your grasp?"

"I do," Zangira said honestly and without hesitation.

"I can imagine," the Jin Dara laughed. "You must hate Eirmon now almost as much as I did then."

Zangira did not say anything to that, and the Jin Dara turned to the small group of people waiting in the back with Devaar. He called, "Come here, Rika."

Rika walked over until she stood beside him, and he put his arm around her waist, gently. The Amhuru did not give much away, but he could see that the man was fighting a war inside himself to maintain his stoic front. "Rika was one of your party for quite some time, was she not?"

"She was," the Amhuru said, again keeping his answer simple and to the point.

"Not so, actually. She was always one of mine, in spirit at least. And, now that she is pregnant with my child," and here, the Jin Dara paused and moved his hand lovingly across Rika's belly, "now she is really one of mine."

The otherwise unflappable Amhuru showed genuine surprise at that, and the Jin Dara watched the shock register in his face, watched the man's eyes flicker and look down at his hand on Rika's stomach, saw the Amhuru have to force himself to pull his eyes away. The Jin Dara patted Rika tenderly and pointed back toward Devaar, and she excused herself and went back to wait with the others.

"Now," the Jin Dara said as he addressed both Zangira and Draagan, who was still bleeding profusely. "I have very special plans for both of you. But first, I want you to witness the moment when I complete my journey and put on the final pieces of the Golden Cord. I want you to witness the moment when your failure is complete. I want you to see my final ascent from mortality to divinity."

He paused and extended his arms wide so that he could place his hands on the outside shoulder of both men. "And then, when I have become your god, I will re-make you into something very, very special."

40

BENEATH THE COLDER MOON

Kaden lay in the grass. The sun was bright and clear overhead, so he didn't understand why it was so cold. He looked over at Nara and Deslo, sitting on the blanket. They were talking and laughing together as though it weren't freezing. They didn't seem to mind the cold, but he didn't understand how this could be, as neither was dressed warmly. Then Kiki came and dropped on top of him, peering into his face and calling, "Yadi! Yadi!"

"Don't lean on him." Kaden heard another voice. Not Kiki's, but also familiar. "Kaden? Kaden?"

Then a pair of hands took his own hand and moved it down onto his side and pressed it against a cloth of some kind, pressed it tightly. The cloth was warm and damp.

"Hold this against your wound if you can. Keep the pressure up. Try to slow the bleeding."

Kaden opened his eyes. Olli was leaning over him, and she smiled when she saw his eyes open. It was a hurried smile, maybe even a worried one, but it was a smile, and he took it as a sign that he had not yet entered the cold embrace of the earth, though if he was losing this much blood from the wound in his side, it wouldn't be long until he did.

"What ..." he started to ask a question, but he was so parched and weak he didn't get any further. Olli took a small handful of snow and gently compacted it together, and then she slipped it inside his mouth so he could suck water from it. As he did, she said, "Save your strength, Kaden. The Jin Dara has allowed us to search the field for any who are wounded and not dead, to bring them back. I think he wants as big an audience as he can get to bear witness to his ultimate triumph."

She turned to Kiki, who was beside her, staring down at Kaden with big, tear-filled eyes. Olli whispered something Kaden couldn't make out, and Kiki nodded and then moved around to his other side and took his other hand.

"I'm sorry I can't do anything right now for your wound, to stop the bleeding, but I don't have my Zerura anymore. They took it. They took it all."

She sounded bitter, and Kaden saw anger and rage mixed with helplessness on her face. When she spoke again, though, she had her voice under control. "We're going to try to get you up on your feet. It's almost dark, and if we can't get you back before the show starts, they'll make me leave you, and I won't be able to come back. You won't make it to morning. You'll freeze to death. So come on, Kaden, up on your feet."

Kiki pulled on his free hand and arm, and Olli tried to get under the shoulder of the arm he was using to put pressure on his wound. He didn't get very far, and after a few attempts, Kaden lay back in the snow, feeling defeated. He was so tired. It didn't look like he was going to be able to stand up, and Olli was right—if he didn't get somewhere warm tonight, in the shape he was in, he wouldn't make it until morning.

He heard Olli whispering something to Kiki again, and she stepped away, but where she went Kaden couldn't see. The next thing he knew, Olli was leaning down, right over his face.

"You need to listen to me, Kaden," Olli said, her voice quiet but urgent. "I can leave you here if you'd prefer. In fact, I don't doubt it would be more merciful than whatever waits for us with the Jin Dara. I almost made that call when we first found you, almost told Kiki we were too late."

She hesitated, but then she continued. "But she was so distraught, Kaden. She's lost everyone else. If you think you can bear it, to come back with us, even if something worse waits for us after, I think it would give her some comfort, and it might give us both a little hope."

"Let's try again," Kaden said weakly, and a moment later they were at it again. It didn't work the first time, but after several attempts, Kaden somehow found himself on his feet, heavily supported by Olli, who had his free arm around her neck.

"Do you think you can walk?" she asked, looking up at him.

"I think so," he said, then added, "I'm sorry, Olli. I saw Maarta fall, but I couldn't help him."

"I've already seen him and said my goodbyes," Olli said, quietly. "I'm sure there was nothing you could have done."

They started hobbling toward the entrance to the corral, which thankfully wasn't far away. When they got there, though, they turned right and headed along the outside of the wall. Before Kaden could ask where they were going, Olli explained that the Jin Dara had given orders for every Amhuru and Cura-Katane who was still alive to join him and his Najin in the large snowfield just beyond the corral to the east for the evening's entertainment. And so they walked until the corral wall started to turn away to the north, but they left the wall and went straight on, passing through the Najin guarding the others, until they had taken their place among the spectators gathered here at the Jin Dara's bidding.

Kaden looked at the Cura-Katane and Amhuru, who made a much smaller crowd than they would have made that morning. A smattering of the Najin encircled them, though most of those soldiers were up front near the Jin Dara. As the Najin now had all the Zerura, they didn't seem to be too worried about a fight or an attempted escape. The Amhuru were defeated at last, and they knew it.

Kaden coughed, and that was enough for him to lose his tenuous grasp on his balance. He staggered down onto one knee, and Olli worked frantically to get him up before they drew the attention of the Najin nearby. A Cura-Katane woman helped her, and Olli thanked her for the hand. "Stay with me, Kaden. As soon as we're done here, I'll get you inside somewhere, and we'll see what we can do for you."

"I don't think there's much to be done," Kaden said softly, but as he spoke to Olli he looked down at Kiki, still holding his hand tightly with both of her own little hands, looking up at him with worry in her eyes. He didn't want to leave her, but he knew. Despite his momentary reprieve, the cold embrace was still waiting for him.

"You just hold on," Olli said, not willing to give up quite as easily.

Several of the Najin had posted lamps on poles to illuminate the field, but just as Olli spoke, the clouds that had been covering the moon moved away and the whole gathering was bathed in the silver gleam of bright moonlight. Kaden looked up and was struck by how bright and clear the cold moon was—and it was a cold moon, for sure, as the mysterious grey halo around it was very distinct tonight.

Marlo had been right, or at least his prophecy had been right. What had been scattered had been brought together. The Jin Dara had gathered together all six original fragments of the Golden Cord, and they had come together, right here, beneath the colder moon, just as Marlo had prophesied.

Kaden didn't understand what the prophecy meant when it said that what had been scattered would be brought together and then scattered again, but he agreed with Marlo that the reference to the long dark was both ominous and upon them. The long dark was coming, but he wasn't going to live to see it. That much he knew.

"There he is," Olli said and pointed up toward the front.

On a small rise, the Jin Dara now stood. He glowed a vibrant golden color, and even from a distance, even to Kaden's weakened eyes, there was no mistaking him. There were a few others up front with him, but Kaden couldn't make any of them out, not that he would have known who they were. He ignored them and kept his eyes on the Jin Dara, who seemed to be preparing to address the assembly.

"Deslo," Olli said, tightening her grip on Kaden's arm. "I think Deslo is up there."

"What?" Kaden said, feeling suddenly faint.

"I could be wrong," Olli said. "But I think they've got Deslo up there, Kaden."

"Delo?" Kiki said, excitedly. "Delo?"

"It might be, Kiki," Olli said, quickly stepping in to contain Kiki's reaction. "But we need to be quiet, sweetie. We don't want to draw any attention to us, all right?"

"I can't see him," Kaden said, trying to make out his son among the faces in the front.

Before Olli could say anything else, the Jin Dara raised his arms, and complete silence swiftly fell over the assembly. "The time has come," he said. "And those of you who are here to see this are here because you have either helped to make this happen or tried to prevent it."

He paused, though not for long, and continued. "Consequently, this moment marks either the consummation of your hopes and dreams or the realization of your nightmares. Those who have served me loyally will reap their reward—as will those who have opposed me."

Kaden's legs buckled under him again, and this time not only did the Cura-Katane woman have to help Olli get him back up, but she stayed with them to give the support on Kaden's other side that Kiki just couldn't provide. Kiki moved in front of Kaden and grabbed his leg, holding him tight around the thigh, and Kaden knew just how she felt. Listening to the Jin Dara speak made Kaden want to do the same.

"The Old Stories tell us the Golden Cord was the gift of a god," the Jin Dara said. "And that this same god is the one who ordered it divided and separated, never to be brought back together. Tonight, as I defy this command from this so-called god and put on the last two fragments of the Cord before you, you will bear witness to the birth of a new god. Tonight, you will bow down and worship me."

The Jin Dara then took off his robe and stood before the assembly in just his undergarments. The night was very cold and Kaden almost shivered to see him standing there all but naked in front of them. Someone nearby handed him two wriggling pieces of Zerura, and the Jin Dara lay down in the snow.

Even though he was lying on a rise out in front of the assembly, Kaden found it hard to see what was going on, so Olli whispered what she could see. "The Zerura is crawling down his right arm—it must be Draagan's fragment."

She confirmed this a moment later when the Zerura wrapped itself around the Jin Dara's right forearm. Not long after this, she told him that the last piece of Zerura had been placed on his chest, and shortly after it was, it made its way down the Jin Dara's left arm until it stopped at his bicep, and then it also wrapped itself around and fastened itself tightly to the Jin Dara's body.

"It's done," Olli said in a hushed tone. "He now wears all six fragments of the Golden Cord."

Kaden was struggling to stay on his feet. His legs were weak and he thought they might give out at any time. He feared that if he fell down again, that this time he would not get back up. He could also tell that his breathing was more difficult and labored. And yet, even though he could feel that time was not on his side, he fought to stay upright—if Olli was right, and Deslo really was alive, he couldn't give up ...

All thoughts of anything but the Jin Dara disappeared as his golden form started to rise off the ground.

"It's, it's … unbelievable!" the Jin Dara called out in the throes of ecstasy. "The music of the Cord! My heart leaps and dances and sings to it!"

As the Jin Dara rose above the ground, first a few feet, and then several, he rotated up from a lying to a standing position. His legs seemed to be held together tightly, whether by the Jin Dara's own will or by a force greater than he, Kaden had no idea. His arms were stretched out wide to both sides, his hands clasped tightly and his muscles bulging. His entire body glowed like bright gold, but still Kaden could see pulsing coming from the six fragments of the Cord—one on each limb and one each around his neck and head.

"I am light!" he called, gazing upward into the night sky. "I am life!"

He was now some ten feet off the ground and still rising slowly, steadily. And while Kaden was struggling, it certainly did seem to his weary eyes that the Jin Dara was getting brighter by the second. In fact, the startlingly bright glow emanating from him reminded him of the lesser sun they had encountered so many years ago on the island of dreadful daylight at the manor house where the Jin Dara grew up.

"You all must bow before me!" the Jin Dara screamed, his voice loud and commanding. "Kneel!"

What happened next was chaotic, as even the Najin seemed confused about how to proceed. Some started immediately to kneel and bow themselves, while others turned their attentions to the captives to make sure they did. Some of these dropped to their knees without needing to be prompted, whether from exhaustion and weakness like that which afflicted Kaden, or from being overwhelmed by what was going on. Indeed, Kaden found the scene playing out in front of him compelling and could almost feel a tangible pull inside himself to simply acquiesce and bow.

At the same time, there were many who very clearly did not bow, nor did they heed the shouts and warnings from the Najin who had turned their attention to the crowd to make them bow. Amid all the small skirmishes that then erupted, Kaden kept trying to see his son, to see Deslo, but he could not make him out, and his focus was soon drawn to a small group of Amhuru up front that looked to include Tchinchura, Zangira and Draagan among others. They were refusing to bow, like many other Amhuru and Cura-Katane, but they were being struck by Najin who had moved in close to them.

He couldn't feel the Arua field being manipulated, but Kaden felt sure the Najin were using that too to force compliance. He felt himself being strangely pulled downward, and though he wanted to resist, he simply couldn't. He dropped down into the snow, onto his knees, as did Kiki before him. Soon Olli joined them, and he turned to her. "I don't think I'll be able to get back up."

"Let's worry about that later," Olli said, not even looking at him. Her eyes were focused on the still-rising golden form of the Jin Dara.

No one was left on his feet now. How the Jin Dara or his Najin near the front had gotten Tchinchura, Zangira and Draagan down, he didn't know, but he imagined it had only happened after the application of irresistible force. All bodies were down, but all faces were uplifted, staring at the Jin Dara as he kept on rising, now perhaps thirty or forty feet in the air.

"Behold your god!" he cried out, and his voice, which seemed magnified many times over, echoed across the snowfield. "Now rise to serve your master and your lord—or to die."

Again, there was confusion in the assembly, but most started to rise. The Najin, no doubt, out of obedience to the Jin Dara, but for many of the Amhuru and the Cura-Katane, it probably had more to do with the fact that they were no longer being compelled to kneel. Kaden, though, as he had suspected, could not rise.

Olli started to try to help him up, but her efforts halted, as did his own fumbling efforts to stagger up. The Jin Dara started to shake and convulse in the air. The pulsing that had been visible before, but only in the fragments of the Golden Cord itself, now seemed to be reverberating throughout his whole body. He shook more and more violently, and his cries, which had obviously been ecstatic shouts of joy at first, became more and more alarmed and even frantic.

Something had gone wrong.

What happened next was very hard for Kaden to understand or describe. The Jin Dara's violent shaking became concentrated, so that his whole body convulsed several times like a gong that has been struck with great force. When his shaking reached fever pitch, something very much like a wave of visible power shot out from him and shot through everything else. It shot through the air, the clouds, and even the distant moon. It shot through the people gathered below, the snow, and the field. It shot through the walls, the houses, and the nearby mountain. The visible wave moved through everything in the quickest of instants.

As soon as it passed outward from the Jin Dara, his golden form lost its bright and shining glow. The Jin Dara dropped like a stone straight down, landing on the snowy rise with a silent thud, where he lay motionless.

And, wherever the visible wave passed through the Najin, they collapsed just as quickly. Soon, the snowy field was dotted with bodies lying still and inert in the snow, all illuminated by the silvery light of the colder moon.

Kaden reeled as he looked around at the carnage. He was feeling faint, and he tried to balance himself, murmuring, "Deslo." And then, finally, though Olli was pulling with all her might in an attempt to get him up, he tilted forward and collapsed into the snow.

41

JUDGEMENT

The Jin Dara's lifeless body struck the ground not far from where Deslo was still kneeling in the snow. His hands and feet were tied, which had slowed his attempt to get up. Now he watched in shock and confusion as the Najin all around him pitched and tumbled over until they too lay lifeless in the snow.

He'd felt the wave as it exploded out of the Jin Dara and ripped right through him, but it had done him no harm. Obviously, the Najin hadn't been so lucky. Everywhere Deslo looked, the Najin were down. Their golden uniforms, a muted echo of the Jin Dara's own golden body, littered the field.

Then Deslo saw them—Rika, and one of the Jin Dara's advisors, the one that always seemed to be with him. They weren't down, like the Najin. In fact, the man had taken Rika's arm and was pulling her away. Rika, for her part, seemed stunned by what she was seeing, but the man was pulling, insistently. Finally, Rika turned to run into the dark with him.

Deslo knew what he had to do. He had to get himself out of these restraints and go after them. There were no Najin to hold him back or stop him. He would finally take his vengeance—but first he had to get free.

He struggled mightily against the ropes that bound him. He could not have done this before when he'd been under the constant surveillance of the Najin, but it felt good to do it now. He was able to work his feet and hands enough to gradually loosen the ropes. He finally got one hand out, and the rest only took a moment. Soon he was up on his feet and free.

He ran to the body of the nearest Najin to find a knife or axe or anything he could wield, so he could go after Rika and finish her. As he bent over the body, though, he heard a voice calling his name. "Deslo! Deslo!"

He looked up, but before he ever saw her face, he knew who it was. He would have known that voice anywhere. "Olli?"

"Deslo," she called again as she ran to him. "You have to come quickly."

"Olli," he said, taking her arms as she started to turn to head back the way she had come, clearly expecting that he would follow. He had to make her understand. "There's something I have to do. It's—"

"Your Yadi," Olli said, cutting him off. "It's Kaden."

"What about him?" Deslo said, knowing that with every moment he delayed, Rika was getting farther and farther away.

"He's dying, Deslo," Olli said. "Please, come quickly."

"Take me to him," Deslo answered her quietly, and then Olli turned and ran. He ran after her, and he did not look back.

. . .

Rika followed Devaar through the dark. It wasn't pitch black, as the light of the moon was still fairly bright, but all felt dark to her. Not only had the literal light of the Jin Dara's bright and glowing body been extinguished, but that amazing sensation of being bathed in the light of his glorious presence was gone. She was stunned, in complete shock. At the moment of his triumph, all had been lost.

She didn't understand. All had gone perfectly. They had defeated the enemy on the field of battle, taken all the replicas of the original fragments of the Cord, rounded up all the living survivors—and most importantly, the Jin Dara had taken to himself and put on the last two fragments of the Golden Cord. She had felt the power course through his veins as he rose up off the ground, felt the glow of it as he ascended into the air. It was like the scent of a fragrant perfume, how it seeped out from him and spread through the air to her, and she had breathed deeply of it and been intoxicated by his wonder.

He had risen, higher and higher, as the rest had knelt. She had knelt too, eagerly, longingly, giving her heart in worship to him—and then something had happened. Something had seized him and shaken him, and out of him had come that wave of death. That somehow-visible wave of death, which had killed all the Najin around her—all save Devaar and her.

Why hadn't it killed her? Why hadn't it killed Devaar?

Devaar was running, pulling her, but she pulled against him until she had wrested her arm free. She stopped in the open field, and he stopped to turn and look at her. His face was pale in the moonlight. He said, "We need to keep going, Rika. We have a long way to go."

"What happened back there, Devaar?"

"Combining the fragments killed him," Devaar said, simply. There was no trace of shock or anguish or anything. It was just a matter-of-fact statement.

"And the Najin?" Rika said. "What killed them? And why didn't it kill us?"

"They were wearing replicas," Devaar said, but he didn't elaborate.

"They died because they were wearing replicas of the Golden Cord?"

"Sa."

"Weren't you?"

"No," Devaar said. "I don't wear any. It probably wouldn't have had the same effect on me, but I thought it better to be safe."

"What are you … I mean, I don't understand," Rika said, her mind reeling. "You're his right hand man—and you don't wear any Zerura? Were you, were you expecting this?"

"Of course," Devaar said, sneering at her. "I worked very hard to engineer this. It would be silly for me not to expect it."

"You did this?"

"In a way," Devaar said. "He desperately wanted it for himself, so all I did was help him get it."

Rika stared at him, her mind racing to keep up. So many threads to follow in what he was saying. She seized one. "What did you mean it wouldn't have had the same effect on you? Wouldn't you have died if you'd been wearing a replica?"

"No," Devaar said, laughing again. "I can't die, Rika."

"Who are you?" Rika asked. "Who are you really?"

"Don't you recognize me?" he said, and in that moment, she thought she saw Gamalian standing in front of her.

"It can't be."

"I beg to differ," he said, and now he was Devaar again.

"What are you?"

"Don't you know?"

"Nekron," she whispered. "You're Nekron."

"I am," he said, smiling. "Very good, Rika, you figured it out at last."

"You were Devaar all along."

"Well, not all along," Nekron said. "But when I decided it was time to get close to the Jin Dara, to have constant access, I arranged an accident for the real Devaar."

Rika's mind snapped back to what had just happened, to the Jin Dara's dead body lying in the snow, and she grabbed a different thread. "Why would you engineer the Jin Dara's death? What was the point of all this?"

"Those are two very different questions," Nekron said. "I didn't want the Jin Dara to die, per se, but I did want the Golden Cord brought back together. Whoever did that was going to die, plain and simple. No one was going to defy Kalos' command and not pay the price."

"Kalos is real?"

"Of course."

Nekron—real. Kalos—real. Rika's whole world was turning upside down.

"What are you going to do to me?" Rika was trembling, from fear and from the cold, but her voice was strangely steady.

"Why, my dear girl," Nekron said. "I'm not going to do anything to you. I have big plans for you, and even bigger plans for your baby. That's why I protected you tonight."

"That's why I didn't die?"

"It's part of why," Nekron said. "That and the fact that I made sure you never wore a fragment of Zerura."

Rika stared at him, trying to make sense of all the things he was telling her. "I don't understand."

"That will take some time," Nekron said, "And as I've already indicated, we have a long way to go. May we get on with it?"

"Wait, why did you want the Cord brought back together?" Rika asked thinking about the wave of power that rippled outward from the Jin Dara.

"Long ago the people of Zeru-Shalim—what your city of Barra-Dohn was once called—learned a lesson about defying Kalos. That lesson pales in comparison with what's coming, but to trigger that judgement, the Cord which was divided and kept apart for the last thousand years had to be gathered together."

"What did it do? What was that wave of power that came out from the Jin Dara?"

"That was judgement, Rika," Nekron said, a wide smile on his face. "That was the moment the Arua field failed."

.   .   .

"Delo!" Kiki called out as she threw her arms around Deslo's waist.

"Hello, Kiki," Deslo said tenderly, hugging her. Then he whispered into her ear, "Let me take a look at Yadi."

Kiki nodded and let go, and Deslo knelt down beside Kaden. He looked to be sleeping, but his breathing was labored and uneasy. He put his hand gently but firmly on Kaden's shoulder and shook, calling to him.

Kaden's eyes opened, and he looked right up into Deslo's face. "My boy," he said. "You're alive."

"Yes, Yadi," Deslo said. "I'm alive."

"I'm so glad," Kaden said, but with obvious effort.

"Yadi," Deslo said. "Olli says we need to get you inside. Do you think you can get up? Or should I carry you?"

"I'm sorry, Deslo," Kaden said. "It's too late for that. I have to go. Nara waits for me."

"Yadi—"

"Please," Kaden said, reaching up and taking Deslo's arm in his hand. "Call me father. One more time."

"Father," Deslo said, and he choked on the word. "We have to move you inside."

"Father," Kaden said, echoing Deslo softly. "I am your father, and I am very proud of you."

Kaden's eyes fluttered shut, and for a moment, Deslo thought he had died, but then he spoke again. "Take care of Kiki, Deslo. Take good care of her."

"I will, father," Deslo whispered, and this time, when Kaden's eyes closed, they did not open again.

.   .   .

There were so many Amhuru and Cura-Katane dead, and the ground was so hard, it took the better part of three days to commit them all into the earth's cold embrace. As for the Najin, they were gathered into a mound & covered with snow, well outside the corral of the Cura-Katane, and only after their bodies had been systematically searched and every trace of Zerura removed from them.

The replicas of the Golden Cord, though, no longer behaved like Zerura. Each piece they recovered remained in the shape it had been in, like ordinary jewelry, and some of them were on so tight they had to be pried or cut off to be removed—but removed they all were.

And the six original fragments? When the Amhuru went to investigate the dead body of the Jin Dara, the man once known as Dagin Orlas, they found no Zerura on him. Rather, around him in the snow lay six golden rods—straight and solid and completely inert. They did not dance to their own inner music in the air, they did not bend or wriggle or respond in any way when laid upon the chest of any of the Amhuru present. They appeared to be, for all intents and purposes, ordinary metallic rods.

Deslo had a chance to examine them himself, as did all the remaining Amhuru. They did not respond to his touch, nor feel any different than meridium or any other metal, and he could not feel through them the Arua field, which was perhaps the greatest mystery of all. Everything in the Cura-Katane corral that depended in some way on the Arua field to work, from the simplest lamp and meridium knife to the great snowships themselves, all of it had ceased to function on the night the Jin Dara combined the fragments and died, and none had worked since.

Now Deslo and the Amhuru, along with Chaarnir and the surviving members of the Cura-Katane Aiden were meeting to discuss what to do about the situation. "To know what to do," Draagan was saying, "do we not first need to understand what happened?"

"Sa," Chaarnir said, agreeing with him.

"Part of what happened should not be a surprise to any of us," Tchinchura said. "The Jin Dara did what Kalos had forbidden, and he paid the price."

"Evil consumes itself," Draagan said, chiming in. "The self-destructive consequences of evil actions aren't always so dramatic, but they are usually there, nonetheless."

Many of those in the gathering nodded in agreement with Draagan, but Olli spoke up. "He had combined fragments before and not been punished. If Kalos was going to punish him for his evil actions, why wait until he had them all?"

"I cannot speak for Kalos," Tchinchura said, "but we should not make the same mistake the Jin Dara made. I suspect that when he first combined fragments—all the way back when he conquered Barra-Dohn and took one from Eirmon—that when nothing happened to him, he came to believe there would be no price for disobeying the command of Kalos.

"But Kalos forbid the reunion of all the fragments, not simply the combination of some of them, and his judgement was not triggered until the Jin Dara put them all on."

"So, Amintuu was right? We were allowed to combine fragments ourselves?" Deslo asked. "Just not all of them."

"I don't think so," Tchinchura said. "Kalos told the sons of Armond to divide the Cord into six fragments and keep them separate. We should not confuse the mercy of Kalos—not judging with ultimate severity the disobedience of this lesser command—with permission to disobey the greater. That Kalos held back his hand, giving the Jin Dara a chance to turn back from his evil course and us a chance to stop him, should also be seen as mercy, I think. It was an opportunity to avoid the situation we now find ourselves in—a world without Arua."

"Do you think it is gone for good?" Zangira asked.

Tchinchura shook his head. "I cannot say, but I hope not."

"What does it mean?" Deslo asked. "The loss of the Arua?"

"It means that many of our tools and most of our technologies no longer work," Chaarnir said. "We will have to relearn many skills, find new ways to do many things."

"It does mean that," Tchinchura said, "but I'm afraid it means far more. The Arua regulates the ecological systems of the world, the growth patterns of all living things. Who can say what happens, now that it is gone?"

"Jin Dara," Deslo muttered, and the others turned to look at him. "My tutor told me the Old Stories, of how Dark Things—'Jin Dara'—walked the world in the days before Kalos made the Arua to set boundaries for the growth patterns of all living things. Maybe, if the Arua is gone, the Dark Things will return."

"Maybe," Tchinchura said. "The prophecy that Marlo, a Kalosene Guardian of Truth made when he was among us, suggested that a long dark was coming. Perhaps this was what he meant."

"So what do we do?" Draagan asked. "To prepare for the long dark? What do we do with these?"

He held up the six inert pieces of the Golden Cord, and the Amhuru and Cura-Katane stared at them. "That is the question," Tchinchura said.

"And the answer?" Chaarnir asked.

"One road forward is to divide the six fragments among us and do what we have always done," Zangira said. "The same prophecy Tchinchura just alluded to said that what was scattered would be gathered together and then scattered again—I think there can be little doubt now that this referred to the fragments of the Golden Cord."

"It may have referred to the Cord," Draagan said, "but it is a tricky business making decisions on what to do based on prophecies, is it not? That the prophecy describes what will happen is not the same thing as saying the prophecy prescribes what should happen—is it?"

"No," Tchinchura agreed. "It isn't, but in the absence of a new word from Kalos, I don't know what else to do other than what we have always done, that is to say, to continue to abide by the command we do have."

"But the Cord is no longer the Cord, is it?" Deslo asked.

"Perhaps not, but I agree with Tchinchura," Draagan said. "We should treat the Cord like it is the Cord until we are told otherwise."

Tchinchura looked around at the gathering. "I think until we know otherwise, this is what we do. Three fragments should stay in the Northlands in the care of the Northland Amhuru, and three should go back south with the Southland Amhuru, across the Madri—if there still is a Madri. Are we agreed?"

There were murmurs of agreement, and soon the meeting adjourned. Tchinchura asked the Southland Amhuru to walk with him. It didn't take any time for them to decide that Tchinchura should keep a fragment, and that Zangira should keep another, but it was far less clear who should keep the third. None of the others had trained for the task of keeping and protecting a fragment of the Golden Cord.

And so, it was a great surprise to Deslo when Tchinchura turned to him and said. "I think you should take the third fragment. Your father died in the quest to make right your family's past wrong. What your grandfather took treacherously, I offer you freely. I think you are the one who should bear it."

Deslo looked at Tchinchura, and tears sprang to his eyes. Tchinchura extended a fragment of the Cord, and Deslo took the cold, smooth metallic rod in his hand. He rolled it in his palm, looking at it thoughtfully. He reflected on his decision to go with Amintuu for all the wrong reasons, on his sudden, deep desire to have the power the Jin Dara had and to wear the fragments himself, and finally, on his capitulation to the Jin Dara when he was warping and mangling Shaline so that he betrayed the remnant of his own who had gone north.

He handed the fragment back.

When Tchinchura took it back into his hand with a look of surprise, Deslo said, "I'm not the one. I don't deserve it. I'll tell you who does, though," and he turned and pointed to Olli. "She does."

Tchinchura looked at Deslo closely, examining him. And after a long moment, he nodded. "You are, I think, too tough on yourself, Deslo. Nevertheless, if you do not want to bear the fragment, I will not make you, and Olli is certainly a worthy choice."

He turned to Olli. "What do you say? Will you bear this burden?"

Olli looked at Tchinchura and the proffered fragment of the Golden Cord. "Sa," she said. "I will—on one condition."

Now she turned to Deslo. "I'll take it, if you come with me. You and Kiki both. I don't want to do this alone."

Deslo looked at Olli, then looked at Tchinchura. "Is that allowed?"

Tchinchura grinned. "Sa, I think we can allow it. So much has changed, I don't see why not."

Deslo turned back to Olli, and for what felt like the first time in a very long time, he smiled. "Sa, we'll come—if you're sure you want us along."

Olli smiled too, a sad smile etched with the pain of all they had lost. "Maarta's gone, and your parents, who were like parents to me too—I don't want lose you and Kiki. I don't want to be alone."

Deslo looked at her for a moment, and then he put his arms around her. "I won't leave you, Olli. Not now. Not ever."

Epilogue

YET TO BE

Marlo stared at the entrance to the small cave in the sheltered cove that lay across the gently lapping water. The rock wall on either side of it was rather sheer, and his faint hope of somehow gaining access to the cave without wading through the freezing water quickly disappeared.

"We will have to go through," he said.

"Sa," Owenn answered.

A moment later, they were wading waist deep through water so cold Marlo couldn't believe it wasn't ice. When they emerged on the pebbly beach of the cove, just in front of the cave, Marlo tried to shake himself like a dog in an effort to cast off as much water as he could. It didn't help. He pointed toward the cave as he shivered, knowing Owenn would take his meaning, and the big man led the way inside.

The cave opened up immediately into a sizable room, and the light coming from the outside lit the front portion fairly well. All the same, beyond the arc of daylight, the room was completely dark. Fortunately, the problem of the dark was one that the hermit who lived here was prepared for, as a small lamp and a pitcher of oil sat not far from the cave entrance.

Owenn picked up the pitcher and poured the oil inside the lamp, and they both waited for the meridium core to respond and begin to shine. They waited, and they waited a little longer, and nothing happened. Owenn bent over the pitcher and smelled the oil, and then he looked at Marlo and shrugged. "Maybe the lamp's broken."

"How does meridium break?" Marlo asked. He'd never heard of a lamp's core failing like that. It was very odd.

Owenn shrugged and said nothing.

Marlo groaned. They'd come so far to get here, and now they were stuck at the threshold to the hermit's cave because a lamp wouldn't work. "Let's search as far in as we can still see anything at all, and look for some other source of light."

Owenn nodded and started immediately to move the other way, and Marlo started to comb his side of the cave. The furnishings this close to the entrance were sparse, and he began to despair of finding anything useful, when Owenn whistled. Marlo turned around to see what he had found. Owenn held up something small and dark in his hand, but Marlo couldn't see what it was, so he walked over to find out.

"Flint?" Marlo said, hazarding a guess about the object in Owenn's hand.

"That's right," Owenn said. "Found it on a small table beside a firepit with some old grey ashes in it. My guess is they cook over the firepit."

"Great," Marlo said. "So now what?"

Owenn responded by stripping off his robe and then another layer or two, until he could pull off a lighter shirt he was wearing underneath. Marlo watched him shivering from the cold and almost told him to stop, but he knew that Owenn wouldn't let some discomfort from the cold stop them now. When he'd put his other layers back on, Owenn tore a strip of the shirt that was wet from their watery crossing and threw it away, and the rest of it he dipped in the pitcher of oil. He broke a wooden chair by the table on which he'd found the flint, took up a leg, and wrapped the oil-soaked cloth around it. Then he struck the flint on a mid-sized rock out on the beach and lit the rag.

"Well done," Marlo said, and Owenn nodded to acknowledge Marlo's appreciation of his resourcefulness. Then Marlo looked up at the torch and shook his head. "Feels downright primitive to have to resort to fire for light, but we'd better get inside since we have no idea how long it will burn."

They walked farther into the cave, into the part that wasn't illuminated by the daylight from the entrance, and their attention was immediately drawn to an altar, right in the middle of the cave. The altar was dedicated to Kalos, as evidenced by the inscription on the front of the stone. Slumped over in front of the altar was the body of a man. They approached cautiously, but it quickly became apparent that the man was dead.

"I guess that's why my vision only talked of coming to the hermit's cave and not of speaking with the hermit," Marlo said as they straightened the hermit's body out as best they could, given its stiffness, thinking it wrong to leave him in the awkward position in which his body had fallen after he died.

"Still," Marlo said, as he ran his hand across the smooth top of the altar of Kalos, "I wonder what we're—"

You have done well, a voice said.

Immediately Marlo dropped to his knees. He had heard that voice before, in his visions, but never while awake. He knew it was time to listen, not to speak.

Some of what I have told you has come to pass. The rest is yet to be. The long dark is upon you, for I have taken back what long ago I gave, that the world might remember what it should never have forgotten.

When the price has been paid and when the truth is remembered, I will restore what has been lost. In the meantime, take the boy and train him in the ways of the Devoted. I have a task that is for him and him alone.

You are a Guardian of Truth, and this truth more than any other I entrust to you that you may know and guard it: when the time is right, I will restore what I have taken, but only when the six fragments of the Golden Cord are restored to me.

The voice was gone, but still Marlo knelt. He was trembling, and for a long time he didn't dare to even look up. Finally, he turned to see that Owenn was kneeling too, with his head down. "You heard that, right?"

Owenn looked up and shook his head. "I knelt when I saw you kneel. I ..." he started. "I felt a presence, but I didn't hear anything."

Marlo related the words of the prophecy, and Owenn listened carefully. They talked about it, but soon they were both fixated on one question.

"Boy?" Marlo said, speaking for them both. "What boy?"

And then they heard it. A child cried out from the dark on the far left side of the room, and using the torch to light their way, they navigated over to the source of the cry. There, wrapped in cloth and lying in a makeshift cradle, was an emaciated baby boy, perhaps six months old.

Marlo picked him up and tried to soothe him, but the child refused to be comforted. "First things first," Marlo said. "We need to give this little fella something to eat and drink."

"Sa," Owenn said, and he started to search the hermit's cave for something to give the child.

Meanwhile, Marlo rocked back and forth and gazed at the baby. "Now I understand why we had to come here. Looks like you're coming with us."

He continued to soothe and rock the baby while Owenn gathered anything he could find that might be edible for them and for the baby. As Marlo gazed down into the baby's beautiful face, he said, "I wonder what kind of world you are going to grow up in?"

For a moment, the question hung in the dark of the cave, a question—like all questions about the future—that had no answer.

"We shall see," Marlo said, cradling the child. "We shall see."

THE END

ACKNOWLEDGEMENTS

Writing a book is one thing. Getting it ready for publication is quite another. In that endeavor, I am very much indebted to several people, too many to satisfactorily acknowledge here. To all who have helped along the way, with my writing in general or with *The Colder Moon* in particular, I appreciate your time and support.

Specifically, I want to thank Daryle Beam/Bright Boy Design and Michael Salter of Chattanooga, TN, for their respective work on the cover design and cover illustration. Their willingness to do the cover made it possible for me to maintain continuity with the covers provided by the original publisher of the first two books, and once again, the work they did is fantastic.

I also want to thank Tegid Bard for his editing and proofreading expertise. I am especially indebted to him and to his generosity. And finally, it has been a pleasure to once again work with 52 Novels for the interior design elements. They are very good at what they do, and I can't recommend them enough.

ABOUT THE AUTHOR

L.B. Graham writes fantasy/sci-fi and contemporary adult fiction. In 2005, his novel *Beyond the Summerland* was a finalist for a Christy, a national fiction award. Check out his website www.lbgraham.com for more information on his previously published works and his forthcoming titles. He lives in Maryland where he is the Director of Beachmont Christian Ministries.

www.ingramcontent.com/pod-product-compliance
Lightning Source LLC
Chambersburg PA
CBHW030620250626
47154CB00006B/1860